John Griffith London (born **John Griffith Chaney**; January 12, 1876 – November 22, 1916) was an American novelist, journalist, and social activist. A pioneer in the world of commercial magazine fiction, he was one of the first writers to become a worldwide celebrity and earn a large fortune from writing. He was also an innovator in the genre that would later become known as science fiction. His most famous works include The Call of the Wild and White Fang, both set in the Klondike Gold Rush, as well as the short stories "To Build a Fire", "An Odyssey of the North", and "Love of Life". He also wrote about the South Pacific in stories such as "The Pearls of Parlay" and "The Heathen". London was part of the radical literary group "The Crowd" in San Francisco and a passionate advocate of unionization, socialism, and the rights of workers. He wrote several powerful works dealing with these topics, such as his dystopian novel The Iron Heel, his non-fiction exposé The People of the Abyss, and The War of the Classes. (Source: Wikipedia)

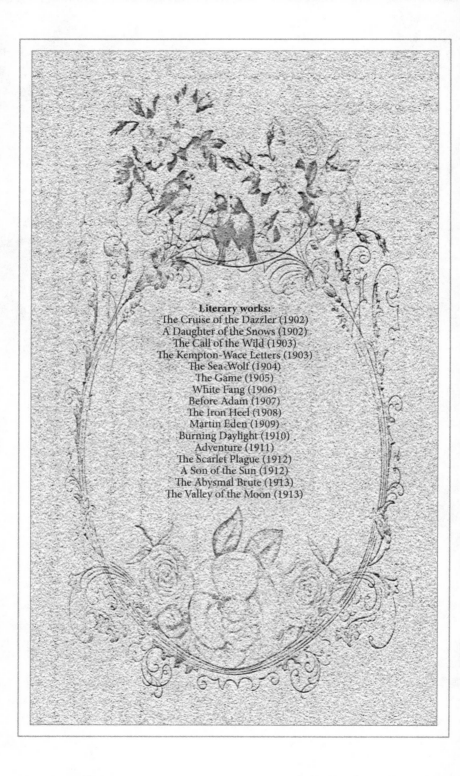

Literary works:
The Cruise of the Dazzler (1902)
A Daughter of the Snows (1902)
The Call of the Wild (1903)
The Kempton-Wace Letters (1903)
The Sea-Wolf (1904)
The Game (1905)
White Fang (1906)
Before Adam (1907)
The Iron Heel (1908)
Martin Eden (1909)
Burning Daylight (1910)
Adventure (1911)
The Scarlet Plague (1912)
A Son of the Sun (1912)
The Abysmal Brute (1913)
The Valley of the Moon (1913)

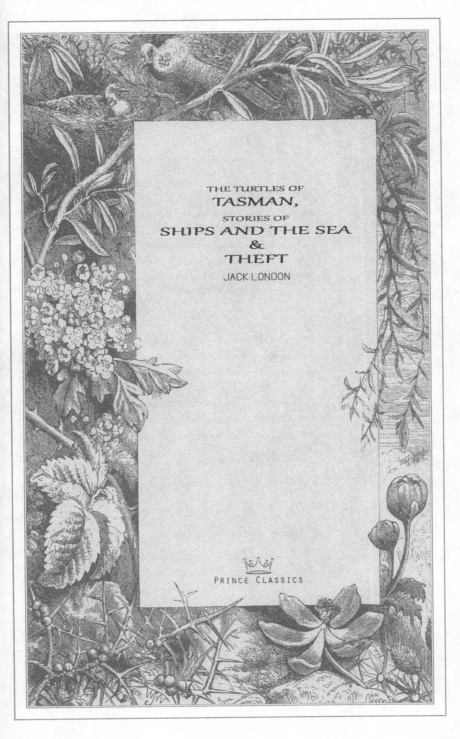

THE TURTLES OF TASMAN,
STORIES OF
SHIPS AND THE SEA
&
THEFT

JACK LONDON

PRINCE CLASSICS

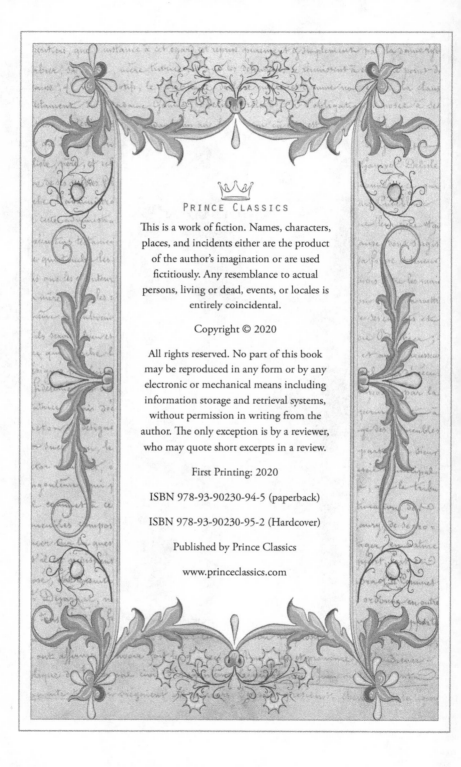

PRINCE CLASSICS

This is a work of fiction. Names, characters, places, and incidents either are the product of the author's imagination or are used fictitiously. Any resemblance to actual persons, living or dead, events, or locales is entirely coincidental.

Copyright © 2020

First Printing: 2020

ISBN 978-93-90230-94-5 (paperback)

ISBN 978-93-90230-95-2 (Hardcover)

Published by Prince Classics

www.princeclassics.com

Contents

THE TURTLES OF TASMAN   11

BY THE TURTLES OF TASMAN   13

THE ETERNITY OF FORMS   42

TOLD IN THE DROOLING WARD   54

THE HOBO AND THE FAIRY   64

THE PRODIGAL FATHER   79

THE FIRST POET   93

FINIS   105

THE END OF THE STORY   123

STORIES OF SHIPS AND THE SEA   **149**

CHRIS FARRINGTON: ABLE SEAMAN   151

TYPHOON OFF THE COAST OF JAPAN   159

THE LOST POACHER   164

THE BANKS OF THE SACRAMENTO   174

IN YEDDO BAY   184

THEFT   193

CHARACTERS   195

ACTORS' DESCRIPTION OF CHARACTERS   197

ACT I. A ROOM IN THE HOUSE OF SENATOR CHALMERS   201

ACT II. Rooms of Howard Knox at Hotel Waltham   256

ACT III. A Room in the Washington House of Anthony Starkweather   282

ACT IV   332

About Author   359

NOTABLE WORKS   381

THE TURTLES OF
TASMAN,
STORIES OF
SHIPS AND THE SEA
&
THEFT

THE TURTLES OF TASMAN

BY THE TURTLES OF TASMAN

Law, order, and restraint had carved Frederick Travers' face. It was the strong, firm face of one used to power and who had used power with wisdom and discretion. Clean living had made the healthy skin, and the lines graved in it were honest lines. Hard and devoted work had left its wholesome handiwork, that was all. Every feature of the man told the same story, from the clear blue of the eyes to the full head of hair, light brown, touched with grey, and smoothly parted and drawn straight across above the strong-domed forehead. He was a seriously groomed man, and the light summer business suit no more than befitted his alert years, while it did not shout aloud that its possessor was likewise the possessor of numerous millions of dollars and property.

For Frederick Travers hated ostentation. The machine that waited outside for him under the porte-cochère was sober black. It was the most expensive machine in the county, yet he did not care to flaunt its price or horse-power in a red flare across the landscape, which also was mostly his, from the sand dunes and the everlasting beat of the Pacific breakers, across the fat bottomlands and upland pastures, to the far summits clad with redwood forest and wreathed in fog and cloud.

A rustle of skirts caused him to look over his shoulder. Just the faintest hint of irritation showed in his manner. Not that his daughter was the object, however. Whatever it was, it seemed to lie on the desk before him.

"What is that outlandish name again?" she asked. "I know I shall never remember it. See, I've brought a pad to write it down."

Her voice was low and cool, and she was a tall, well-formed, clear-skinned young woman. In her voice and complacence she, too, showed the drill-marks of order and restraint.

Frederick Travers scanned the signature of one of two letters on the desk. "Bronislawa Plaskoweitzkaia Travers," he read; then spelled the difficult first portion, letter by letter, while his daughter wrote it down.

"Now, Mary," he added, "remember Tom was always harum scarum, and you must make allowances for this daughter of his. Her very name is—ah—disconcerting. I haven't seen him for years, and as for her...." A shrug epitomised his apprehension. He smiled with an effort at wit. "Just the same, they're as much your family as mine. If he *is* my brother, he is your uncle. And if she's my niece, you're both cousins."

Mary nodded. "Don't worry, father. I'll be nice to her, poor thing. What nationality was her mother?—to get such an awful name."

"I don't know. Russian, or Polish, or Spanish, or something. It was just like Tom. She was an actress or singer—I don't remember. They met in Buenos Ayres. It was an elopement. Her husband—"

"Then she was already married!"

Mary's dismay was unfeigned and spontaneous, and her father's irritation grew more pronounced. He had not meant that. It had slipped out.

"There was a divorce afterward, of course. I never knew the details. Her mother died out in China—no; in Tasmania. It was in China that Tom—" His lips shut with almost a snap. He was not going to make any more slips. Mary waited, then turned to the door, where she paused.

"I've given her the rooms over the rose court," she said. "And I'm going now to take a last look."

Frederick Travers turned back to the desk, as if to put the letters away, changed his mind, and slowly and ponderingly reread them.

"Dear Fred:

"It's been a long time since I was so near to the old home, and I'd like to take a run up. Unfortunately, I played ducks and drakes with my Yucatan project—I think I wrote about it—and I'm broke as usual. Could you advance me funds for the run? I'd like to arrive first class. Polly is with me, you know. I wonder how you two will get along.

"Tom.

"P.S. If it doesn't bother you too much, send it along next mail."

"Dear Uncle Fred":

the other letter ran, in what seemed to him a strange, foreign-taught, yet distinctly feminine hand.

"Dad doesn't know I am writing this. He told me what he said to you. It is not true. He is coming home to die. He doesn't know it, but I've talked with the doctors. And he'll have to come home, for we have no money. We're in a stuffy little boarding house, and it is not the place for Dad. He's helped other persons all his life, and now is the time to help him. He didn't play ducks and drakes in Yucatan. I was with him, and I know. He dropped all he had there, and he was robbed. He can't play the business game against New Yorkers. That explains it all, and I am proud he can't.

"He always laughs and says I'll never be able to get along with you. But I don't agree with him. Besides, I've never seen a really, truly blood relative in my life, and there's your daughter. Think of it!—a real live cousin!

"In anticipation,

"Your niece,

"Bronislawa Plaskoweitzkaia Travers.

"P.S. You'd better telegraph the money, or you won't see Dad at all. He doesn't know how sick he is, and if he meets any of his old friends he'll be off and away on some wild goose chase. He's

15

beginning to talk Alaska. Says it will get the fever out of his bones. Please know that we must pay the boarding house, or else we'll arrive without luggage.

"B.P.T."

Frederick Travers opened the door of a large, built-in safe and methodically put the letters away in a compartment labelled "Thomas Travers."

"Poor Tom! Poor Tom!" he sighed aloud.

II

The big motor car waited at the station, and Frederick Travers thrilled as he always thrilled to the distant locomotive whistle of the train plunging down the valley of Isaac Travers River. First of all westering white-men, had Isaac Travers gazed on that splendid valley, its salmon-laden waters, its rich bottoms, and its virgin forest slopes. Having seen, he had grasped and never let go. "Land-poor," they had called him in the mid-settler period. But that had been in the days when the placers petered out, when there were no wagon roads nor tugs to draw in sailing vessels across the perilous bar, and when his lonely grist mill had been run under armed guards to keep the marauding Klamaths off while wheat was ground. Like father, like son, and what Isaac Travers had grasped, Frederick Travers had held. It had been the same tenacity of hold. Both had been far-visioned. Both had foreseen the transformation of the utter West, the coming of the railroad, and the building of the new empire on the Pacific shore.

Frederick Travers thrilled, too, at the locomotive whistle, because, more than any man's, it was his railroad. His father had died still striving to bring the railroad in across the mountains that averaged a hundred thousand dollars to the mile. He, Frederick, had brought it in. He had sat up nights over that railroad; bought newspapers, entered politics, and subsidised party machines; and he had made pilgrimages, more than once, at his own expense, to the railroad chiefs of the East. While all the county knew how many miles of his land were crossed by the right of way, none of the county guessed nor dreamed the number of his dollars which had gone into guaranties and railroad bonds. He had done much for his county, and the railroad was his last and greatest achievement, the capstone of the Travers' effort, the momentous and marvellous thing that had been brought about just yesterday. It had been running two years, and, highest proof of all of his judgment, dividends were in sight. And farther reaching reward was in sight. It was written in the books that the next Governor of California was to be spelled, Frederick A. Travers.

Twenty years had passed since he had seen his elder brother, and then it had been after a gap of ten years. He remembered that night well. Tom was the only man who dared run the bar in the dark, and that last time, between nightfall and the dawn, with a southeaster breezing up, he had sailed his schooner in and out again. There had been no warning of his coming—a clatter of hoofs at midnight, a lathered horse in the stable, and Tom had appeared, the salt of the sea on his face as his mother attested. An hour only he remained, and on a fresh horse was gone, while rain squalls rattled upon the windows and the rising wind moaned through the redwoods, the memory of his visit a whiff, sharp and strong, from the wild outer world. A week later, sea-hammered and bar-bound for that time, had arrived the revenue cutter *Bear*, and there had been a column of conjecture in the local paper, hints of a heavy landing of opium and of a vain quest for the mysterious schooner *Halcyon*. Only Fred and his mother, and the several house Indians, knew of the stiffened horse in the barn and of the devious way it was afterward smuggled back to the fishing village on the beach.

Despite those twenty years, it was the same old Tom Travers that alighted from the Pullman. To his brother's eyes, he did not look sick. Older he was of course. The Panama hat did not hide the grey hair, and though indefinably hinting of shrunkenness, the broad shoulders were still broad and erect. As for the young woman with him, Frederick Travers experienced an immediate shock of distaste. He felt it vitally, yet vaguely. It was a challenge and a mock, yet he could not name nor place the source of it. It might have been the dress, of tailored linen and foreign cut, the shirtwaist, with its daring stripe, the black wilfulness of the hair, or the flaunt of poppies on the large straw hat

17

or it might have been the flash and colour of her—the black eyes and brows, the flame of rose in the cheeks, the white of the even teeth that showed too readily. "A spoiled child," was his thought, but he had no time to analyse, for his brother's hand was in his and he was making his niece's acquaintance.

There it was again. She flashed and talked like her colour, and she talked with her hands as well. He could not avoid noting the smallness of them. They were absurdly small, and his eyes went to her feet to make the same discovery. Quite oblivious of the curious crowd on the station platform, she had intercepted his attempt to lead to the motor car and had ranged the brothers side by side. Tom had been laughingly acquiescent, but his younger brother was ill at ease, too conscious of the many eyes of his townspeople. He knew only the old Puritan way. Family displays were for the privacy of the family, not for the public. He was glad she had not attempted to kiss him. It was remarkable she had not. Already he apprehended anything of her.

She embraced them and penetrated them with sun-warm eyes that seemed to see through them, and over them, and all about them.

"You're really brothers," she cried, her hands flashing with her eyes. "Anybody can see it. And yet there is a difference—I don't know. I can't explain."

In truth, with a tact that exceeded Frederick Travers' farthest disciplined forbearance, she did not dare explain. Her wide artist-eyes had seen and sensed the whole trenchant and essential difference. Alike they looked, of the unmistakable same stock, their features reminiscent of a common origin; and there resemblance ceased. Tom was three inches taller, and well-greyed was the long, Viking moustache. His was the same eagle-like nose as his brother's, save that it was more eagle-like, while the blue eyes were pronouncedly so. The lines of the face were deeper, the cheek-bones higher, the hollows larger, the weather-beat darker. It was a volcanic face. There had been fire there, and the fire still lingered. Around the corners of the eyes were more laughter-wrinkles and in the eyes themselves a promise of deadlier seriousness than the younger brother possessed. Frederick was bourgeois in his carriage, but in Tom's was a certain careless ease and distinction. It was the same pioneer blood of Isaac

18

Travers in both men, but it had been retorted in widely different crucibles. Frederick represented the straight and expected line of descent. His brother expressed a vast and intangible something that was unknown in the Travers stock. And it was all this that the black-eyed girl saw and knew on the instant. All that had been inexplicable in the two men and their relationship cleared up in the moment she saw them side by side.

"Wake me up," Tom was saying. "I can't believe I arrived on a train. And the population? There were only four thousand thirty years ago."

"Sixty thousand now," was the other's answer. "And increasing by leaps and bounds. Want to spin around for a look at the city? There's plenty of time."

As they sped along the broad, well-paved streets, Tom persisted in his Rip Van Winkle pose. The waterfront perplexed him. Where he had once anchored his sloop in a dozen feet of water, he found solid land and railroad yards, with wharves and shipping still farther out.

"Hold on! Stop!" he cried, a few blocks on, looking up at a solid business block. "Where is this, Fred?"

"Fourth and Travers—don't you remember?"

Tom stood up and gazed around, trying to discern the anciently familiar configuration of the land under its clutter of buildings.

"I ... I think...." he began hesitantly. "No; by George, I'm sure of it. We used to hunt cottontails over that ground, and shoot blackbirds in the brush. And there, where the bank building is, was a pond." He turned to Polly. "I built my first raft there, and got my first taste of the sea."

"Heaven knows how many gallons of it," Frederick laughed, nodding to the chauffeur. "They rolled you on a barrel, I remember."

"Oh! More!" Polly cried, clapping her hands.

"There's the park," Frederick pointed out a little later, indicating a mass of virgin redwoods on the first dip of the bigger hills.

"Father shot three grizzlies there one afternoon," was Tom's remark.

"I presented forty acres of it to the city," Frederick went on. "Father bought the quarter section for a dollar an acre from Leroy."

Tom nodded, and the sparkle and flash in his eyes, like that of his daughter, were unlike anything that ever appeared in his brother's eyes.

"Yes," he affirmed, "Leroy, the negro squawman. I remember the time he carried you and me on his back to Alliance, the night the Indians burned the ranch. Father stayed behind and fought."

"But he couldn't save the grist mill. It was a serious setback to him."

"Just the same he nailed four Indians."

In Polly's eyes now appeared the flash and sparkle.

"An Indian-fighter!" she cried. "Tell me about him."

"Tell her about Travers Ferry," Tom said.

"That's a ferry on the Klamath River on the way to Orleans Bar and Siskiyou. There was great packing into the diggings in those days, and, among other things, father had made a location there. There was rich bench farming land, too. He built a suspension bridge—wove the cables on the spot with sailors and materials freighted in from the coast. It cost him twenty thousand dollars. The first day it was open, eight hundred mules crossed at a dollar a head, to say nothing of the toll for foot and horse. That night the river rose. The bridge was one hundred and forty feet above low water mark. Yet the freshet rose higher than that, and swept the bridge away. He'd have made a fortune there otherwise."

"That wasn't it at all," Tom blurted out impatiently. "It was at Travers Ferry that father and old Jacob Vance were caught by a war party of Mad River Indians. Old Jacob was killed right outside the door of the log cabin. Father dragged the body inside and stood the Indians off for a week. Father was some shot. He buried Jacob under the cabin floor."

"I still run the ferry," Frederick went on, "though there isn't so much travel as in the old days. I freight by wagon-road to the Reservation, and then mule-back on up the Klamath and clear in to the forks of Little Salmon. I have twelve stores on that chain now, a stage-line to the Reservation, and a hotel there. Quite a tourist trade is beginning to pick up."

And the girl, with curious brooding eyes, looked from brother to brother as they so differently voiced themselves and life.

"Ay, he was some man, father was," Tom murmured.

There was a drowsy note in his speech that drew a quick glance of anxiety from her. The machine had turned into the cemetery, and now halted before a substantial vault on the crest of the hill.

"I thought you'd like to see it," Frederick was saying. "I built that mausoleum myself, most of it with my own hands. Mother wanted it. The estate was dreadfully encumbered. The best bid I could get out of the contractors was eleven thousand. I did it myself for a little over eight."

"Must have worked nights," Tom murmured admiringly and more sleepily than before.

"I did, Tom, I did. Many a night by lantern-light. I was so busy. I was reconstructing the water works then—the artesian wells had failed—and mother's eyes were troubling her. You remember—cataract—I wrote you. She was too weak to travel, and I brought the specialists up from San Francisco. Oh, my hands were full. I was just winding up the disastrous affairs of the steamer line father had established to San Francisco, and I was keeping up the interest on mortgages to the tune of one hundred and eighty thousand dollars."

A soft stertorous breathing interrupted him. Tom, chin on chest, was asleep. Polly, with a significant look, caught her uncle's eye. Then her father, after an uneasy restless movement, lifted drowsy lids.

"Deuced warm day," he said with a bright apologetic laugh. "I've been actually asleep. Aren't we near home?"

Frederick nodded to the chauffeur, and the car rolled on.

21

III

The house that Frederick Travers had built when his prosperity came, was large and costly, sober and comfortable, and with no more pretence than was naturally attendant on the finest country home in the county. Its atmosphere was just the sort that he and his daughter would create. But in the days that followed his brother's home-coming, all this was changed. Gone was the subdued and ordered repose. Frederick was neither comfortable nor happy. There was an unwonted flurry of life and violation of sanctions and traditions. Meals were irregular and protracted, and there were midnight chafing-dish suppers and bursts of laughter at the most inappropriate hours.

Frederick was abstemious. A glass of wine at dinner was his wildest excess. Three cigars a day he permitted himself, and these he smoked either on the broad veranda or in the smoking room. What else was a smoking room for? Cigarettes he detested. Yet his brother was ever rolling thin, brown-paper cigarettes and smoking them wherever he might happen to be. A litter of tobacco crumbs was always to be found in the big easy chair he frequented and among the cushions of the window-seats. Then there were the cocktails. Brought up under the stern tutelage of Isaac and Eliza Travers, Frederick looked upon liquor in the house as an abomination. Ancient cities had been smitten by God's wrath for just such practices. Before lunch and dinner, Tom, aided and abetted by Polly, mixed an endless variety of drinks, she being particularly adept with strange swivel-stick concoctions learned at the ends of the earth. To Frederick, at such times, it seemed that his butler's pantry and dining room had been turned into bar-rooms. When he suggested this, under a facetious show, Tom proclaimed that when he made his pile he would build a liquor cabinet in every living room of his house.

And there were more young men at the house than formerly, and they helped in disposing of the cocktails. Frederick would have liked to account in that manner for their presence, but he knew better. His brother and his brother's daughter did what he and Mary had failed to do. They were the magnets. Youth and joy and laughter drew to them. The house was lively with young life. Ever, day and night, the motor cars honked up and down the gravelled drives. There were picnics and expeditions in the summer weather, moonlight sails on the bay, starts before dawn or home-comings at midnight, and often, of nights, the many bedrooms were filled as they had never been before. Tom must cover all his boyhood ramblings, catch trout again on Bull Creek, shoot quail over Walcott's Prairie, get a deer on Round Mountain. That deer was a cause of pain and shame to Frederick. What if it was closed season? Tom had triumphantly brought home the buck and gleefully called it sidehill-salmon when it was served and eaten at Frederick's own table.

They had clambakes at the head of the bay and musselbakes down by the roaring surf; and Tom told shamelessly of the *Halcyon*, and of the run of contraband, and asked Frederick before them all how he had managed to smuggle the horse back to the fishermen without discovery. All the young men were in the conspiracy with Polly to pamper Tom to his heart's desire. And Frederick heard the true inwardness of the killing of the deer; of its purchase from the overstocked Golden Gate Park; of its crated carriage by train, horse-team and mule-back to the fastnesses of Round Mountain; of Tom falling asleep beside the deer-run the first time it was driven by; of the pursuit by the young men, the jaded saddle horses, the scrambles and the falls, and the roping of it at Burnt Ranch Clearing; and, finally, of the triumphant culmination, when it was driven past a second time and Tom had dropped it at fifty yards. To Frederick there was a vague hurt in it all. When had such consideration been shown him?

There were days when Tom could not go out, postponements of outdoor frolics, when, still the centre, he sat and drowsed in the big chair, waking, at times, in that unexpected queer, bright way of his, to roll a cigarette and call for his *ukulele*—a sort of miniature guitar of Portuguese invention. Then, with strumming and tumtuming, the live cigarette laid aside to the imminent peril of polished wood, his full baritone would roll out in South Sea *hulas* and sprightly French and Spanish songs.

One, in particular, had pleased Frederick at first. The favourite song of a Tahitian king, Tom explained—the last of the Pomares, who had himself composed it and was wont to lie on his mats by the hour singing it. It consisted of the repetition of a few syllables. "*E meu ru ru a vau*," it ran, and that was all of it, sung in a stately, endless, ever-varying chant, accompanied by solemn chords from the *ukelele*. Polly took great joy in teaching it to her uncle, but when, himself questing for some of this genial flood of life that bathed about his brother, Frederick essayed the song, he noted suppressed glee on the part of his listeners, which increased, through giggles and snickers, to a great outburst of laughter. To his disgust and dismay, he learned that the simple phrase he had repeated and repeated was nothing else than "I am so drunk." He had been made a fool of. Over and over, solemnly and gloriously, he, Frederick Travers, had announced how drunk he was. After that, he slipped quietly out of the room whenever it was sung. Nor could Polly's later explanation that the last word was "happy," and not "drunk," reconcile him; for she had been compelled to admit that the old king was a toper, and that he was always in his cups when he struck up the chant.

Frederick was constantly oppressed by the feeling of being out of it all. He was a social being, and he liked fun, even if it were of a more wholesome and dignified brand than that to which his brother was addicted. He could not understand why in the past the young people had voted his house a bore and come no more, save on state and formal occasions, until now, when they flocked to it and to his brother, but not to him. Nor could he like the way the young women petted his brother, and called him Tom, while it was intolerable to see them twist and pull his buccaneer moustache in mock punishment when his sometimes too-jolly banter sank home to them.

Such conduct was a profanation to the memory of Isaac and Eliza Travers. There was too much an air of revelry in the house. The long table was never shortened, while there was extra help in the kitchen. Breakfast extended from four until eleven, and the midnight suppers, entailing raids on the pantry and complaints from the servants, were a vexation to Frederick. The house had become a restaurant, a hotel, he sneered bitterly to himself; and there were times when he was sorely tempted to put his foot down and reassert the old ways. But somehow the ancient sorcery of his masterful brother was too strong upon him; and at times he gazed upon him with a sense almost of awe, groping to fathom the alchemy of charm, baffled by the strange lights and fires in his brother's eyes, and by the wisdom of far places and of wild nights and days written in his face. What was it? What lordly vision had the other glimpsed?—he, the irresponsible and careless one? Frederick remembered a line of an old song—"Along the shining ways he came." Why did his brother remind him of that line? Had he, who in boyhood had known no law, who in manhood had exalted himself above law, in truth found the shining ways?

There was an unfairness about it that perplexed Frederick, until he found solace in dwelling upon the failure Tom had made of life. Then it was, in quiet intervals, that he got some comfort and stiffened his own pride by showing Tom over the estate.

"You have done well, Fred," Tom would say. "You have done very well."

He said it often, and often he drowsed in the big smooth-running machine.

"Everything orderly and sanitary and spick and span—not a blade of grass out of place," was Polly's comment. "How do you ever manage it? I should not like to be a blade of grass on your land," she concluded, with a little shivery shudder.

"You have worked hard," Tom said.

"Yes, I have worked hard," Frederick affirmed. "It was worth it."

He was going to say more, but the strange flash in the girl's eyes brought him to an uncomfortable pause. He felt that she measured him, challenged him. For the first time his honourable career of building a county commonwealth had been questioned—and by a chit of a girl, the daughter of a wastrel, herself but a flighty, fly-away, foreign creature.

Conflict between them was inevitable. He had disliked her from the first moment of meeting. She did not have to speak. Her mere presence made him uncomfortable. He felt her unspoken disapproval, though there were times when she did not stop at that. Nor did she mince language. She spoke forthright, like a man, and as no man had ever dared to speak to him.

"I wonder if you ever miss what you've missed," she told him. "Did you ever, once in your life, turn yourself loose and rip things up by the roots? Did you ever once get drunk? Or smoke yourself black in the face? Or dance a hoe-down on the ten commandments? Or stand up on your hind legs and wink like a good fellow at God?"

"Isn't she a rare one!" Tom gurgled. "Her mother over again."

Outwardly smiling and calm, there was a chill of horror at Frederick's heart. It was incredible.

"I think it is the English," she continued, "who have a saying that a man has not lived until he has kissed his woman and struck his man. I wonder—confess up, now—if you ever struck a man."

"Have you?" he countered.

She nodded, an angry reminiscent flash in her eyes, and waited.

"No, I have never had that pleasure," he answered slowly. "I early learned control."

Later, irritated by his self-satisfied complacence and after listening to a recital of how he had cornered the Klamath salmon-packing, planted the first oysters on the bay and established that lucrative monopoly, and of how, after exhausting litigation and a campaign of years he had captured the water front of Williamsport and thereby won to control of the Lumber Combine, she returned to the charge.

"You seem to value life in terms of profit and loss," she said. "I wonder if you have ever known love."

The shaft went home. He had not kissed his woman. His marriage had been one of policy. It had saved the estate in the days when he had been almost beaten in the struggle to disencumber the vast holdings Isaac Travers' wide hands had grasped. The girl was a witch. She had probed an old wound and made it hurt again. He had never had time to love. He had worked hard. He had been president of the chamber of commerce, mayor of the city, state senator, but he had missed love. At chance moments he had come upon Polly, openly and shamelessly in her father's arms, and he had noted the warmth and tenderness in their eyes. Again he knew that he had missed love. Wanton as was the display, not even in private did he and Mary so behave. Normal, formal, and colourless, she was what was to be expected of a loveless marriage. He even puzzled to decide whether the feeling he felt for her was love. Was he himself loveless as well?

In the moment following Polly's remark, he was aware of a great emptiness. It seemed that his hands had grasped ashes, until, glancing into the other room, he saw Tom asleep in the big chair, very grey and aged and tired. He remembered all that he had done, all that he possessed. Well, what did Tom possess? What had Tom done?—save play ducks and drakes with life and wear it out until all that remained was that dimly flickering spark in a dying body.

What bothered Frederick in Polly was that she attracted him as well as repelled him. His own daughter had never interested him in that way. Mary moved along frictionless grooves, and to forecast her actions was so effortless that it was automatic. But Polly! many-hued, protean-natured, he never knew what she was going to do next.

"Keeps you guessing, eh?" Tom chuckled.

She was irresistible. She had her way with Frederick in ways that in Mary would have been impossible. She took liberties with him, cosened him or hurt him, and compelled always in him a sharp awareness of her existence.

Once, after one of their clashes, she devilled him at the piano, playing a mad damned thing that stirred and irritated him and set his pulse pounding wild and undisciplined fancies in the ordered chamber of his brain. The worst of it was she saw and knew just what she was doing. She was aware before he was, and she made him aware, her face turned to look at him, on her lips a mocking, contemplative smile that was almost a superior sneer. It was this that shocked him into consciousness of the orgy his imagination had been playing him. From the wall above her, the stiff portraits of Isaac and Eliza Travers looked down like reproachful spectres. Infuriated, he left the room. He had never dreamed such potencies resided in music. And then, and he remembered it with shame, he had stolen back outside to listen, and she had known, and once more she had devilled him.

When Mary asked him what he thought of Polly's playing, an unbidden contrast leaped to his mind. Mary's music reminded him of church. It was cold and bare as a Methodist meeting house. But Polly's was like the mad and lawless ceremonial of some heathen temple where incense arose and nautch girls writhed.

"She plays like a foreigner," he answered, pleased with the success and oppositeness of his evasion.

"She is an artist," Mary affirmed solemnly. "She is a genius. When does she ever practise? When did she ever practise? You know how I have. My best is like a five-finger exercise compared with the foolishest thing she ripples off. Her music tells me things—oh, things wonderful and unutterable. Mine tells me, 'one-two-three, one-two-three.' Oh, it is maddening! I work and work and get nowhere. It is unfair. Why should she be born that way, and not I?"

"Love," was Frederick's immediate and secret thought; but before he could dwell upon the conclusion, the unprecedented had happened and Mary was sobbing in a break-down of tears. He would have liked to take her in his arms, after Tom's fashion, but he did not know how. He tried, and found Mary as unschooled as himself. It resulted only in an embarrassed awkwardness for both of them.

The contrasting of the two girls was inevitable. Like father like daughter. Mary was no more than a pale camp-follower of a gorgeous, conquering general. Frederick's thrift had been sorely educated in the matter of clothes. He knew just how expensive Mary's clothes were, yet he could not blind himself to the fact that Polly's vagabond makeshifts, cheap and apparently haphazard, were always all right and far more successful. Her taste was unerring. Her ways with a shawl were inimitable. With a scarf she performed miracles.

"She just throws things together," Mary complained. "She doesn't even try. She can dress in fifteen minutes, and when she goes swimming she beats the boys out of the dressing rooms." Mary was honest and incredulous in her admiration. "I can't see how she does it. No one could dare those colours, but they look just right on her."

"She's always threatened that when I became finally flat broke she'd set up dressmaking and take care of both of us," Tom contributed.

Frederick, looking over the top of a newspaper, was witness to an illuminating scene; Mary, to his certain knowledge, had been primping for an hour ere she appeared.

"Oh! How lovely!" was Polly's ready appreciation. Her eyes and face glowed with honest pleasure, and her hands wove their delight in the air. "But why not wear that bow so and thus?"

Her hands flashed to the task, and in a moment the miracle of taste and difference achieved by her touch was apparent even to Frederick.

Polly was like her father, generous to the point of absurdity with her meagre possessions. Mary admired a Spanish fan—a Mexican treasure that had come down from one of the grand ladies of the Court of the Emperor Maximilian. Polly's delight flamed like wild-fire. Mary found herself the immediate owner of the fan, almost labouring under the fictitious impression that she had conferred an obligation by accepting it. Only a foreign woman could do such things, and Polly was guilty of similar gifts to all the young women. It was her way. It might be a lace handkerchief, a pink Paumotan pearl, or a comb of hawksbill turtle. It was all the same. Whatever their eyes rested on in joy was theirs. To women, as to men, she was irresistible.

"I don't dare admire anything any more," was Mary's plaint. "If I do she always gives it to me."

Frederick had never dreamed such a creature could exist. The women of his own race and place had never adumbrated such a possibility. He knew that whatever she did—her quick generosities, her hot enthusiasms or angers, her birdlike caressing ways—was unbelievably sincere. Her extravagant moods at the same time shocked and fascinated him. Her voice was as mercurial as her feelings. There were no even tones, and she talked with her hands. Yet, in her mouth, English was a new and beautiful language, softly limpid, with an audacity of phrase and tellingness of expression that conveyed subtleties and nuances as unambiguous and direct as they were unexpected from one of such childlikeness and simplicity. He woke up of nights and on his darkened eyelids saw bright memory-pictures of the backward turn of her vivid, laughing face.

IV

Like daughter like father. Tom, too, had been irresistible. All the world still called to him, and strange men came from time to time with its messages. Never had there been such visitors to the Travers home. Some came with the reminiscent roll of the sea in their gait. Others were black-browed ruffians; still others were fever-burnt and sallow; and about all of them was something bizarre and outlandish. Their talk was likewise bizarre and outlandish, of things to Frederick unguessed and undreamed, though he recognised the men for what they were—soldiers of fortune, adventurers, free lances of the world. But the big patent thing was the love and loyalty they bore their leader. They named him variously?—Black Tom, Blondine, Husky Travers, Malemute Tom, Swiftwater Tom—but most of all he was Captain Tom. Their projects and propositions were equally various, from the South Sea trader with the discovery of a new guano island and the Latin-American with a nascent revolution on his hands, on through Siberian gold chases and the prospecting of the placer benches of the upper Kuskokeem, to darker things that were mentioned only in whispers. And Captain Tom regretted the temporary indisposition that prevented immediate departure with them, and continued to sit and drowse more and more in the big chair. It was Polly, with a camaraderie distasteful to her uncle, who got these men aside and broke the news that Captain Tom would never go out on the shining ways again. But not all of them came with projects. Many made love-calls on their leader of old and unforgetable days, and Frederick sometimes was a witness to their meeting, and he marvelled anew at the mysterious charm in his brother that drew all men to him.

"By the turtles of Tasman!" cried one, "when I heard you was in California, Captain Tom, I just had to come and shake hands. I reckon you ain't forgot Tasman, eh?—nor the scrap at Thursday Island. Say—old Tasman was killed by his niggers only last year up German New Guinea way. Remember his cook-boy?—Ngani-Ngani? He was the ringleader. Tasman swore by him, but Ngani-Ngani hatcheted him just the same."

"Shake hands with Captain Carlsen, Fred," was Tom's introduction of his brother to another visitor. "He pulled me out of a tight place on the West Coast once. I'd have cashed in, Carlsen, if you hadn't happened along."

Captain Carlsen was a giant hulk of a man, with gimlet eyes of palest blue, a slash-scarred mouth that a blazing red beard could not quite hide, and a grip in his hand that made Frederick squirm.

A few minutes later, Tom had his brother aside.

"Say, Fred, do you think it will bother to advance me a thousand?"

"Of course," Frederick answered splendidly. "You know half of that I have is yours, Tom."

And when Captain Carlsen departed, Frederick was morally certain that the thousand dollars departed with him.

Small wonder Tom had made a failure of life—and come home to die. Frederick sat at his own orderly desk taking stock of the difference between him and his brother. Yes, and if it hadn't been for him, there would have been no home for Tom to die in.

Frederick cast back for solace through their joint history. It was he who had always been the mainstay, the dependable one. Tom had laughed and rollicked, played hooky from school, disobeyed Isaac's commandments. To the mountains or the sea, or in hot water with the neighbours and the town authorities—it was all the same; he was everywhere save where the dull plod of work obtained. And work was work in those backwoods days, and he, Frederick, had done the work. Early and late and all days he had been at it. He remembered the season when Isaac's wide plans had taken one of their smashes, when food had been scarce on the table of a man who owned a hundred thousand acres, when there had been no money to hire harvesters for the hay, and when Isaac would not let go his grip on a single one of his acres. He, Frederick, had pitched the hay, while Isaac mowed and raked. Tom had lain in bed and run up a doctor bill with a broken leg, gained by falling off the ridge-pole of the barn—which place was the last in the world to which any one would expect to go to pitch hay. About the only work Tom had ever done, it seemed to him, was to fetch in venison and bear-oil, to break colts, and to raise a din in the valley pastures and wooded canyons with his bear-hounds.

Tom was the elder, yet when Isaac died, the estate, with all its vast possibilities would have gone to ruin, had not he, Frederick, buckled down to it and put the burden on his back. Work! He remembered the enlargement of the town water-system—how he had manoeuvred and financed, persuaded small loans at ruinous interest, and laid pipe and made joints by lantern light while the workmen slept, and then been up ahead of them to outline and direct and rack his brains over the raising of the next week-end wages. For he had carried on old Isaac's policy. He would not let go. The future would vindicate.

And Tom!—with a bigger pack of bear dogs ranging the mountains and sleeping out a week at a time. Frederick remembered the final conference in the kitchen—Tom, and he, and Eliza Travers, who still cooked and baked and washed dishes on an estate that carried a hundred and eighty thousand dollars in mortgages.

"Don't divide," Eliza Travers had pleaded, resting her soap-flecked, parboiled arms. "Isaac was right. It will be worth millions. The country is opening up. We must all pull together."

"I don't want the estate," Tom cried. "Let Frederick have it. What I want...."

He never completed the sentence, but all the vision of the world burned in his eyes.

32

"I can't wait," he went on. "You can have the millions when they come. In the meantime let me have ten thousand. I'll sign off quitclaim to everything. And give me the old schooner, and some day I'll be back with a pot of money to help you out."

Frederick could see himself, in that far past day, throwing up his arms in horror and crying:

"Ten thousand!—when I'm strained to the breaking point to raise this quarter's interest!"

"There's the block of land next to the court house," Tom had urged. "I know the bank has a standing offer for ten thousand."

"But it will be worth a hundred thousand in ten years," Frederick had objected.

"Call it so. Say I quitclaim everything for a hundred thousand. Sell it for ten and let me have it. It's all I want, and I want it now. You can have the rest."

And Tom had had his will as usual (the block had been mortgaged instead of sold), and sailed away in the old schooner, the benediction of the town upon his head, for he had carried away in his crew half the riff-raff of the beach.

The bones of the schooner had been left on the coast of Java. That had been when Eliza Travers was being operated on for her eyes, and Frederick had kept it from her until indubitable proof came that Tom was still alive.

Frederick went over to his files and drew out a drawer labelled "Thomas Travers." In it were packets, methodically arranged. He went over the letters. They were from everywhere—China, Rangoon, Australia, South Africa, the Gold Coast, Patagonia, Armenia, Alaska. Briefly and infrequently written, they epitomised the wanderer's life. Frederick ran over in his mind a few of the glimpsed highlights of Tom's career. He had fought in some sort of foreign troubles in Armenia. He had been an officer in the Chinese army, and it was a certainty that the trade he later drove in the China Seas was illicit. He had been caught running arms into Cuba. It seemed he had always been running something somewhere that it ought not to have been run. And he had never outgrown it. One letter, on crinkly tissue paper, showed that as late as the Japanese-Russian War he had been caught running coal into Port Arthur and been taken to the prize court at Sasebo, where his steamer was confiscated and he remained a prisoner until the end of the war.

Frederick smiled as he read a paragraph: "*How do you prosper? Let me know any time a few thousands will help you.*" He looked at the date, April 18, 1883, and opened another packet. "*May 5th,*" 1883, was the dated sheet he drew out. "*Five thousand will put me on my feet again. If you can, and love me, send it along pronto—that's Spanish for rush.*"

He glanced again at the two dates. It was evident that somewhere between April 18th and May 5th Tom had come a cropper. With a smile, half bitter, Frederick skimmed on through the correspondence: "*There's a wreck on Midway Island. A fortune in it, salvage you know. Auction in two days. Cable me four thousand.*" The last he examined, ran: "*A deal I can swing with a little cash. It's big, I tell you. It's so big I don't dare tell you.*" He remembered that deal—a Latin-American revolution. He had sent the cash, and Tom had swung it, and himself as well, into a prison cell and a death sentence.

Tom had meant well, there was no denying that. And he had always religiously forwarded his I O U's. Frederick musingly weighed the packet of them in his hand, as though to determine if any relation existed between the weight of paper and the sums of money represented on it.

He put the drawer back in the cabinet and passed out. Glancing in at the big chair he saw Polly just tiptoeing from the room. Tom's head lay back, and his breathing was softly heavy, the sickness pronouncedly apparent on his relaxed face.

V

"I have worked hard," Frederick explained to Polly that evening on the veranda, unaware that when a man explains it is a sign his situation is growing parlous. "I have done what came to my hand—how creditably it is for others to say. And I have been paid for it. I have taken care of others and taken care of myself. The doctors say they have never seen such a constitution in a man of my years. Why, almost half my life is yet before me, and we Travers are a long-lived stock. I took care of myself, you see, and I have myself to show for it. I was not a waster. I conserved my heart and my arteries, and yet there are few men who can boast having done as much work as I have done. Look at that hand. Steady, eh? It will be as steady twenty years from now. There is nothing in playing fast and loose with oneself."

And all the while Polly had been following the invidious comparison that lurked behind his words.

"You can write 'Honourable' before your name," she flashed up proudly. "But my father has been a king. He has lived. Have you lived? What have you got to show for it? Stocks and bonds, and houses and servants—pouf! Heart and arteries and a steady hand—is that all? Have you lived merely to live? Were you afraid to die? I'd rather sing one wild song and burst my heart with it, than live a thousand years watching my digestion and being afraid of the wet. When you are dust, my father will be ashes. That is the difference."

"But my dear child—" he began.

"What have you got to show for it?" she flamed on. "Listen!"

From within, through the open window, came the tinkling of Tom's *ukulele* and the rollicking lilt of his voice in an Hawaiian *hula*. It ended in a throbbing, primitive love-call from the sensuous tropic night that no one could mistake. There was a burst of young voices, and a clamour for more. Frederick did not speak. He had sensed something vague and significant.

Turning, he glanced through the window at Tom, flushed and royal, surrounded by the young men and women, under his Viking moustache lighting a cigarette from a match held to him by one of the girls. It abruptly struck Frederick that never had he lighted a cigar at a match held in a woman's hand.

"Doctor Tyler says he oughtn't to smoke—it only aggravates," he said; and it was all he could say.

As the fall of the year came on, a new type of men began to frequent the house. They proudly called themselves "sour-doughs," and they were arriving in San Francisco on the winter's furlough from the gold-diggings of Alaska. More and more of them came, and they pre-empted a large portion of one of the down-town hotels. Captain Tom was fading with the season, and almost lived in the big chair. He drowsed oftener and longer, but whenever he awoke he was surrounded by his court of young people, or there was some comrade waiting to sit and yarn about the old gold days and plan for the new gold days.

For Tom—Husky Travers, the Yukoners named him—never thought that the end approached. A temporary illness, he called it, the natural enfeeblement following upon a prolonged bout with Yucatan fever. In the spring he would be right and fit again. Cold weather was what he needed. His blood had been cooked. In the meantime it was a case of take it easy and make the most of the rest.

And no one undeceived him—not even the Yukoners, who smoked pipes and black cigars and chewed tobacco on Frederick's broad verandas until he felt like an intruder in his own house. There was no touch with them. They regarded him as a stranger to be tolerated. They came to see Tom. And their manner of seeing him was provocative of innocent envy pangs to Frederick. Day after day he watched them. He would see the Yukoners meet, perhaps one just leaving the sick room and one just going in. They would clasp hands, solemnly and silently, outside the door. The newcomer would question with his eyes, and the other would shake his head. And more than once Frederick noted the moisture in their eyes. Then the newcomer would enter and draw his chair up to Tom's, and with jovial voice proceed to plan the outfitting for the exploration of the upper Kuskokeem; for it was there Tom was bound in the spring. Dogs could be had at Larabee's—a clean breed, too, with no taint of the soft Southland strains. It was rough country, it was reported, but if sour-doughs couldn't make the traverse from Larabee's in forty days they'd like to see a *chechako* do it in sixty.

And so it went, until Frederick wondered, when he came to die, if there was one man in the county, much less in the adjoining county, who would come to him at his bedside.

Seated at his desk, through the open windows would drift whiffs of strong tobacco and rumbling voices, and he could not help catching snatches of what the Yukoners talked.

"D'ye recollect that Koyokuk rush in the early nineties?" he would hear one say. "Well, him an' me was pardners then, tradin' an' such. We had a dinky little steamboat, the *Blatterbat*. He named her that, an' it stuck. He was a caution. Well, sir, as I was sayin', him an' me loaded the little *Blatterbat* to the guards an' started up the Koyokuk, me firin' an' engineerin' an' him steerin', an' both of us deck-handin'. Once in a while we'd tie to the bank an' cut firewood. It was the fall, an' mush-ice was comin' down, an' everything gettin' ready for the freeze up. You see, we was north of the Arctic Circle then an' still headin' north. But they was two hundred miners in there needin' grub if they wintered, an' we had the grub.

"Well, sir, pretty soon they begun to pass us, driftin' down the river in canoes an' rafts. They was pullin' out. We kept track of them. When a hundred an' ninety-four had passed, we didn't see no reason for keepin' on. So we turned tail and started down. A cold snap had come, an' the water was fallin' fast, an' dang me if we didn't ground on a bar—up-stream side. The *Blatterbat* hung up solid. Couldn't budge her. 'It's a shame to waste all that grub,' says I, just as we was pullin' out in a canoe. 'Let's stay an' eat it,' says he. An' dang me if we didn't. We wintered right there on the *Blatterbat*, huntin' and tradin' with the Indians, an' when the river broke next year we brung down eight thousand dollars' worth of skins. Now a whole winter, just two of us, is goin' some. But never a cross word out of him. Best-tempered pardner I ever seen. But fight!"

"Huh!" came the other voice. "I remember the winter Oily Jones allowed he'd clean out Forty Mile. Only he didn't, for about the second yap he let off he ran afoul of Husky Travers. It was in the White Caribou. 'I'm a wolf!' yaps Jones. You know his style, a gun in his belt, fringes on his moccasins, and long hair down his back. 'I'm a wolf,' he yaps, 'an' this is my night to howl. Hear me, you long lean makeshift of a human critter?'—an' this to Husky Travers."

"Well?" the other voice queried, after a pause.

"In about a second an' a half Oily Jones was on the floor an' Husky on top askin' somebody kindly to pass him a butcher knife. What's he do but plumb hack off all of Oily Jones' long hair. 'Now howl, damn you, howl,' says Husky, gettin' up."

"He was a cool one, for a wild one," the first voice took up. "I seen him buck roulette in the Little Wolverine, drop nine thousand in two hours, borrow some more, win it back in fifteen minutes, buy the drinks, an' cash in—dang me, all in fifteen minutes."

One evening Tom was unusually brightly awake, and Frederick, joining the rapt young circle, sat and listened to his brother's serio-comic narrative of the night of wreck on the island of Blang; of the swim through the sharks where half the crew was lost; of the great pearl which Desay brought ashore with him; of the head-decorated palisade that surrounded the grass palace wherein dwelt the Malay queen with her royal consort, a shipwrecked Chinese Eurasian; of the intrigue for the pearl of Desay; of mad feasts and dances in the barbaric night, and quick dangers and sudden deaths; of the queen's love-making to Desay, of Desay's love-making to the queen's daughter, and of Desay, every joint crushed, still alive, staked out on the reef at low tide to be eaten by the sharks; of the coming of the plague; of the beating of tom-toms and the exorcising of the devil-devil doctors; of the flight over the man-trapped, wild-pig runs of the mountain bush-men; and of the final rescue by Tasman, he who was hatcheted only last year and whose head reposed in some Melanesian stronghold—and all breathing of the warmth and abandon and savagery of the burning islands of the sun.

And despite himself, Frederick sat entranced; and when all the tale was told, he was aware of a queer emptiness. He remembered back to his boyhood, when he had pored over the illustrations in the old-fashioned geography. He, too, had dreamed of amazing adventure in far places and desired to go out on the shining ways. And he had planned to go; yet he had known only work and duty. Perhaps that was the difference. Perhaps that was the secret of the strange wisdom in his brother's eyes. For the moment, faint and far, vicariously, he glimpsed the lordly vision his brother had seen. He remembered a sharp saying of Polly's. "You have missed romance. You traded it for dividends." She was right, and yet, not fair. He had wanted romance, but the work had been placed ready to his hand. He had toiled and moiled, day and night, and been faithful to his trust. Yet he had missed love and the world-living that was forever a-whisper in his brother. And what had Tom done to deserve it?—a wastrel and an idle singer of songs.

His place was high. He was going to be the next governor of California. But what man would come to him and lie to him out of love? The thought of all his property seemed to put a dry and gritty taste in his mouth. Property! Now that he looked at it, one thousand dollars was like any other thousand dollars; and one day (of his days) was like any other day. He had never made the pictures in the geography come true. He had not struck his man, nor lighted his cigar at a match held in a woman's hand. A man could sleep in only one bed at a time—Tom had said that. He shuddered as he strove to estimate how many beds he owned, how many blankets he had bought. And all the beds and blankets would not buy one man to come from the end of the earth, and grip his hand, and cry, "By the turtles of Tasman!"

Something of all this he told Polly, an undercurrent of complaint at the unfairness of things in his tale. And she had answered:

"It couldn't have been otherwise. Father bought it. He never drove bargains. It was a royal thing, and he paid for it royally. You grudged the price, don't you see. You saved your arteries and your money and kept your feet dry."

VI

On an afternoon in the late fall all were gathered about the big chair and Captain Tom. Though he did not know it, he had drowsed the whole day through and only just awakened to call for his *ukulele* and light a cigarette at Polly's hand. But the *ukulele* lay idle on his arm, and though the pine logs crackled in the huge fireplace he shivered and took note of the cold.

"It's a good sign," he said, unaware that the faintness of his voice drew the heads of his listeners closer. "The cold weather will be a tonic. It's a hard job to work the tropics out of one's blood. But I'm beginning to shape up now for the Kuskokeem. In the spring, Polly, we start with the dogs, and you'll see the midnight sun. How your mother would have liked the trip. She was a game one. Forty sleeps with the dogs, and we'll be shaking out yellow nuggets from the moss-roots. Larabee has some fine animals. I know the breed. They're timber wolves, that's what they are, big grey timber wolves, though they sport brown about one in a litter—isn't that right, Bennington?"

"One in a litter, that's just about the average," Bennington, the Yukoner, replied promptly, but in a voice hoarsely unrecognisable.

"And you must never travel alone with them," Captain Tom went on. "For if you fall down they'll jump you. Larabee's brutes only respect a man when he stands upright on his legs. When he goes down, he's meat. I remember coming over the divide from Tanana to Circle City. That was before the Klondike strike. It was in '94 ... no, '95, and the bottom had dropped out of the thermometer. There was a young Canadian with the outfit. His name was it was ... a peculiar one ... wait a minute it will come to me...."

His voice ceased utterly, though his lips still moved. A look of unbelief and vast surprise dawned on his face. Followed a sharp, convulsive shudder. And in that moment, without warning, he saw Death. He looked clear-eyed and steady, as if pondering, then turned to Polly. His hand moved impotently, as if to reach hers, and when he found it, his fingers could not close. He gazed at her with a great smile that slowly faded. The eyes drooped as the life went out, and remained a face of quietude and repose. The *ukulele* clattered to the floor. One by one they went softly from the room, leaving Polly alone.

From the veranda, Frederick watched a man coming up the driveway. By the roll of the sea in his walk, Frederick could guess for whom the stranger came. The face was swarthy with sun and wrinkled with age that was given the lie by the briskness of his movements and the alertness in the keen black eyes. In the lobe of each ear was a tiny circlet of gold.

"How do you do, sir," the man said, and it was patent that English was not the tongue he had learned at his mother's knee. "How's Captain Tom? They told me in the town that he was sick."

"My brother is dead," Frederick answered.

The stranger turned his head and gazed out over the park-like grounds and up to the distant redwood peaks, and Frederick noted that he swallowed with an effort.

"By the turtles of Tasman, he was a man," he said, in a deep, changed voice.

"By the turtles of Tasman, he was a man," Frederick repeated; nor did he stumble over the unaccustomed oath.

THE ETERNITY OF FORMS

A strange life has come to an end in the death of Mr. Sedley Crayden, of Crayden Hill.

Mild, harmless, he was the victim of a strange delusion that kept him pinned, night and day, in his chair for the last two years of his life. The mysterious death, or, rather, disappearance, of his elder brother, James Crayden, seems to have preyed upon his mind, for it was shortly after that event that his delusion began to manifest itself.

Mr. Crayden never vouchsafed any explanation of his strange conduct. There was nothing the matter with him physically; and, mentally, the alienists found him normal in every way save for his one remarkable idiosyncrasy. His remaining in his chair was purely voluntary, an act of his own will. And now he is dead, and the mystery remains unsolved.

—*Extract from the Newton Courier-Times.*

Briefly, I was Mr. Sedley Crayden's confidential servant and valet for the last eight months of his life. During that time he wrote a great deal in a manuscript that he kept always beside him, except when he drowsed or slept, at which times he invariably locked it in a desk drawer close to his hand.

I was curious to read what the old gentleman wrote, but he was too cautious and cunning. I never got a peep at the manuscript. If he were engaged upon it when I attended on him, he covered the top sheet with a large blotter. It was I who found him dead in his chair, and it was then that I took the liberty of abstracting the manuscript. I was very curious to read it, and I have no excuses to offer.

After retaining it in my secret possession for several years, and after ascertaining that Mr. Crayden left no surviving relatives, I have decided to make the nature of the manuscript known. It is very long, and I have omitted nearly all of it, giving only the more lucid fragments. It bears all the earmarks of a disordered mind, and various experiences are repeated over and over, while much is so vague and incoherent as to defy comprehension. Nevertheless, from reading it myself, I venture to predict that if an excavation is made in the main basement, somewhere in the vicinity of the foundation of the great chimney, a collection of bones will be found which should very closely resemble those which James Crayden once clothed in mortal flesh.

—*Statement of Rudolph Heckler.*

Here follows the excerpts from the manuscript, made and arranged by Rudolph Heckler:

I never killed my brother. Let this be my first word and my last. Why should I kill him? We lived together in unbroken harmony for twenty years. We were old men, and the fires and tempers of youth had long since burned out. We never disagreed even over the most trivial things. Never was there such amity as ours. We were scholars. We cared nothing for the outside world. Our companionship and our books were all-satisfying. Never were there such talks as we held. Many a night we have sat up till two and three in the morning, conversing, weighing opinions and judgments, referring to authorities—in short, we lived at high and friendly intellectual altitudes.

He disappeared. I suffered a great shock. Why should he have disappeared? Where could he have gone? It was very strange. I was stunned. They say I was very sick for weeks. It was brain fever. This was caused by his inexplicable disappearance. It was at the beginning of the experience I hope here to relate, that he disappeared.

How I have endeavoured to find him. I am not an excessively rich man, yet have I offered continually increasing rewards. I have advertised in all the papers, and sought the aid of all the detective bureaus. At the present moment, the rewards I have out aggregate over fifty thousand dollars.

They say he was murdered. They also say murder will out. Then I say, why does not his murder come out? Who did it? Where is he? Where is Jim? My Jim?

We were so happy together. He had a remarkable mind, a most remarkable mind, so firmly founded, so widely informed, so rigidly logical, that it was not at all strange that we agreed in all things. Dissension was unknown between us. Jim was the most truthful man I have ever met. In this, too, we were similar, as we were similar in our intellectual honesty. We never sacrificed truth to make a point. We had no points to make, we so thoroughly agreed. It is absurd to think that we could disagree on anything under the sun.

I wish he would come back. Why did he go? Who can ever explain it? I am lonely now, and depressed with grave forebodings—frightened by terrors that are of the mind and that put at naught all that my mind has ever conceived. Form is mutable. This is the last word of positive science. The dead do not come back. This is incontrovertible. The dead are dead, and that is the end of it, and of them. And yet I have had experiences here—here, in this very room, at this very desk, that—But wait. Let me put it down in black and white, in words simple and unmistakable. Let me ask some questions. Who mislays my pen? That is what I desire to know. Who uses up my ink so rapidly? Not I. And yet the ink goes.

The answer to these questions would settle all the enigmas of the universe. I know the answer. I am not a fool. And some day, if I am plagued too desperately, I shall give the answer myself. I shall give the name of him who mislays my pen and uses up my ink. It is so silly to think that I could use such a quantity of ink. The servant lies. I know.

I have got me a fountain pen. I have always disliked the device, but my old stub had to go. I burned it in the fireplace. The ink I keep under lock and key. I shall see if I cannot put a stop to these lies that are being written about me. And I have other plans. It is not true that I have recanted. I still believe that I live in a mechanical universe. It has not been proved otherwise to me, for all that I have peered over his shoulder and read his malicious statement to the contrary. He gives me credit for no less than average stupidity. He thinks I think he is real. How silly. I know he is a brain-figment, nothing more.

There are such things as hallucinations. Even as I looked over his shoulder and read, I knew that this was such a thing. If I were only well it would be interesting. All my life I have wanted to experience such phenomena. And now it has come to me. I shall make the most of it. What is imagination? It can make something where there is nothing. How can anything be something where there is nothing? How can anything be something and nothing at the same time? I leave it for the metaphysicians to ponder. I know better. No scholastics for me. This is a real world, and everything in it is real. What is not real, is not. Therefore he is not. Yet he tries to fool me into believing that he is ... when all the time I know he has no existence outside of my own brain cells.

I saw him to-day, seated at the desk, writing. It gave me quite a shock, because I had thought he was quite dispelled. Nevertheless, on looking steadily, I found that he was not there—the old familiar trick of the brain. I have dwelt too long on what has happened. I am becoming morbid, and my old indigestion is hinting and muttering. I shall take exercise. Each day I shall walk for two hours.

It is impossible. I cannot exercise. Each time I return from my walk, he is sitting in my chair at the desk. It grows more difficult to drive him away. It is my chair. Upon this I insist. It *was* his, but he is dead and it is no longer his. How one can be befooled by the phantoms of his own imagining! There is nothing real in this apparition. I know it. I am firmly grounded with my fifty years of study. The dead are dead.

And yet, explain one thing. To-day, before going for my walk, I carefully put the fountain pen in my pocket before leaving the room. I remember it distinctly. I looked at the clock at the time. It was twenty minutes past ten. Yet on my return there was the pen lying on the desk. Some one had been using it. There was very little ink left. I wish he would not write so much. It is disconcerting.

There was one thing upon which Jim and I were not quite agreed. He believed in the eternity of the forms of things. Therefore, entered in immediately the consequent belief in immortality, and all the other notions of the metaphysical philosophers. I had little patience with him in this. Painstakingly I have traced to him the evolution of his belief in the eternity of forms, showing him how it has arisen out of his early infatuation with logic and mathematics. Of course, from that warped, squinting, abstract viewpoint, it is very easy to believe in the eternity of forms.

I laughed at the unseen world. Only the real was real, I contended, and what one did not perceive, was not, could not be. I believed in a mechanical universe. Chemistry and physics explained everything. "Can no being be?" he demanded in reply. I said that his question was but the major promise of a fallacious Christian Science syllogism. Oh, believe me, I know my logic, too. But he was very stubborn. I never had any patience with philosophic idealists.

Once, I made to him my confession of faith. It was simple, brief, unanswerable. Even as I write it now I know that it is unanswerable. Here it is. I told him: "I assert, with Hobbes, that it is impossible to separate thought from matter that thinks. I assert, with Bacon, that all human understanding arises from the world of sensations. I assert, with Locke, that all human ideas are due to the functions of the senses. I assert, with Kant, the mechanical origin of the universe, and that creation is a natural and historical process. I assert, with Laplace, that there is no need of the hypothesis of a creator. And, finally, I assert, because of all the foregoing, that form is ephemeral. Form passes. Therefore we pass."

I repeat, it was unanswerable. Yet did he answer with Paley's notorious fallacy of the watch. Also, he talked about radium, and all but asserted that the very existence of matter had been exploded by these later-day laboratory researches. It was childish. I had not dreamed he could be so immature.

How could one argue with such a man? I then asserted the reasonableness of all that is. To this he agreed, reserving, however, one exception. He looked at me, as he said it, in a way I could not mistake. The inference was obvious.

46

That he should be guilty of so cheap a quip in the midst of a serious discussion, astounded me.

The eternity of forms. It is ridiculous. Yet is there a strange magic in the words. If it be true, then has he not ceased to exist. Then does he exist. This is impossible.

I have ceased exercising. As long as I remain in the room, the hallucination does not bother me. But when I return to the room after an absence, he is always there, sitting at the desk, writing. Yet I dare not confide in a physician. I must fight this out by myself.

He grows more importunate. To-day, consulting a book on the shelf, I turned and found him again in the chair. This is the first time he has dared do this in my presence. Nevertheless, by looking at him steadily and sternly for several minutes, I compelled him to vanish. This proves my contention. He does not exist. If he were an eternal form I could not make him vanish by a mere effort of my will.

This is getting damnable. To-day I gazed at him for an entire hour before I could make him leave. Yet it is so simple. What I see is a memory picture. For twenty years I was accustomed to seeing him there at the desk. The present phenomenon is merely a recrudescence of that memory picture—a picture which was impressed countless times on my consciousness.

I gave up to-day. He exhausted me, and still he would not go. I sat and watched him hour after hour. He takes no notice of me, but continually writes. I know what he writes, for I read it over his shoulder. It is not true. He is taking an unfair advantage.

Query: He is a product of my consciousness; is it possible, then, that entities may be created by consciousness?

We did not quarrel. To this day I do not know how it happened. Let me tell you. Then you will see. We sat up late that never-to-be-forgotten last night of his existence. It was the old, old discussion—the eternity of forms. How many hours and how many nights we had consumed over it!

On this night he had been particularly irritating, and all my nerves were screaming. He had been maintaining that the human soul was itself a form, an eternal form, and that the light within his brain would go on forever and always. I took up the poker.

"Suppose," I said, "I should strike you dead with this?"

"I would go on," he answered.

"As a conscious entity?" I demanded.

"Yes, as a conscious entity," was his reply. "I should go on, from plane to plane of higher existence, remembering my earth-life, you, this very argument—ay, and continuing the argument with you."

It was only argument[1]. I swear it was only argument. I never lifted a hand. How could I? He was my brother, my elder brother, Jim.

I cannot remember. I was very exasperated. He had always been so obstinate in this metaphysical belief of his. The next I knew, he was lying on the hearth. Blood was running. It was terrible. He did not speak. He did not move. He must have fallen in a fit and struck his head. I noticed there was blood on the poker. In falling he must have struck upon it with his head. And yet I fail to see how this can be, for I held it in my hand all the time. I was still holding it in my hand as I looked at it.

It is an hallucination. That is a conclusion of common sense. I have watched the growth of it. At first it was only in the dimmest light that I could see him sitting in the chair. But as the time passed, and the hallucination, by repetition, strengthened, he was able to appear in the chair under the strongest lights. That is the explanation. It is quite satisfactory.

I shall never forget the first time I saw it. I had dined alone downstairs. I never drink wine, so that what happened was eminently normal. It was in the summer twilight that I returned to the study. I glanced at the desk. There he was, sitting. So natural was it, that before I knew I cried out "Jim!" Then I remembered all that had happened. Of course it was an hallucination. I knew that. I took the poker and went over to it. He did not move nor vanish. The poker cleaved through the non-existent substance of the thing and struck the back of the chair. Fabric of fancy, that is all it was. The mark is there on the chair now where the poker struck. I pause from my writing and turn and look at it—press the tips of my fingers into the indentation.

He *did* continue the argument. I stole up to-day and looked over his shoulder. He was writing the history of our discussion. It was the same old nonsense about the eternity of forms. But as I continued to read, he wrote down the practical test I had made with the poker. Now this is unfair and untrue. I made no test. In falling he struck his head on the poker.

Some day, somebody will find and read what he writes. This will be terrible. I am suspicious of the servant, who is always peeping and peering, trying to see what I write. I must do something. Every servant I have had is curious about what I write.

Fabric of fancy. That is all it is. There is no Jim who sits in the chair. I know that. Last night, when the house was asleep, I went down into the cellar and looked carefully at the soil around the chimney. It was untampered with. The dead do not rise up.

Yesterday morning, when I entered the study, there he was in the chair. When I had dispelled him, I sat in the chair myself all day. I had my meals brought to me. And thus I escaped the sight of him for many hours, for he appears only in the chair. I was weary, but I sat late, until eleven o'clock. Yet, when I stood up to go to bed, I looked around, and there he was. He had slipped into the chair on the instant. Being only fabric of fancy, all day he had resided in my brain. The moment it was unoccupied, he took up his residence in the chair. Are these his boasted higher planes of existence—his brother's brain and a chair? After all, was he not right? Has his eternal form become so attenuated as to be an hallucination? Are hallucinations real entities? Why not? There is food for thought here. Some day I shall come to a conclusion upon it.

He was very much disturbed to-day. He could not write, for I had made the servant carry the pen out of the room in his pocket But neither could I write.

The servant never sees him. This is strange. Have I developed a keener sight for the unseen? Or rather does it not prove the phantom to be what it is—a product of my own morbid consciousness?

He has stolen my pen again. Hallucinations cannot steal pens. This is unanswerable. And yet I cannot keep the pen always out of the room. I want to write myself.

I have had three different servants since my trouble came upon me, and not one has seen him. Is the verdict of their senses right? And is that of mine wrong? Nevertheless, the ink goes too rapidly. I fill my pen more often than is necessary. And furthermore, only to-day I found my pen out of order. I did not break it.

I have spoken to him many times, but he never answers. I sat and watched him all morning. Frequently he looked at me, and it was patent that he knew me.

By striking the side of my head violently with the heel of my hand, I can shake the vision of him out of my eyes. Then I can get into the chair; but I have learned that I must move very quickly in order to accomplish this. Often he fools me and is back again before I can sit down.

It is getting unbearable. He is a jack-in-the-box the way he pops into the chair. He does not assume form slowly. He pops. That is the only way to describe it. I cannot stand looking at him much more. That way lies madness, for it compels me almost to believe in the reality of what I know is not. Besides, hallucinations do not pop.

Thank God he only manifests himself in the chair. As long as I occupy the chair I am quit of him.

My device for dislodging him from the chair by striking my head, is failing. I have to hit much more violently, and I do not succeed perhaps more than once in a dozen trials. My head is quite sore where I have so repeatedly struck it. I must use the other hand.

My brother was right. There is an unseen world. Do I not see it? Am I not cursed with the seeing of it all the time? Call it a thought, an idea, anything you will, still it is there. It is unescapable. Thoughts are entities. We create with every act of thinking. I have created this phantom that sits in my chair and uses my ink. Because I have created him is no reason that he is any the less real. He is an idea; he is an entity: ergo, ideas are entities, and an entity is a reality.

Query: If a man, with the whole historical process behind him, can create an entity, a real thing, then is not the hypothesis of a Creator made substantial? If the stuff of life can create, then it is fair to assume that there can be a He who created the stuff of life. It is merely a difference of degree. I have not yet made a mountain nor a solar system, but I have made a something that sits in my chair. This being so, may I not some day be able to make a mountain or a solar system?

All his days, down to to-day, man has lived in a maze. He has never seen the light. I am convinced that I am beginning to see the light—not as my brother saw it, by stumbling upon it accidentally, but deliberately and rationally. My brother is dead. He has ceased. There is no doubt about it, for I have made another journey down into the cellar to see. The ground was untouched. I broke it myself to make sure, and I saw what made me sure. My brother has ceased, yet have I recreated him. This is not my old brother, yet it is something as nearly resembling him as I could fashion it. I am unlike other men. I am a god. I have created.

Whenever I leave the room to go to bed, I look back, and there is my brother sitting in the chair. And then I cannot sleep because of thinking of him sitting through all the long night-hours. And in the morning, when I open the study door, there he is, and I know he has sat there the night long.

I am becoming desperate from lack of sleep. I wish I could confide in a physician.

Blessed sleep! I have won to it at last. Let me tell you. Last night I was so worn that I found myself dozing in my chair. I rang for the servant and ordered him to bring blankets. I slept. All night was he banished from my thoughts as he was banished from my chair. I shall remain in it all day. It is a wonderful relief.

It is uncomfortable to sleep in a chair. But it is more uncomfortable to lie in bed, hour after hour, and not sleep, and to know that he is sitting there in the cold darkness.

It is no use. I shall never be able to sleep in a bed again. I have tried it now, numerous times, and every such night is a horror. If I could but only persuade him to go to bed! But no. He sits there, and sits there—I know he does—while I stare and stare up into the blackness and think and think, continually think, of him sitting there. I wish I had never heard of the eternity of forms.

The servants think I am crazy. That is but to be expected, and it is why I have never called in a physician.

I am resolved. Henceforth this hallucination ceases. From now on I shall remain in the chair. I shall never leave it. I shall remain in it night and day and always.

I have succeeded. For two weeks I have not seen him. Nor shall I ever see him again. I have at last attained the equanimity of mind necessary for philosophic thought. I wrote a complete chapter to-day.

It is very wearisome, sitting in a chair. The weeks pass, the months come and go, the seasons change, the servants replace each other, while I remain. I only remain. It is a strange life I lead, but at least I am at peace.

He comes no more. There is no eternity of forms. I have proved it. For nearly two years now, I have remained in this chair, and I have not seen him once. True, I was severely tried for a time. But it is clear that what I thought I saw was merely hallucination. He never was. Yet I do not leave the chair. I am afraid to leave the chair.

FOOTNOTES:

[1] (Forcible—ha! ha!—comment of Rudolph Heckler on margin.)

TOLD IN THE DROOLING WARD

Me? I'm not a drooler. I'm the assistant, I don't know what Miss Jones or Miss Kelsey could do without me. There are fifty-five low-grade droolers in this ward, and how could they ever all be fed if I wasn't around? I like to feed droolers. They don't make trouble. They can't. Something's wrong with most of their legs and arms, and they can't talk. They're very low-grade. I can walk, and talk, and do things. You must be careful with the droolers and not feed them too fast. Then they choke. Miss Jones says I'm an expert. When a new nurse comes I show her how to do it. It's funny watching a new nurse try to feed them. She goes at it so slow and careful that supper time would be around before she finished shoving down their breakfast. Then I show her, because I'm an expert. Dr. Dalrymple says I am, and he ought to know. A drooler can eat twice as fast if you know how to make him.

My name's Tom. I'm twenty-eight years old. Everybody knows me in the institution. This is an institution, you know. It belongs to the State of California and is run by politics. I know. I've been here a long time. Everybody trusts me. I run errands all over the place, when I'm not busy with the droolers. I like droolers. It makes me think how lucky I am that I ain't a drooler.

I like it here in the Home. I don't like the outside. I know. I've been around a bit, and run away, and adopted. Me for the Home, and for the drooling ward best of all. I don't look like a drooler, do I? You can tell the difference soon as you look at me. I'm an assistant, expert assistant. That's going some for a feeb. Feeb? Oh, that's feeble-minded. I thought you knew. We're all feebs in here.

But I'm a high-grade feeb. Dr. Dalrymple says I'm too smart to be in the Home, but I never let on. It's a pretty good place. And I don't throw fits like lots of the feebs. You see that house up there through the trees. The high-grade epilecs all live in it by themselves. They're stuck up because they ain't just ordinary feebs. They call it the club house, and they say they're just as good as anybody outside, only they're sick. I don't like them much. They laugh at me, when they ain't busy throwing fits. But I don't care. I never have to be scared about falling down and busting my head. Sometimes they run around in circles trying to find a place to sit down quick, only they don't. Low-grade epilecs are disgusting, and high-grade epilecs put on airs. I'm glad I ain't an epilec. There ain't anything to them. They just talk big, that's all.

Miss Kelsey says I talk too much. But I talk sense, and that's more than the other feebs do. Dr. Dalrymple says I have the gift of language. I know it. You ought to hear me talk when I'm by myself, or when I've got a drooler to listen. Sometimes I think I'd like to be a politician, only it's too much trouble. They're all great talkers; that's how they hold their jobs.

Nobody's crazy in this institution. They're just feeble in their minds. Let me tell you something funny. There's about a dozen high-grade girls that set the tables in the big dining room. Sometimes when they're done ahead of time, they all sit down in chairs in a circle and talk. I sneak up to the door and listen, and I nearly die to keep from laughing. Do you want to know what they talk? It's like this. They don't say a word for a long time. And then one says, "Thank God I'm not feeble-minded." And all the rest nod their heads and look pleased. And then nobody says anything for a time. After which the next girl in the circle says, "Thank God I'm not feeble-minded," and they nod their heads all over again. And it goes on around the circle, and they never say anything else. Now they're real feebs, ain't they? I leave it to you. I'm not that kind of a feeb, thank God.

Sometimes I don't think I'm a feeb at all. I play in the band and read music. We're all supposed to be feebs in the band except the leader. He's crazy. We know it, but we never talk about it except amongst ourselves. His job is politics, too, and we don't want him to lose it. I play the drum. They can't get along without me in this institution. I was sick once, so I know. It's a wonder the drooling ward didn't break down while I was in hospital.

I could get out of here if I wanted to. I'm not so feeble as some might think. But I don't let on. I have too good a time. Besides, everything would run down if I went away. I'm afraid some time they'll find out I'm not a feeb and send me out into the world to earn my own living. I know the world, and I don't like it. The Home is fine enough for me.

You see how I grin sometimes. I can't help that. But I can put it on a lot. I'm not bad, though. I look at myself in the glass. My mouth is funny, I know that, and it lops down, and my teeth are bad. You can tell a feeb anywhere by looking at his mouth and teeth. But that doesn't prove I'm a feeb. It's just because I'm lucky that I look like one.

I know a lot. If I told you all I know, you'd be surprised. But when I don't want to know, or when they want me to do something I don't want to do, I just let my mouth lop down and laugh and make foolish noises. I watch the foolish noises made by the low-grades, and I can fool anybody. And I know a lot of foolish noises. Miss Kelsey called me a fool the other day. She was very angry, and that was where I fooled her.

Miss Kelsey asked me once why I don't write a book about feebs. I was telling her what was the matter with little Albert. He's a drooler, you know, and I can always tell the way he twists his left eye what's the matter with him. So I was explaining it to Miss Kelsey, and, because she didn't know, it made her mad. But some day, mebbe, I'll write that book. Only it's so much trouble. Besides, I'd sooner talk.

Do you know what a micro is? It's the kind with the little heads no bigger than your fist. They're usually droolers, and they live a long time. The hydros don't drool. They have the big heads, and they're smarter. But they never grow up. They always die. I never look at one without thinking he's going to die. Sometimes, when I'm feeling lazy, or the nurse is mad at me, I wish I was a drooler with nothing to do and somebody to feed me. But I guess I'd sooner talk and be what I am.

Only yesterday Doctor Dalrymple said to me, "Tom," he said, "I just don't know what I'd do without you." And he ought to know, seeing as he's had the bossing of a thousand feebs for going on two years. Dr. Whatcomb was before him. They get appointed, you know. It's politics. I've seen a whole lot of doctors here in my time. I was here before any of them. I've been in this institution twenty-five years. No, I've got no complaints. The institution couldn't be run better.

It's a snap to be a high-grade feeb. Just look at Doctor Dalrymple. He has troubles. He holds his job by politics. You bet we high-graders talk politics. We know all about it, and it's bad. An institution like this oughtn't to be run on politics. Look at Doctor Dalrymple. He's been here two years and learned a lot. Then politics will come along and throw him out and send a new doctor who don't know anything about feebs.

I've been acquainted with just thousands of nurses in my time. Some of them are nice. But they come and go. Most of the women get married. Sometimes I think I'd like to get married. I spoke to Dr. Whatcomb about it once, but he told me he was very sorry, because feebs ain't allowed to get married. I've been in love. She was a nurse. I won't tell you her name. She had blue eyes, and yellow hair, and a kind voice, and she liked me. She told me so. And she always told me to be a good boy. And I was, too, until afterward, and then I ran away. You see, she went off and got married, and she didn't tell me about it.

I guess being married ain't what it's cracked up to be. Dr. Anglin and his wife used to fight. I've seen them. And once I heard her call him a feeb. Now nobody has a right to call anybody a feeb that ain't. Dr. Anglin got awful mad when she called him that. But he didn't last long. Politics drove him out, and Doctor Mandeville came. He didn't have a wife. I heard him talking one time with the engineer. The engineer and his wife fought like cats and dogs, and that day Doctor Mandeville told him he was damn glad he wasn't tied to no petticoats. A petticoat is a skirt. I knew what he meant, if I was a feeb. But I never let on. You hear lots when you don't let on.

I've seen a lot in my time. Once I was adopted, and went away on the railroad over forty miles to live with a man named Peter Bopp and his wife. They had a ranch. Doctor Anglin said I was strong and bright, and I said I was, too. That was because I wanted to be adopted. And Peter Bopp said he'd give me a good home, and the lawyers fixed up the papers.

But I soon made up my mind that a ranch was no place for me. Mrs. Bopp was scared to death of me and wouldn't let me sleep in the house. They fixed up the woodshed and made me sleep there. I had to get up at four o'clock and feed the horses, and milk cows, and carry the milk to the neighbours. They called it chores, but it kept me going all day. I chopped wood, and cleaned chicken houses, and weeded vegetables, and did most everything on the place. I never had any fun. I hadn't no time.

Let me tell you one thing. I'd sooner feed mush and milk to feebs than milk cows with the frost on the ground. Mrs. Bopp was scared to let me play with her children. And I was scared, too. They used to make faces at me when nobody was looking, and call me "Looney." Everybody called me Looney Tom. And the other boys in the neighbourhood threw rocks at me. You never see anything like that in the Home here. The feebs are better behaved.

Mrs. Bopp used to pinch me and pull my hair when she thought I was too slow, and I only made foolish noises and went slower. She said I'd be the death of her some day. I left the boards off the old well in the pasture, and the pretty new calf fell in and got drowned. Then Peter Bopp said he was going to give me a licking. He did, too. He took a strap halter and went at me. It was awful. I'd never had a licking in my life. They don't do such things in the Home, which is why I say the Home is the place for me.

I know the law, and I knew he had no right to lick me with a strap halter. That was being cruel, and the guardianship papers said he mustn't be cruel. I didn't say anything. I just waited, which shows you what kind of a feeb I am. I waited a long time, and got slower, and made more foolish noises; but he wouldn't, send me back to the Home, which was what I wanted. But one day, it was the first of the month, Mrs. Brown gave me three dollars, which was for her milk bill with Peter Bopp. That was in the morning. When I brought the milk in the evening I was to bring back the receipt. But I didn't. I just walked down to the station, bought a ticket like any one, and rode on the train back to the Home. That's the kind of a feeb I am.

Doctor Anglin was gone then, and Doctor Mandeville had his place. I walked right into his office. He didn't know me. "Hello," he said, "this ain't visiting day." "I ain't a visitor," I said. "I'm Tom. I belong here." Then he whistled and showed he was surprised. I told him all about it, and showed him the marks of the strap halter, and he got madder and madder all the time and said he'd attend to Mr. Peter Bopp's case.

And mebbe you think some of them little droolers weren't glad to see me.

I walked right into the ward. There was a new nurse feeding little Albert. "Hold on," I said. "That ain't the way. Don't you see how he's twisting that left eye? Let me show you." Mebbe she thought I was a new doctor, for she just gave me the spoon, and I guess I filled little Albert up with the most comfortable meal he'd had since I went away. Droolers ain't bad when you understand them. I heard Miss Jones tell Miss Kelsey once that I had an amazing gift in handling droolers.

Some day, mebbe, I'm going to talk with Doctor Dalrymple and get him to give me a declaration that I ain't a feeb. Then I'll get him to make me a real assistant in the drooling ward, with forty dollars a month and my board. And then I'll marry Miss Jones and live right on here. And if she won't have me, I'll marry Miss Kelsey or some other nurse. There's lots of them that want to get married. And I won't care if my wife gets mad and calls me a feeb. What's the good? And I guess when one's learned to put up with droolers a wife won't be much worse.

I didn't tell you about when I ran away. I hadn't no idea of such a thing, and it was Charley and Joe who put me up to it. They're high-grade epilecs, you know. I'd been up to Doctor Wilson's office with a message, and was going back to the drooling ward, when I saw Charley and Joe hiding around the corner of the gymnasium and making motions to me. I went over to them.

"Hello," Joe said. "How's droolers?"

"Fine," I said. "Had any fits lately?"

That made them mad, and I was going on, when Joe said, "We're running away. Come on."

"What for?" I said.

"We're going up over the top of the mountain," Joe said.

"And find a gold mine," said Charley. "We don't have fits any more. We're cured."

"All right," I said. And we sneaked around back of the gymnasium and in among the trees. Mebbe we walked along about ten minutes, when I stopped.

"What's the matter?" said Joe.

"Wait," I said. "I got to go back."

"What for?" said Joe.

And I said, "To get little Albert."

And they said I couldn't, and got mad. But I didn't care. I knew they'd wait. You see, I've been here twenty-five years, and I know the back trails that lead up the mountain, and Charley and Joe didn't know those trails. That's why they wanted me to come.

So I went back and got little Albert. He can't walk, or talk, or do anything except drool, and I had to carry him in my arms. We went on past the last hayfield, which was as far as I'd ever gone. Then the woods and brush got so thick, and me not finding any more trail, we followed the cow-path down to a big creek and crawled through the fence which showed where the Home land stopped.

We climbed up the big hill on the other side of the creek. It was all big trees, and no brush, but it was so steep and slippery with dead leaves we could hardly walk. By and by we came to a real bad place. It was forty feet across, and if you slipped you'd fall a thousand feet, or mebbe a hundred. Anyway, you wouldn't fall—just slide. I went across first, carrying little Albert. Joe came next. But Charley got scared right in the middle and sat down.

"I'm going to have a fit," he said.

"No, you're not," said Joe. "Because if you was you wouldn't 'a' sat down. You take all your fits standing."

"This is a different kind of a fit," said Charley, beginning to cry.

He shook and shook, but just because he wanted to he couldn't scare up the least kind of a fit.

60

Joe got mad and used awful language. But that didn't help none. So I talked soft and kind to Charley. That's the way to handle feebs. If you get mad, they get worse. I know. I'm that way myself. That's why I was almost the death of Mrs. Bopp. She got mad.

It was getting along in the afternoon, and I knew we had to be on our way, so I said to Joe:

"Here, stop your cussing and hold Albert. I'll go back and get him."

And I did, too; but he was so scared and dizzy he crawled along on hands and knees while I helped him. When I got him across and took Albert back in my arms, I heard somebody laugh and looked down. And there was a man and woman on horseback looking up at us. He had a gun on his saddle, and it was her who was laughing.

"Who in hell's that?" said Joe, getting scared. "Somebody to catch us?"

"Shut up your cussing," I said to him. "That is the man who owns this ranch and writes books."

"How do you do, Mr. Endicott," I said down to him.

"Hello," he said. "What are you doing here?"

"We're running away," I said.

And he said, "Good luck. But be sure and get back before dark."

"But this is a real running away," I said.

And then both he and his wife laughed.

"All right," he said. "Good luck just the same. But watch out the bears and mountain lions don't get you when it gets dark."

Then they rode away laughing, pleasant like; but I wished he hadn't said that about the bears and mountain lions.

After we got around the hill, I found a trail, and we went much faster. Charley didn't have any more signs of fits, and began laughing and talking about gold mines. The trouble was with little Albert. He was almost as big as me. You see, all the time I'd been calling him little Albert, he'd been growing up. He was so heavy I couldn't keep up with Joe and Charley. I was all out of breath. So I told them they'd have to take turns in carrying him, which they said they wouldn't. Then I said I'd leave them and they'd get lost, and the mountain lions and bears would eat them. Charley looked like he was going to have a fit right there, and Joe said, "Give him to me." And after that we carried him in turn.

We kept right on up that mountain. I don't think there was any gold mine, but we might 'a' got to the top and found it, if we hadn't lost the trail, and if it hadn't got dark, and if little Albert hadn't tired us all out carrying him. Lots of feebs are scared of the dark, and Joe said he was going to have a fit right there. Only he didn't. I never saw such an unlucky boy. He never could throw a fit when he wanted to. Some of the feebs can throw fits as quick as a wink.

By and by it got real black, and we were hungry, and we didn't have no fire. You see, they don't let feebs carry matches, and all we could do was just shiver. And we'd never thought about being hungry. You see, feebs always have their food ready for them, and that's why it's better to be a feeb than earning your living in the world.

And worse than everything was the quiet. There was only one thing worse, and it was the noises. There was all kinds of noises every once in a while, with quiet spells in between. I reckon they were rabbits, but they made noises in the brush like wild animals—you know, rustle rustle, thump, bump, crackle crackle, just like that. First Charley got a fit, a real one, and Joe threw a terrible one. I don't mind fits in the Home with everybody around. But out in the woods on a dark night is different. You listen to me, and never go hunting gold mines with epilecs, even if they are high-grade.

I never had such an awful night. When Joe and Charley weren't throwing fits they were making believe, and in the darkness the shivers from the cold which I couldn't see seemed like fits, too. And I shivered so hard I thought I was getting fits myself. And little Albert, with nothing to eat, just drooled and drooled. I never seen him as bad as that before. Why, he twisted that left eye of his until it ought to have dropped out. I couldn't see it, but I could tell from the movements he made. And Joe just lay and cussed and cussed, and Charley cried and wished he was back in the Home.

We didn't die, and next morning we went right back the way we'd come. And little Albert got awful heavy. Doctor Wilson was mad as could be, and said I was the worst feeb in the institution, along with Joe and Charley. But Miss Striker, who was a nurse in the drooling ward then, just put her arms around me and cried, she was that happy I'd got back. I thought right there that mebbe I'd marry her. But only a month afterward she got married to the plumber that came up from the city to fix the gutter-pipes of the new hospital. And little Albert never twisted his eye for two days, it was that tired.

Next time I run away I'm going right over that mountain. But I ain't going to take epilecs along. They ain't never cured, and when they get scared or excited they throw fits to beat the band. But I'll take little Albert. Somehow I can't get along without him. And anyway, I ain't going to run away. The drooling ward's a better snap than gold mines, and I hear there's a new nurse coming. Besides, little Albert's bigger than I am now, and I could never carry him over a mountain. And he's growing bigger every day. It's astonishing.

THE HOBO AND THE FAIRY

He lay on his back. So heavy was his sleep that the stamp of hoofs and cries of the drivers from the bridge that crossed the creek did not rouse him. Wagon after wagon, loaded high with grapes, passed the bridge on the way up the valley to the winery, and the coming of each wagon was like an explosion of sound and commotion in the lazy quiet of the afternoon.

But the man was undisturbed. His head had slipped from the folded newspaper, and the straggling unkempt hair was matted with the foxtails and burrs of the dry grass on which it lay. He was not a pretty sight. His mouth was open, disclosing a gap in the upper row where several teeth at some time had been knocked out. He breathed stertorously, at times grunting and moaning with the pain of his sleep. Also, he was very restless, tossing his arms about, making jerky, half-convulsive movements, and at times rolling his head from side to side in the burrs. This restlessness seemed occasioned partly by some internal discomfort, and partly by the sun that streamed down on his face and by the flies that buzzed and lighted and crawled upon the nose and cheeks and eyelids. There was no other place for them to crawl, for the rest of the face was covered with matted beard, slightly grizzled, but greatly dirt-stained and weather-discoloured.

The cheek-bones were blotched with the blood congested by the debauch that was evidently being slept off. This, too, accounted for the persistence with which the flies clustered around the mouth, lured by the alcohol-laden exhalations. He was a powerfully built man, thick-necked, broad-shouldered, with sinewy wrists and toil-distorted hands. Yet the distortion was not due to recent toil, nor were the callouses other than ancient that showed under the dirt of the one palm upturned. From time to time this hand clenched tightly and spasmodically into a fist, large, heavy-boned and wicked-looking.

The man lay in the dry grass of a tiny glade that ran down to the tree-fringed bank of the stream. On either side of the glade was a fence, of the old stake-and-rider type, though little of it was to be seen, so thickly was it overgrown by wild blackberry bushes, scrubby oaks and young madrono trees. In the rear, a gate through a low paling fence led to a snug, squat bungalow, built in the California Spanish style and seeming to have been compounded directly from the landscape of which it was so justly a part. Neat and trim and modestly sweet was the bungalow, redolent of comfort and repose, telling with quiet certitude of some one that knew, and that had sought and found.

Through the gate and into the glade came as dainty a little maiden as ever stepped out of an illustration made especially to show how dainty little maidens may be. Eight years she might have been, and, possibly, a trifle more, or less. Her little waist and little black-stockinged calves showed how delicately fragile she was; but the fragility was of mould only. There was no hint of anæmia in the clear, healthy complexion nor in the quick, tripping step. She was a little, delicious blond, with hair spun of gossamer gold and wide blue eyes that were but slightly veiled by the long lashes. Her expression was of sweetness and happiness; it belonged by right to any face that sheltered in the bungalow.

She carried a child's parasol, which she was careful not to tear against the scrubby branches and bramble bushes as she sought for wild poppies along the edge of the fence. They were late poppies, a third generation, which had been unable to resist the call of the warm October sun.

Having gathered along one fence, she turned to cross to the opposite fence. Midway in the glade she came upon the tramp. Her startle was merely a startle. There was no fear in it. She stood and looked long and curiously at the forbidding spectacle, and was about to turn back when the sleeper moved restlessly and rolled his hand among the burrs. She noted the sun on his face, and the buzzing flies; her face grew solicitous, and for a moment she debated with herself. Then she tiptoed to his side, interposed the parasol between him and the sun, and brushed away the flies. After a time, for greater ease, she sat down beside him.

An hour passed, during which she occasionally shifted the parasol from one tired hand to the other. At first the sleeper had been restless, but, shielded from the flies and the sun, his breathing became gentler and his movements ceased. Several times, however, he really frightened her. The first was the worst, coming abruptly and without warning. "Christ! How deep! How deep!" the man murmured from some profound of dream. The parasol was agitated; but the little girl controlled herself and continued her self-appointed ministrations.

Another time it was a gritting of teeth, as of some intolerable agony. So terribly did the teeth crunch and grind together that it seemed they must crash into fragments. A little later he suddenly stiffened out. The hands clenched and the face set with the savage resolution of the dream. The eyelids trembled from the shock of the fantasy, seemed about to open, but did not. Instead, the lips muttered:

"No; by God, no. And once more no. I won't peach." The lips paused, then went on. "You might as well tie me up, warden, and cut me to pieces. That's all you can get outa me—blood. That's all any of you-uns has ever got outa me in this hole."

After this outburst the man slept gently on, while the little girl still held the parasol aloft and looked down with a great wonder at the frowsy, unkempt creature, trying to reconcile it with the little part of life that she knew. To her ears came the cries of men, the stamp of hoofs on the bridge, and the creak and groan of wagons heavy-laden. It was a breathless California Indian summer day. Light fleeces of cloud drifted in the azure sky, but to the west heavy cloud banks threatened with rain. A bee droned lazily by. From farther thickets came the calls of quail, and from the fields the songs of meadow larks. And oblivious to it all slept Ross Shanklin—Ross Shanklin, the tramp and outcast, ex-convict 4379, the bitter and unbreakable one who had defied all keepers and survived all brutalities.

Texas-born, of the old pioneer stock that was always tough and stubborn, he had been unfortunate. At seventeen years of age he had been apprehended for horse-stealing. Also, he had been convicted of stealing seven horses which he had not stolen, and he had been sentenced to fourteen years' imprisonment. This was severe under any circumstances, but with him it had been especially severe, because there had been no prior convictions against him. The sentiment of the people who believed him guilty had been that two years was adequate punishment for the youth, but the county attorney, paid according to the convictions he secured, had made seven charges against him and earned seven fees. Which goes to show that the county attorney valued twelve years of Ross Shanklin's life at less than a few dollars.

Young Ross Shanklin had toiled in hell; he had escaped, more than once; and he had been caught and sent back to toil in other and various hells. He had been triced up and lashed till he fainted, had been revived and lashed again. He had been in the dungeon ninety days at a time. He had experienced the torment of the straightjacket. He knew what the humming bird was. He had been farmed out as a chattel by the state to the contractors. He had been trailed through swamps by blood hounds. Twice he had been shot. For six years on end he had cut a cord and a half of wood each day in a convict lumber camp. Sick or well, he had cut that cord and a half or paid for it under a whip-lash knotted and pickled.

And Ross Shanklin had not sweetened under the treatment. He had sneered, and cursed, and defied. He had seen convicts, after the guards had manhandled them, crippled in body for life, or left to maunder in mind to the end of their days. He had seen convicts, even his own cell-mate, goaded to murder by their keepers, go to the gallows cursing God. He had been in a break in which eleven of his kind were shot down. He had been through a mutiny, where, in the prison yard, with gatling guns trained upon them, three hundred convicts had been disciplined with pick-handles wielded by brawny guards.

He had known every infamy of human cruelty, and through it all he had never been broken. He had resented and fought to the last, until, embittered and bestial, the day came when he was discharged. Five dollars were given him in payment for the years of his labour and the flower of his manhood. And he had worked little in the years that followed. Work he hated and despised. He tramped, begged and stole, lied or threatened as the case might warrant, and drank to besottedness whenever he got the chance.

The little girl was looking at him when he awoke. Like a wild animal, all of him was awake the instant he opened his eyes. The first he saw was the parasol, strangely obtruded between him and the sky. He did not start nor move, though his whole body seemed slightly to tense. His eyes followed down the parasol handle to the tight-clutched little fingers, and along the arm to the child's face. Straight and unblinking, he looked into her eyes, and she, returning the look, was chilled and frightened by his glittering eyes, cold and harsh, withal bloodshot, and with no hint in them of the warm humanness she had been accustomed to see and feel in human eyes. They were the true prison eyes—the eyes of a man who had learned to talk little, who had forgotten almost how to talk.

"Hello," he said finally, making no effort to change his position. "What game are you up to?"

His voice was gruff and husky, and at first it had been harsh; but it had softened queerly in a feeble attempt at forgotten kindliness.

"How do you do?" she said. "I'm not playing. The sun was on your face, and mamma says one oughtn't to sleep in the sun."

The sweet clearness of her child's voice was pleasant to him, and he wondered why he had never noticed it in children's voices before. He sat up slowly and stared at her. He felt that he ought to say something, but speech with him was a reluctant thing.

"I hope you slept well," she said gravely.

"I sure did," he answered, never taking his eyes from her, amazed at the fairness and delicacy of her. "How long was you holdin' that contraption up over me?"

"O-oh," she debated with herself, "a long, long time. I thought you would never wake up."

"And I thought you was a fairy when I first seen you."

He felt elated at his contribution to the conversation.

"No, not a fairy," she smiled.

He thrilled in a strange, numb way at the immaculate whiteness of her small even teeth.

"I was just the good Samaritan," she added.

"I reckon I never heard of that party."

He was cudgelling his brains to keep the conversation going. Never having been at close quarters with a child since he was man-grown, he found it difficult.

"What a funny man not to know about the good Samaritan. Don't you remember? A certain man went down to Jericho—"

"I reckon I've been there," he interrupted.

"I knew you were a traveller!" she cried, clapping her hands. "Maybe you saw the exact spot."

"What spot?"

"Why, where he fell among thieves and was left half dead. And then the good Samaritan went to him, and bound up his wounds, and poured in oil and wine—was that olive oil, do you think?"

He shook his head slowly.

"I reckon you got me there. Olive oil is something the dagoes cooks with. I never heard of it for busted heads."

She considered his statement for a moment.

"Well," she announced, "we use olive oil in our cooking, so we must be dagoes. I never knew what they were before. I thought it was slang."

"And the Samaritan dumped oil on his head," the tramp muttered reminiscently. "Seems to me I recollect a sky pilot sayin' something about that old gent. D'ye know, I've been looking for him off n' on all my life, and never scared up hide or hair of him. They ain't no more Samaritans."

"Wasn't I one?" she asked quickly.

He looked at her steadily, with a great curiosity and wonder. Her ear, by a movement exposed to the sun, was transparent. It seemed he could almost see through it. He was amazed at the delicacy of her colouring, at the blue of her eyes, at the dazzle of the sun-touched golden hair. And he was astounded by her fragility. It came to him that she was easily broken. His eye went quickly from his huge, gnarled paw to her tiny hand in which it seemed to him he could almost see the blood circulate. He knew the power in his muscles, and he knew the tricks and turns by which men use their bodies to ill-treat men. In fact, he knew little else, and his mind for the time ran in its customary channel. It was his way of measuring the beautiful strangeness of her. He calculated a grip, and not a strong one, that could grind her little fingers to pulp. He thought of fist-blows he had given to men's heads, and received on his own head, and felt that the least of them could shatter hers like an eggshell. He scanned her little shoulders and slim waist, and knew in all certitude that with his two hands he could rend her to pieces.

"Wasn't I one?" she insisted again.

He came back to himself with a shock—or away from himself, as the case happened. He was loth that the conversation should cease.

"What?" he answered. "Oh, yes; you bet you was a Samaritan, even if you didn't have no olive oil." He remembered what his mind had been dwelling on, and asked, "But ain't you afraid?"

She looked at him uncomprehendingly.

"Of ... of me?" he added lamely.

She laughed merrily.

"Mamma says never to be afraid of anything. She says that if you're good, and you think good of other people, they'll be good, too."

"And you was thinkin' good of me when you kept the sun off," he marvelled.

"But it's hard to think good of bees and nasty crawly things," she confessed.

"But there's men that is nasty and crawly things," he argued.

"Mamma says no. She says there's good in every one."

"I bet you she locks the house up tight at night just the same," he proclaimed triumphantly.

"But she doesn't. Mamma isn't afraid of anything. That's why she lets me play out here alone when I want. Why, we had a robber once. Mamma got right up and found him. And what do you think! He was only a poor hungry man. And she got him plenty to eat from the pantry, and afterward she got him work to do."

Ross Shanklin was stunned. The vista shown him of human nature was unthinkable. It had been his lot to live in a world of suspicion and hatred, of evil-believing and evil-doing. It had been his experience, slouching along village streets at nightfall, to see little children, screaming with fear, run from him to their mothers. He had even seen grown women shrink aside from him as he passed along the sidewalk.

He was aroused by the girl clapping her hands as she cried out.

"I know what you are! You're an open air crank. That's why you were sleeping here in the grass."

He felt a grim desire to laugh, but repressed it.

"And that's what tramps are—open air cranks," she continued. "I often wondered. Mamma believes in the open air. I sleep on the porch at night. So does she. This is our land. You must have climbed the fence. Mamma lets me when I put on my climbers—they're bloomers, you know. But you ought to be told something. A person doesn't know when they snore because they're asleep. But you do worse than that. You grit your teeth. That's bad. Whenever you are going to sleep you must think to yourself, 'I won't grit my teeth, I won't grit my teeth,' over and over, just like that, and by and by you'll get out of the habit.

"All bad things are habits. And so are all good things. And it depends on us what kind our habits are going to be. I used to pucker my eyebrows— wrinkle them all up, but mamma said I must overcome that habit. She said that when my eyebrows were wrinkled it was an advertisement that my brain was wrinkled inside, and that it wasn't good to have wrinkles in the brain. And then she smoothed my eyebrows with her hand and said I must always think *smooth—smooth* inside, and *smooth* outside. And do you know, it was easy. I haven't wrinkled my brows for ever so long. I've heard about filling teeth by thinking. But I don't believe that. Neither does mamma."

She paused, rather out of breath. Nor did he speak. Her flow of talk had been too much for him. Also, sleeping drunkenly, with open mouth, had made him very thirsty. But, rather than lose one precious moment, he endured the torment of his scorching throat and mouth. He licked his dry lips and struggled for speech.

"What is your name?" he managed at last.

"Joan."

She looked her own question at him, and it was not necessary to voice it.

"Mine is Ross Shanklin," he volunteered, for the first time in forgotten years giving his real name.

"I suppose you've travelled a lot."

"I sure have, but not as much as I might have wanted to."

"Papa always wanted to travel, but he was too busy at the office. He never could get much time. He went to Europe once with mamma. That was before I was born. It takes money to travel."

Ross Shanklin did not know whether to agree with this statement or not.

"But it doesn't cost tramps much for expenses," she took the thought away from him. "Is that why you tramp?"

He nodded and licked his lips.

"Mamma says it's too bad that men must tramp to look for work. But there's lots of work now in the country. All the farmers in the valley are trying to get men. Have you been working?"

He shook his head, angry with himself that he should feel shame at the confession when his savage reasoning told him he was right in despising work. But this was followed by another thought. This beautiful little creature was some man's child. She was one of the rewards of work.

"I wish I had a little girl like you," he blurted out, stirred by a sudden consciousness of passion for paternity. "I'd work my hands off. I ... I'd do anything."

She considered his case with fitting gravity.

"Then you aren't married?"

"Nobody would have me."

"Yes they would, if...."

She did not turn up her nose, but she favoured his dirt and rags with a look of disapprobation he could not mistake.

"Go on," he half-shouted. "Shoot it into me. If I was washed—if I wore good clothes—if I was respectable—if I had a job and worked regular—if I wasn't what I am."

To each statement she nodded.

"Well, I ain't that kind," he rushed on.

"I'm no good. I'm a tramp. I don't want to work, that's what. And I like dirt."

Her face was eloquent with reproach as she said, "Then you were only making believe when you wished you had a little girl like me?"

This left him speechless, for he knew, in all the deeps of his new-found passion, that that was just what he did want.

With ready tact, noting his discomfort, she sought to change the subject.

"What do you think of God?" she asked.

"I ain't never met him. What do you think about him?"

His reply was evidently angry, and she was frank in her disapproval.

"You are very strange," she said. "You get angry so easily. I never saw anybody before that got angry about God, or work, or being clean."

"He never done anything for me," he muttered resentfully. He cast back in quick review of the long years of toil in the convict camps and mines. "And work never done anything for me neither."

An embarrassing silence fell.

He looked at her, numb and hungry with the stir of the father-love, sorry for his ill temper, puzzling his brain for something to say. She was looking off and away at the clouds, and he devoured her with his eyes. He reached out stealthily and rested one grimy hand on the very edge of her little dress. It seemed to him that she was the most wonderful thing in the world. The quail still called from the coverts, and the harvest sounds seemed abruptly to become very loud. A great loneliness oppressed him.

"I'm ... I'm no good," he murmured huskily and repentantly.

But, beyond a glance from her blue eyes, she took no notice. The silence was more embarrassing than ever. He felt that he could give the world just to touch with his lips that hem of her dress where his hand rested. But he was afraid of frightening her. He fought to find something to say, licking his parched lips and vainly attempting to articulate something, anything.

"This ain't Sonoma Valley," he declared finally. "This is fairy land, and you're a fairy. Mebbe I'm asleep and dreaming. I don't know. You and me don't know how to talk together, because, you see, you're a fairy and don't know nothing but good things, and I'm a man from the bad, wicked world."

Having achieved this much, he was left gasping for ideas like a stranded fish.

"And you're going to tell me about the bad, wicked world," she cried, clapping her hands. "I'm just dying to know."

He looked at her, startled, remembering the wreckage of womanhood he had encountered on the sunken ways of life. She was no fairy. She was flesh and blood, and the possibilities of wreckage were in her as they had been in him even when he lay at his mother's breast. And there was in her eagerness to know.

"Nope," he said lightly, "this man from the bad, wicked world ain't going to tell you nothing of the kind. He's going to tell you of the good things in that world. He's going to tell you how he loved hosses when he was a shaver, and about the first hoss he straddled, and the first hoss he owned. Hosses ain't like men. They're better. They're clean—clean all the way through and back again. And, little fairy, I want to tell you one thing—there sure ain't nothing in the world like when you're settin' a tired hoss at the end of a long day, and when you just speak, and that tired animal lifts under you willing and hustles along. Hosses! They're my long suit. I sure dote on hosses. Yep. I used to be a cowboy once."

She clapped her hands in the way that tore so delightfully to his heart, and her eyes were dancing, as she exclaimed:

"A Texas cowboy! I always wanted to see one! I heard papa say once that cowboys are bow-legged. Are you?"

"I sure was a Texas cowboy," he answered. "But it was a long time ago. And I'm sure bow-legged. You see, you can't ride much when you're young and soft without getting the legs bent some. Why, I was only a three-year-old when I begun. He was a three-year-old, too, fresh-broken. I led him up alongside the fence, clumb to the top rail, and dropped on. He was a pinto, and a real devil at bucking, but I could do anything with him. I reckon he knowed I was only a little shaver. Some hosses knows lots more 'n' you think."

For half an hour Ross Shanklin rambled on with his horse reminiscences, never unconscious for a moment of the supreme joy that was his through the touch of his hand on the hem of her dress. The sun dropped slowly into the cloud bank, the quail called more insistently, and empty wagon after empty wagon rumbled back across the bridge. Then came a woman's voice.

"Joan! Joan!" it called. "Where are you, dear?"

The little girl answered, and Ross Shanklin saw a woman, clad in a soft, clinging gown, come through the gate from the bungalow. She was a slender, graceful woman, and to his charmed eyes she seemed rather to float along than walk like ordinary flesh and blood.

"What have you been doing all afternoon?" the woman asked, as she came up.

"Talking, mamma," the little girl replied "I've had a very interesting time."

Ross Shanklin scrambled to his feet and stood watchfully and awkwardly. The little girl took the mother's hand, and she, in turn, looked at him frankly and pleasantly, with a recognition of his humanness that was a new thing to him. In his mind ran the thought: *the woman who ain't afraid*. Not a hint was there of the timidity he was accustomed to seeing in women's eyes. And he was quite aware, and never more so, of his bleary-eyed, forbidding appearance.

"How do you do?" she greeted him sweetly and naturally.

"How do you do, ma'am," he responded, unpleasantly conscious of the huskiness and rawness of his voice.

"And did you have an interesting time, too?" she smiled.

"Yes, ma'am. I sure did. I was just telling your little girl about hosses."

"He was a cowboy, once, mamma," she cried.

The mother smiled her acknowledgment to him, and looked fondly down at the little girl. The thought that came into Ross Shanklin's mind was the awfulness of the crime if any one should harm either of the wonderful pair. This was followed by the wish that some terrible danger should threaten, so that he could fight, as he well knew how, with all his strength and life, to defend them.

76

"You'll have to come along, dear," the mother said. "It's growing late." She looked at Ross Shanklin hesitantly. "Would you care to have something to eat?"

"No, ma'am, thanking you kindly just the same. I ... I ain't hungry."

"Then say good-bye, Joan," she counselled.

"Good-bye." The little girl held out her hand, and her eyes lighted roguishly. "Good-bye, Mr. Man from the bad, wicked world."

To him, the touch of her hand as he pressed it in his was the capstone of the whole adventure.

"Good-bye, little fairy," he mumbled. "I reckon I got to be pullin' along."

But he did not pull along. He stood staring after his vision until it vanished through the gate. The day seemed suddenly empty. He looked about him irresolutely, then climbed the fence, crossed the bridge, and slouched along the road. He was in a dream. He did not note his feet nor the way they led him. At times he stumbled in the dust-filled ruts.

A mile farther on, he aroused at the crossroads. Before him stood the saloon. He came to a stop and stared at it, licking his lips. He sank his hand into his pants pocket and fumbled a solitary dime. "God!" he muttered. "God!" Then, with dragging, reluctant feet, went on along the road.

He came to a big farm. He knew it must be big, because of the bigness of the house and the size and number of the barns and outbuildings. On the porch, in shirt sleeves, smoking a cigar, keen-eyed and middle-aged, was the farmer.

"What's the chance for a job?" Ross Shanklin asked.

The keen eyes scarcely glanced at him.

"A dollar a day and grub," was the answer.

Ross Shanklin swallowed and braced himself.

"I'll pick grapes all right, or anything. But what's the chance for a steady job? You've got a big ranch here. I know hosses. I was born on one. I can drive team, ride, plough, break, do anything that anybody ever done with hosses."

The other looked him over with an appraising, incredulous eye.

"You don't look it," was the judgment.

"I know I don't. Give me a chance. That's all. I'll prove it."

The farmer considered, casting an anxious glance at the cloud bank into which the sun had sunk.

"I'm short a teamster, and I'll give you the chance to make good. Go and get supper with the hands."

Ross Shanklin's voice was very husky, and be spoke with an effort.

"All right. I'll make good. Where can I get a drink of water and wash up?"

THE PRODIGAL FATHER

I

Josiah Childs was ordinarily an ordinary-appearing, prosperous business man. He wore a sixty-dollar, business-man's suit, his shoes were comfortable and seemly and made from the current last, his tie, collars and cuffs were just what all prosperous business men wore, and an up-to-date, business-man's derby was his wildest adventure in head-gear. Oakland, California, is no sleepy country town, and Josiah Childs, as the leading grocer of a rushing Western metropolis of three hundred thousand, appropriately lived, acted, and dressed the part.

But on this morning, before the rush of custom began, his appearance at the store, while it did not cause a riot, was sufficiently startling to impair for half an hour the staff's working efficiency. He nodded pleasantly to the two delivery drivers loading their wagons for the first trip of the morning, and cast upward the inevitable, complacent glance at the sign that ran across the front of the building—CHILDS' CASH STORE. The lettering, not too large, was of dignified black and gold, suggestive of noble spices, aristocratic condiments, and everything of the best (which was no more than to be expected of a scale of prices ten per cent. higher than any other grocery in town). But what Josiah Childs did not see as he turned his back on the drivers and entered, was the helpless and mutual fall of surprise those two worthies perpetrated on each other's necks. They clung together for support.

"Did you catch the kicks, Bill?" one moaned.

"Did you pipe the head-piece?" Bill moaned back.

"Now if he was goin' to a masquerade ball...."

"Or attendin' a reunion of the Rough Riders...."

"Or goin' huntin' bear...."

"Or swearin' off his taxes...."

"Instead of goin' all the way to the effete East—Monkton says he's going clear to Boston...."

The two drivers held each other apart at arm's length, and fell limply together again.

For Josiah Childs' outfit was all their actions connotated. His hat was a light fawn, stiff-rimmed John B. Stetson, circled by a band of Mexican stamped leather. Over a blue flannel shirt, set off by a drooping Windsor tie, was a rough-and-ready coat of large-ribbed corduroy. Pants of the same material were thrust into high-laced shoes of the sort worn by surveyors, explorers, and linemen.

A clerk at a near counter almost petrified at sight of his employer's bizarre rig. Monkton, recently elevated to the managership, gasped, swallowed, and maintained his imperturbable attentiveness. The lady bookkeeper, glancing down from her glass eyrie on the inside balcony, took one look and buried her giggles in the day book. Josiah Childs saw most of all this, but he did not mind. He was starting on his vacation, and his head and heart were buzzing with plans and anticipations of the most adventurous vacation he had taken in ten years. Under his eyelids burned visions of East Falls, Connecticut, and of all the home scenes he had been born to and brought up in. Oakland, he was thoroughly aware, was more modern than East Falls, and the excitement caused by his garb was only to be expected. Undisturbed by the sensation he knew he was creating among his employés, he moved about, accompanied by his manager, making last suggestions, giving final instructions, and radiating fond, farewell glances at all the loved details of the business he had built out of nothing.

He had a right to be proud of Childs' Cash Store. Twelve years before he had landed in Oakland with fourteen dollars and forty-three cents. Cents did not circulate so far West, and after the fourteen dollars were gone, he continued to carry the three pennies in his pocket for a weary while. Later, when he had got a job clerking in a small grocery for eleven dollars a week, and had begun sending a small monthly postal order to one, Agatha Childs, East Falls, Connecticut, he invested the three coppers in postage stamps. Uncle Sam could not reject his own lawful coin of the realm.

Having spent all his life in cramped New England, where sharpness and shrewdness had been whetted to razor-edge on the harsh stone of meagre circumstance, he had found himself abruptly in the loose and free-and-easy West, where men thought in thousand-dollar bills and newsboys dropped dead at sight of copper cents. Josiah Childs bit like fresh acid into the new industrial and business conditions. He had vision. He saw so many ways of making money all at once, that at first his brain was in a whirl.

At the same time, being sane and conservative, he had resolutely avoided speculation. The solid and substantial called to him. Clerking at eleven dollars a week, he took note of the lost opportunities, of the openings for safe enterprise, of the countless leaks in the business. If, despite all this, the boss could make a good living, what couldn't he, Josiah Childs, do with his Connecticut training? It was like a bottle of wine to a thirsty hermit, this coming to the active, generous-spending West after thirty-five years in East Falls, the last fifteen of which had been spent in humdrum clerking in the humdrum East Falls general store. Josiah Childs' head buzzed with the easy possibilities he saw. But he did not lose his head. No detail was overlooked. He spent his spare hours in studying Oakland, its people, how they made their money, and why they spent it and where. He walked the central streets, watching the drift of the buying crowds, even counting them and compiling the statistics in various notebooks. He studied the general credit system of the trade, and the particular credit systems of the different districts. He could tell to a dot the average wage or salary earned by the householders of any locality, and he made it a point of thoroughness to know every locality from the waterfront slums to the aristocratic Lake Merritt and Piedmont sections, from West Oakland, where dwelt the railroad employés, to the semi-farmers of Fruitvale at the opposite end of the city.

Broadway, on the main street and in the very heart of the shopping district, where no grocer had ever been insane enough to dream of establishing a business, was his ultimate selection. But that required money, while he had to start from the smallest of beginnings. His first store was on lower Filbert, where lived the nail-workers. In half a year, three other little corner groceries went out of business while he was compelled to enlarge his premises. He understood the principle of large sales at small profits, of stable qualities of goods, and of a square deal. He had glimpsed, also, the secret of advertising. Each week he set forth one article that sold at a loss to him. This was not an advertised loss, but an absolute loss. His one clerk prophesied impending bankruptcy when butter, that cost Childs thirty cents, was sold for twenty-five cents, when twenty-two-cent coffee was passed across the counter at eighteen cents. The neighbourhood housewives came for these bargains and remained to buy other articles that sold at a profit. Moreover, the whole neighbourhood came quickly to know Josiah Childs, and the busy crowd of buyers in his store was an attraction in itself.

But Josiah Childs made no mistake. He knew the ultimate foundation on which his prosperity rested. He studied the nail works until he came to know as much about them as the managing directors. Before the first whisper had stirred abroad, he sold his store, and with a modest sum of ready cash went in search of a new location. Six months later the nail works closed down, and closed down forever.

His next store was established on Adeline Street, where lived a comfortable, salaried class. Here, his shelves carried a higher-grade and a more diversified stock. By the same old method, he drew his crowd. He established a delicatessen counter. He dealt directly with the farmers, so that his butter and eggs were not only always dependable but were a shade better than those sold by the finest groceries in the city. One of his specialties was Boston baked beans, and so popular did it become that the Twin Cabin Bakery paid him better than handsomely for the privilege of taking it over. He made time to study the farmers, the very apples they grew, and certain farmers he taught how properly to make cider. As a side-line, his New England apple cider proved his greatest success, and before long, after he had invaded San Francisco, Berkeley, and Alameda, he ran it as an independent business.

But always his eyes were fixed on Broadway. Only one other intermediate move did he make, which was to as near as he could get to the Ashland Park Tract, where every purchaser of land was legally pledged to put up no home that should cost less than four thousand dollars. After that came Broadway. A strange swirl had come in the tide of the crowd. The drift was to Washington

Street, where real estate promptly soared while on Broadway it was as if the bottom had fallen out. One big store after another, as the leases expired, moved to Washington.

The crowd will come back, Josiah Childs said, but he said it to himself. He knew the crowd. Oakland was growing, and he knew why it was growing. Washington Street was too narrow to carry the increasing traffic. Along Broadway, in the physical nature of things, the electric cars, ever in greater numbers, would have to run. The realty dealers said that the crowd would never come back, while the leading merchants followed the crowd. And then it was, at a ridiculously low figure, that Josiah Childs got a long lease on a modern, Class A building on Broadway, with a buying option at a fixed price. It was the beginning of the end for Broadway, said the realty dealers, when a grocery was established in its erstwhile sacred midst. Later, when the crowd did come back, they said Josiah Childs was lucky. Also, they whispered among themselves that he had cleared at least fifty thousand on the transaction.

It was an entirely different store from his previous ones. There were no more bargains. Everything was of the superlative best, and superlative best prices were charged. He catered to the most expensive trade in town. Only those who could carelessly afford to pay ten per cent. more than anywhere else, patronised him, and so excellent was his service that they could not afford to go elsewhere. His horses and delivery wagons were more expensive and finer than any one else's in town. He paid his drivers, and clerks, and bookkeepers higher wages than any other store could dream of paying. As a result, he got more efficient men, and they rendered him and his patrons a more satisfying service. In short, to deal at Childs' Cash Store became almost the infallible index of social status.

To cap everything, came the great San Francisco earthquake and fire, which caused one hundred thousand people abruptly to come across the Bay and live in Oakland. Not least to profit from so extraordinary a boom, was Josiah Childs. And now, after twelve years' absence, he was departing on a visit to East Falls, Connecticut. In the twelve years he had not received a letter from Agatha, nor had he seen even a photograph of his and Agatha's boy.

Agatha and he had never got along together. Agatha was masterful. Agatha had a tongue. She was strong on old-fashioned morality. She was unlovely in her rectitude. Josiah never could quite make out how he had happened to marry her. She was two years his senior, and had long ranked as an old maid She had taught school, and was known by the young generation as the sternest disciplinarian in its experience. She had become set in her ways, and when she married it was merely an exchange of a number of pupils for one. Josiah had to stand the hectoring and nagging that thitherto had been distributed among many. As to how the marriage came about, his Uncle Isaac nearly hit it off one day when he said in confidence: "Josiah, when Agatha married you it was a case of marrying a struggling young man. I reckon you was overpowered. Or maybe you broke your leg and couldn't get away."

"Uncle Isaac," Josiah answered, "I didn't break my leg. I ran my dangdest, but she just plum run me down and out of breath."

"Strong in the wind, eh?" Uncle Isaac chuckled.

"We've ben married five years now," Josiah agreed, "and I've never known her to lose it."

"And never will," Uncle Isaac added.

This conversation had taken place in the last days, and so dismal an outlook proved too much for Josiah Childs. Meek he was, under Agatha's firm tuition, but he was very healthy, and his promise of life was too long for his patience. He was only thirty-three, and he came of a long-lived stock. Thirty-three more years with Agatha and Agatha's nagging was too hideous to contemplate. So, between a sunset and a rising, Josiah Childs disappeared from East Falls. And from that day, for twelve years, he had received no letter from her. Not that it was her fault. He had carefully avoided letting her have his address. His first postal money orders were sent to her from Oakland, but in the years that followed he had arranged his remittances so that they bore the scattered postmarks of most of the states west of the Rockies.

But twelve years, and the confidence born of deserved success, had softened his memories. After all, she was the mother of his boy, and it was incontestable that she had always meant well. Besides, he was not working so hard now, and he had more time to think of things besides his business. He wanted to see the boy, whom he had never seen and who had turned three before his father ever learned he was a father. Then, too, homesickness had begun to crawl in him. In a dozen years he had not seen snow, and he was always wondering if New England fruits and berries had not a finer tang than those of California. Through hazy vistas he saw the old New England life, and he wanted to see it again in the flesh before he died.

And, finally, there was duty. Agatha was his wife. He would bring her back with him to the West. He felt that he could stand it. He was a man, now, in the world of men. He ran things, instead of being run, and Agatha would quickly find it out. Nevertheless, he wanted Agatha to come to him for his own sake. So it was that he had put on his frontier rig. He would be the prodigal father, returning as penniless as when he left, and it would be up to her whether or not she killed the fatted calf. Empty of hand, and looking it, he would come back wondering if he could get his old job in the general store. Whatever followed would be Agatha's affair.

By the time he said good-bye to his staff and emerged on the sidewalk, five more of his delivery wagons were backed up and loading.

He ran his eye proudly over them, took a last fond glance at the black-and-gold letters, and signalled the electric car at the corner.

II

He ran up to East Falls from New York. In the Pullman smoker he became acquainted with several business men. The conversation, turning on the West, was quickly led by him. As president of the Oakland Chamber of Commerce, he was an authority. His words carried weight, and he knew what he was talking about, whether it was Asiatic trade, the Panama Canal, or the Japanese coolie question. It was very exhilarating, this stimulus of respectful attention accorded him by these prosperous Eastern men, and before he knew it he was at East Falls.

He was the only person who alighted, and the station was deserted. Nobody was there expecting anybody. The long twilight of a January evening was beginning, and the bite of the keen air made him suddenly conscious that his clothing was saturated with tobacco smoke. He shuddered involuntarily. Agatha did not tolerate tobacco. He half-moved to toss the fresh-lighted cigar away, then it was borne in upon him that this was the old East Falls atmosphere overpowering him, and he resolved to combat it, thrusting the cigar between his teeth and gripping it with the firmness of a dozen years of Western resolution.

A few steps brought him into the little main street. The chilly, stilted aspect of it shocked him. Everything seemed frosty and pinched, just as the cutting air did after the warm balminess of California. Only several persons, strangers to his recollection, were abroad, and they favoured him with incurious glances. They were wrapped in an uncongenial and frosty imperviousness. His first impression was surprise at his surprise. Through the wide perspective of twelve years of Western life, he had consistently and steadily discounted the size and importance of East Falls; but this was worse than all discounting. Things were more meagre than he had dreamed. The general store took his breath away. Countless myriads of times he had contrasted it with his own spacious emporium, but now he saw that in justice he had overdone it. He felt certain that it could not accommodate two of his delicatessen counters, and he knew that he could lose all of it in one of his storerooms.

He took the familiar turning to the right at the head of the street, and as he plodded along the slippery walk he decided that one of the first things he must do was to buy sealskin cap and gloves. The thought of sleighing cheered him for a moment, until, now on the outskirts of the village, he was sanitarily perturbed by the adjacency of dwelling houses and barns. Some were even connected. Cruel memories of bitter morning chores oppressed him. The thought of chapped hands and chilblains was almost terrifying, and his heart sank at sight of the double storm-windows, which he knew were solidly fastened and unraisable, while the small ventilating panes, the size of ladies' handkerchiefs, smote him with sensations of suffocation. Agatha'll like California, he thought, calling to his mind visions of roses in dazzling sunshine and the wealth of flowers that bloomed the twelve months round.

And then, quite illogically, the years were bridged and the whole leaden weight of East Falls descended upon him like a damp sea fog. He fought it from him, thrusting it off and aside by sentimental thoughts on the "honest snow," the "fine elms," the "sturdy New England spirit," and the "great homecoming." But at sight of Agatha's house he wilted. Before he knew it, with a recrudescent guilty pang, he had tossed the half-smoked cigar away and slackened his pace until his feet dragged in the old lifeless, East Falls manner. He tried to remember that he was the owner of Childs' Cash Store, accustomed to command, whose words were listened to with respect in the Employers' Association, and who wielded the gavel at the meetings of the Chamber of Commerce. He strove to conjure visions of the letters in black and gold, and of the string of delivery wagons backed up to the sidewalk. But Agatha's New England spirit was as sharp as the frost, and it travelled to him through solid house-walls and across the intervening hundred yards.

Then he became aware that despite his will he had thrown the cigar away. This brought him an awful vision. He saw himself going out in the frost to the woodshed to smoke. His memory of Agatha he found less softened by the lapse of years than it had been when three thousand miles intervened. It was unthinkable. No; he couldn't do it. He was too old, too used to smoking all over the house, to do the woodshed stunt now. And everything depended on how he began. He would put his foot down. He would smoke in the house that very night ... in the kitchen, he feebly amended. No, by George, he would smoke now. He would arrive smoking. Mentally imprecating the cold, he exposed his bare hands and lighted another cigar. His manhood seemed to flare up with the match. He would show her who was boss. Right from the drop of the hat he would show her.

Josiah Childs had been born in this house. And it was long before he was born that his father had built it. Across the low stone fence, Josiah could see the kitchen porch and door, the connected woodshed, and the several outbuildings. Fresh from the West, where everything was new and in constant flux, he was astonished at the lack of change. Everything was as it had always been. He could almost see himself, a boy, doing the chores. There, in the woodshed, how many cords of wood had he bucksawed and split! Well, thank the Lord, that was past.

The walk to the kitchen showed signs of recent snow-shovelling. That had been one of his tasks. He wondered who did it now, and suddenly remembered that his own son must be twelve. In another moment he would have knocked at the kitchen door, but the *skreek* of a bucksaw from the woodshed led him aside. He looked in and saw a boy hard at work. Evidently, this was his son. Impelled by the wave of warm emotion that swept over him, he all but rushed in upon the lad. He controlled himself with an effort.

"Father here?" he asked curtly, though from under the stiff brim of his John B. Stetson he studied the boy closely.

Sizable for his age, he thought. A mite spare in the ribs maybe, and that possibly due to rapid growth. But the face strong and pleasing and the eyes like Uncle Isaac's. When all was said, a darn good sample.

"No, sir," the boy answered, resting on the saw-buck.

"Where is he?"

"At sea," was the answer.

Josiah Childs felt a something very akin to relief and joy tingle through him. Agatha had married again—evidently a seafaring man. Next, came an ominous, creepy sensation. Agatha had committed bigamy. He remembered Enoch Arden, read aloud to the class by the teacher in the old schoolhouse, and began to think of himself as a hero. He would do the heroic. By George, he would. He would sneak away and get the first train for California. She would never know.

But there was Agatha's New England morality, and her New England conscience. She received a regular remittance. She knew he was alive. It was impossible that she could have done this thing. He groped wildly for a solution. Perhaps she had sold the old home, and this boy was somebody else's boy.

"What is your name?" Josiah asked.

"Johnnie," came the reply.

"Last name I mean?"

"Childs, Johnnie Childs."

"And your father's name?—first name?"

"Josiah Childs."

"And he's away at sea, you say?"

"Yes, sir."

This set Josiah wondering again.

"What kind of a man is he?"

"Oh, he's all right—a good provider, Mom says. And he is. He always sends his money home, and he works hard for it, too, Mom says. She says he always was a good worker, and he's better'n other men she ever saw. He don't smoke, or drink, or swear, or do anything he oughtn't. And he never did. He was always that way, Mom says, and she knew him all her life before ever they got married. He's a very kind man, and never hurts anybody's feelings. Mom says he's the most considerate man she ever knew."

Josiah's heart went weak. Agatha had done it after all—had taken a second husband when she knew her first was still alive. Well, he had learned charity in the West, and he could be charitable. He would go quietly away. Nobody would ever know. Though it was rather mean of her, the thought flashed through him, that she should go on cashing his remittances when she was married to so model and steady-working a seafaring husband who brought his wages home. He cudgelled his brains in an effort to remember such a man out of all the East Falls men he had known.

"What's he look like?"

"Don't know. Never saw him. He's at sea all the time. But I know how tall he is. Mom says I'm goin' to be bigger'n him, and he was five feet eleven. There's a picture of him in the album. His face is thin, and he has whiskers."

A great illumination came to Josiah. He was himself five feet eleven. He had worn whiskers, and his face had been thin in those days. And Johnnie had said his father's name was Josiah Childs. He, Josiah, was this model husband who neither smoked, swore, nor drank. He was this seafaring man whose memory had been so carefully shielded by Agatha's forgiving fiction. He warmed toward her. She must have changed mightily since he left. He glowed with penitence. Then his heart sank as he thought of trying to live up to this reputation Agatha had made for him. This boy with the trusting blue eyes would expect it of him. Well, he'd have to do it. Agatha had been almighty square with him. He hadn't thought she had it in her.

The resolve he might there and then have taken was doomed never to be, for he heard the kitchen door open to give vent to a woman's nagging, irritable voice.

"Johnnie!—you!" it cried.

How often had he heard it in the old days: "Josiah!—you!" A shiver went through him. Involuntarily, automatically, with a guilty start, he turned his hand back upward so that the cigar was hidden. He felt himself shrinking and shrivelling as she stepped out on the stoop. It was his unchanged wife, the same shrew wrinkles, with the same sour-drooping corners to the thin-lipped mouth. But there was more sourness, an added droop, the lips were thinner, and the shrew wrinkles were deeper. She swept Josiah with a hostile, withering stare.

"Do you think your father would stop work to talk to tramps?" she demanded of the boy, who visibly quailed, even as Josiah.

"I was only answering his questions," Johnnie pleaded doggedly but hopelessly. "He wanted to know—"

"And I suppose you told him," she snapped. "What business is it of his prying around? No, and he gets nothing to eat. As for you, get to work at once. I'll teach you, idling at your chores. Your father wa'n't like that. Can't I ever make you like him?"

Johnnie bent his back, and the bucksaw resumed its protesting skreek. Agatha surveyed Josiah sourly. It was patent she did not recognise him.

90

"You be off," she commanded harshly. "None of your snooping around here."

Josiah felt the numbness of paralysis creeping over him. He moistened his lips and tried to say something, but found himself bereft of speech.

"You be off, I say," she rasped in her high-keyed voice, "or I'll put the constable after you."

Josiah turned obediently. He heard the door slam as he went down the walk. As in a nightmare he opened the gate he had opened ten thousand times and stepped out on the sidewalk. He felt dazed. Surely it was a dream. Very soon he would wake up with a sigh of relief. He rubbed his forehead and paused indecisively. The monotonous complaint of the bucksaw came to his ears. If that boy had any of the old Childs spirit in him, sooner or later he'd run away. Agatha was beyond the endurance of human flesh. She had not changed, unless for the worse, if such a thing were possible. That boy would surely run for it, maybe soon. Maybe now.

Josiah Childs straightened up and threw his shoulders back. The great-spirited West, with its daring and its carelessness of consequences when mere obstacles stand in the way of its desire, flamed up in him. He looked at his watch, remembered the time table, and spoke to himself, solemnly, aloud. It was an affirmation of faith:

"I don't care a hang about the law. That boy can't be crucified. I'll give her a double allowance, four times, anything, but he goes with me. She can follow on to California if she wants, but I'll draw up an agreement, in which what's what, and she'll sign it, and live up to it, by George, if she wants to stay. And she will," he added grimly. "She's got to have somebody to nag."

He opened the gate and strode back to the woodshed door. Johnnie looked up, but kept on sawing.

"What'd you like to do most of anything in the world?" Josiah demanded in a tense, low voice.

Johnnie hesitated, and almost stopped sawing. Josiah made signs for him to keep it up.

"Go to sea," Johnnie answered. "Along with my father."

Josiah felt himself trembling.

"Would you?" he asked eagerly.

"Would I!"

The look of joy on Johnnie's face decided everything.

"Come here, then. Listen. I'm your father. I'm Josiah Childs. Did you ever want to run away?"

Johnnie nodded emphatically.

"That's what I did," Josiah went on. "I ran away." He fumbled for his watch hurriedly. "We've just time to catch the train for California. I live there now. Maybe Agatha, your mother, will come along afterward. I'll tell you all about it on the train. Come on."

He gathered the half-frightened, half-trusting boy into his arms for a moment, then, hand in hand, they fled across the yard, out of the gate, and down the street. They heard the kitchen door open, and the last they heard was:

"Johnnie!—you! Why ain't you sawing? I'll attend to your case directly!"

THE FIRST POET

SCENE: *A summer plain, the eastern side of which is bounded by grassy hills of limestone, the other sides by a forest. The hill nearest to the plain terminates in a cliff, in the face of which, nearly at the level of the ground, are four caves, with low, narrow entrances. Before the caves, and distant from them less than one hundred feet, is a broad, flat rock, on which are laid several sharp slivers of flint, which, like the rock, are blood-stained. Between the rock and the cave-entrances, on a low pile of stones, is squatted a man, stout and hairy. Across his knees is a thick club, and behind him crouches a woman. At his right and left are two men somewhat resembling him, and like him, bearing wooden clubs. These four face the west, and between them and the bloody rock squat some threescore of cave-folk, talking loudly among themselves. It is late afternoon. The name of him on the pile of stones is Uk, the name of his mate, Ala; and of those at his right and left, Ok and Un.*

Uk:

Be still!

(Turning to the woman behind him)

Thou seest that they become still. None save me can make his kind be still, except perhaps the chief of the apes, when in the night he deems he hears a serpent.... At whom dost thou stare so long? At Oan? Oan, come to me!

Oan:

I am thy cub.

Uk:

Oan, thou art a fool!

Ok and Un:

Ho! ho! Oan is a fool!

All the Tribe:

Ho! ho! Oan is a fool!

Oan:

Why am I a fool?

Uk:

Dost thou not chant strange words? Last night I heard thee chant strange words at the mouth of thy cave.

Oan:

Ay! they are marvellous words; they were born within me in the dark.

Uk:

Art thou a woman, that thou shouldst bring forth? Why dost thou not sleep when it is dark?

Oan:

I did half sleep; perhaps I dreamed.

Uk:

And why shouldst thou dream, not having had more than thy portion of flesh? Hast thou slain a deer in the forest and brought it not to the Stone?

All the Tribe:

Wa! Wa! He hath slain in the forest, and brought not the meat to the Stone!

Uk:

Be still, ye!

(To Ala)

Thou seest that they become still.... Oan, hast thou slain and kept to thyself?

Oan:

Nay, thou knowest that I am not apt at the chase. Also it irks me to squat on a branch all day above a path, bearing a rock upon my thighs. Those words did but awaken within me when I was peaceless in the night.

Uk:

And why wast thou peaccless in the night?

Oan:

Thy mate wept, for that thou didst heat her.

Uk:

Ay! she lamented loudly. But thou shalt make thy half-sleep henceforth at the mouth of the cave, so that when Gurr the tiger cometh, thou shalt hear him sniff between the boulders, and shalt strike the flints, whose stare he hatest. Gurr cometh nightly to the caves.

One of the Tribe:

Ay! Gurr smelleth the Stone!

Uk:

Be still!

(To Ala)

Had he not become still, Ok and Un would have beaten him with their clubs.... But, Oan, tell us those words that were born to thee when Ala did weep.

Oan (*arising*):

They are wonderful words. They are such:

The bright day is gone—

Uk:

Now I see thou art liar as well as fool: behold, the day is not gone!

Oan:

But the day was gone in that hour when my song was born to me.

Uk:

Then shouldst thou have sung it only at that time, and not when it is yet day. But beware lest thou awaken me in the night. Make thou many stars, that they fly in the whiskers of Gurr.

Oan:

My song is even of stars.

Uk:

It was Ul, thy father's wont, ere I slew him with four great stones, to climb to the tops of the tallest trees and reach forth his hand, to see if he might not pluck a star. But I said: "Perhaps they be as chestnut-burs." And all the tribe did laugh. Ul was also a fool. But what dost thou sing of stars?

Oan:

I will begin again:

> The bright day is gone.
>
> The night maketh me sad, sad, sad—

Uk:

Nay, the night maketh thee sad; not sad, sad, sad. For when I say to Ala, "Gather thou dried leaves," I say not, "Gather thou dried leaves, leaves, leaves." Thou art a fool!

96

Ok and Un:

Thou art a fool!

All the Tribe:

Thou art a fool!

Uk:

Yea, he is a fool. But say on, Oan, and tell us of thy chestnut-burs.

Oan:

I will begin again:

> The bright day is gone—

Uk:

Thou dost not say, "gone, gone, gone!"

Oan:

I am thy cub. Suffer that I speak: so shall the tribe admire greatly.

Uk:

Speak on!

Oan:

I will begin once more:

> The bright day is gone.
>
> The night maketh me sad, sad—

Uk:

Said I not that "sad" should be spoken but once? Shall I set Ok and Un upon thee with their branches?

Oan:

But it was so born within me—even "sad, sad—"

Uk:

If again thou twice or thrice say "sad," thou shalt be dragged to the Stone.

Oan:

Owl Ow! I am thy cub! Yet listen:

> The bright day is gone.
>
> The night maketh me sad—

Ow! Ow! thou makest me more sad than the night doth! The song—

Uk:

Ok! Un! Be prepared!

Oan (*hastily*):

Nay! have mercy! I will begin afresh:

> The bright day is gone.
>
> The night maketh me sad.
>
> The—the—the—

Uk:

Thou hast forgotten, and art a fool! See, Ala, he is a fool!

Ok and Un:

He is a fool!

All the Tribe:

He is a fool!

Oan:

I am not a fool! This is a new thing. In the past, when ye did chant, O men, ye did leap about the Stone, beating your breasts and crying, "Hai, hai, hai!" Or, if the moon was great, "Hai, hai! hai, hai, hai!" But this song is made even with such words as ye do speak, and is a great wonder. One may sit at the cave's mouth, and moan it many times as the light goeth out of the sky.

One of the Tribe:

Ay! even thus doth he sit at the mouth of our cave, making us marvel, and more especially the women.

Uk:

Be still!... When I would make women marvel, I do show them a wolf's brains upon my club, or the great stone that I cast, or perhaps do whirl my arms mightily, or bring home much meat. How should a man do otherwise? I will have no songs in this place.

Oan:

Yet suffer that I sing my song unto the tribe. Such things have not been before. It may be that they shall praise thee, seeing that I who do make this song am thy cub.

Uk:

Well, let us have the song.

Oan (*facing the tribe*):

> The bright day is gone.
>
> The night maketh me sa—sad.
>
> But the stars are very white.
>
> They whisper that the day shall return.
>
> O stars; little pieces of the day!

Uk:

This is indeed madness. Hast thou heard a star whisper? Did Ul, thy father, tell thee that he heard the stars whisper when he was in the tree-top? And of what moment is it that a star be a piece of the day, seeing that its light is of no value? Thou art a fool!

Ok and Un:

Thou art a fool!

All the Tribe:

Thou art a fool!

Oan:

But it was so born unto me. And at that birth it was as though I would weep, yet had not been stricken; I was moreover glad, yet none had given me a gift of meat.

Uk:

It is a madness. How shall the stars profit us? Will they lead us to a bear's den, or where the deer foregather, or break for us great bones that we come at their marrow? Will they tell us anything at all? Wait thou until the night, and we shall peer forth from between the boulders, and all men shall take note that the stars cannot whisper.... Yet it may be that they are pieces of the day. This is a deep matter.

Oan:

Ay! they are pieces of the moon!

Uk:

What further madness is this? How shall they be pieces of two things that are not the same? Also it was not thus in the song.

Oan:

I will make me a new song. We do change the shape of wood and stone, but a song is made out of nothing. Ho! ho! I can fashion things from nothing! Also I say that the stars come down at morning and become the dew.

Uk:

Let us have no more of these stars. It may be that a song is a good thing, if it be of what a man knoweth. Thus, if thou singest of my club, or of the bear that I slew, of the stain on the Stone, or the cave and the warm leaves in the cave, it might be well.

Oan:

I will make thee a song of Ala!

Uk (*furiously*):

Thou shalt make me no such song! Thou shalt make me a song of the deer-liver that thou hast eaten! Did I not give to thee of the liver of the she-deer, because thou didst bring me crawfish?

Oan:

Truly I did eat of the liver of the she-deer; but to sing thereof is another matter.

101

Uk:

It was no labour for thee to sing of the stars. See now our clubs and casting-stones, with which we slay flesh to eat; also the caves in which we dwell, and the Stone whereon we make sacrifice; wilt thou sing no song of those?

Oan:

It may be that I shall sing thee songs of them. But now, as I strive here to sing of the doe's liver, no words are born unto me: I can but sing, "O liver! O red liver!"

Uk:

That is a good song: thou seest that the liver is red. It is red as blood.

Oan:

But I love not the liver, save to eat of it.

Uk:

Yet the song of it is good. When the moon is full we shall sing it about the Stone. We shall beat upon our breasts and sing, "O liver! O red liver!" And all the women in the caves shall be affrighted.

Oan:

I will not have that song of the liver! It shall be Ok's song; the tribe must say, "Ok hath made the song!"

Ok:

Ay! I shall be a great singer; I shall sing of a wolf's heart, and say, "Behold, it is red!"

Uk:

Thou art a fool, and shalt sing only, "Hai, hai!" as thy father before thee. But Oan shall make me a song of my club, for the women listen to his songs.

102

Oan:

I will make thee no songs, neither of thy club, nor thy cave, nor thy doe's-liver. Yea! though thou give me no more flesh, yet will I live alone in the forest, and eat the seed of grasses, and likewise rabbits, that are easily snared. And I will sleep in a tree-top, and I will sing nightly:

> The bright day is gone.
>
> The night maketh me sad, sad, sad,
>
> > sad, sad, sad—

Uk:

Ok and Un, arise and slay!

(Ok and Un rush upon Oan, who stoops and picks up two casting-stones, with one of which he strikes Ok between the eyes, and with the other mashes the hand of Un, so that he drops his club. Uk arises.)

Uk:

Behold! Gurr cometh! he cometh swiftly from the wood!

(The Tribe, including Oan and Ala, rush for the cave-mouths. As Oan passes Uk, the latter runs behind Oan and crushes his skull with a blow of his club.)

Uk:

O men! O men with the heart of hyenas! Behold, Gurr cometh not! I did but strive to deceive you, that I might the more easily slay this singer, who is very swift of foot.... Gather ye before me, for I would speak wisdom.... It is not well that there be any song among us other than what our fathers sang in the past, or, if there be songs, let them be of such matters as are of common understanding. If a man sing of a deer, so shall he be drawn, it may be, to go forth and slay a deer, or even a moose. And if he sing of his casting-stones,

103

it may be that he become more apt in the use thereof. And if he sing of his cave, it may be that he shall defend it more stoutly when Gurr teareth at the boulders. But it is a vain thing to make songs of the stars, that seem scornful even of me; or of the moon, which is never two nights the same; or of the day, which goeth about its business and will not linger though one pierce a she-babe with a flint. But as for me, I would have none of these songs. For if I sing of such in the council, how shall I keep my wits? And if I think thereof, when at the chase, it may be that I babble it forth, and the meat hear and escape. And ere it be time to eat, I do give my mind solely to the care of my hunting-gear. And if one sing when eating, he may fall short of his just portion. And when, one hath eaten, doth not he go straightway to sleep? So where shall men find a space for singing? But do ye as ye will: as for me, I will have none of these songs and stars.

Be it also known to all the women that if, remembering these wild words of Oan, they do sing them to themselves, or teach them to the young ones, they shall be beaten with brambles. Cause swiftly that the wife of Ok cease from her wailing, and bring hither the horses that were slain yesterday, that I may apportion them. Had Oan wisdom, he might have eaten thereof; and had a mammoth fallen into our pit, he might have feasted many days. But Oan was a fool!

Un:

Oan was a fool!

All the Tribe:

Oan was a fool!

FINIS

It was the last of Morganson's bacon. In all his life he had never pampered his stomach. In fact, his stomach had been a sort of negligible quantity that bothered him little, and about which he thought less. But now, in the long absence of wonted delights, the keen yearning of his stomach was tickled hugely by the sharp, salty bacon.

His face had a wistful, hungry expression. The cheeks were hollow, and the skin seemed stretched a trifle tightly across the cheek-bones. His pale blue eyes were troubled. There was that in them that showed the haunting imminence of something terrible. Doubt was in them, and anxiety and foreboding. The thin lips were thinner than they were made to be, and they seemed to hunger towards the polished frying-pan.

He sat back and drew forth a pipe. He looked into it with sharp scrutiny, and tapped it emptily on his open palm. He turned the hair-seal tobacco pouch inside out and dusted the lining, treasuring carefully each flake and mite of tobacco that his efforts gleaned. The result was scarce a thimbleful. He searched in his pockets, and brought forward, between thumb and forefinger, tiny pinches of rubbish. Here and there in this rubbish were crumbs of tobacco. These he segregated with microscopic care, though he occasionally permitted small particles of foreign substance to accompany the crumbs to the hoard in his palm. He even deliberately added small, semi-hard woolly fluffs, that had come originally from the coat lining, and that had lain for long months in the bottoms of the pockets.

At the end of fifteen minutes he had the pipe part filled. He lighted it from the camp fire, and sat forward on the blankets, toasting his moccasined feet and smoking parsimoniously. When the pipe was finished he sat on, brooding into the dying flame of the fire. Slowly the worry went out of his eyes and resolve came in. Out of the chaos of his fortunes he had finally achieved a way. But it was not a pretty way. His face had become stern and wolfish, and the thin lips were drawn very tightly.

With resolve came action. He pulled himself stiffly to his feet and proceeded to break camp. He packed the rolled blankets, the frying-pan, rifle, and axe on the sled, and passed a lashing around the load. Then he warmed his hands at the fire and pulled on his mittens. He was foot-sore, and limped noticeably as he took his place at the head of the sled. When he put the looped haul-rope over his shoulder, and leant his weight against it to start the sled, he winced. His flesh was galled by many days of contact with the haul-rope.

The trail led along the frozen breast of the Yukon. At the end of four hours he came around a bend and entered the town of Minto. It was perched on top of a high earth bank in the midst of a clearing, and consisted of a road house, a saloon, and several cabins. He left his sled at the door and entered the saloon.

"Enough for a drink?" he asked, laying an apparently empty gold sack upon the bar.

The barkeeper looked sharply at it and him, then set out a bottle and a glass.

"Never mind the dust," he said.

"Go on and take it," Morganson insisted.

The barkeeper held the sack mouth downward over the scales and shook it, and a few flakes of gold dust fell out. Morganson took the sack from him, turned it inside out, and dusted it carefully.

"I thought there was half-a-dollar in it," he said.

"Not quite," answered the other, "but near enough. I'll get it back with the down weight on the next comer."

Morganson shyly poured the whisky into the glass, partly filling it.

"Go on, make it a man's drink," the barkeeper encouraged.

Morganson tilted the bottle and filled the glass to the brim. He drank the liquor slowly, pleasuring in the fire of it that bit his tongue, sank hotly down his throat, and with warm, gentle caresses permeated his stomach.

"Scurvy, eh?" the barkeeper asked.

"A touch of it," he answered. "But I haven't begun to swell yet. Maybe I can get to Dyea and fresh vegetables, and beat it out."

"Kind of all in, I'd say," the other laughed sympathetically. "No dogs, no money, and the scurvy. I'd try spruce tea if I was you."

At the end of half-an-hour, Morganson said good-bye and left the saloon. He put his galled shoulder to the haul-rope and took the river-trail south. An hour later he halted. An inviting swale left the river and led off to the right at an acute angle. He left his sled and limped up the swale for half a mile. Between him and the river was three hundred yards of flat ground covered with cottonwoods. He crossed the cottonwoods to the bank of the Yukon. The trail went by just beneath, but he did not descend to it. South toward Selkirk he could see the trail widen its sunken length through the snow for over a mile. But to the north, in the direction of Minto, a tree-covered out-jut in the bank a quarter of a mile away screened the trail from him.

He seemed satisfied with the view and returned to the sled the way he had come. He put the haul-rope over his shoulder and dragged the sled up the swale. The snow was unpacked and soft, and it was hard work. The runners clogged and stuck, and he was panting severely ere he had covered the half-mile. Night had come on by the time he had pitched his small tent, set up the sheet-iron stove, and chopped a supply of firewood. He had no candles, and contented himself with a pot of tea before crawling into his blankets.

In the morning, as soon as he got up, he drew on his mittens, pulled the flaps of his cap down over his ears, and crossed through the cottonwoods to the Yukon. He took his rifle with him. As before, he did not descend the bank. He watched the empty trail for an hour, beating his hands and stamping his feet to keep up the circulation, then returned to the tent for breakfast. There was little tea left in the canister—half a dozen drawings at most; but so meagre a pinch did he put in the teapot that he bade fair to extend the lifetime of the tea indefinitely. His entire food supply consisted of half-a-sack of flour and a part-full can of baking powder. He made biscuits, and ate them slowly, chewing each mouthful with infinite relish. When he had had three he called a halt. He debated a while, reached for another biscuit, then hesitated. He turned to the part sack of flour, lifted it, and judged its weight.

"I'm good for a couple of weeks," he spoke aloud.

"Maybe three," he added, as he put the biscuits away.

Again he drew on his mittens, pulled down his ear-flaps, took the rifle, and went out to his station on the river bank. He crouched in the snow, himself unseen, and watched. After a few minutes of inaction, the frost began to bite in, and he rested the rifle across his knees and beat his hands back and forth. Then the sting in his feet became intolerable, and he stepped back from the bank and tramped heavily up and down among the trees. But he did not tramp long at a time. Every several minutes he came to the edge of the bank and peered up and down the trail, as though by sheer will he could materialise the form of a man upon it. The short morning passed, though it had seemed century-long to him, and the trail remained empty.

It was easier in the afternoon, watching by the bank. The temperature rose, and soon the snow began to fall—dry and fine and crystalline. There was no wind, and it fell straight down, in quiet monotony. He crouched with eyes closed, his head upon his knees, keeping his watch upon the trail with his ears. But no whining of dogs, churning of sleds, nor cries of drivers broke the silence. With twilight he returned to the tent, cut a supply of firewood, ate two biscuits, and crawled into his blankets. He slept restlessly, tossing about and groaning; and at midnight he got up and ate another biscuit.

Each day grew colder. Four biscuits could not keep up the heat of his body, despite the quantities of hot spruce tea he drank, and he increased his allowance, morning and evening, to three biscuits. In the middle of the day he ate nothing, contenting himself with several cups of excessively weak real tea. This programme became routine. In the morning three biscuits, at noon real tea, and at night three biscuits. In between he drank spruce tea for his scurvy. He caught himself making larger biscuits, and after a severe struggle with himself went back to the old size.

108

On the fifth day the trail returned to life. To the south a dark object appeared, and grew larger. Morganson became alert. He worked his rifle, ejecting a loaded cartridge from the chamber, by the same action replacing it with another, and returning the ejected cartridge into the magazine. He lowered the trigger to half-cock, and drew on his mitten to keep the trigger-hand warm. As the dark object came nearer he made it out to be a man, without dogs or sled, travelling light. He grew nervous, cocked the trigger, then put it back to half-cock again. The man developed into an Indian, and Morganson, with a sigh of disappointment, dropped the rifle across his knees. The Indian went on past and disappeared towards Minto behind the out-jutting clump of trees.

But Morganson conceived an idea. He changed his crouching spot to a place where cottonwood limbs projected on either side of him. Into these with his axe he chopped two broad notches. Then in one of the notches he rested the barrel of his rifle and glanced along the sights. He covered the trail thoroughly in that direction. He turned about, rested the rifle in the other notch, and, looking along the sights, swept the trail to the clump of trees behind which it disappeared.

He never descended to the trail. A man travelling the trail could have no knowledge of his lurking presence on the bank above. The snow surface was unbroken. There was no place where his tracks left the main trail.

As the nights grew longer, his periods of daylight watching of the trail grew shorter. Once a sled went by with jingling bells in the darkness, and with sullen resentment he chewed his biscuits and listened to the sounds. Chance conspired against him. Faithfully he had watched the trail for ten days, suffering from the cold all the prolonged torment of the damned, and nothing had happened. Only an Indian, travelling light, had passed in. Now, in the night, when it was impossible for him to watch, men and dogs and a sled loaded with life, passed out, bound south to the sea and the sun and civilisation.

So it was that he conceived of the sled for which he waited. It was loaded with life, his life. His life was fading, fainting, gasping away in the tent in the snow. He was weak from lack of food, and could not travel of himself. But on the sled for which he waited were dogs that would drag him, food that would fan up the flame of his life, money that would furnish sea and sun and civilisation. Sea and sun and civilisation became terms interchangeable with life, his life, and they were loaded there on the sled for which he waited. The idea became an obsession, and he grew to think of himself as the rightful and deprived owner of the sled-load of life.

His flour was running short, and he went back to two biscuits in the morning and two biscuits at night. Because, of this his weakness increased and the cold bit in more savagely, and day by day he watched by the dead trail that would not live for him. At last the scurvy entered upon its next stage. The skin was unable longer to cast off the impurity of the blood, and the result was that the body began to swell. His ankles grew puffy, and the ache in them kept him awake long hours at night. Next, the swelling jumped to his knees, and the sum of his pain was more than doubled.

Then there came a cold snap. The temperature went down and down—forty, fifty, sixty degrees below zero. He had no thermometer, but this he knew by the signs and natural phenomena understood by all men in that country—the crackling of water thrown on the snow, the swift sharpness of the bite of the frost, and the rapidity with which his breath froze and coated the canvas walls and roof of the tent. Vainly he fought the cold and strove to maintain his watch on the bank. In his weak condition he was an easy prey, and the frost sank its teeth deep into him before he fled away to the tent and crouched by the fire. His nose and cheeks were frozen and turned black, and his left thumb had frozen inside the mitten. He concluded that he would escape with the loss of the first joint.

Then it was, beaten into the tent by the frost, that the trail, with monstrous irony, suddenly teemed with life. Three sleds went by the first day, and two the second. Once, during each day, he fought his way out to the bank only to succumb and retreat, and each of the two times, within half-an-hour after he retreated, a sled went by.

The cold snap broke, and he was able to remain by the bank once more, and the trail died again. For a week he crouched and watched, and never life stirred along it, not a soul passed in or out. He had cut down to one biscuit night and morning, and somehow he did not seem to notice it. Sometimes he marvelled at the way life remained in him. He never would have thought it possible to endure so much.

When the trail fluttered anew with life it was life with which he could not cope. A detachment of the North-West police went by, a score of them, with many sleds and dogs; and he cowered down on the bank above, and they were unaware of the menace of death that lurked in the form of a dying man beside the trail.

His frozen thumb gave him a great deal of trouble. While watching by the bank he got into the habit of taking his mitten off and thrusting the hand inside his shirt so as to rest the thumb in the warmth of his arm-pit. A mail carrier came over the trail, and Morganson let him pass. A mail carrier was an important person, and was sure to be missed immediately.

On the first day after his last flour had gone it snowed. It was always warm when the snow fell, and he sat out the whole eight hours of daylight on the bank, without movement, terribly hungry and terribly patient, for all the world like a monstrous spider waiting for its prey. But the prey did not come, and he hobbled back to the tent through the darkness, drank quarts of spruce tea and hot water, and went to bed.

The next morning circumstance eased its grip on him. As he started to come out of the tent he saw a huge bull-moose crossing the swale some four hundred yards away. Morganson felt a surge and bound of the blood in him, and then went unaccountably weak. A nausea overpowered him, and he was compelled to sit down a moment to recover. Then he reached for his rifle and took careful aim. The first shot was a hit: he knew it; but the moose turned and broke for the wooded hillside that came down to the swale. Morganson pumped bullets wildly among the trees and brush at the fleeing animal, until it dawned upon him that he was exhausting the ammunition he needed for the sled-load of life for which he waited.

111

He stopped shooting, and watched. He noted the direction of the animal's flight, and, high up on the hillside in an opening among the trees, saw the trunk of a fallen pine. Continuing the moose's flight in his mind he saw that it must pass the trunk. He resolved on one more shot, and in the empty air above the trunk he aimed and steadied his wavering rifle. The animal sprang into his field of vision, with lifted fore-legs as it took the leap. He pulled the trigger. With the explosion the moose seemed to somersault in the air. It crashed down to earth in the snow beyond and flurried the snow into dust.

Morganson dashed up the hillside—at least he started to dash up. The next he knew he was coming out of a faint and dragging himself to his feet. He went up more slowly, pausing from time to time to breathe and to steady his reeling senses. At last he crawled over the trunk. The moose lay before him. He sat down heavily upon the carcass and laughed. He buried his face in his mittened hands and laughed some more.

He shook the hysteria from him. He drew his hunting knife and worked as rapidly as his injured thumb and weakness would permit him. He did not stop to skin the moose, but quartered it with its hide on. It was a Klondike of meat.

When he had finished he selected a piece of meat weighing a hundred pounds, and started to drag it down to the tent. But the snow was soft, and it was too much for him. He exchanged it for a twenty-pound piece, and, with many pauses to rest, succeeded in getting it to the tent. He fried some of the meat, but ate sparingly. Then, and automatically, he went out to his crouching place on the bank. There were sled-tracks in the fresh snow on the trail. The sled-load of life had passed by while he had been cutting up the moose.

But he did not mind. He was glad that the sled had not passed before the coming of the moose. The moose had changed his plans. Its meat was worth fifty cents a pound, and he was but little more than three miles from Minto. He need no longer wait for the sled-load of life. The moose was the sled-load of life. He would sell it. He would buy a couple of dogs at Minto, some food and some tobacco, and the dogs would haul him south along the trail to the sea, the sun, and civilisation.

He felt hungry. The dull, monotonous ache of hunger had now become a sharp and insistent pang. He hobbled back to the tent and fried a slice of meat. After that he smoked two whole pipefuls of dried tea leaves. Then he fried another slice of moose. He was aware of an unwonted glow of strength, and went out and chopped some firewood. He followed that up with a slice of meat. Teased on by the food, his hunger grew into an inflammation. It became imperative every little while to fry a slice of meat. He tried smaller slices and found himself frying oftener.

In the middle of the day he thought of the wild animals that might eat his meat, and he climbed the hill, carrying along his axe, the haul rope, and a sled lashing. In his weak state the making of the cache and storing of the meat was an all-afternoon task. He cut young saplings, trimmed them, and tied them together into a tall scaffold. It was not so strong a cache as he would have desired to make, but he had done his best. To hoist the meat to the top was heart-breaking. The larger pieces defied him until he passed the rope over a limb above, and, with one end fast to a piece of meat, put all his weight on the other end.

Once in the tent, he proceeded to indulge in a prolonged and solitary orgy. He did not need friends. His stomach and he were company. Slice after slice and many slices of meat he fried and ate. He ate pounds of the meat. He brewed real tea, and brewed it strong. He brewed the last he had. It did not matter. On the morrow he would be buying tea in Minto. When it seemed he could eat no more, he smoked. He smoked all his stock of dried tea leaves. What of it? On the morrow he would be smoking tobacco. He knocked out his pipe, fried a final slice, and went to bed. He had eaten so much he seemed bursting, yet he got out of his blankets and had just one more mouthful of meat.

In the morning he awoke as from the sleep of death. In his ears were strange sounds. He did not know where he was, and looked about him stupidly until he caught sight of the frying-pan with the last piece of meat in it, partly eaten. Then he remembered all, and with a quick start turned his attention to the strange sounds. He sprang from the blankets with an oath. His scurvy-ravaged legs gave under him and he winced with the pain. He proceeded more slowly to put on his moccasins and leave the tent.

From the cache up the hillside arose a confused noise of snapping and snarling, punctuated by occasional short, sharp yelps. He increased his speed at much expense of pain, and cried loudly and threateningly. He saw the wolves hurrying away through the snow and underbrush, many of them, and he saw the scaffold down on the ground. The animals were heavy with the meat they had eaten, and they were content to slink away and leave the wreckage.

The way of the disaster was clear to him. The wolves had scented his cache. One of them had leapt from the trunk of the fallen tree to the top of the cache. He could see marks of the brute's paws in the snow that covered the trunk. He had not dreamt a wolf could leap so far. A second had followed the first, and a third and fourth, until the flimsy scaffold had gone down under their weight and movement.

His eyes were hard and savage for a moment as he contemplated the extent of the calamity; then the old look of patience returned into them, and he began to gather together the bones well picked and gnawed. There was marrow in them, he knew; and also, here and there, as he sifted the snow, he found scraps of meat that had escaped the maws of the brutes made careless by plenty.

He spent the rest of the morning dragging the wreckage of the moose down the hillside. In addition, he had at least ten pounds left of the chunk of meat he had dragged down the previous day.

"I'm good for weeks yet," was his comment as he surveyed the heap.

He had learnt how to starve and live. He cleaned his rifle and counted the cartridges that remained to him. There were seven. He loaded the weapon and hobbled out to his crouching-place on the bank. All day he watched the dead trail. He watched all the week, but no life passed over it.

Thanks to the meat he felt stronger, though his scurvy was worse and more painful. He now lived upon soup, drinking endless gallons of the thin product of the boiling of the moose bones. The soup grew thinner and thinner as he cracked the bones and boiled them over and over; but the hot water with the essence of the meat in it was good for him, and he was more vigorous than he had been previous to the shooting of the moose.

It was in the next week that a new factor entered into Morganson's life. He wanted to know the date. It became an obsession. He pondered and calculated, but his conclusions were rarely twice the same. The first thing in the morning and the last thing at night, and all day as well, watching by the trail, he worried about it. He awoke at night and lay awake for hours over the problem. To have known the date would have been of no value to him; but his curiosity grew until it equalled his hunger and his desire to live. Finally it mastered him, and he resolved to go to Minto and find out.

It was dark when he arrived at Minto, but this served him. No one saw him arrive. Besides, he knew he would have moonlight by which to return. He climbed the bank and pushed open the saloon door. The light dazzled him. The source of it was several candles, but he had been living for long in an unlighted tent. As his eyes adjusted themselves, he saw three men sitting around the stove. They were trail-travellers—he knew it at once; and since they had not passed in, they were evidently bound out. They would go by his tent next morning.

The barkeeper emitted a long and marvelling whistle.

"I thought you was dead," he said.

"Why?" Morganson asked in a faltering voice.

He had become unused to talking, and he was not acquainted with the sound of his own voice. It seemed hoarse and strange.

"You've been dead for more'n two months, now," the barkeeper explained. "You left here going south, and you never arrived at Selkirk. Where have you been?"

115

"Chopping wood for the steamboat company," Morganson lied unsteadily.

He was still trying to become acquainted with his own voice. He hobbled across the floor and leant against the bar. He knew he must lie consistently; and while he maintained an appearance of careless indifference, his heart was beating and pounding furiously and irregularly, and he could not help looking hungrily at the three men by the stove. They were the possessors of life—his life.

"But where in hell you been keeping yourself all this time?" the barkeeper demanded.

"I located across the river," he answered. "I've got a mighty big stack of wood chopped."

The barkeeper nodded. His face beamed with understanding.

"I heard sounds of chopping several times," he said. "So that was you, eh? Have a drink?"

Morganson clutched the bar tightly. A drink! He could have thrown his arms around the man's legs and kissed his feet. He tried vainly to utter his acceptance; but the barkeeper had not waited and was already passing out the bottle.

"But what did you do for grub?" the latter asked. "You don't look as if you could chop wood to keep yourself warm. You look terribly bad, friend."

Morganson yearned towards the delayed bottle and gulped dryly.

"I did the chopping before the scurvy got bad," he said. "Then I got a moose right at the start. I've been living high all right. It's the scurvy that's run me down."

He filled the glass, and added, "But the spruce tea's knocking it, I think."

"Have another," the barkeeper said.

The action of the two glasses of whisky on Morganson's empty stomach and weak condition was rapid. The next he knew he was sitting by the stove on a box, and it seemed as though ages had passed. A tall, broad-shouldered, black-whiskered man was paying for drinks. Morganson's swimming eyes saw him drawing a greenback from a fat roll, and Morganson's swimming eyes cleared on the instant. They were hundred-dollar bills. It was life! His life! He felt an almost irresistible impulse to snatch the money and dash madly out into the night.

The black-whiskered man and one of his companions arose.

"Come on, Oleson," the former said to the third one of the party, a fair-haired, ruddy-faced giant.

Oleson came to his feet, yawning and stretching.

"What are you going to bed so soon for?" the barkeeper asked plaintively. "It's early yet."

"Got to make Selkirk to-morrow," said he of the black whiskers.

"On Christmas Day!" the barkeeper cried.

"The better the day the better the deed," the other laughed.

As the three men passed out of the door it came dimly to Morganson that it was Christmas Eve. That was the date. That was what he had come to Minto for. But it was overshadowed now by the three men themselves, and the fat roll of hundred-dollar bills.

The door slammed.

"That's Jack Thompson," the barkeeper said. "Made two millions on Bonanza and Sulphur, and got more coming. I'm going to bed. Have another drink first."

Morganson hesitated.

"A Christmas drink," the other urged. "It's all right. I'll get it back when you sell your wood."

Morganson mastered his drunkenness long enough to swallow the whisky, say good night, and get out on the trail. It was moonlight, and he hobbled along through the bright, silvery quiet, with a vision of life before him that took the form of a roll of hundred-dollar bills.

He awoke. It was dark, and he was in his blankets. He had gone to bed in his moccasins and mittens, with the flaps of his cap pulled down over his ears. He got up as quickly as his crippled condition would permit, and built the fire and boiled some water. As he put the spruce-twigs into the teapot he noted the first glimmer of the pale morning light. He caught up his rifle and hobbled in a panic out to the bank. As he crouched and waited, it came to him that he had forgotten to drink his spruce tea. The only other thought in his mind was the possibility of John Thompson changing his mind and not travelling Christmas Day.

Dawn broke and merged into day. It was cold and clear. Sixty below zero was Morganson's estimate of the frost. Not a breath stirred the chill Arctic quiet. He sat up suddenly, his muscular tensity increasing the hurt of the scurvy. He had heard the far sound of a man's voice and the faint whining of dogs. He began beating his hands back and forth against his sides. It was a serious matter to bare the trigger hand to sixty degrees below zero, and against that time he needed to develop all the warmth of which his flesh was capable.

They came into view around the outjutting clump of trees. To the fore was the third man whose name he had not learnt. Then came eight dogs drawing the sled. At the front of the sled, guiding it by the gee-pole, walked John Thompson. The rear was brought up by Oleson, the Swede. He was certainly a fine man, Morganson thought, as he looked at the bulk of him in his squirrel-skin *parka*. The men and dogs were silhouetted sharply against the white of the landscape. They had the seeming of two dimension, cardboard figures that worked mechanically.

Morganson rested his cocked rifle in the notch in the tree. He became abruptly aware that his fingers were cold, and discovered that his right hand was bare. He did not know that he had taken off the mitten. He slipped it on again hastily. The men and dogs drew closer, and he could see their breaths spouting into visibility in the cold air. When the first man was fifty yards away, Morganson slipped the mitten from his right hand. He placed the first finger on the trigger and aimed low. When he fired the first man whirled half around and went down on the trail.

In the instant of surprise, Morganson pulled the trigger on John Thompson—too low, for the latter staggered and sat down suddenly on the sled. Morganson raised his aim and fired again. John Thompson sank down backward along the top of the loaded sled.

Morganson turned his attention to Oleson. At the same time that he noted the latter running away towards Minto he noted that the dogs, coming to where the first man's body blocked the trail, had halted. Morganson fired at the fleeing man and missed, and Oleson swerved. He continued to swerve back and forth, while Morganson fired twice in rapid succession and missed both shots. Morganson stopped himself just as he was pulling the trigger again. He had fired six shots. Only one more cartridge remained, and it was in the chamber. It was imperative that he should not miss his last shot.

He held his fire and desperately studied Oleson's flight. The giant was grotesquely curving and twisting and running at top speed along the trail, the tail of his *parka* flapping smartly behind. Morganson trained his rifle on the man and with a swaying action followed his erratic flight. Morganson's finger was getting numb. He could scarcely feel the trigger. "God help me," he breathed a prayer aloud, and pulled the trigger. The running man pitched forward on his face, rebounded from the hard trail, and slid along, rolling over and over. He threshed for a moment with his arms and then lay quiet.

Morganson dropped his rifle (worthless now that the last cartridge was gone) and slid down the bank through the soft snow. Now that he had sprung the trap, concealment of his lurking-place was no longer necessary. He hobbled along the trail to the sled, his fingers making involuntary gripping and clutching movements inside the mittens.

The snarling of the dogs halted him. The leader, a heavy dog, half Newfoundland and half Hudson Bay, stood over the body of the man that lay

119

on the trail, and menaced Morganson with bristling hair and bared fangs. The other seven dogs of the team were likewise bristling and snarling. Morganson approached tentatively, and the team surged towards him. He stopped again and talked to the animals, threatening and cajoling by turns. He noticed the face of the man under the leader's feet, and was surprised at how quickly it had turned white with the ebb of life and the entrance of the frost. John Thompson lay back along the top of the loaded sled, his head sunk in a space between two sacks and his chin tilted upwards, so that all Morganson could see was the black beard pointing skyward.

Finding it impossible to face the dogs Morganson stepped off the trail into the deep snow and floundered in a wide circle to the rear of the sled. Under the initiative of the leader, the team swung around in its tangled harness. Because of his crippled condition, Morganson could move only slowly. He saw the animals circling around on him and tried to retreat. He almost made it, but the big leader, with a savage lunge, sank its teeth into the calf of his leg. The flesh was slashed and torn, but Morganson managed to drag himself clear.

He cursed the brutes fiercely, but could not cow them. They replied with neck-bristling and snarling, and with quick lunges against their breastbands. He remembered Oleson, and turned his back upon them and went along the trail. He scarcely took notice of his lacerated leg. It was bleeding freely; the main artery had been torn, but he did not know it.

Especially remarkable to Morganson was the extreme pallor of the Swede, who the preceding night had been so ruddy-faced. Now his face was like white marble. What with his fair hair and lashes he looked like a carved statue rather than something that had been a man a few minutes before. Morganson pulled off his mittens and searched the body. There was no money-belt around the waist next to the skin, nor did he find a gold-sack. In a breast pocket he lit on a small wallet. With fingers that swiftly went numb with the frost, he hurried through the contents of the wallet. There were letters with foreign stamps and postmarks on them, and several receipts and memorandum accounts, and a letter of credit for eight hundred dollars. That was all. There was no money.

120

He made a movement to start back toward the sled, but found his foot rooted to the trail. He glanced down and saw that he stood in a fresh deposit of frozen red. There was red ice on his torn pants leg and on the moccasin beneath. With a quick effort he broke the frozen clutch of his blood and hobbled along the trail to the sled. The big leader that had bitten him began snarling and lunging, and was followed in this conduct by the whole team.

Morganson wept weakly for a space, and weakly swayed from one side to the other. Then he brushed away the frozen tears that gemmed his lashes. It was a joke. Malicious chance was having its laugh at him. Even John Thompson, with his heaven-aspiring whiskers, was laughing at him.

He prowled around the sled demented, at times weeping and pleading with the brutes for his life there on the sled, at other times raging impotently against them. Then calmness came upon him. He had been making a fool of himself. All he had to do was to go to the tent, get the axe, and return and brain the dogs. He'd show them.

In order to get to the tent he had to go wide of the sled and the savage animals. He stepped off the trail into the soft snow. Then he felt suddenly giddy and stood still. He was afraid to go on for fear he would fall down. He stood still for a long time, balancing himself on his crippled legs that were trembling violently from weakness. He looked down and saw the snow reddening at his feet. The blood flowed freely as ever. He had not thought the bite was so severe. He controlled his giddiness and stooped to examine the wound. The snow seemed rushing up to meet him, and he recoiled from it as from a blow. He had a panic fear that he might fall down, and after a struggle he managed to stand upright again. He was afraid of that snow that had rushed up to him.

Then the white glimmer turned black, and the next he knew he was awakening in the snow where he had fallen. He was no longer giddy. The cobwebs were gone. But he could not get up. There was no strength in his limbs. His body seemed lifeless. By a desperate effort he managed to roll over on his side. In this position he caught a glimpse of the sled and of John Thompson's black beard pointing skyward. Also he saw the lead dog licking

121

the face of the man who lay on the trail. Morganson watched curiously. The dog was nervous and eager. Sometimes it uttered short, sharp yelps, as though to arouse the man, and surveyed him with ears cocked forward and wagging tail. At last it sat down, pointed its nose upward, and began to howl. Soon all the team was howling.

Now that he was down, Morganson was no longer afraid. He had a vision of himself being found dead in the snow, and for a while he wept in self-pity. But he was not afraid. The struggle had gone out of him. When he tried to open his eyes he found that the wet tears had frozen them shut. He did not try to brush the ice away. It did not matter. He had not dreamed death was so easy. He was even angry that he had struggled and suffered through so many weary weeks. He had been bullied and cheated by the fear of death. Death did not hurt. Every torment he had endured had been a torment of life. Life had defamed death. It was a cruel thing.

But his anger passed. The lies and frauds of life were of no consequence now that he was coming to his own. He became aware of drowsiness, and felt a sweet sleep stealing upon him, balmy with promises of easement and rest. He heard faintly the howling of the dogs, and had a fleeting thought that in the mastering of his flesh the frost no longer bit. Then the light and the thought ceased to pulse beneath the tear-gemmed eyelids, and with a tired sigh of comfort he sank into sleep.

THE END OF THE STORY

I

The table was of hand-hewn spruce boards, and the men who played whist had frequent difficulties in drawing home their tricks across the uneven surface. Though they sat in their undershirts, the sweat noduled and oozed on their faces; yet their feet, heavily moccasined and woollen-socked, tingled with the bite of the frost. Such was the difference of temperature in the small cabin between the floor level and a yard or more above it. The sheet-iron Yukon Stove roared red-hot, yet, eight feet away, on the meat-shelf, placed low and beside the door, lay chunks of solidly frozen moose and bacon. The door, a third of the way up from the bottom, was a thick rime. In the chinking between the logs at the back of the bunks the frost showed white and glistening. A window of oiled paper furnished light. The lower portion of the paper, on the inside, was coated an inch deep with the frozen moisture of the men's breath.

They played a momentous rubber of whist, for the pair that lost was to dig a fishing hole through the seven feet of ice and snow that covered the Yukon.

"It's mighty unusual, a cold snap like this in March," remarked the man who shuffled. "What would you call it, Bob?"

"Oh, fifty-five or sixty below—all of that. What do you make it, Doc?"

Doc turned his head and glanced at the lower part of the door with a measuring eye.

"Not a bit worse than fifty. If anything, slightly under—say forty-nine. See the ice on the door. It's just about the fifty mark, but you'll notice the upper edge is ragged. The time she went seventy the ice climbed a full four inches higher." He picked up his hand, and without ceasing from sorting called "Come in," to a knock on the door.

The man who entered was a big, broad-shouldered Swede, though his nationality was not discernible until he had removed his ear-flapped cap and thawed away the ice which had formed on beard and moustache and which served to mask his face. While engaged in this, the men at the table played out the hand.

"I hear one doctor faller stop this camp," the Swede said inquiringly, looking anxiously from face to face, his own face haggard and drawn from severe and long endured pain. "I come long way. North fork of the Whyo."

"I'm the doctor. What's the matter?"

In response, the man held up his left hand, the second finger of which was monstrously swollen. At the same time he began a rambling, disjointed history of the coming and growth of his affliction.

"Let me look at it," the doctor broke in impatiently. "Lay it on the table. There, like that."

Tenderly, as if it were a great boil, the man obeyed.

"Humph," the doctor grumbled. "A weeping sinew. And travelled a hundred miles to have it fixed. I'll fix it in a jiffy. You watch me, and next time you can do it yourself."

Without warning, squarely and at right angles, and savagely, the doctor brought the edge of his hand down on the swollen crooked finger. The man yelled with consternation and agony. It was more like the cry of a wild beast, and his face was a wild beast's as he was about to spring on the man who had perpetrated the joke.

"That's all right," the doctor placated sharply and authoritatively. "How do you feel? Better, eh? Of course. Next time you can do it yourself—Go on and deal, Strothers. I think we've got you."

Slow and ox-like, on the face of the Swede dawned relief and comprehension. The pang over, the finger felt better. The pain was gone. He examined the finger curiously, with wondering eyes, slowly crooking it back and forth. He reached into his pocket and pulled out a gold-sack.

"How much?"

The doctor shook his head impatiently. "Nothing. I'm not practising— Your play, Bob."

The Swede moved heavily on his feet, re-examined the finger, then turned an admiring gaze on the doctor.

"You are good man. What your name?"

"Linday, Doctor Linday," Strothers answered, as if solicitous to save his opponent from further irritation.

"The day's half done," Linday said to the Swede, at the end of the hand, while he shuffled. "Better rest over to-night. It's too cold for travelling. There's a spare bunk."

He was a slender brunette of a man, lean-cheeked, thin-lipped, and strong. The smooth-shaven face was a healthy sallow. All his movements were quick and precise. He did not fumble his cards. The eyes were black, direct, and piercing, with the trick of seeming to look beneath the surfaces of things. His hands, slender, fine and nervous, appeared made for delicate work, and to the most casual eye they conveyed an impression of strength.

"Our game," he announced, drawing in the last trick. "Now for the rub and who digs the fishing hole."

A knock at the door brought a quick exclamation from him.

"Seems we just can't finish this rubber," he complained, as the door opened. "What's the matter with *you?*"—this last to the stranger who entered.

The newcomer vainly strove to move his icebound jaws and jowls. That he had been on trail for long hours and days was patent. The skin across the cheekbones was black with repeated frost-bite. From nose to chin was a mass of solid ice perforated by the hole through which he breathed. Through this he had also spat tobacco juice, which had frozen, as it trickled, into an amber-coloured icicle, pointed like a Van Dyke beard.

He shook his head dumbly, grinned with his eyes, and drew near to the stove to thaw his mouth to speech. He assisted the process with his fingers, clawing off fragments of melting ice which rattled and sizzled on the stove.

"Nothing the matter with me," he finally announced. "But if they's a doctor in the outfit he's sure needed. They's a man up the Little Peco that's had a ruction with a panther, an' the way he's clawed is something scand'lous."

"How far up?" Doctor Linday demanded.

"A matter of a hundred miles."

"How long since?"

"I've ben three days comin' down."

"Bad?"

"Shoulder dislocated. Some ribs broke for sure. Right arm broke. An' clawed clean to the bone most all over but the face. We sewed up two or three bad places temporary, and tied arteries with twine."

"That settles it," Linday sneered. "Where were they?"

"Stomach."

"He's a sight by now."

"Not on your life. Washed clean with bug-killin' dope before we stitched. Only temporary anyway. Had nothin' but linen thread, but washed that, too."

"He's as good as dead," was Linday's judgment, as he angrily fingered the cards.

"Nope. That man ain't goin' to die. He knows I've come for a doctor, an' he'll make out to live until you get there. He won't let himself die. I know him."

"Christian Science and gangrene, eh?" came the sneer. "Well, I'm not practising. Nor can I see myself travelling a hundred miles at fifty below for a dead man."

126

"I can see you, an' for a man a long ways from dead."

Linday shook his head. "Sorry, you had your trip for nothing. Better stop over for the night."

"Nope. We'll be pullin' out in ten minutes."

"What makes you so cocksure?" Linday demanded testily.

Then it was that Tom Daw made the speech of his life.

"Because he's just goin' on livin' till you get there, if it takes you a week to make up your mind. Besides, his wife's with him, not sheddin' a tear, or nothin', an' she's helpin' him live till you come. They think a almighty heap of each other, an' she's got a will like hisn. If he weakened, she'd just put her immortal soul into hisn an' make him live. Though he ain't weakenin' none, you can stack on that. I'll stack on it. I'll lay you three to one, in ounces, he's alive when you get there. I got a team of dawgs down the bank. You ought to allow to start in ten minutes, an' we ought to make it back in less'n three days because the trail's broke. I'm goin' down to the dawgs now, an' I'll look for you in ten minutes."

Tom Daw pulled down his earflaps, drew on his mittens, and passed out.

"Damn him!" Linday cried, glaring vindictively at the closed door.

II

That night, long after dark, with twenty-five miles behind them, Linday and Tom Daw went into camp. It was a simple but adequate affair: a fire built in the snow; alongside, their sleeping-furs spread in a single bed on a mat of spruce boughs; behind the bed an oblong of canvas stretched to refract the heat. Daw fed the dogs and chopped ice and firewood. Linday's cheeks burned with frost-bite as he squatted over the cooking. They ate heavily, smoked a pipe and talked while they dried their moccasins before the fire, and turned in to sleep the dead sleep of fatigue and health.

Morning found the unprecedented cold snap broken. Linday estimated the temperature at fifteen below and rising. Daw was worried. That day would see them in the canyon, he explained, and if the spring thaw set in the canyon would run open water. The walls of the canyon were hundreds to thousands of feet high. They could be climbed, but the going would be slow.

Camped well in the dark and forbidding gorge, over their pipe that evening they complained of the heat, and both agreed that the thermometer must be above zero—the first time in six months.

"Nobody ever heard tell of a panther this far north," Daw was saying. "Rocky called it a cougar. But I shot a-many of 'em down in Curry County, Oregon, where I come from, an' we called 'em panther. Anyway, it was a bigger cat than ever I seen. It was sure a monster cat. Now how'd it ever stray to such out of the way huntin' range?—that's the question."

Linday made no comment. He was nodding. Propped on sticks, his moccasins steamed unheeded and unturned. The dogs, curled in furry balls, slept in the snow. The crackle of an ember accentuated the profound of silence that reigned. He awoke with a start and gazed at Daw, who nodded and returned the gaze. Both listened. From far off came a vague disturbance that increased to a vast and sombre roaring. As it neared, ever-increasing, riding the mountain tops as well as the canyon depths, bowing the forest before it, bending the meagre, crevice-rooted pines on the walls of the gorge, they knew it for what it was. A wind, strong and warm, a balmy gale, drove past them, flinging a rocket-shower of sparks from the fire. The dogs, aroused, sat on their haunches, bleak noses pointed upward, and raised the long wolf howl.

"It's the Chinook," Daw said.

"It means the river trail, I suppose?"

"Sure thing. And ten miles of it is easier than one over the tops." Daw surveyed Linday for a long, considering minute. "We've just had fifteen hours of trail," he shouted above the wind, tentatively, and again waited. "Doc," he said finally, "are you game?"

For answer, Linday knocked out his pipe and began to pull on his damp moccasins. Between them, and in few minutes, bending to the force of the wind, the dogs were harnessed, camp broken, and the cooking outfit and unused sleeping furs lashed on the sled. Then, through the darkness, for a night of travel, they churned out on the trail Daw had broken nearly a week before. And all through the night the Chinook roared and they urged the weary dogs and spurred their own jaded muscles. Twelve hours of it they made, and stopped for breakfast after twenty-seven hours on trail.

"An hour's sleep," said Daw, when they had wolfed pounds of straight moose-meat fried with bacon.

Two hours he let his companion sleep, afraid himself to close his eyes. He occupied himself with making marks upon the soft-surfaced, shrinking snow. Visibly it shrank. In two hours the snow level sank three inches. From every side, faintly heard and near, under the voice of the spring wind, came the trickling of hidden waters. The Little Peco, strengthened by the multitudinous streamlets, rose against the manacles of winter, riving the ice with crashings and snappings.

Daw touched Linday on the shoulder; touched him again; shook, and shook violently.

"Doc," he murmured admiringly. "You can sure go some."

The weary black eyes, under heavy lids, acknowledged the compliment.

"But that ain't the question. Rocky is clawed something scand'lous. As I said before, I helped sew up his in'ards. Doc...." He shook the man, whose eyes had again closed. "I say, Doc! The question is: can you go some more?—hear me? I say, can you go some more?"

The weary dogs snapped and whimpered when kicked from their sleep. The going was slow, not more than two miles an hour, and the animals took every opportunity to lie down in the wet snow.

"Twenty miles of it, and we'll be through the gorge," Daw encouraged. "After that the ice can go to blazes, for we can take to the bank, and it's only ten more miles to camp. Why, Doc, we're almost there. And when you get Rocky fixed up, you can come down in a canoe in one day."

But the ice grew more uneasy under them, breaking loose from the shore-line and rising steadily inch by inch. In places where it still held to the shore, the water overran and they waded and slushed across. The Little Peco growled and muttered. Cracks and fissures were forming everywhere as they battled on for the miles that each one of which meant ten along the tops.

"Get on the sled, Doc, an' take a snooze," Daw invited.

The glare from the black eyes prevented him from repeating the suggestion.

As early as midday they received definite warning of the beginning of the end. Cakes of ice, borne downward in the rapid current, began to thunder beneath the ice on which they stood. The dogs whimpered anxiously and yearned for the bank.

"That means open water above," Daw explained. "Pretty soon she'll jam somewheres, an' the river'll raise a hundred feet in a hundred minutes. It's us for the tops if we can find a way to climb out. Come on! Hit her up I! An' just to think, the Yukon'll stick solid for weeks."

Unusually narrow at this point, the great walls of the canyon were too precipitous to scale. Daw and Linday had to keep on; and they kept on till the disaster happened. With a loud explosion, the ice broke asunder midway under the team. The two animals in the middle of the string went into the fissure, and the grip of the current on their bodies dragged the lead-dog backward and in. Swept downstream under the ice, these three bodies began to drag to the edge the two whining dogs that remained. The men held back frantically on the sled, but were slowly drawn along with it. It was all over in the space of seconds. Daw slashed the wheel-dog's traces with his sheath-knife, and the animal whipped over the ice-edge and was gone. The ice on which they stood, broke into a large and pivoting cake that ground and splintered against the shore ice and rocks. Between them they got the sled ashore and up into a crevice in time to see the ice-cake up-edge, sink, and down-shelve from view.

Meat and sleeping furs were made into packs, and the sled was abandoned. Linday resented Daw's taking the heavier pack, but Daw had his will.

"You got to work as soon as you get there. Come on."

It was one in the afternoon when they started to climb. At eight that evening they cleared the rim and for half an hour lay where they had fallen. Then came the fire, a pot of coffee, and an enormous feed of moosemeat. But first Linday hefted the two packs, and found his own lighter by half.

"You're an iron man, Daw," he admired.

"Who? Me? Oh, pshaw! You ought to see Rocky. He's made out of platinum, an' armour plate, an' pure gold, an' all strong things. I'm mountaineer, but he plumb beats me out. Down in Curry County I used to 'most kill the boys when we run bear. So when I hooks up with Rocky on our first hunt I had a mean idea to show 'm a few. I let out the links good an' generous, 'most nigh keepin' up with the dawgs, an' along comes Rocky a-treadin' on my heels. I knowed he couldn't last that way, and I just laid down an' did my dangdest. An' there he was, at the end of another hour, a-treadin' steady an' regular on my heels. I was some huffed. 'Mebbe you'd like to come to the front an' show me how to travel,' I says. 'Sure,' says he. An' he done it! I stayed with 'm, but let me tell you I was plumb tuckered by the time the bear tree'd."

"They ain't no stoppin' that man. He ain't afraid of nothin'. Last fall, before the freeze-up, him an' me was headin' for camp about twilight. I was clean shot out—ptarmigan—an' he had one cartridge left. An' the dawgs tree'd a she grizzly. Small one. Only weighed about three hundred, but you know what grizzlies is. 'Don't do it,' says I, when he ups with his rifle. 'You only got that one shot, an' it's too dark to see the sights.'

"'Climb a tree,' says he. I didn't climb no tree, but when that bear come down a-cussin' among the dawgs, an' only creased, I want to tell you I was sure hankerin' for a tree. It was some ruction. Then things come on real bad. The bear slid down a hollow against a big log. Downside, that log was four feet up

131

an' down. Dawgs couldn't get at bear that way. Upside was steep gravel, an' the dawgs'd just naturally slide down into the bear. They was no jumpin' back, an' the bear was a-manglin' 'em fast as they come. All underbrush, gettin' pretty dark, no cartridges, nothin'.

"What's Rocky up an' do? He goes downside of log, reaches over with his knife, an' begins slashin'. But he can only reach bear's rump, an' dawgs bein' ruined fast, one-two-three time. Rocky gets desperate. He don't like to lose his dawgs. He jumps on top log, grabs bear by the slack of the rump, an' heaves over back'ard right over top of that log. Down they go, kit an' kaboodle, twenty feet, bear, dawgs, an' Rocky, slidin', cussin', an' scratchin', ker-plump into ten feet of water in the bed of stream. They all swum out different ways. Nope, he didn't get the bear, but he saved the dawgs. That's Rocky. They's no stoppin' him when his mind's set."

It was at the next camp that Linday heard how Rocky had come to be injured.

"I'd ben up the draw, about a mile from the cabin, lookin' for a piece of birch likely enough for an axe-handle. Comin' back I heard the darndest goings-on where we had a bear trap set. Some trapper had left the trap in an old cache an' Rocky'd fixed it up. But the goings-on. It was Rocky an' his brother Harry. First I'd hear one yell and laugh, an' then the other, like it was some game. An' what do you think the fool game was? I've saw some pretty nervy cusses down in Curry County, but they beat all. They'd got a whoppin' big panther in the trap an' was takin' turns rappin' it on the nose with a light stick. But that wa'n't the point. I just come out of the brush in time to see Harry rap it. Then he chops six inches off the stick an' passes it to Rocky. You see, that stick was growin' shorter all the time. It ain't as easy as you think. The panther'd slack back an' hunch down an' spit, an' it was mighty lively in duckin' the stick. An' you never knowed when it'd jump. It was caught by the hind leg, which was curious, too, an' it had some slack I'm tellin' you.

"It was just a game of dare they was playin', an' the stick gettin' shorter an' shorter an' the panther madder 'n madder. Bimeby they wa'n't no stick left—only a nubbin, about four inches long, an' it was Rocky's turn. 'Better quit now,' says Harry. 'What for?' says Rocky. 'Because if you rap him again they won't be no stick left for me,' Harry answers. 'Then you'll quit an' I win,' says Rocky with a laugh, an' goes to it.

"An' I don't want to see anything like it again. That cat'd bunched back an' down till it had all of six feet slack in its body. An' Rocky's stick four inches long. The cat got him. You couldn't see one from t'other. No chance to shoot. It was Harry, in the end, that got his knife into the panther's jugular."

"If I'd known how he got it I'd never have come," was Linday's comment.

Daw nodded concurrence.

"That's what she said. She told me sure not to whisper how it happened."

"Is he crazy?" Linday demanded in his wrath.

"They're all crazy. Him an' his brother are all the time devilin' each other to tom-fool things. I seen them swim the riffle last fall, bad water an' mush-ice runnin'—on a dare. They ain't nothin' they won't tackle. An' she's 'most as bad. Not afraid some herself. She'll do anything Rocky'll let her. But he's almighty careful with her. Treats her like a queen. No camp-work or such for her. That's why another man an' me are hired on good wages. They've got slathers of money an' they're sure dippy on each other. 'Looks like good huntin',' says Rocky, when they struck that section last fall. 'Let's make a camp then,' says Harry. An' me all the time thinkin' they was lookin' for gold. Ain't ben a prospect pan washed the whole winter."

Linday's anger mounted. "I haven't any patience with fools. For two cents I'd turn back."

"No you wouldn't," Daw assured him confidently. "They ain't enough grub to turn back, an' we'll be there to-morrow. Just got to cross that last divide an' drop down to the cabin. An' they's a better reason. You're too far from home, an' I just naturally wouldn't let you turn back."

Exhausted as Linday was, the flash in his black eyes warned Daw that he had overreached himself. His hand went out.

"My mistake, Doc. Forget it. I reckon I'm gettin' some cranky what of losin' them dawgs."

III

Not one day, but three days later, the two men, after being snowed in on the summit by a spring blizzard, staggered up to a cabin that stood in a fat bottom beside the roaring Little Peco. Coming in from the bright sunshine to the dark cabin, Linday observed little of its occupants. He was no more than aware of two men and a woman. But he was not interested in them. He went directly to the bunk where lay the injured man. The latter was lying on his back, with eyes closed, and Linday noted the slender stencilling of the brows and the kinky silkiness of the brown hair. Thin and wan, the face seemed too small for the muscular neck, yet the delicate features, despite their waste, were firmly moulded.

"What dressings have you been using?" Linday asked of the woman.

"Corrosive, sublimate, regular solution," came the answer.

He glanced quickly at her, shot an even quicker glance at the face of the injured man, and stood erect. She breathed sharply, abruptly biting off the respiration with an effort of will. Linday turned to the men.

"You clear out—chop wood or something. Clear out."

One of them demurred.

"This is a serious case," Linday went on. "I want to talk to his wife."

"I'm his brother," said the other.

To him the woman looked, praying him with her eyes. He nodded reluctantly and turned toward the door.

"Me, too?" Daw queried from the bench where he had flung himself down.

"You, too."

Linday busied himself with a superficial examination of the patient while the cabin was emptying.

"So?" he said. "So that's your Rex Strang."

She dropped her eyes to the man in the bunk as if to reassure herself of his identity, and then in silence returned Linday's gaze.

"Why don't you speak?"

She shrugged her shoulders. "What is the use? You know it is Rex Strang."

"Thank you. Though I might remind you that it is the first time I have ever seen him. Sit down." He waved her to a stool, himself taking the bench. "I'm really about all in, you know. There's no turnpike from the Yukon here."

He drew a penknife and began extracting a thorn from his thumb.

"What are you going to do?" she asked, after a minute's wait.

"Eat and rest up before I start back."

"What are you going to do about...." She inclined her head toward the unconscious man.

"Nothing."

She went over to the bunk and rested her fingers lightly on the tight-curled hair.

"You mean you will kill him," she said slowly. "Kill him by doing nothing, for you can save him if you will."

"Take it that way." He considered a moment, and stated his thought with a harsh little laugh. "From time immemorial in this weary old world it has been a not uncommon custom so to dispose of wife-stealers."

"You are unfair, Grant," she answered gently. "You forget that I was willing and that I desired. I was a free agent. Rex never stole me. It was you who lost me. I went with him, willing and eager, with song on my lips. As well accuse me of stealing him. We went together."

135

"A good way of looking at it," Linday conceded. "I see you are as keen a thinker as ever, Madge. That must have bothered him."

"A keen thinker can be a good lover—"

"And not so foolish," he broke in.

"Then you admit the wisdom of my course?"

He threw up his hands. "That's the devil of it, talking with clever women. A man always forgets and traps himself. I wouldn't wonder if you won him with a syllogism."

Her reply was the hint of a smile in her straight-looking blue eyes and a seeming emanation of sex pride from all the physical being of her.

"No, I take that back, Madge. If you'd been a numbskull you'd have won him, or any one else, on your looks, and form, and carriage. I ought to know. I've been through that particular mill, and, the devil take me, I'm not through it yet."

His speech was quick and nervous and irritable, as it always was, and, as she knew, it was always candid. She took her cue from his last remark.

"Do you remember Lake Geneva?"

"I ought to. I was rather absurdly happy."

She nodded, and her eyes were luminous. "There is such a thing as old sake. Won't you, Grant, please, just remember back ... a little ... oh, so little ... of what we were to each other ... then?"

"Now you're taking advantage," he smiled, and returned to the attack on his thumb. He drew the thorn out, inspected it critically, then concluded. "No, thank you. I'm not playing the Good Samaritan."

"Yet you made this hard journey for an unknown man," she urged.

His impatience was sharply manifest. "Do you fancy I'd have moved a step had I known he was my wife's lover?"

136

"But you are here ... now. And there he lies. What are you going to do?"

"Nothing. Why should I? I am not at the man's service. He pilfered me."

She was about to speak, when a knock came on the door.

"Get out!" he shouted.

"If you want any assistance—"

"Get out! Get a bucket of water! Set it down outside!"

"You are going to....?" she began tremulously.

"Wash up."

She recoiled from the brutality, and her lips tightened.

"Listen, Grant," she said steadily. "I shall tell his brother. I know the Strang breed. If you can forget old sake, so can I. If you don't do something, he'll kill you. Why, even Tom Daw would if I asked."

"You should know me better than to threaten," he reproved gravely, then added, with a sneer: "Besides, I don't see how killing me will help your Rex Strang."

She gave a low gasp, closed her lips tightly, and watched his quick eyes take note of the trembling that had beset her.

"It's not hysteria, Grant," she cried hastily and anxiously, with clicking teeth. "You never saw me with hysteria. I've never had it. I don't know what it is, but I'll control it. I am merely beside myself. It's partly anger—with you. And it's apprehension and fear. I don't want to lose him. I do love him, Grant. He is my king, my lover. And I have sat here beside him so many dreadful days now. Oh, Grant, please, please."

"Just nerves," he commented drily. "Stay with it. You can best it. If you were a man I'd say take a smoke."

She went unsteadily back to the stool, where she watched him and fought for control. From the rough fireplace came the singing of a cricket. Outside two wolf-dogs bickered. The injured man's chest rose and fell

137

perceptibly under the fur robes. She saw a smile, not altogether pleasant, form on Linday's lips.

"How much do you love him?" he asked.

Her breast filled and rose, and her eyes shone with a light unashamed and proud. He nodded in token that he was answered.

"Do you mind if I take a little time?" He stopped, casting about for the way to begin. "I remember reading a story—Herbert Shaw wrote it, I think. I want to tell you about it. There was a woman, young and beautiful; a man magnificent, a lover of beauty and a wanderer. I don't know how much like your Rex Strang he was, but I fancy a sort of resemblance. Well, this man was a painter, a bohemian, a vagabond. He kissed—oh, several times and for several weeks—and rode away. She possessed for him what I thought you possessed for me ... at Lake Geneva. In ten years she wept the beauty out of her face. Some women turn yellow, you know, when grief upsets their natural juices.

"Now it happened that the man went blind, and ten years afterward, led as a child by the hand, he stumbled back to her. There was nothing left. He could no longer paint. And she was very happy, and glad he could not see her face. Remember, he worshipped beauty. And he continued to hold her in his arms and believe in her beauty. The memory of it was vivid in him. He never ceased to talk about it, and to lament that he could not behold it.

"One day he told her of five great pictures he wished to paint. If only his sight could be restored to paint them, he could write *finis* and be content. And then, no matter how, there came into her hands an elixir. Anointed on his eyes, the sight would surely and fully return."

Linday shrugged his shoulders.

"You see her struggle. With sight, he could paint his five pictures. Also, he would leave her. Beauty was his religion. It was impossible that he could abide her ruined face. Five days she struggled. Then she anointed his eyes."

138

Linday broke off and searched her with his eyes, the high lights focused sharply in the brilliant black.

"The question is, do you love Rex Strang as much as that?"

"And if I do?" she countered.

"Do you?"

"Yes."

"You can sacrifice? You can give him up?"

Slow and reluctant was her "Yes."

"And you will come with me?"

"Yes." This time her voice was a whisper. "When he is well—yes."

"You understand. It must be Lake Geneva over again. You will be my wife."

She seemed to shrink and droop, but her head nodded.

"Very well." He stood up briskly, went to his pack, and began unstrapping. "I shall need help. Bring his brother in. Bring them all in. Boiling water—let there be lots of it. I've brought bandages, but let me see what you have in that line.—Here, Daw, build up that fire and start boiling all the water you can.—Here you," to the other man, "get that table out and under the window there. Clean it; scrub it; scald it. Clean, man, clean, as you never cleaned a thing before. You, Mrs. Strang, will be my helper. No sheets, I suppose. Well, we'll manage somehow.—You're his brother, sir. I'll give the anæsthetic, but you must keep it going afterward. Now listen, while I instruct you. In the first place—but before that, can you take a pulse?..."

IV

Noted for his daring and success as a surgeon, through the days and weeks that followed Linday exceeded himself in daring and success. Never, because of the frightful mangling and breakage, and because of the long delay, had he encountered so terrible a case. But he had never had a healthier specimen of human wreck to work upon. Even then he would have failed, had it not been for the patient's catlike vitality and almost uncanny physical and mental grip on life.

There were days of high temperature and delirium; days of heart-sinking when Strang's pulse was barely perceptible; days when he lay conscious, eyes weary and drawn, the sweat of pain on his face. Linday was indefatigable, cruelly efficient, audacious and fortunate, daring hazard after hazard and winning. He was not content to make the man live. He devoted himself to the intricate and perilous problem of making him whole and strong again.

"He will be a cripple?" Madge queried.

"He will not merely walk and talk and be a limping caricature of his former self," Linday told her. "He shall run and leap, swim riffles, ride bears, fight panthers, and do all things to the top of his fool desire. And, I warn you, he will fascinate women just as of old. Will you like that? Are you content? Remember, you will not be with him."

"Go on, go on," she breathed. "Make him whole. Make him what he was."

More than once, whenever Strang's recuperation permitted, Linday put him under the anæsthetic and did terrible things, cutting and sewing, rewiring and connecting up the disrupted organism. Later, developed a hitch in the left arm. Strang could lift it so far, and no farther. Linday applied himself to the problem. It was a case of more wires, shrunken, twisted, disconnected. Again it was cut and switch and ease and disentangle. And all that saved Strang was his tremendous vitality and the health of his flesh.

"You will kill him," his brother complained. "Let him be. For God's sake let him be. A live and crippled man is better than a whole and dead one."

Linday flamed in wrath. "You get out! Out of this cabin with you till you can come back and say that I make him live. Pull—by God, man, you've got to pull with me with all your soul. Your brother's travelling a hairline razor-edge. Do you understand? A thought can topple him off. Now get out, and come back sweet and wholesome, convinced beyond all absoluteness that he will live and be what he was before you and he played the fool together. Get out, I say."

The brother, with clenched hands and threatening eyes, looked to Madge for counsel.

"Go, go, please," she begged. "He is right. I know he is right."

Another time, when Strang's condition seemed more promising, the brother said:

"Doc, you're a wonder, and all this time I've forgotten to ask your name."

"None of your damn business. Don't bother me. Get out."

The mangled right arm ceased from its healing, burst open again in a frightful wound.

"Necrosis," said Linday.

"That does settle it," groaned the brother.

"Shut up!" Linday snarled. "Get out! Take Daw with you. Take Bill, too. Get rabbits—alive—healthy ones. Trap them. Trap everywhere."

"How many?" the brother asked.

"Forty of them—four thousand—forty thousand—all you can get. You'll help me, Mrs. Strang. I'm going to dig into that arm and size up the damage. Get out, you fellows. You for the rabbits."

And he dug in, swiftly, unerringly, scraping away disintegrating bone, ascertaining the extent of the active decay.

"It never would have happened," he told Madge, "if he hadn't had so many other things needing vitality first. Even he didn't have vitality enough to go around. I was watching it, but I had to wait and chance it. That piece must go. He could manage without it, but rabbit-bone will make it what it was."

From the hundreds of rabbits brought in, he weeded out, rejected, selected, tested, selected and tested again, until he made his final choice. He used the last of his chloroform and achieved the bone-graft—living bone to living bone, living man and living rabbit immovable and indissolubly bandaged and bound together, their mutual processes uniting and reconstructing a perfect arm.

And through the whole trying period, especially as Strang mended, occurred passages of talk between Linday and Madge. Nor was he kind, nor she rebellious.

"It's a nuisance," he told her. "But the law is the law, and you'll need a divorce before we can marry again. What do you say? Shall we go to Lake Geneva?"

"As you will," she said.

And he, another time: "What the deuce did you see in him anyway? I know he had money. But you and I were managing to get along with some sort of comfort. My practice was averaging around forty thousand a year then—I went over the books afterward. Palaces and steam yachts were about all that was denied you."

"Perhaps you've explained it," she answered. "Perhaps you were too interested in your practice. Maybe you forgot me."

"Humph," he sneered. "And may not your Rex be too interested in panthers and short sticks?"

He continually girded her to explain what he chose to call her infatuation for the other man.

"There is no explanation," she replied. And, finally, she retorted, "No one can explain love, I least of all. I only knew love, the divine and irrefragable fact, that is all. There was once, at Fort Vancouver, a baron of the Hudson Bay Company who chided the resident Church of England parson. The dominie had written home to England complaining that the Company folk, from the head factor down, were addicted to Indian wives. 'Why didn't you explain the extenuating circumstances?' demanded the baron. Replied the dominie: 'A cow's tail grows downward. I do not attempt to explain why the cow's tail grows downward. I merely cite the fact.'"

"Damn clever women!" cried Linday, his eyes flashing his irritation.

"What brought you, of all places, into the Klondike?" she asked once.

"Too much money. No wife to spend it. Wanted a rest. Possibly overwork. I tried Colorado, but their telegrams followed me, and some of them did themselves. I went on to Seattle. Same thing. Ransom ran his wife out to me in a special train. There was no escaping it. Operation successful. Local newspapers got wind of it. You can imagine the rest. I had to hide, so I ran away to Klondike. And—well, Tom Daw found me playing whist in a cabin down on the Yukon."

Came the day when Strang's bed was carried out of doors and into the sunshine.

"Let me tell him now," she said to Linday.

"No; wait," he answered.

Later, Strang was able to sit up on the edge of the bed, able to walk his first giddy steps, supported on either side.

"Let me tell him now," she said.

"No. I'm making a complete job of this. I want no set-backs. There's a slight hitch still in that left arm. It's a little thing, but I am going to remake him as God made him. Tomorrow I've planned to get into that arm and take out the kink. It will mean a couple of days on his back. I'm sorry there's no more chloroform. He'll just have to bite his teeth on a spike and hang on. He can do it. He's got grit for a dozen men."

Summer came on. The snow disappeared, save on the far peaks of the Rockies to the east. The days lengthened till there was no darkness, the sun dipping at midnight, due north, for a few minutes beneath the horizon. Linday never let up on Strang. He studied his walk, his body movements, stripped him again and again and for the thousandth time made him flex all his muscles. Massage was given him without end, until Linday declared that Tom Daw, Bill, and the brother were properly qualified for Turkish bath and osteopathic hospital attendants. But Linday was not yet satisfied. He put Strang through his whole repertoire of physical feats, searching him the while for hidden weaknesses. He put him on his back again for a week, opened up his leg, played a deft trick or two with the smaller veins, scraped a spot of bone no larger than a coffee grain till naught but a surface of healthy pink remained to be sewed over with the living flesh.

"Let me tell him," Madge begged.

"Not yet," was the answer. "You will tell him only when I am ready."

July passed, and August neared its end, when he ordered Strang out on trail to get a moose. Linday kept at his heels, watching him, studying him. He was slender, a cat in the strength of his muscles, and he walked as Linday had seen no man walk, effortlessly, with all his body, seeming to lift the legs with supple muscles clear to the shoulders. But it was without heaviness, so easy that it invested him with a peculiar grace, so easy that to the eye the speed was deceptive. It was the killing pace of which Tom Daw had complained. Linday toiled behind, sweating and panting; from time to time, when the ground favoured, making short runs to keep up. At the end of ten miles he called a halt and threw himself down on the moss.

"Enough!" he cried. "I can't keep up with you."

He mopped his heated face, and Strang sat down on a spruce log, smiling at the doctor, and, with the camaraderie of a pantheist, at all the landscape.

"Any twinges, or hurts, or aches, or hints of aches?" Linday demanded.

Strang shook his curly head and stretched his lithe body, living and joying in every fibre of it.

"You'll do, Strang. For a winter or two you may expect to feel the cold and damp in the old wounds. But that will pass, and perhaps you may escape it altogether."

144

"God, Doctor, you have performed miracles with me. I don't know how to thank you. I don't even know your name."

"Which doesn't matter. I've pulled you through, and that's the main thing."

"But it's a name men must know out in the world," Strang persisted. "I'll wager I'd recognise it if I heard it."

"I think you would," was Linday's answer. "But it's beside the matter. I want one final test, and then I'm done with you. Over the divide at the head of this creek is a tributary of the Big Windy. Daw tells me that last year you went over, down to the middle fork, and back again, in three days. He said you nearly killed him, too. You are to wait here and camp to-night. I'll send Daw along with the camp outfit. Then it's up to you to go to the middle fork and back in the same time as last year."

V

"Now," Linday said to Madge. "You have an hour in which to pack. I'll go and get the canoe ready. Bill's bringing in the moose and won't get back till dark. We'll make my cabin to-day, and in a week we'll be in Dawson."

"I was in hope...." She broke off proudly.

"That I'd forego the fee?"

"Oh, a compact is a compact, but you needn't have been so hateful in the collecting. You have not been fair. You have sent him away for three days, and robbed me of my last words to him."

"Leave a letter."

"I shall tell him all."

"Anything less than all would be unfair to the three of us," was Linday's answer.

When he returned from the canoe, her outfit was packed, the letter written.

"Let me read it," he said, "if you don't mind."

Her hesitation was momentary, then she passed it over.

"Pretty straight," he said, when he had finished it. "Now, are you ready?"

He carried her pack down to the bank, and, kneeling, steadied the canoe with one hand while he extended the other to help her in. He watched her closely, but without a tremor she held out her hand to his and prepared to step on board.

"Wait," he said. "One moment. You remember the story I told you of the elixir. I failed to tell you the end. And when she had anointed his eyes and was about to depart, it chanced she saw in the mirror that her beauty had been restored to her. And he opened his eyes, and cried out with joy at the sight of her beauty, and folded her in his arms."

She waited, tense but controlled, for him to continue, a dawn of wonder faintly beginning to show in her face and eyes.

"You are very beautiful, Madge." He paused, then added drily, "The rest is obvious. I fancy Rex Strang's arms won't remain long empty. Good-bye."

"Grant...." she said, almost whispered, and in her voice was all the speech that needs not words for understanding.

He gave a nasty little laugh. "I just wanted to show you I wasn't such a bad sort. Coals of fire, you know."

"Grant...."

He stepped into the canoe and put out a slender, nervous hand.

"Good-bye," he said.

She folded both her own hands about his.

"Dear, strong hand," she murmured, and bent and kissed it.

He jerked it away, thrust the canoe out from the bank, dipped the paddle in the swift rush of the current, and entered the head of the riffle where the water poured glassily ere it burst into a white madness of foam.

STORIES OF SHIPS AND
THE SEA

CHRIS FARRINGTON: ABLE SEAMAN

"If you vas in der old country ships, a liddle shaver like you vood pe only der boy, und you vood wait on der able seamen. Und ven der able seaman sing out, 'Boy, der water-jug!' you vood jump quick, like a shot, und bring der water-jug. Und ven der able seaman sing out, 'Boy, my boots!' you vood get der boots. Und you vood pe politeful, und say 'Yessir' und 'No sir.' But you pe in der American ship, and you t'ink you are so good as der able seamen. Chris, mine boy, I haf ben a sailorman for twenty-two years, und do you t'ink you are so good as me? I vas a sailorman pefore you vas borned, und I knot und reef und splice ven you play mit topstrings und fly kites."

"But you are unfair, Emil!" cried Chris Farrington, his sensitive face flushed and hurt. He was a slender though strongly built young fellow of seventeen, with Yankee ancestry writ large all over him.

"Dere you go vonce again!" the Swedish sailor exploded. "My name is Mister Johansen, und a kid of a boy like you call me 'Emil!' It vas insulting, und comes pecause of der American ship!"

"But you call me 'Chris'!" the boy expostulated, reproachfully.

"But you vas a boy."

"Who does a man's work," Chris retorted. "And because I do a man's work I have as much right to call you by your first name as you me. We are all equals in this fo'castle, and you know it. When we signed for the voyage in San Francisco, we signed as sailors on the *Sophie Sutherland* and there was no difference made with any of us. Haven't I always done my work? Did I ever shirk? Did you or any other man ever have to take a wheel for me? Or a lookout? Or go aloft?"

"Chris is right," interrupted a young English sailor. "No man has had to do a tap of his work yet. He signed as good as any of us and he's shown himself as good—"

"Better!" broke in a Novia Scotia man. "Better than some of us! When we struck the sealing-grounds he turned out to be next to the best boat-steerer aboard. Only French Louis, who'd been at it for years, could beat him. I'm only a boat-puller, and you're only a boat-puller, too, Emil Johansen, for all your twenty-two years at sea. Why don't you become a boat-steerer?"

"Too clumsy," laughed the Englishman, "and too slow."

"Little that counts, one way or the other," joined in Dane Jurgensen, coming to the aid of his Scandinavian brother. "Emil is a man grown and an able seaman; the boy is neither."

And so the argument raged back and forth, the Swedes, Norwegians and Danes, because of race kinship, taking the part of Johansen, and the English, Canadians and Americans taking the part of Chris. From an unprejudiced point of view, the right was on the side of Chris. As he had truly said, he did a man's work, and the same work that any of them did. But they were prejudiced, and badly so, and out of the words which passed rose a standing quarrel which divided the forecastle into two parties.

The *Sophie Sutherland* was a seal-hunter, registered out of San Francisco, and engaged in hunting the furry sea-animals along the Japanese coast north to Bering Sea. The other vessels were two-masted schooners, but she was a three-master and the largest in the fleet. In fact, she was a full-rigged, three-topmast schooner, newly built.

Although Chris Farrington knew that justice was with him, and that he performed all his work faithfully and well, many a time, in secret thought, he longed for some pressing emergency to arise whereby he could demonstrate to the Scandinavian seamen that he also was an able seaman.

But one stormy night, by an accident for which he was in nowise accountable, in overhauling a spare anchor-chain he had all the fingers of his left hand badly crushed. And his hopes were likewise crushed, for it was impossible for him to continue hunting with the boats, and he was forced to stay idly aboard until his fingers should heal. Yet, although he little dreamed it, this very accident was to give him the long-looked-for-opportunity.

One afternoon in the latter part of May the *Sophie Sutherland* rolled sluggishly in a breathless calm. The seals were abundant, the hunting good, and the boats were all away and out of sight. And with them was almost every man of the crew. Besides Chris, there remained only the captain, the sailing-master and the Chinese cook.

The captain was captain only by courtesy. He was an old man, past eighty, and blissfully ignorant of the sea and its ways; but he was the owner of the vessel, and hence the honorable title. Of course the sailing-master, who was really captain, was a thorough-going seaman. The mate, whose post was aboard, was out with the boats, having temporarily taken Chris's place as boat-steerer.

When good weather and good sport came together, the boats were accustomed to range far and wide, and often did not return to the schooner until long after dark. But for all that it was a perfect hunting day, Chris noted a growing anxiety on the part of the sailing-master. He paced the deck nervously, and was constantly sweeping the horizon with his marine glasses. Not a boat was in sight. As sunset arrived, he even sent Chris aloft to the mizzen-topmast-head, but with no better luck. The boats could not possibly be back before midnight.

Since noon the barometer had been falling with startling rapidity, and all the signs were ripe for a great storm—how great, not even the sailing-master anticipated. He and Chris set to work to prepare for it. They put storm gaskets on the furled topsails, lowered and stowed the foresail and spanker and took in the two inner jibs. In the one remaining jib they put a single reef, and a single reef in the mainsail.

Night had fallen before they finished, and with the darkness came the storm. A low moan swept over the sea, and the wind struck the *Sophie Sutherland* flat. But she righted quickly, and with the sailing-master at the wheel, sheered her bow into within five points of the wind. Working as well as he could with his bandaged hand, and with the feeble aid of the Chinese cook, Chris went forward and backed the jib over to the weather side. This with the flat mainsail, left the schooner hove to.

"God help the boats! It's no gale! It's a typhoon!" the sailing-master shouted to Chris at eleven o'clock. "Too much canvas! Got to get two more reefs into the mainsail, and got to do it right away!" He glanced at the old captain, shivering in oilskins at the binnacle and holding on for dear life. "There's only you and I, Chris—and the cook; but he's next to worthless!"

In order to make the reef, it was necessary to lower the mainsail, and the removal of this after pressure was bound to make the schooner fall off before the wind and sea because of the forward pressure of the jib.

"Take the wheel!" the sailing-master directed. "And when I give the word, hard up with it! And when she's square before it, steady her! And keep her there! We'll heave to again as soon as I get the reefs in!"

Gripping the kicking spokes, Chris watched him and the reluctant cook go forward into the howling darkness. The *Sophie Sutherland* was plunging into the huge head-seas and wallowing tremendously, the tense steel stays and taut rigging humming like harp-strings to the wind. A buffeted cry came to his ears, and he felt the schooner's bow paying off of its own accord. The mainsail was down!

He ran the wheel hard-over and kept anxious track of the changing direction of the wind on his face and of the heave of the vessel. This was the crucial moment. In performing the evolution she would have to pass broadside to the surge before she could get before it. The wind was blowing directly on his right cheek, when he felt the *Sophie Sutherland* lean over and begin to rise toward the sky—up—up—an infinite distance! Would she clear the crest of the gigantic wave?

Again by the feel of it, for he could see nothing, he knew that a wall of water was rearing and curving far above him along the whole weather side. There was an instant's calm as the liquid wall intervened and shut off the wind. The schooner righted, and for that instant seemed at perfect rest. Then she rolled to meet the descending rush.

Chris shouted to the captain to hold tight, and prepared himself for the shock. But the man did not live who could face it. An ocean of water smote

154

Chris's back and his clutch on the spokes was loosened as if it were a baby's. Stunned, powerless, like a straw on the face of a torrent, he was swept onward he knew not whither. Missing the corner of the cabin, he was dashed forward along the poop runway a hundred feet or more, striking violently against the foot of the foremast. A second wave, crushing inboard, hurled him back the way he had come, and left him half-drowned where the poop steps should have been.

Bruised and bleeding, dimly conscious, he felt for the rail and dragged himself to his feet. Unless something could be done, he knew the last moment had come. As he faced the poop, the wind drove into his mouth with suffocating force. This brought him back to his senses with a start. The wind was blowing from dead aft! The schooner was out of the trough and before it! But the send of the sea was bound to breach her to again. Crawling up the runway, he managed to get to the wheel just in time to prevent this. The binnacle light was still burning. They were safe!

That is, he and the schooner were safe. As to the welfare of his three companions he could not say. Nor did he dare leave the wheel in order to find out, for it took every second of his undivided attention to keep the vessel to her course. The least fraction of carelessness and the heave of the sea under the quarter was liable to thrust her into the trough. So, a boy of one hundred and forty pounds, he clung to his herculean task of guiding the two hundred straining tons of fabric amid the chaos of the great storm forces.

Half an hour later, groaning and sobbing, the captain crawled to Chris's feet. All was lost, he whimpered. He was smitten unto death. The galley had gone by the board, the mainsail and running-gear, the cook, every thing!

"Where's the sailing-master?" Chris demanded when he had caught his breath after steadying a wild lurch of the schooner. It was no child's play to steer a vessel under single reefed jib before a typhoon.

"Clean up for'ard," the old man replied "Jammed under the fo'c'sle-head, but still breathing. Both his arms are broken, he says and he doesn't know how many ribs. He's hurt bad."

"Well, he'll drown there the way she's shipping water through the hawse-pipes. Go for'ard!" Chris commanded, taking charge of things as a matter of course. "Tell him not to worry; that I'm at the wheel. Help him as much as you can, and make him help"—he stopped and ran the spokes to starboard as a tremendous billow rose under the stern and yawed the schooner to port—"and make him help himself for the rest. Unship the fo'castle hatch and get him down into a bunk. Then ship the hatch again."

The captain turned his aged face forward and wavered pitifully. The waist of the ship was full of water to the bulwarks. He had just come through it, and knew death lurked every inch of the way.

"Go!" Chris shouted, fiercely. And as the fear-stricken man started, "And take another look for the cook!"

Two hours later, almost dead from suffering, the captain returned. He had obeyed orders. The sailing-master was helpless, although safe in a bunk; the cook was gone. Chris sent the captain below to the cabin to change his clothes.

After interminable hours of toil day broke cold and gray. Chris looked about him. The *Sophie Sutherland* was racing before the typhoon like a thing possessed. There was no rain, but the wind whipped the spray of the sea mast-high, obscuring everything except in the immediate neighborhood.

Two waves only could Chris see at a time—the one before and the one behind. So small and insignificant the schooner seemed on the long Pacific roll! Rushing up a maddening mountain, she would poise like a cockle-shell on the giddy summit, breathless and rolling, leap outward and down into the yawning chasm beneath, and bury herself in the smother of foam at the bottom. Then the recovery, another mountain, another sickening upward rush, another poise, and the downward crash. Abreast of him, to starboard, like a ghost of the storm, Chris saw the cook dashing apace with the schooner. Evidently, when washed overboard, he had grasped and become entangled in a trailing halyard.

156

For three hours more, alone with this gruesome companion, Chris held the *Sophie Sutherland* before the wind and sea. He had long since forgotten his mangled fingers. The bandages had been torn away, and the cold, salt spray had eaten into the half-healed wounds until they were numb and no longer pained. But he was not cold. The terrific labor of steering forced the perspiration from every pore. Yet he was faint and weak with hunger and exhaustion, and hailed with delight the advent on deck of the captain, who fed him all of a pound of cake-chocolate. It strengthened him at once.

He ordered the captain to cut the halyard by which the cook's body was towing, and also to go forward and cut loose the jib-halyard and sheet. When he had done so, the jib fluttered a couple of moments like a handkerchief, then tore out of the bolt-ropes and vanished. The *Sophie Sutherland* was running under bare poles.

By noon the storm had spent itself, and by six in the evening the waves had died down sufficiently to let Chris leave the helm. It was almost hopeless to dream of the small boats weathering the typhoon, but there is always the chance in saving human life, and Chris at once applied himself to going back over the course along which he had fled. He managed to get a reef in one of the inner jibs and two reefs in the spanker, and then, with the aid of the watch-tackle, to hoist them to the stiff breeze that yet blew. And all through the night, tacking back and forth on the back track, he shook out canvas as fast as the wind would permit.

The injured sailing-master had turned delirious and between tending him and lending a hand with the ship, Chris kept the captain busy. "Taught me more seamanship," as he afterward said, "than I'd learned on the whole voyage." But by daybreak the old man's feeble frame succumbed, and he fell off into exhausted sleep on the weather poop.

Chris, who could now lash the wheel, covered the tired man with blankets from below, and went fishing in the lazaretto for something to eat. But by the day following he found himself forced to give in, drowsing fitfully by the wheel and waking ever and anon to take a look at things.

On the afternoon of the third day he picked up a schooner, dismasted and battered. As he approached, close-hauled on the wind, he saw her decks crowded by an unusually large crew, and on sailing in closer, made out among others the faces of his missing comrades. And he was just in the nick of time, for they were fighting a losing fight at the pumps. An hour later they, with the crew of the sinking craft were aboard the *Sophie Sutherland*.

Having wandered so far from their own vessel, they had taken refuge on the strange schooner just before the storm broke. She was a Canadian sealer on her first voyage, and as was now apparent, her last.

The captain of the *Sophie Sutherland* had a story to tell, also, and he told it well—so well, in fact, that when all hands were gathered together on deck during the dog-watch, Emil Johansen strode over to Chris and gripped him by the hand.

"Chris," he said, so loudly that all could hear, "Chris, I gif in. You vas yoost so good a sailorman as I. You vas a bully boy und able seaman, und I pe proud for you!

"Und Chris!" He turned as if he had forgotten something, and called back, "From dis time always you call me 'Emil' mitout der 'Mister'!"

TYPHOON OFF THE COAST OF JAPAN

Jack London's First Story, Published at the Age of Seventeen.

It was four bells in the morning watch. We had just finished breakfast when the order came forward for the watch on deck to stand by to heave her to and all hands stand by the boats.

"Port! hard a port!" cried our sailing-master. "Clew up the topsails! Let the flying jib run down! Back the jib over to windward and run down the foresail!" And so was our schooner *Sophie Sutherland* hove to off the Japan coast, near Cape Jerimo, on April 10, 1893.

Then came moments of bustle and confusion. There were eighteen men to man the six boats. Some were hooking on the falls, others casting off the lashings; boat-steerers appeared with boat-compasses and water-breakers, and boat-pullers with the lunch boxes. Hunters were staggering under two or three shotguns, a rifle and heavy ammunition box, all of which were soon stowed away with their oilskins and mittens in the boats.

The sailing-master gave his last orders, and away we went, pulling three pairs of oars to gain our positions. We were in the weather boat, and so had a longer pull than the others. The first, second and third lee boats soon had all sail set and were running off to the southward and westward with the wind beam, while the schooner was running off to leeward of them, so that in case of accident the boats would have fair wind home.

It was a glorious morning, but our boat steerer shook his head ominously as he glanced at the rising sun and prophetically muttered: "Red sun in the morning, sailor take warning." The sun had an angry look, and a few light, fleecy "nigger-heads" in that quarter seemed abashed and frightened and soon disappeared.

Away off to the northward Cape Jerimo reared its black, forbidding head like some huge monster rising from the deep. The winter's snow, not yet entirely dissipated by the sun, covered it in patches of glistening white, over which the light wind swept on its way out to sea. Huge gulls rose slowly, fluttering their wings in the light breeze and striking their webbed feet on the surface of the water for over half a mile before they could leave it. Hardly had the patter, patter died away when a flock of sea quail rose, and with whistling wings flew away to windward, where members of a large band of whales were disporting themselves, their blowings sounding like the exhaust of steam engines. The harsh, discordant cries of a sea-parrot grated unpleasantly on the ear, and set half a dozen alert in a small band of seals that were ahead of us. Away they went, breaching and jumping entirely out of water. A sea-gull with slow, deliberate flight and long, majestic curves circled round us, and as a reminder of home a little English sparrow perched impudently on the fo'castle head, and, cocking his head on one side, chirped merrily. The boats were soon among the seals, and the bang! bang! of the guns could be heard from down to leeward.

The wind was slowly rising, and by three o'clock as, with a dozen seals in our boat, we were deliberating whether to go on or turn back, the recall flag was run up at the schooner's mizzen—a sure sign that with the rising wind the barometer was falling and that our sailing-master was getting anxious for the welfare of the boats.

Away we went before the wind with a single reef in our sail. With clenched teeth sat the boat-steerer, grasping the steering oar firmly with both hands, his restless eyes on the alert—a glance at the schooner ahead, as we rose on a sea, another at the mainsheet, and then one astern where the dark ripple of the wind on the water told him of a coming puff or a large white-cap that threatened to overwhelm us. The waves were holding high carnival, performing the strangest antics, as with wild glee they danced along in fierce pursuit—now up, now down, here, there, and everywhere, until some great sea of liquid green with its milk-white crest of foam rose from the ocean's throbbing bosom and drove the others from view. But only for a moment, for again under new forms they reappeared. In the sun's path they wandered, where every ripple, great or small, every little spit or spray looked like molten silver, where the water lost its dark green color and became a dazzling, silvery flood, only to vanish and become a wild waste of sullen turbulence, each dark foreboding sea rising and breaking, then rolling on again. The dash, the sparkle, the silvery light soon vanished with the sun, which became obscured by black clouds that were rolling swiftly in from the west, northwest; apt heralds of the coming storm.

We soon reached the schooner and found ourselves the last aboard. In a few minutes the seals were skinned, boats and decks washed, and we were down below by the roaring fo'castle fire, with a wash, change of clothes, and a hot, substantial supper before us. Sail had been put on the schooner, as we had a run of seventy-five miles to make to the southward before morning, so as to get in the midst of the seals, out of which we had strayed during the last two days' hunting.

We had the first watch from eight to midnight. The wind was soon blowing half a gale, and our sailing-master expected little sleep that night as he paced up and down the poop. The topsails were soon clewed up and made fast, then the flying jib run down and furled. Quite a sea was rolling by this time, occasionally breaking over the decks, flooding them and threatening to smash the boats. At six bells we were ordered to turn them over and put on storm lashings. This occupied us till eight bells, when we were relieved by the mid-watch. I was the last to go below, doing so just as the watch on deck was furling the spanker. Below all were asleep except our green hand, the "bricklayer," who was dying of consumption. The wildly dancing movements of the sea lamp cast a pale, flickering light through the fo'castle and turned to golden honey the drops of water on the yellow oilskins. In all the corners dark shadows seemed to come and go, while up in the eyes of her, beyond the pall bits, descending from deck to deck, where they seemed to lurk like some dragon at the cavern's mouth, it was dark as Erebus. Now and again, the light seemed to penetrate for a moment as the schooner rolled heavier than usual, only to recede, leaving it darker and blacker than before. The roar of the wind through the rigging came to the ear muffled like the distant rumble of a train crossing a trestle or the surf on the beach, while the loud crash of the seas on her weather bow seemed almost to rend the beams and planking asunder as it resounded through the fo'castle. The creaking and groaning of the timbers, stanchions, and bulkheads, as the strain the vessel was undergoing was felt,

161

served to drown the groans of the dying man as he tossed uneasily in his bunk. The working of the foremast against the deck beams caused a shower of flaky powder to fall, and sent another sound mingling with the tumultuous storm. Small cascades of water streamed from the pall bits from the fo'castle head above, and, joining issue with the streams from the wet oilskins, ran along the floor and disappeared aft into the main hold.

At two bells in the middle watch—that is, in land parlance one o'clock in the morning;—the order was roared out on the fo'castle: "All hands on deck and shorten sail!"

Then the sleepy sailors tumbled out of their bunk and into their clothes, oilskins and sea-boots and up on deck. 'Tis when that order comes on cold, blustering nights that "Jack" grimly mutters: "Who would not sell a farm and go to sea?"

It was on deck that the force of the wind could be fully appreciated, especially after leaving the stifling fo'castle. It seemed to stand up against you like a wall, making it almost impossible to move on the heaving decks or to breathe as the fierce gusts came dashing by. The schooner was hove to under jib, foresail and mainsail. We proceeded to lower the foresail and make it fast. The night was dark, greatly impeding our labor. Still, though not a star or the moon could pierce the black masses of storm clouds that obscured the sky as they swept along before the gale, nature aided us in a measure. A soft light emanated from the movement of the ocean. Each mighty sea, all phosphorescent and glowing with the tiny lights of myriads of animalculae, threatened to overwhelm us with a deluge of fire. Higher and higher, thinner and thinner, the crest grew as it began to curve and overtop preparatory to breaking, until with a roar it fell over the bulwarks, a mass of soft glowing light and tons of water which sent the sailors sprawling in all directions and left in each nook and cranny little specks of light that glowed and trembled till the next sea washed them away, depositing new ones in their places. Sometimes several seas following each other with great rapidity and thundering down on our decks filled them full to the bulwarks, but soon they were discharged through the lee scuppers.

To reef the mainsail we were forced to run off before the gale under the single reefed jib. By the time we had finished the wind had forced up such a tremendous sea that it was impossible to heave her to. Away we flew on the wings of the storm through the muck and flying spray. A wind sheer to starboard, then another to port as the enormous seas struck the schooner astern and nearly broached her to. As day broke we took in the jib, leaving not a sail unfurled. Since we had begun scudding she had ceased to take the seas over her bow, but amidships they broke fast and furious. It was a dry storm in the matter of rain, but the force of the wind filled the air with fine spray, which flew as high as the crosstrees and cut the face like a knife, making it impossible to see over a hundred yards ahead. The sea was a dark lead color as with long, slow, majestic roll it was heaped up by the wind into liquid mountains of foam. The wild antics of the schooner were sickening as she forged along. She would almost stop, as though climbing a mountain, then rapidly rolling to right and left as she gained the summit of a huge sea, she steadied herself and paused for a moment as though affrighted at the yawning precipice before her. Like an avalanche, she shot forward and down as the sea astern struck her with the force of a thousand battering rams, burying her bow to the cat-heads in the milky foam at the bottom that came on deck in all directions—forward, astern, to right and left, through the hawse-pipes and over the rail.

The wind began to drop, and by ten o'clock we were talking of heaving her to. We passed a ship, two schooners and a four-masted barkentine under the smallest canvas, and at eleven o'clock, running up the spanker and jib, we hove her to, and in another hour we were beating back again against the aftersea under full sail to regain the sealing ground away to the westward.

Below, a couple of men were sewing the "bricklayer's" body in canvas preparatory to the sea burial. And so with the storm passed away the "bricklayer's" soul.

THE LOST POACHER

"But they won't take excuses. You're across the line, and that's enough. They'll take you. In you go, Siberia and the salt mines. And as for Uncle Sam, why, what's he to know about it? Never a word will get back to the States. 'The *Mary Thomas*,' the papers will say, 'the *Mary Thomas* lost with all hands. Probably in a typhoon in the Japanese seas.' That's what the papers will say, and people, too. In you go, Siberia and the salt mines. Dead to the world and kith and kin, though you live fifty years."

In such manner John Lewis, commonly known as the "sea-lawyer," settled the matter out of hand.

It was a serious moment in the forecastle of the *Mary Thomas*. No sooner had the watch below begun to talk the trouble over, than the watch on deck came down and joined them. As there was no wind, every hand could be spared with the exception of the man at the wheel, and he remained only for the sake of discipline. Even "Bub" Russell, the cabin-boy, had crept forward to hear what was going on.

However, it was a serious moment, as the grave faces of the sailors bore witness. For the three preceding months the *Mary Thomas* sealing schooner, had hunted the seal pack along the coast of Japan and north to Bering Sea. Here, on the Asiatic side of the sea, they were forced to give over the chase, or rather, to go no farther; for beyond, the Russian cruisers patrolled forbidden ground, where the seals might breed in peace.

A week before she had fallen into a heavy fog accompanied by calm. Since then the fog-bank had not lifted, and the only wind had been light airs and catspaws. This in itself was not so bad, for the sealing schooners are never in a hurry so long as they are in the midst of the seals; but the trouble lay in the fact that the current at this point bore heavily to the north. Thus the *Mary Thomas* had unwittingly drifted across the line, and every hour she was penetrating, unwillingly, farther and farther into the dangerous waters where the Russian bear kept guard.

How far she had drifted no man knew. The sun had not been visible for a week, nor the stars, and the captain had been unable to take observations in order to determine his position. At any moment a cruiser might swoop down and hale the crew away to Siberia. The fate of other poaching seal-hunters was too well known to the men of the *Mary Thomas*, and there was cause for grave faces.

"Mine friends," spoke up a German boat-steerer, "it vas a pad piziness. Shust as ve make a big catch, und all honest, somedings go wrong, und der Russians nab us, dake our skins and our schooner, und send us mit der anarchists to Siberia. Ach! a pretty pad piziness!"

"Yes, that's where it hurts," the sea lawyer went on. "Fifteen hundred skins in the salt piles, and all honest, a big pay-day coming to every man Jack of us, and then to be captured and lose it all! It'd be different if we'd been poaching, but it's all honest work in open water."

"But if we haven't done anything wrong, they can't do anything to us, can they?" Bub queried.

"It strikes me as 'ow it ain't the proper thing for a boy o' your age shovin' in when 'is elders is talkin'," protested an English sailor, from over the edge of his bunk.

"Oh, that's all right, Jack," answered the sea-lawyer. "He's a perfect right to. Ain't he just as liable to lose his wages as the rest of us?"

"Wouldn't give thruppence for them!" Jack sniffed back. He had been planning to go home and see his family in Chelsea when he was paid off, and he was now feeling rather blue over the highly possible loss, not only of his pay, but of his liberty.

"How are they to know?" the sea-lawyer asked in answer to Bub's previous question. "Here we are in forbidden water. How do they know but what we came here of our own accord? Here we are, fifteen hundred skins in the hold. How do they know whether we got them in open water or in the closed sea? Don't you see, Bub, the evidence is all against us. If you caught a man with his pockets full of apples like those which grow on your tree, and if you caught him in your tree besides, what'd you think if he told you he couldn't help it, and had just been sort of blown there, and that anyway those apples came from some other tree—what'd you think, eh?"

Bub saw it clearly when put in that light, and shook his head despondently.

"You'd rather be dead than go to Siberia," one of the boat-pullers said. "They put you into the salt-mines and work you till you die. Never see daylight again. Why, I've heard tell of one fellow that was chained to his mate, and that mate died. And they were both chained together! And if they send you to the quicksilver mines you get salivated. I'd rather be hung than salivated."

"Wot's salivated?" Jack asked, suddenly sitting up in his bunk at the hint of fresh misfortunes.

"Why, the quicksilver gets into your blood; I think that's the way. And your gums all swell like you had the scurvy, only worse, and your teeth get loose in your jaws. And big ulcers forms, and then you die horrible. The strongest man can't last long a-mining quicksilver."

"A pad piziness," the boat-steerer reiterated, dolorously, in the silence which followed. "A pad piziness. I vish I vas in Yokohama. Eh? Vot vas dot?"

The vessel had suddenly heeled over. The decks were aslant. A tin pannikin rolled down the inclined plane, rattling and banging. From above came the slapping of canvas and the quivering rat-tat-tat of the after leech of the loosely stretched foresail. Then the mate's voice sang down the hatch, "All hands on deck and make sail!"

Never had such summons been answered with more enthusiasm. The calm had broken. The wind had come which was to carry them south into safety. With a wild cheer all sprang on deck. Working with mad haste, they flung out topsails, flying jibs and staysails. As they worked, the fog-bank lifted and the black vault of heaven, bespangled with the old familiar stars, rushed into view. When all was shipshape, the *Mary Thomas* was lying gallantly over on her side to a beam wind and plunging ahead due south.

"Steamer's lights ahead on the port bow, sir!" cried the lookout from his station on the forecastle-head. There was excitement in the man's voice.

166

The captain sent Bub below for his night-glasses. Everybody crowded to the lee-rail to gaze at the suspicious stranger, which already began to loom up vague and indistinct. In those unfrequented waters the chance was one in a thousand that it could be anything else than a Russian patrol. The captain was still anxiously gazing through the glasses, when a flash of flame left the stranger's side, followed by the loud report of a cannon. The worst fears were confirmed. It was a patrol, evidently firing across the bows of the *Mary Thomas* in order to make her heave to.

"Hard down with your helm!" the captain commanded the steersman, all the life gone out of his voice. Then to the crew, "Back over the jib and foresail! Run down the flying jib! Clew up the foretopsail! And aft here and swing on to the main-sheet!"

The *Mary Thomas* ran into the eye of the wind, lost headway, and fell to courtesying gravely to the long seas rolling up from the west.

The cruiser steamed a little nearer and lowered a boat. The sealers watched in heartbroken silence. They could see the white bulk of the boat as it was slacked away to the water, and its crew sliding aboard. They could hear the creaking of the davits and the commands of the officers. Then the boat sprang away under the impulse of the oars, and came toward them. The wind had been rising, and already the sea was too rough to permit the frail craft to lie alongside the tossing schooner; but watching their chance, and taking advantage of the boarding ropes thrown to them, an officer and a couple of men clambered aboard. The boat then sheered off into safety and lay to its oars, a young midshipman, sitting in the stern and holding the yoke-lines, in charge.

The officer, whose uniform disclosed his rank as that of second lieutenant in the Russian navy went below with the captain of the *Mary Thomas* to look at the ship's papers. A few minutes later he emerged, and upon his sailors removing the hatch-covers, passed down into the hold with a lantern to inspect the salt piles. It was a goodly heap which confronted him—fifteen hundred fresh skins, the season's catch; and under the circumstances he could have had but one conclusion.

"I am very sorry," he said, in broken English to the sealing captain, when he again came on deck, "but it is my duty, in the name of the tsar, to seize your vessel as a poacher caught with fresh skins in the closed sea. The penalty, as you may know, is confiscation and imprisonment."

The captain of the *Mary Thomas* shrugged his shoulders in seeming indifference, and turned away. Although they may restrain all outward show, strong men, under unmerited misfortune, are sometimes very close to tears. Just then the vision of his little California home, and of the wife and two yellow-haired boys, was strong upon him, and there was a strange, choking sensation in his throat, which made him afraid that if he attempted to speak he would sob instead.

And also there was upon him the duty he owed his men. No weakness before them, for he must be a tower of strength to sustain them in misfortune. He had already explained to the second lieutenant, and knew the hopelessness of the situation. As the sea-lawyer had said, the evidence was all against him. So he turned aft, and fell to pacing up and down the poop of the vessel over which he was no longer commander.

The Russian officer now took temporary charge. He ordered more of his men aboard, and had all the canvas clewed up and furled snugly away. While this was being done, the boat plied back and forth between the two vessels, passing a heavy hawser, which was made fast to the great towing-bitts on the schooner's forecastle-head. During all this work the sealers stood about in sullen groups. It was madness to think of resisting, with the guns of a man-of-war not a biscuit-toss away; but they refused to lend a hand, preferring instead to maintain a gloomy silence.

Having accomplished his task, the lieutenant ordered all but four of his men back into the boat. Then the midshipman, a lad of sixteen, looking strangely mature and dignified in his uniform and sword, came aboard to take command of the captured sealer. Just as the lieutenant prepared to depart his eye chanced to alight upon Bub. Without a word of warning, he seized him by the arm and dropped him over the rail into the waiting boat; and then, with a parting wave of his hand, he followed him.

It was only natural that Bub should be frightened at this unexpected happening. All the terrible stories he had heard of the Russians served to make him fear them, and now returned to his mind with double force. To be captured by them was bad enough, but to be carried off by them, away from his comrades, was a fate of which he had not dreamed.

"Be a good boy, Bub," the captain called to him, as the boat drew away from the *Mary Thomas*'s side, "and tell the truth!"

"Aye, aye, sir!" he answered, bravely enough by all outward appearance. He felt a certain pride of race, and was ashamed to be a coward before these strange enemies, these wild Russian bears.

"Und be politeful!" the German boat-steerer added, his rough voice lifting across the water like a fog-horn.

Bub waved his hand in farewell, and his mates clustered along the rail as they answered with a cheering shout. He found room in the stern-sheets, where he fell to regarding the lieutenant. He didn't look so wild or bearish after all—very much like other men, Bub concluded, and the sailors were much the same as all other man-of-war's men he had ever known. Nevertheless, as his feet struck the steel deck of the cruiser, he felt as if he had entered the portals of a prison.

For a few minutes he was left unheeded. The sailors hoisted the boat up, and swung it in on the davits. Then great clouds of black smoke poured out of the funnels, and they were under way—to Siberia, Bub could not help but think. He saw the *Mary Thomas* swing abruptly into line as she took the pressure from the hawser, and her side-lights, red and green, rose and fell as she was towed through the sea.

Bub's eyes dimmed at the melancholy sight, but—but just then the lieutenant came to take him down to the commander, and he straightened up and set his lips firmly, as if this were a very commonplace affair and he were used to being sent to Siberia every day in the week. The cabin in which the commander sat was like a palace compared to the humble fittings of the *Mary Thomas*, and the commander himself, in gold lace and dignity, was a most august personage, quite unlike the simple man who navigated his schooner on the trail of the seal pack.

169

Bub now quickly learned why he had been brought aboard, and in the prolonged questioning which followed, told nothing but the plain truth. The truth was harmless; only a lie could have injured his cause. He did not know much, except that they had been sealing far to the south in open water, and that when the calm and fog came down upon them, being close to the line, they had drifted across. Again and again he insisted that they had not lowered a boat or shot a seal in the week they had been drifting about in the forbidden sea; but the commander chose to consider all that he said to be a tissue of falsehoods, and adopted a bullying tone in an effort to frighten the boy. He threatened and cajoled by turns, but failed in the slightest to shake Bub's statements, and at last ordered him out of his presence.

By some oversight, Bub was not put in anybody's charge, and wandered up on deck unobserved. Sometimes the sailors, in passing, bent curious glances upon him, but otherwise he was left strictly alone. Nor could he have attracted much attention, for he was small, the night dark, and the watch on deck intent on its own business. Stumbling over the strange decks, he made his way aft where he could look upon the side-lights of the *Mary Thomas*, following steadily in the rear.

For a long while he watched, and then lay down in the darkness close to where the hawser passed over the stern to the captured schooner. Once an officer came up and examined the straining rope to see if it were chafing, but Bub cowered away in the shadow undiscovered. This, however, gave him an idea which concerned the lives and liberties of twenty-two men, and which was to avert crushing sorrow from more than one happy home many thousand miles away.

In the first place, he reasoned, the crew were all guiltless of any crime, and yet were being carried relentlessly away to imprisonment in Siberia—a living death, he had heard, and he believed it implicitly. In the second place, he was a prisoner, hard and fast, with no chance to escape. In the third, it was possible for the twenty-two men on the *Mary Thomas* to escape. The only thing which bound them was a four-inch hawser. They dared not cut it at their end, for a watch was sure to be maintained upon it by their Russian captors; but at this end, ah! at his end—

Bub did not stop to reason further. Wriggling close to the hawser, he opened his jack-knife and went to work. The blade was not very sharp, and he sawed away, rope-yarn by rope-yarn, the awful picture of the solitary Siberian exile he must endure growing clearer and more terrible at every stroke. Such a fate was bad enough to undergo with one's comrades, but to face it alone seemed frightful. And besides, the very act he was performing was sure to bring greater punishment upon him.

In the midst of such somber thoughts, he heard footsteps approaching. He wriggled away into the shadow. An officer stopped where he had been working, half-stooped to examine the hawser, then changed his mind and straightened up. For a few minutes he stood there, gazing at the lights of the captured schooner, and then went forward again.

Now was the time! Bub crept back and went on sawing. Now two parts were severed. Now three. But one remained. The tension upon this was so great that it readily yielded. Splash the freed end went overboard. He lay quietly, his heart in his mouth, listening. No one on the cruiser but himself had heard.

He saw the red and green lights of the *Mary Thomas* grow dimmer and dimmer. Then a faint hallo came over the water from the Russian prize crew. Still nobody heard. The smoke continued to pour out of the cruiser's funnels, and her propellers throbbed as mightily as ever.

What was happening on the *Mary Thomas*? Bub could only surmise; but of one thing he was certain: his comrades would assert themselves and overpower the four sailors and the midshipman. A few minutes later he saw a small flash, and straining his ears heard the very faint report of a pistol. Then, oh joy! both the red and green lights suddenly disappeared. The *Mary Thomas* was retaken!

Just as an officer came aft, Bub crept forward, and hid away in one of the boats. Not an instant too soon. The alarm was given. Loud voices rose in command. The cruiser altered her course. An electric search-light began to throw its white rays across the sea, here, there, everywhere; but in its flashing path no tossing schooner was revealed.

Bub went to sleep soon after that, nor did he wake till the gray of dawn. The engines were pulsing monotonously, and the water, splashing noisily, told him the decks were being washed down. One sweeping glance, and he saw that they were alone on the expanse of ocean. The *Mary Thomas* had escaped. As he lifted his head, a roar of laughter went up from the sailors. Even the officer, who ordered him taken below and locked up, could not quite conceal the laughter in his eyes. Bub thought often in the days of confinement which followed that they were not very angry with him for what he had done.

He was not far from right. There is a certain innate nobility deep down in the hearts of all men, which forces them to admire a brave act, even if it is performed by an enemy. The Russians were in nowise different from other men. True, a boy had outwitted them; but they could not blame him, and they were sore puzzled as to what to do with him. It would never do to take a little mite like him in to represent all that remained of the lost poacher.

So, two weeks later, a United States man-of-war, steaming out of the Russian port of Vladivostok, was signaled by a Russian cruiser. A boat passed between the two ships, and a small boy dropped over the rail upon the deck of the American vessel. A week later he was put ashore at Hakodate, and after some telegraphing, his fare was paid on the railroad to Yokohama.

From the depot he hurried through the quaint Japanese streets to the harbor, and hired a sampan boatman to put him aboard a certain vessel whose familiar rigging had quickly caught his eye. Her gaskets were off, her sails unfurled; she was just starting back to the United States. As he came closer, a crowd of sailors sprang upon the forecastle head, and the windlass-bars rose and fell as the anchor was torn from its muddy bottom.

"'Yankee ship come down the ribber!'" the sea-lawyer's voice rolled out as he led the anchor song.

"'Pull, my bully boys, pull!'" roared back the old familiar chorus, the men's bodies lifting and bending to the rhythm.

Bub Russell paid the boatman and stepped on deck. The anchor was forgotten. A mighty cheer went up from the men, and almost before he could catch his breath he was on the shoulders of the captain, surrounded by his mates, and endeavoring to answer twenty questions to the second.

The next day a schooner hove to off a Japanese fishing village, sent ashore four sailors and a little midshipman, and sailed away. These men did not talk English, but they had money and quickly made their way to Yokohama. From that day the Japanese village folk never heard anything more about them, and they are still a much-talked-of mystery. As the Russian government never said anything about the incident, the United States is still ignorant of the whereabouts of the lost poacher, nor has she ever heard, officially, of the way in which some of her citizens "shanghaied" five subjects of the tsar. Even nations have secrets sometimes.

THE BANKS OF THE SACRAMENTO

"And it's blow, ye winds, heigh-ho,

For Cal-i-for-ni-o;

For there's plenty of gold so I've been told,

On the banks of the Sacramento!"

It was only a little boy, singing in a shrill treble the sea chantey which seamen sing the wide world over when they man the capstan bars and break the anchors out for "Frisco" port. It was only a little boy who had never seen the sea, but two hundred feet beneath him rolled the Sacramento. "Young" Jerry he was called, after "Old" Jerry, his father, from whom he had learned the song, as well as received his shock of bright-red hair, his blue, dancing eyes, and his fair and inevitably freckled skin.

For Old Jerry had been a sailor, and had followed the sea till middle life, haunted always by the words of the ringing chantey. Then one day he had sung the song in earnest, in an Asiatic port, swinging and thrilling round the capstan-circle with twenty others. And at San Francisco he turned his back upon his ship and upon the sea, and went to behold with his own eyes the banks of the Sacramento.

He beheld the gold, too, for he found employment at the Yellow Dream mine, and proved of utmost usefulness in rigging the great ore-cables across the river and two hundred feet above its surface.

After that he took charge of the cables and kept them in repair, and ran them and loved them, and became himself an indispensable fixture of the Yellow Dream mine. Then he loved pretty Margaret Kelly; but she had left him and Young Jerry, the latter barely toddling, to take up her last long sleep in the little graveyard among the great sober pines.

Old Jerry never went back to the sea. He remained by his cables, and lavished upon them and Young Jerry all the love of his nature. When evil days came to the Yellow Dream, he still remained in the employ of the company as watchman over the all but abandoned property.

But this morning he was not visible. Young Jerry only was to be seen, sitting on the cabin step and singing the ancient chantey. He had cooked and eaten his breakfast all by himself, and had just come out to take a look at the world. Twenty feet before him stood the steel drum round which the endless cable worked. By the drum, snug and fast, was the ore-car. Following with his eyes the dizzy flight of the cables to the farther bank, he could see the other drum and the other car.

The contrivance was worked by gravity, the loaded car crossing the river by virtue of its own weight, and at the same time dragging the empty car back. The loaded car being emptied, and the empty car being loaded with more ore, the performance could be repeated—a performance which had been repeated tens of thousands of times since the day Old Jerry became the keeper of the cables.

Young Jerry broke off his song at the sound of approaching footsteps. A tall, blue-shirted man, a rifle across the hollow of his arm, came out from the gloom of the pine-trees. It was Hall, watchman of the Yellow Dragon mine, the cables of which spanned the Sacramento a mile farther up.

"Yello, younker!" was his greeting. "What you doin' here by your lonesome?"

"Oh, bachin'," Jerry tried to answer unconcernedly, as if it were a very ordinary sort of thing. "Dad's away, you see."

"Where's he gone?" the man asked.

"San Francisco. Went last night. His brother's dead in the old country, and he's gone down to see the lawyers. Won't be back till tomorrow night."

So spoke Jerry, and with pride, because of the responsibility which had fallen to him of keeping an eye on the property of the Yellow Dream, and the glorious adventure of living alone on the cliff above the river and of cooking his own meals.

"Well, take care of yourself," Hall said, "and don't monkey with the cables. I'm goin' to see if I can pick up a deer in the Cripple Cow Cañon."

"It's goin' to rain, I think," Jerry said, with mature deliberation.

"And it's little I mind a wettin'," Hall laughed, as he strode away among the trees.

Jerry's prediction concerning rain was more than fulfilled. By ten o'clock the pines were swaying and moaning, the cabin windows rattling, and the rain driving by in fierce squalls. At half past eleven he kindled a fire, and promptly at the stroke of twelve sat down to his dinner.

No out-of-doors for him that day, he decided, when he had washed the few dishes and put them neatly away; and he wondered how wet Hall was and whether he had succeeded in picking up a deer.

At one o'clock there came a knock at the door, and when he opened it a man and a woman staggered in on the breast of a great gust of wind. They were Mr. and Mrs. Spillane, ranchers, who lived in a lonely valley a dozen miles back from the river.

"Where's Hall?" was Spillane's opening speech, and he spoke sharply and quickly.

Jerry noted that he was nervous and abrupt in his movements, and that Mrs. Spillane seemed laboring under some strong anxiety. She was a thin, washed-out, worked-out woman, whose life of dreary and unending toil had stamped itself harshly upon her face. It was the same life that had bowed her husband's shoulders and gnarled his hands and turned his hair to a dry and dusty gray.

"He's gone hunting up Cripple Cow," Jerry answered. "Did you want to cross?"

The woman began to weep quietly, while Spillane dropped a troubled exclamation and strode to the window. Jerry joined him in gazing out to where the cables lost themselves in the thick downpour.

176

It was the custom of the backwoods people in that section of country to cross the Sacramento on the Yellow Dragon cable. For this service a small toll was charged, which tolls the Yellow Dragon Company applied to the payment of Hall's wages.

"We've got to get across, Jerry," Spillane said, at the same time jerking his thumb over his shoulder in the direction of his wife. "Her father's hurt at the Clover Leaf. Powder explosion. Not expected to live. We just got word."

Jerry felt himself fluttering inwardly. He knew that Spillane wanted to cross on the Yellow Dream cable, and in the absence of his father he felt that he dared not assume such a responsibility, for the cable had never been used for passengers; in fact, had not been used at all for a long time.

"Maybe Hall will be back soon," he said.

Spillane shook his head, and demanded, "Where's your father?"

"San Francisco," Jerry answered, briefly.

Spillane groaned, and fiercely drove his clenched fist into the palm of the other hand. His wife was crying more audibly, and Jerry could hear her murmuring, "And daddy's dyin', dyin'!"

The tears welled up in his own eyes, and he stood irresolute, not knowing what he should do. But the man decided for him.

"Look here, kid," he said, with determination, "the wife and me are goin' over on this here cable of yours! Will you run it for us?"

Jerry backed slightly away. He did it unconsciously, as if recoiling instinctively from something unwelcome.

"Better see if Hall's back," he suggested.

"And if he ain't?"

Again Jerry hesitated.

"I'll stand for the risk," Spillane added. "Don't you see, kid, we've simply got to cross!"

Jerry nodded his head reluctantly.

"And there ain't no use waitin' for Hall," Spillane went on. "You know as well as me he ain't back from Cripple Cow this time of day! So come along and let's get started."

No wonder that Mrs. Spillane seemed terrified as they helped her into the ore-car—so Jerry thought, as he gazed into the apparently fathomless gulf beneath her. For it was so filled with rain and cloud, hurtling and curling in the fierce blast, that the other shore, seven hundred feet away, was invisible, while the cliff at their feet dropped sheer down and lost itself in the swirling vapor. By all appearances it might be a mile to bottom instead of two hundred feet.

"All ready?" he asked.

"Let her go!" Spillane shouted, to make himself heard above the roar of the wind.

He had clambered in beside his wife, and was holding one of her hands in his.

Jerry looked upon this with disapproval. "You'll need all your hands for holdin' on, the way the wind's yowlin'."

The man and the woman shifted their hands accordingly, tightly gripping the sides of the car, and Jerry slowly and carefully released the brake. The drum began to revolve as the endless cable passed round it, and the car slid slowly out into the chasm, its trolley wheels rolling on the stationary cable overhead, to which it was suspended.

It was not the first time Jerry had worked the cable, but it was the first time he had done so away from the supervising eye of his father. By means of the brake he regulated the speed of the car. It needed regulating, for at times, caught by the stronger gusts of wind, it swayed violently back and forth; and once, just before it was swallowed up in a rain squall, it seemed about to spill out its human contents.

178

After that Jerry had no way of knowing where the car was except by means of the cable. This he watched keenly as it glided around the drum. "Three hundred feet," he breathed to himself, as the cable markings went by, "three hundred and fifty, four hundred; four hundred and——"

The cable had stopped. Jerry threw off the brake, but it did not move. He caught the cable with his hands and tried to start it by tugging smartly. Something had gone wrong. What? He could not guess; he could not see. Looking up, he could vaguely make out the empty car, which had been crossing from the opposite cliff at a speed equal to that of the loaded car. It was about two hundred and fifty feet away. That meant, he knew, that somewhere in the gray obscurity, two hundred feet above the river and two hundred and fifty feet from the other bank, Spillane and his wife were suspended and stationary.

Three times Jerry shouted with all the shrill force of his lungs, but no answering cry came out of the storm. It was impossible for him to hear them or to make himself heard. As he stood for a moment, thinking rapidly, the flying clouds seemed to thin and lift. He caught a brief glimpse of the swollen Sacramento beneath, and a briefer glimpse of the car and the man and woman. Then the clouds descended thicker than ever.

The boy examined the drum closely, and found nothing the matter with it. Evidently it was the drum on the other side that had gone wrong. He was appalled at the thought of the man and woman out there in the midst of the storm, hanging over the abyss, rocking back and forth in the frail car and ignorant of what was taking place on shore. And he did not like to think of their hanging there while he went round by the Yellow Dragon cable to the other drum.

But he remembered a block and tackle in the tool-house, and ran and brought it. They were double blocks, and he murmured aloud, "A purchase of four," as he made the tackle fast to the endless cable. Then he heaved upon it, heaved until it seemed that his arms were being drawn out from their sockets and that his shoulder muscles would be ripped asunder. Yet the cable did not budge. Nothing remained but to cross over to the other side.

He was already soaking wet, so he did not mind the rain as he ran over the trail to the Yellow Dragon. The storm was with him, and it was easy going, although there was no Hall at the other end of it to man the brake for him and regulate the speed of the car. This he did for himself, however, by means of a stout rope, which he passed, with a turn, round the stationary cable.

As the full force of the wind struck him in mid-air, swaying the cable and whistling and roaring past it, and rocking and careening the car, he appreciated more fully what must be the condition of mind of Spillane and his wife. And this appreciation gave strength to him, as, safely across, he fought his way up the other bank, in the teeth of the gale, to the Yellow Dream cable.

To his consternation, he found the drum in thorough working order. Everything was running smoothly at both ends. Where was the hitch? In the middle, without a doubt.

From this side, the car containing Spillane was only two hundred and fifty feet away. He could make out the man and woman through the whirling vapor, crouching in the bottom of the car and exposed to the pelting rain and the full fury of the wind. In a lull between the squalls he shouted to Spillane to examine the trolley of the car.

Spillane heard, for he saw him rise up cautiously on his knees, and with his hands go over both trolley-wheels. Then he turned his face toward the bank.

"She's all right, kid!"

Jerry heard the words, faint and far, as from a remote distance. Then what was the matter? Nothing remained but the other and empty car, which he could not see, but which he knew to be there, somewhere in that terrible gulf two hundred feet beyond Spillane's car.

His mind was made up on the instant. He was only fourteen years old, slightly and wirily built; but his life had been lived among the mountains, his father had taught him no small measure of "sailoring," and he was not particularly afraid of heights.

In the tool-box by the drum he found an old monkey-wrench and a short bar of iron, also a coil of fairly new Manila rope. He looked in vain for a piece of board with which to rig a "boatswain's chair." There was nothing at hand but large planks, which he had no means of sawing, so he was compelled to do without the more comfortable form of saddle.

The saddle he rigged was very simple. With the rope he made merely a large loop round the stationary cable, to which hung the empty car. When he sat in the loop his hands could just reach the cable conveniently, and where the rope was likely to fray against the cable he lashed his coat, in lieu of the old sack he would have used had he been able to find one.

These preparations swiftly completed, he swung out over the chasm, sitting in the rope saddle and pulling himself along the cable by his hands. With him he carried the monkey-wrench and short iron bar and a few spare feet of rope. It was a slightly up-hill pull, but this he did not mind so much as the wind. When the furious gusts hurled him back and forth, sometimes half twisting him about, and he gazed down into the gray depths, he was aware that he was afraid. It was an old cable. What if it should break under his weight and the pressure of the wind?

It was fear he was experiencing, honest fear, and he knew that there was a "gone" feeling in the pit of his stomach, and a trembling of the knees which he could not quell.

But he held himself bravely to the task. The cable was old and worn, sharp pieces of wire projected from it, and his hands were cut and bleeding by the time he took his first rest, and held a shouted conversation with Spillane. The car was directly beneath him and only a few feet away, so he was able to explain the condition of affairs and his errand.

"Wish I could help you," Spillane shouted at him as he started on, "but the wife's gone all to pieces! Anyway, kid, take care of yourself! I got myself in this fix, but it's up to you to get me out!"

"Oh, I'll do it!" Jerry shouted back. "Tell Mrs. Spillane that she'll be ashore now in a jiffy!"

In the midst of pelting rain, which half-blinded him, swinging from side to side like a rapid and erratic pendulum, his torn hands paining him severely and his lungs panting from his exertions and panting from the very air which the wind sometimes blew into his mouth with strangling force, he finally arrived at the empty car.

A single glance showed him that he had not made the dangerous journey in vain. The front trolley-wheel, loose from long wear, had jumped the cable, and the cable was now jammed tightly between the wheel and the sheave-block.

One thing was clear—the wheel must be removed from the block. A second thing was equally clear—while the wheel was being removed the car would have to be fastened to the cable by the rope he had brought.

At the end of a quarter of an hour, beyond making the car secure, he had accomplished nothing. The key which bound the wheel on its axle was rusted and jammed. He hammered at it with one hand and held on the best he could with the other, but the wind persisted in swinging and twisting his body, and made his blows miss more often than not. Nine-tenths of the strength he expended was in trying to hold himself steady. For fear that he might drop the monkey-wrench he made it fast to his wrist with his handkerchief.

At the end of half an hour Jerry had hammered the key clear, but he could not draw it out. A dozen times it seemed that he must give up in despair, that all the danger and toil he had gone through were for nothing. Then an idea came to him, and he went through his pockets with feverish haste, and found what he sought—a ten-penny nail.

But for that nail, put in his pocket he knew not when or why, he would have had to make another trip over the cable and back. Thrusting the nail through the looped head of the key, he at last had a grip, and in no time the key was out.

Then came punching and prying with the iron bar to get the wheel itself free from where it was jammed by the cable against the side of the block. After that Jerry replaced the wheel, and by means of the rope, heaved up on the car till the trolley once more rested properly on the cable.

All this took time. More than an hour and a half had elapsed since his arrival at the empty car. And now, for the first time, he dropped out of his saddle and down into the car. He removed the detaining ropes, and the trolley-wheel began slowly to revolve. The car was moving, and he knew that somewhere beyond, although he could not see, the car of Spillane was likewise moving, and in the opposite direction.

There was no need for a brake, for his weight sufficiently counterbalanced the weight in the other car; and soon he saw the cliff rising out of the cloud depths and the old familiar drum going round and round.

Jerry climbed out and made the car securely fast. He did it deliberately and carefully, and then, quite unhero-like, he sank down by the drum, regardless of the pelting storm, and burst out sobbing.

There were many reasons why he sobbed—partly from the pain of his hand, which was excruciating; partly from exhaustion; partly from relief and release from the nerve-tension he had been under for so long; and in a large measure for thankfulness that the man and woman were saved.

They were not there to thank him; but somewhere beyond that howling, storm-driven gulf he knew they were hurrying over the trail toward the Clover Leaf.

Jerry staggered to the cabin, and his hand left the white knob red with blood as he opened the door, but he took no notice of it.

He was too proudly contented with himself, for he was certain that he had done well, and he was honest enough to admit to himself that he had done well. But a small regret arose and persisted in his thoughts—if his father had only been there to see!

IN YEDDO BAY

Somewhere along Theater Street he had lost it. He remembered being hustled somewhat roughly on the bridge over one of the canals that cross that busy thoroughfare. Possibly some slant-eyed, light-fingered pickpocket was even then enjoying the fifty-odd yen his purse had contained. And then again, he thought, he might have lost it himself, just lost it carelessly.

Hopelessly, and for the twentieth time, he searched in all his pockets for the missing purse. It was not there. His hand lingered in his empty hip-pocket, and he woefully regarded the voluble and vociferous restaurant-keeper, who insanely clamored: "Twenty-five sen! You pay now! Twenty-five sen!"

"But my purse!" the boy said. "I tell you I've lost it somewhere."

Whereupon the restaurant-keeper lifted his arms indignantly and shrieked: "Twenty-five sen! Twenty-five sen! You pay now!"

Quite a crowd had collected, and it was growing embarrassing for Alf Davis.

It was so ridiculous and petty, Alf thought. Such a disturbance about nothing! And, decidedly, he must be doing something. Thoughts of diving wildly through that forest of legs, and of striking out at whomsoever opposed him, flashed through his mind; but, as though divining his purpose, one of the waiters, a short and chunky chap with an evil-looking cast in one eye, seized him by the arm.

"You pay now! You pay now! Twenty-five sen!" yelled the proprietor, hoarse with rage.

Alf was red in the face, too, from mortification; but he resolutely set out on another exploration. He had given up the purse, pinning his last hope on stray coins. In the little change-pocket of his coat he found a ten-sen piece and five-copper sen; and remembering having recently missed a ten-sen piece, he cut the seam of the pocket and resurrected the coin from the depths of the lining. Twenty-five sen he held in his hand, the sum required to pay for the supper he had eaten. He turned them over to the proprietor, who counted them, grew suddenly calm, and bowed obsequiously—in fact, the whole crowd bowed obsequiously and melted away.

Alf Davis was a young sailor, just turned sixteen, on board the *Annie Mine*, an American sailing-schooner, which had run into Yokohama to ship its season's catch of skins to London. And in this, his second trip ashore, he was beginning to snatch his first puzzling glimpses of the Oriental mind. He laughed when the bowing and kotowing was over, and turned on his heel to confront another problem. How was he to get aboard ship? It was eleven o'clock at night, and there would be no ship's boats ashore, while the outlook for hiring a native boatman, with nothing but empty pockets to draw upon, was not particularly inviting.

Keeping a sharp lookout for shipmates, he went down to the pier. At Yokohama there are no long lines of wharves. The shipping lies out at anchor, enabling a few hundred of the short-legged people to make a livelihood by carrying passengers to and from the shore.

A dozen sampan men and boys hailed Alf and offered their services. He selected the most favorable-looking one, an old and beneficent-appearing man with a withered leg. Alf stepped into his sampan and sat down. It was quite dark and he could not see what the old fellow was doing, though he evidently was doing nothing about shoving off and getting under way. At last he limped over and peered into Alf's face.

"Ten sen," he said.

"Yes, I know, ten sen," Alf answered carelessly. "But hurry up. American schooner."

"Ten sen. You pay now," the old fellow insisted.

Alf felt himself grow hot all over at the hateful words "pay now." "You take me to American schooner; then I pay," he said.

But the man stood up patiently before him, held out his hand, and said, "Ten sen. You pay now."

Alf tried to explain. He had no money. He had lost his purse. But he would pay. As soon as he got aboard the American schooner, then he would pay. No; he would not even go aboard the American schooner. He would call to his shipmates, and they would give the sampan man the ten sen first. After that he would go aboard. So it was all right, of course.

To all of which the beneficent-appearing old man replied: "You pay now. Ten sen." And, to make matters worse, the other sampan men squatted on the pier steps, listening.

Alf, chagrined and angry, stood up to step ashore. But the old fellow laid a detaining hand on his sleeve. "You give shirt now. I take you 'Merican schooner," he proposed.

Then it was that all of Alf's American independence flamed up in his breast. The Anglo-Saxon has a born dislike of being imposed upon, and to Alf this was sheer robbery! Ten sen was equivalent to six American cents, while his shirt, which was of good quality and was new, had cost him two dollars.

He turned his back on the man without a word, and went out to the end of the pier, the crowd, laughing with great gusto, following at his heels. The majority of them were heavy-set, muscular fellows, and the July night being one of sweltering heat, they were clad in the least possible raiment. The water-people of any race are rough and turbulent, and it struck Alf that to be out at midnight on a pier-end with such a crowd of wharfmen, in a big Japanese city, was not as safe as it might be.

One burly fellow, with a shock of black hair and ferocious eyes, came up. The rest shoved in after him to take part in the discussion.

"Give me shoes," the man said. "Give me shoes now. I take you 'Merican schooner."

Alf shook his head, whereat the crowd clamored that he accept the proposal. Now the Anglo-Saxon is so constituted that to browbeat or bully him is the last way under the sun of getting him to do any certain thing. He will dare willingly, but he will not permit himself to be driven. So this attempt of the boatmen to force Alf only aroused all the dogged stubbornness of his race. The same qualities were in him that are in men who lead forlorn hopes; and there, under the stars, on the lonely pier, encircled by the jostling and shouldering gang, he resolved that he would die rather than submit to the indignity of being robbed of a single stitch of clothing. Not value, but principle, was at stake.

Then somebody thrust roughly against him from behind. He whirled about with flashing eyes, and the circle involuntarily gave ground. But the crowd was growing more boisterous. Each and every article of clothing he had on was demanded by one or another, and these demands were shouted simultaneously at the tops of very healthy lungs.

Alf had long since ceased to say anything, but he knew that the situation was getting dangerous, and that the only thing left to him was to get away. His face was set doggedly, his eyes glinted like points of steel, and his body was firmly and confidently poised. This air of determination sufficiently impressed the boatmen to make them give way before him When he started to walk toward the shore-end of the pier. But they trooped along beside more noisily than ever. One of the youngsters about Alf's size and build, impudently snatched his cap from his head; and before he could put it on his own head, Alf struck out from the shoulder, and sent the fellow rolling on the stones.

The cap flew out of his hand and disappeared among the many legs. Alf did some quick thinking, his sailor pride would not permit him to leave the cap in their hands. He followed in the direction it had sped, and soon found it under the bare foot of a stalwart fellow, who kept his weight stolidly upon it. Alf tried to get the cap by a sudden jerk, but failed. He shoved against the man's leg, but the man only grunted. It was challenge direct, and Alf accepted it. Like a flash one leg was behind the man and Alf had thrust strongly with his shoulder against the fellow's chest. Nothing could save the man from the fierce vigorousness of the trick, and he was hurled over and backward.

Next, the cap was on Alf's head and his fists were up before him. Then he whirled about to prevent attack from behind, and all those in that quarter fled precipitately. This was what he wanted. None remained between him and the shore end. The pier was narrow. Facing them and threatening with his fist those who attempted to pass him on either side, he continued his retreat. It was exciting work, walking backward and at the same time checking that surging mass of men. But the dark-skinned peoples, the world over, have learned to respect the white man's fist; and it was the battles fought by many sailors, more than his own warlike front, that gave Alf the victory.

Where the pier adjoins the shore was the station of the harbor police, and Alf backed into the electric-lighted office, very much to the amusement of the dapper lieutenant in charge. The sampan men, grown quiet and orderly, clustered like flies by the open door, through which they could see and hear what passed.

Alf explained his difficulty in few words, and demanded, as the privilege of a stranger in a strange land, that the lieutenant put him aboard in the police-boat. The lieutenant, in turn, who knew all the "rules and regulations" by heart, explained that the harbor police were not ferrymen, and that the police-boats had other functions to perform than that of transporting belated and penniless sailormen to their ships. He also said he knew the sampan men to be natural-born robbers, but that so long as they robbed within the law he was powerless. It was their right to collect fares in advance, and who was he to command them to take a passenger and collect fare at the journey's end? Alf acknowledged the justice of his remarks, but suggested that while he could not command he might persuade. The lieutenant was willing to oblige, and went to the door, from where he delivered a speech to the crowd. But they, too, knew their rights, and, when the officer had finished, shouted in chorus their abominable "Ten sen! You pay now! You pay now!"

"You see, I can do nothing," said the lieutenant, who, by the way, spoke perfect English. "But I have warned them not to harm or molest you, so you will be safe, at least. The night is warm and half over. Lie down somewhere and go to sleep. I would permit you to sleep here in the office, were it not against the rules and regulations."

Alf thanked him for his kindness and courtesy; but the sampan men had aroused all his pride of race and doggedness, and the problem could not be solved that way. To sleep out the night on the stones was an acknowledgment of defeat.

"The sampan men refuse to take me out?"

The lieutenant nodded.

"And you refuse to take me out?"

Again the lieutenant nodded.

"Well, then, it's not in the rules and regulations that you can prevent my taking myself out?"

The lieutenant was perplexed. "There is no boat," he said.

"That's not the question," Alf proclaimed hotly. "If I take myself out, everybody's satisfied and no harm done?"

"Yes; what you say is true," persisted the puzzled lieutenant. "But you cannot take yourself out."

"You just watch me," was the retort.

Down went Alf's cap on the office floor. Right and left he kicked off his low-cut shoes. Trousers and shirt followed.

"Remember," he said in ringing tones, "I, as a citizen of the United States, shall hold you, the city of Yokohama, and the government of Japan responsible for those clothes. Good night."

He plunged through the doorway, scattering the astounded boatmen to either side, and ran out on the pier. But they quickly recovered and ran after him, shouting with glee at the new phase the situation had taken on. It was a night long remembered among the water-folk of Yokohama town. Straight to the end Alf ran, and, without pause, dived off cleanly and neatly into the water. He struck out with a lusty, single-overhand stroke till curiosity prompted him to halt for a moment. Out of the darkness, from where the pier should be, voices were calling to him.

He turned on his back, floated, and listened.

"All right! All right!" he could distinguish from the babel. "No pay now; pay bime by! Come back! Come back now; pay bime by!"

"No, thank you," he called back. "No pay at all. Good night."

Then he faced about in order to locate the *Annie Mine*. She was fully a mile away, and in the darkness it was no easy task to get her bearings. First, he settled upon a blaze of lights which he knew nothing but a man-of-war could make. That must be the United States war-ship *Lancaster*. Somewhere to the left and beyond should be the *Annie Mine*. But to the left he made out three lights close together. That could not be the schooner. For the moment he was confused. He rolled over on his back and shut his eyes, striving to construct a mental picture of the harbor as he had seen it in daytime. With a snort of satisfaction he rolled back again. The three lights evidently belonged to the big English tramp steamer. Therefore the schooner must lie somewhere between the three lights and the *Lancaster*. He gazed long and steadily, and there, very dim and low, but at the point he expected, burned a single light— the anchor-light of the *Annie Mine*.

And it was a fine swim under the starshine. The air was warm as the water, and the water as warm as tepid milk. The good salt taste of it was in his mouth, the tingling of it along his limbs; and the steady beat of his heart, heavy and strong, made him glad for living.

But beyond being glorious the swim was uneventful. On the right hand he passed the many-lighted *Lancaster*, on the left hand the English tramp, and ere long the *Annie Mine* loomed large above him. He grasped the hanging rope-ladder and drew himself noiselessly on deck. There was no one in sight. He saw a light in the galley, and knew that the captain's son, who kept the lonely anchor-watch, was making coffee. Alf went forward to the forecastle. The men were snoring in their bunks, and in that confined space the heat seemed to him insufferable. So he put on a thin cotton shirt and a pair of dungaree trousers, tucked blanket and pillow under his arm, and went up on deck and out on the forecastle-head.

Hardly had he begun to doze when he was roused by a boat coming alongside and hailing the anchor-watch. It was the police-boat, and to Alf it was given to enjoy the excited conversation that ensued. Yes, the captain's son recognized the clothes. They belonged to Alf Davis, one of the seamen.

What had happened? No; Alf Davis had not come aboard. He was ashore. He was not ashore? Then he must be drowned. Here both the lieutenant and the captain's son talked at the same time, and Alf could make out nothing. Then he heard them come forward and rouse out the crew. The crew grumbled sleepily and said that Alf Davis was not in the forecastle; whereupon the captain's son waxed indignant at the Yokohama police and their ways, and the lieutenant quoted rules and regulations in despairing accents.

Alf rose up from the forecastle-head and extended his hand, saying:

"I guess I'll take those clothes. Thank you for bringing them aboard so promptly."

"I don't see why he couldn't have brought you aboard inside of them," said the captain's son.

And the police lieutenant said nothing, though he turned the clothes over somewhat sheepishly to their rightful owner.

The next day, when Alf started to go ashore, he found himself surrounded by shouting and gesticulating, though very respectful, sampan men, all extraordinarily anxious to have him for a passenger. Nor did the one he selected say, "You pay now," when he entered his boat. When Alf prepared to step out on to the pier, he offered the man the customary ten sen. But the man drew himself up and shook his head.

"You all right," he said. "You no pay. You never no pay. You bully boy and all right."

And for the rest of the *Annie Mine*'s stay in port, the sampan men refused money at Alf Davis's hand. Out of admiration for his pluck and independence, they had given him the freedom of the harbor.

THEFT

Time of Play, To-Day, in Washington, D. C.

It Occurs in Twenty Hours

CHARACTERS

Margaret Chalmers

Howard Knox

Thomas Chalmers

Master Thomas Chalmers

Ellery Jackson Hubbard

Anthony Starkweather

Mrs Starkweather

Connie Starkweather

Felix Dobleman

Linda Davis

Julius Rutland

John Gieford

Matsu Sakari

Dolores Ortega

Senator Dowsett Mrs Dowsett

Housekeeper, Servs

Wife of Senator Chalmers

A Congressman from Oregon

A United States Senator and several times millionaire

Son of Margaret and Senator Chalmers

A Journalist

A great magnate, and father of Margaret Chalmers

His wife

Their younger daughter

Secretary to Anthony Starkweather

Maid to Margaret Chalmers

Episcopalian Minister

Labor Agitator

Secretary of Japanese Embassy

Wife of Peruvian Minister

Agents, etc

ACTORS' DESCRIPTION OF CHARACTERS

Margaret Chalmers. Twenty-seven years of age; a strong, mature woman, but quite feminine where her heart or sense of beauty are concerned. Her eyes are wide apart. Has a dazzling smile, which she knows how to use on occasion. Also, on occasion, she can be firm and hard, even cynical An intellectual woman, and at the same time a very womanly woman, capable of sudden tendernesses, flashes of emotion, and abrupt actions. She is a finished product of high culture and refinement, and at the same time possesses robust vitality and instinctive rijkkjght-promptings that augur well for the future of the race.

Howard Knox. He might have been a poet, but was turned politician. Inflamed with love for humanity. Thirty-five years of age. He has his vision, and must follow it. He has suffered ostracism because of it, and has followed his vision in spite of abuse and ridicule. Physically, a well-built, powerful man. Strong-featured rather than handsome. Very much in earnest, and, despite his university training, a trifle awkward in carriage and demeanor, lacking in social ease. He has been elected to Congress on a reform ticket, and is almost alone in fight he is making. He has no party to back him, though he has a following of a few independents and insurgents.

Thomas Chalmers. Forty-five to fifty years of age. Iron-gray mustache. Slightly stout. A good liver, much given to Scotch and soda, with a weak heart. Is liable to collapse any time. If anything, slightly lazy or lethargic in his emotional life. One of the "owned" senators representing a decadent New England state, himself master of the state political machine. Also, he is nobody's fool. He possesses the brain and strength of character to play his part. His most distinctive feature is his temperamental opportunism.

Master Thomas Chalmers. Six years of age. Sturdy and healthy despite his grandmother's belief to the contrary.

Ellery Jackson Hubbard. Thirty-eight to forty years of age. Smooth-shaven. A star journalist with a national reputation; a large, heavy-set man, with large head, large hands—everything about him is large. A man radiating prosperity, optimism and selfishness. Has no morality whatever. Is a conscious individualist, cold-blooded, pitiless, working only for himself, and believing in nothing but himself.

Anthony Starkweather. An elderly, well preserved gentleman, slenderly built, showing all the signs of a man who has lived clean and has been almost an ascetic. One to whom the joys of the flesh have had little meaning. A cold, controlled man whose one passion is for power. Distinctively a man of power. An eagle-like man, who, by keenness of brain and force of character, has carved out a fortune of hundreds of millions. In short, an industrial and financial magnate of the first water and of the finest type to be found in the United States. Essentially a moral man, his rigid New England morality has suffered a sea change and developed into the morality of the master-man of affairs, equally rigid, equally uncompromising, but essentially Jesuitical in that he believes in doing wrong that right may come of it. He is absolutely certain that civilization and progress rest on his shoulders and upon the shoulders of the small group of men like him.

Mrs. Starkweather. Of the helpless, comfortably stout, elderly type. She has not followed her husband in his moral evolution. She is the creature of old customs, old prejudices, old New England ethics. She is rather confused by the modern rush of life.

Connie Starkweather. Margaret's younger sister, twenty years old. She is nothing that Margaret is, and everything that Margaret is not. No essential evil in her, but has no mind of her own—hopelessly a creature of convention. Gay, laughing, healthy, buxom—a natural product of her care-free environment.

Feux Dobleman. Private secretary to Anthony Starkweather. A young man of correct social deportment, thoroughly and in all things just the sort of private secretary a man like Anthony Starkweather would have. He is a weak-souled creature, timorous, almost effeminate.

Linda Davis. Maid to Margaret. A young woman of twenty-five or so, blond, Scandinavian, though American-born. A cold woman, almost featureless because of her long years of training, but with a hot heart deep down, and characterized by an intense devotion to her mistress. Wild horses could drag nothing from her where her mistress is concerned.

Junus Rutland. Having no strong features about him, the type realizes itself.

John Gifford. A labor agitator. A man of the people, rough-hewn, narrow as a labor-leader may well be, earnest and sincere. He is a proper, better type of labor-leader.

Matsu Sakari. Secretary of Japanese Embassy. He is the perfection of politeness and talks classical book-English. He bows a great deal.

Dolores Ortega. Wife of Peruvian Minister; bright and vivacious, and uses her hands a great deal as she talks, in the Latin-American fashion.

Senator Dowsett. Fifty years of age; well preserved.

Mrs. Dowsett. Stout and middle-aged.

ACT I. A ROOM IN THE HOUSE OF SENATOR CHALMERS

Scene. *In Senator Chalmers' home. It is four o'clock in the afternoon, in a modern living room with appropriate furnishings. In particular, in front, on left, a table prepared for the serving of tea, all excepting the tea urn itself. At rear, right of center, is main entrance to the room. Also, doorways at sides, on left and right. Curtain discloses Chalmers and Hubbard seated loungingly at the right front.*

Hubbard

(*After an apparent pause for cogitation.*) I can't understand why an old wheel-horse like Elsworth should kick over the traces that way.

Chalmers

Disgruntled. Thinks he didn't get his fair share of plums out of the Tariff Committee. Besides, it's his last term. He's announced that he's going to retire.

Hubbard

(*Snorting contemptuously, mimicking an old man's pompous enunciation.*) "A Resolution to Investigate the High Cost of Living!"—old Senator Elsworth introducing a measure like that! The old buck!—— How are you going to handle it?

Chalmers

It's already handled.

Hubbard

Yes?

Chalmers

(*Pulling his mustache.*) Turned it over to the Committee to Audit and Control the Contingent Expenses of the Senate.

Hubbard

(*Grinning his appreciation.*) And you're chairman. Poor old Elsworth. This way to the lethal chamber, and the bill's on its way.

Chalmers

Elsworth will be retired before it's ever reported. In the meantime, say after a decent interval, Senator Hodge will introduce another resolution to investigate the high cost of living. It will be like Elsworth's, only it won't.

Hubbard

(*Nodding his head and anticipating.*) And it will go to the Committee on Finance and come back for action inside of twenty-four hours.

Chalmers

By the way, I see *Cartwright's Magazine* has ceased muck-raking.

Hubbard

Cartwrights never did muck-rake—that is, not the big Interests—only the small independent businesses that didn't advertise.

Chalmers

Yes, it deftly concealed its reactionary tendencies.

Hubbard

And from now on the concealment will be still more deft. I've gone into it myself. I have a majority of the stock right now.

Chalmers

I thought I had noticed a subtle change in the last two numbers.

Hubbard

(*Nodding.*) We're still going on muck-raking. We have a splendid series on Aged Paupers, demanding better treatment and more sanitary conditions. Also we are going to run "Barbarous Venezuela" and show up thoroughly the rotten political management of that benighted country.

Chalmers

(*Nods approvingly, and, after a pause.*) And now concerning Knox. That's what I sent for you about. His speech comes off tomorrow per schedule. At last we've got him where we want him.

Hubbard

I have the ins and outs of it pretty well. Everything's arranged. The boys have their cue, though they don't know just what's going to be pulled off; and this time to-morrow afternoon their dispatches will be singing along the wires.

Chalmers

(*Firmly and harshly.*) This man Knox must be covered with ridicule, swamped with ridicule, annihilated with ridicule.

Hubbard

It is to laugh. Trust the great American people for that. We'll make those little Western editors sit up. They've been swearing by Knox, like a little tin god. Roars of laughter for them.

Chalmers

Do you do anything yourself?

Hubbard

Trust me. I have my own article for Cartwright's blocked out. They're holding the presses for it. I shall wire it along hot-footed to-morrow evening. Say——?

Chalmers

(*After a pause.*) Well?

Hubbard

Wasn't it a risky thing to give him his chance with that speech?

Chalmers

It was the only feasible thing. He never has given us an opening. Our service men have camped on his trail night and day. Private life as unimpeachable as his public life. But now is our chance. The gods have given him into our hands. That speech will do more to break his influence—

Hubbard

(*Interrupting.*) Than a Fairbanks cocktail.

(*Both laugh.*) But don't forget that this Knox is a live wire. Somebody might get stung. Are you sure, when he gets up to make that speech, that he won't be able to back it up?

Chalmers

No danger at all.

Hubbard

But there are hooks and crooks by which facts are sometimes obtained.

Chalmers

(*Positively.*) Knox has nothing to go on but suspicions and hints, and unfounded assertions from the yellow press.

(*Man-servant enters, goes to tea-table, looks it over, and makes slight rearrangements.*) (*Lowering his voice.*) He will make himself a laughing stock. His charges will turn into boomerangs. His speech will be like a sheet from a Sunday supplement, with not a fact to back it up. (*Glances at Servant.*) We'd better be getting out of here. They're going to have tea.

(*The Servant, however, makes exit.*) Come to the library and have a high-ball. (*They pause as Hubbard speaks.*)

Hubbard

(*With quiet glee.*) And to-morrow Ali Baba gets his.

204

Chalmers

Ali Baba?

Hubbard

That's what your wife calls him—Knox.

Chalmers

Oh, yes, I believe I've heard it before. It's about time he hanged himself, and now we've given him the rope.

Hubbard

(*Sinking voice and becoming deprecatingly confidential.*)

Oh, by the way, just a little friendly warning, Senator Chalmers. Not so fast and loose up New York way. That certain lady, not to be mentioned—there's gossip about it in the New York newspaper offices. Of course, all such stories are killed. But be discreet, be discreet If Gherst gets hold of it, he'll play it up against the Administration in all his papers.

(*Chalmers, who throughout this speech is showing a growing resentment, is about to speak, when voices are heard without and he checks himself.*)

(*Enter. Mrs. Starkweather, rather flustered and imminently in danger of a collapse, followed by Connie Starkweather, fresh, radiant, and joyous.*)

Mrs. Starkweather

(*With appeal and relief.*)

Oh——Tom!

(*Chalmers takes her hand sympathetically and protectingly.*)

Connie

(*Who is an exuberant young woman, bursts forth.*) Oh, brother-in-law! Such excitement! That's what's the matter with mother. We ran into a go-cart. Our chauffeur was not to blame. It was the woman's fault. She tried to cross just as we were turning the corner. But we hardly grazed it. Fortunately the baby was not hurt—only spilled. It was ridiculous. *(Catching sight of Hubbard.)* Oh, there you are, Mr. Hubbard. How de do.

(Steps half way to meet him and shakes hands with him.) (Mrs. Starkweather looks around helplessly for a chair, and Chalmers conducts her to one soothingly.)

Mrs. Starkweather

Oh, it was terrible! The little child might have been killed. And such persons love their babies, I know.

Connie

(To Chalmers.) Has father come? We were to pick him up here. Where's Madge?

Mrs. Starkweather

(Espying Hubbard, faintly.) Oh, there is Mr. Hubbard.

(Hubbard comes to her and shakes hands.) I simply can't get used to these rapid ways of modern life. The motor-car is the invention of the devil. Everything is *too* quick. When I was a girl, we lived sedately, decorously. There was time for meditation and repose. But in this age there is time for nothing. How Anthony keeps his head is more than I can understand. But, then, Anthony is a wonderful man.

Hubbard

I am sure Mr. Starkweather never lost his head in his life.

Chalmers

Unless when he was courting you, mother.

Mrs. Starkweather

(A trifle grimly.) I'm not so sure about that.

Connie

(*Imitating a grave, business-like enunciation.*) Father probably conferred first with his associates, then turned the affair over for consideration by his corporation lawyers, and, when they reported no flaws, checked the first spare half hour in his notebook to ask mother if she would have him.

(*They laugh.*) And looked at his watch at least twice while he was proposing.

Mrs. Starkweather

Anthony was not so busy then as all that.

Hubbard

He hadn't yet taken up the job of running the United States.

Mrs. Starkweather

I'm sure I don't know what he is running, but he is a very busy man—business, politics, and madness; madness, politics, and business.

(*She stops breathlessly and glances at tea-table.*) Tea. I should like a cup of tea. Connie, I shall stay for a cup of tea, and then, if your father hasn't come, we'll go home. (*To Chalmers.*) Where is Tommy?

Chalmers

Out in the car with Madge.

(*Glances at tea-table and consults watch.*) She should be back now.

Connie

Mother, you mustn't stay long. I have to dress.

Chalmers

Oh, yes, that dinner.

(*Yawns.*) I wish I could loaf to-night.

Connie

207

(*Explaining to Hubbard.*) The Turkish Charge d'Affaires—I never can remember his name. But he's great fun—a positive joy. He's giving the dinner to the British Ambassador.

Mrs. Starkweather

(*Starting forward in her chair and listening intently.*) There's Tommy, now.

(*Voices of Margaret Chalmers and of Tommy heard from without. Hers is laughingly protesting, while Tommy's is gleefully insistent.*) (*Margaret and Tommy appear and pause just outside door, holding each other's hands, facing each other, too immersed in each other to be aware of the presence of those inside the room. Margaret and Tommy are in street costume.*)

Tommy

(*Laughing.*)

But mama.

Margaret

(*Herself laughing, but shaking her head.*) No. Tommy First—

Margaret

No; you must run along to Linda, now, mother's boy. And we'll talk about that some other time.

(*Tommy notices for the first time that there are persons in the room. He peeps in around the door and espies Mrs. Starkweather. At the same moment, impulsively, he withdraws his hands and runs in to Mrs. Starkweather.*)

Tommy

(*Who is evidently fond of his grandmother.*) Grandma!

(*They embrace and make much of each other.*)

(*Margaret enters, appropriately greeting the others—a kiss* (maybe) *to Connie, and a slightly cold handshake to Hubbard.*)

208

Margaret

(*To Chalmers.*) Now that you're here, Tom, you mustn't run away.

(*Greets Mrs. Starkweather.*)

Mrs. Starkweather

(*Turning Tommy's face to the light and looking at it anxiously.*) A trifle thin, Margaret.

Margaret

On the contrary, mother——

Mrs. Starkweather

(*To Chalmers.*) Don't you think so, Tom?

Connie

(*Aside to Hubbard.*) Mother continually worries about his health.

Hubbard

A sturdy youngster, I should say.

Tommy

(*To Chalmers.*) I'm an Indian, aren't I, daddy?

Chalmers

(*Nodding his head emphatically.*) And the stoutest-hearted in the tribe.

(*Linda appears in doorway, evidently looking for Tommy, and Chalmers notices her.*) There's Linda looking for you, young stout heart.

Margaret

Take Tommy, Linda. Run along, mother's boy.

Tommy

Come along, grandma. I want to show you something.

(*He catches Mrs. Starkweather by the hand. Protesting, but highly pleased, she allows him to lead her to the door, where he extends his other hand to Linda. Thus, pausing in doorway, leading a woman by either hand, he looks back at Margaret.*) (*Roguishly.*) Remember, mama, we're going to scout in a little while.

Margaret

(*Going to Tommy, and bending down with her arms around him.*) No, Tommy. Mama has to go to that horrid dinner to-night. But to-morrow we'll play.

(*Tommy is cast down and looks as if he might pout.*) Where is my little Indian now?

Hubbard

Be an Indian, Tommy.

Tommy

(*Brightening up.*)

All right, mama. To-morrow.——if you can't find time to-day.

(*Margaret kisses him.*) (*Exit Tommy, Mrs. Starkweather, and Linda, Tommy leading them by a hand in each of theirs.*)

Chalmers

(*Nodding to Hubbard, in low voice to Hubbard and starting to make exit to right.*) That high-ball.

(*Hubbard disengages himself from proximity of Connie, and starts to follow.*)

Connie

(*Reproachfully.*) If you run away, I won't stop for tea.

Margaret

Do stop, Tom. Father will be here in a few minutes.

Connie

A regular family party.

Chalmers

All right. We'll be back. We're just going to have a little talk.

(*Chalmers and Hubbard make exit to right.*) (*Margaret puts her arm impulsively around Connie—a sheerly spontaneous act of affection—kisses her, and at same time evinces preparation to leave.*)

Margaret

I've got to get my things off. Won't you wait here, dear, in case anybody comes? It's nearly time.

(*Starts toward exit to rear, but is stopped by Connie.*) Madge.

(*Margaret immediately pauses and waits expectantly, smiling, while Connie is hesitant.*)

I want to speak to you about something, Madge. You don't mind?

(*Margaret, still smiling, shakes her head.*) Just a warning. Not that anybody could believe for a moment, there is anything wrong, but——

Margaret

(*Dispelling a shadow of irritation that has crossed her face.*)

If it concerns Tom, don't tell me, please. You know he does do ridiculous things at times. But I don't let him worry me any more; so don't worry me about him.

(*Connie remains silent, and Margaret grows curious.*) Well?

Connie

It's not about Tom—

(*Pauses.*) It's about you.

Margaret

Oh.

Connie

I don't know how to begin.

Margaret

By coming right out with it, the worst of it, all at once, first.

Connie

It isn't serious at all, but—well, mother is worrying about it. You know how old-fashioned she is. And when you consider our position—father's and Tom's, I mean—it doesn't seem just right for you to be seeing so much of such an enemy of theirs. He has abused them dreadfully, you know. And there's that dreadful speech he is going to give to-morrow. You haven't seen the afternoon papers. He has made the most terrible charges against everybody—all of us, our friends, everybody.

Margaret

You mean Mr. Knox, of course. But he wouldn't harm anybody, Connie, dear.

Connie

(*Bridling,*) Oh, he wouldn't? He as good as publicly called father a thief.

Margaret

When did that happen? I never heard of it.

Connie

Well, he said that the money magnates had grown so unprincipled, sunk so low, that they would steal a mouse from a blind kitten.

212

Margaret

I don't see what father has to do with that.

Connie

He meant him just the same.

Margaret

You silly goose. He couldn't have meant father. Father? Why, father wouldn't look at anything less than fifty or a hundred millions.

Connie

And you speak to him and make much of him when you meet him places. You talked with him for half an hour at that Dugdale reception. You have him here in your own house—Tom's house—when he's such a bitter enemy of Tom's. (*During the foregoing speech, Anthony Starkweather makes entrance from rear. His face is grave, and he is in a brown study, as if pondering weighty problems. At sight of the two women he pauses and surveys them. They are unaware of his presence.*)

Margaret

You are wrong, Connie. He is nobody's enemy. He is the truest, cleanest, most right-seeking man I have ever seen.

Connie

(*Interrupting.*) He is a trouble-maker, a disturber of the public peace, a shallow-pated demagogue—

Margaret

(*Reprovingly.*)

Now you're quoting somebody—— father, I suppose. To think of him being so abused—poor, dear Ali Baba—

Starkweather

(*Clearing his throat in advertisement of his presence.*) A-hem.

(*Margaret and Connie turn around abruptly and discover him.*)

Margaret

And Connie Father!

(*Both come forward to greet him, Margaret leading.*)

Starkweather

(*Anticipating, showing the deliberate method of the busy man saving time by eliminating the superfluous.*) Fine, thank you. Quite well in every particular. This Ali Baba? Who is Ali Baba?

(*Margaret looks amused reproach at Connie.*)

Connie

Mr. Howard Knox.

Starkweather

And why is he called Ali Baba?

Margaret

That is my nickname for him. In the den of thieves, you know. You remember your Arabian Nights.

Starkweather

(*Severely.*) I have been wanting to speak to you for some time, Margaret, about that man. You know that I have never interfered with your way of life since your marriage, nor with your and Tom's housekeeping arrangements. But this man Knox. I understand that you have even had him here in your house—

Margaret

(*Interrupting.*) He is very liable to be here this afternoon, any time, now.

214

(*Connie displays irritation at Margaret.*)

Starkweather

(*Continuing imperturbably.*) *Your* house—*you*, my daughter, and the wife of Senator Chalmers. As I said, I have not interfered with you since your marriage. But this Knox affair transcends household arrangements. It is of political importance. The man is an enemy to our class, a firebrand. Why do you have him here?

Margaret

Because I like him. Because he is a man I am proud to call "friend." Because I wish there were more men like him, many more men like him, in the world. Because I have ever seen in him nothing but the best and highest. And, besides, it's such good fun to see how one virtuous man can so disconcert you captains of industry and arbiters of destiny. Confess that you are very much disconcerted, father, right now. He will be here in a few minutes, and you will be more disconcerted. Why? Because it is an affair that transcends family arrangements. And it is your affair, not mine.

Starkweather

This man Knox is a dangerous character—one that I am not pleased to see any of my family take up with. He is not a gentleman.

Margaret

He is a self-made man, if that is what you mean, and he certainly hasn't any money.

Connie

(*Interrupting.*) He says that money is theft—at least when it is in the hands of a wealthy person.

Starkweather

He is uncouth—ignorant.

Margaret

I happen to know that he is a graduate of the University of Oregon.

Starkweather

(*Sneeringly.*) A cow college. But that is not what I mean. He is a demagogue, stirring up the wild-beast passions of the people.

Margaret

Surely you would not call his advocacy of that child labor bill and of the conservation of the forest and coal lands stirring up the wild-beast passions of the people?

Starkweather

(*Wearily.*) You don't understand. When I say he is dangerous it is because he threatens all the stabilities, because he threatens us who have made this country and upon whom this country and its prosperity rest.

(*Connie, scenting trouble, walks across stage away from them.*)

Margaret

The captains of industry—the banking magnates and the mergers?

Starkweather

Call it so. Call it what you will. Without us the country falls into the hands of scoundrels like that man Knox and smashes to ruin.

Margaret

(*Reprovingly.*) Not a scoundrel, father.

Starkweather

He is a sentimental dreamer, a hair-brained enthusiast. It is the foolish utterances of men like him that place the bomb and the knife in the hand of the assassin.

Margaret

216

He is at least a good man, even if he does disagree with you on political and industrial problems. And heaven knows that good men are rare enough these days.

Starkweather

I impugn neither his morality nor his motives—only his rationality. Really, Margaret, there is nothing inherently vicious about him. I grant that. And it is precisely that which makes him such a power for evil.

Margaret

When I think of all the misery and pain which he is trying to remedy—I can see in him only a power for good. He is not working for himself but for the many. That is why he has no money. You have heaven alone knows how many millions—you don't; you have worked for yourself.

Starkweather

I, too, work for the many. I give work to the many. I make life possible for the many. I am only too keenly alive to the responsibilities of my stewardship of wealth.

Margaret

But what of the child laborers working at the machines? Is that necessary, O steward of wealth? How my heart has ached for them! How I have longed to do something for them—to change conditions so that it will no longer be necessary for the children to toil, to have the playtime of childhood stolen away from them. Theft—that is what it is, the playtime of the children coined into profits. That is why I like Howard Knox. He calls theft theft. He is trying to do something for those children. What are you trying to do for them?

Starkweather

Sentiment. Sentiment. The question is too vast and complicated, and you cannot understand. No woman can understand. That is why you run to sentiment. That is what is the matter with this Knox—sentiment. You can't run a government of ninety millions of people on sentiment, nor on abstract ideas of justice and right.

Margaret

But if you eliminate justice and right, what remains?

Starkweather

This is a practical world, and it must be managed by practical men—by thinkers, not by near-thinkers whose heads are addled with the half-digested ideas of the French Encyclopedists and Revolutionists of a century and a half ago.

(*Margaret shows signs of impatience—she is not particularly perturbed by this passage-at-arms with her father, and is anxious to get off her street things.*)

Don't forget, my daughter, that your father knows the books as well as any cow college graduate from Oregon. I, too, in my student days, dabbled in theories of universal happiness and righteousness, saw my vision and dreamed my dream. I did not know then the weakness, and frailty, and grossness of the human clay. But I grew out of that and into a man. Some men never grow out of that stage. That is what is the trouble with Knox. He is still a dreamer, and a dangerous one.

(*He pauses a moment, and then his thin lips shut grimly. But he has just about shot his bolt.*)

Margaret

What do you mean?

Starkweather

He has let himself in to give a speech to-morrow, wherein he will be called upon to deliver the proofs of all the lurid charges he has made against the Administration—against us, the stewards of wealth if you please. He will be unable to deliver the proofs, and the nation will laugh. And that will be the political end of Mr. Ali Baba and his dream.

218

Margaret

It is a beautiful dream. Were there more like him the dream would come true. After all, it is the dreamers that build and that never die. Perhaps you will find that he is not so easily to be destroyed. But I can't stay and argue with you, father. I simply must go and get my things off.

(*To Connie.*) You'll have to receive, dear. I'll be right back.

(*Julius Rutland enters. Margaret advances to meet him, shaking his hand.*) You must forgive me for deserting for a moment.

Rutland

(*Greeting the others.*) A family council, I see.

Margaret

(*On way to exit at rear.*) No; a discussion on dreams and dreamers. I leave you to bear my part.

Rutland

(*Bowing.*) With pleasure. The dreamers are the true architects. But—a—what is the dream and who is the dreamer?

Margaret

(*Pausing in the doorway.*) The dream of social justice, of fair play and a square deal to everybody. The dreamer—Mr. Knox.

(*Rutland is so patently irritated, that Margaret lingers in the doorway to enjoy.*)

Rutland

That man! He has insulted and reviled the Church—my calling. He—

Connie

(*Interrupting.*) He said the churchmen stole from God. I remember he once said there had been only one true Christian and that He died on the Cross.

Margaret

He quoted that from Nietzsche.

Starkweather

(*To Rutland, in quiet glee.*) He had you there.

Rutland

(*In composed fury.*) Nietzsche is a blasphemer, sir. Any man who reads Nietzsche or quotes Nietzsche is a blasphemer. It augurs ill for the future of America when such pernicious literature has the vogue it has.

Margaret

(*Interrupting, laughing.*) I leave the quarrel in your hands, sir knight. Remember—the dreamer and the dream. (*Margaret makes exit.*)

Rutland

(*Shaking his head.*) I cannot understand what is coming over the present generation. Take your daughter, for instance. Ten years ago she was an earnest, sincere lieutenant of mine in all our little charities.

Starkweather

Has she given charity up?

Connie

It's settlement work, now, and kindergartens.

Rutland

(*Ominously.*) It's writers like Nietzsche, and men who read him, like Knox, who are responsible.

(*Senator Dowsett and Mrs. Dowsett enter from rear.*)

(*Connie advances to greet them. Rutland knows Mrs. Dowsett, and Connie introduces him to Senator Dowsett.*)

(*In the meantime, not bothering to greet anybody, evincing his own will and way, Starkweather goes across to right front, selects one of several chairs, seats himself, pulls a thin note-book from inside coat pocket, and proceeds to immerse himself in contents of same.*) (*Dowsett and Rutland pair and stroll to left rear and seat themselves, while Connie and Mrs. Dowsett seat themselves at tea-table to left front. Connie rings the bell for Servant.*)

Mrs. Dowsett

(*Glancing significantly at Starkweather, and speaking in a low voice.*) That's your father, isn't it? I have so wanted to meet him.

Connie

(*Softly.*) You know he's peculiar. He is liable to ignore everybody here this afternoon, and get up and go away abruptly, without saying good-bye.

Mrs. Dowsett

(*Sympathetically. *) Yes, I know, a man of such large affairs. He must have so much on his mind. He is a wonderful man—my husband says the greatest in contemporary history—more powerful than a dozen presidents, the King of England, and the Kaiser, all rolled into one.

(*Servant enters with tea urn and accessories, and Connie proceeds to serve tea, all accompanied by appropriate patter—"Two lumps?" "One, please." "Lemon;" etc.*)

(*Rutland and Dowsett come forward to table for their tea, where they remain.*)

(*Connie, glancing apprehensively across at her father and debating a moment, prepares a cup for him and a small plate with crackers, and hands them to Dowsett, who likewise betrays apprehensiveness.*)

Connie

Take it to father, please, senator.

(*Note:—Throughout the rest of this act, Starkweather is like a being apart, a king sitting on his throne. He divides the tea function with Margaret. Men come up to him and speak with him. He sends for men. They come and go at his bidding. The whole attitude, perhaps unconsciously on his part, is that wherever he may be he is master. This attitude is accepted by all the others; forsooth, he is indeed a great man and master. The only one who is not really afraid of him is Margaret; yet she gives in to him in so far as she lets him do as he pleases at her afternoon tea.*) (*Dowsett carries the cup of tea and small plate across stage to Starkweather. Starkweather does not notice him at first.*)

Connie

(*Who has been watching.*) Tea, father, won't you have a cup of tea?

(*Through the following scene between Starkweather and Dowsett, the latter holds cup of tea and crackers, helplessly, at a disadvantage. At the same time Rutland is served with tea and remains at the table, talking with the two women.*)

Starkweather

(*Looking first at Connie, then peering into cup of tea. He grunts refusal, and for the first time looks up into the other man's face. He immediately closes note-book down on finger to keep the place.*) Oh, it's you. Dowsett.

(*Painfully endeavoring to be at ease.*) A pleasure, Mr. Starkweather, an entirely unexpected pleasure to meet you here. I was not aware you frequented frivolous gatherings of this nature.

Starkweather

(*Abruptly and peremptorily.*) Why didn't you come when you were sent for this morning?

Dowsett

I was sick—I was in bed.

Starkweather

222

That is no excuse, sir. When you are sent for you are to come. Understand? That bill was reported back. Why was it reported back? You told Dobleman you would attend to it.

Dowsett

It was a slip up. Such things will happen.

Starkweather

What was the matter with that committee? Have you no influence with the Senate crowd? If not, say so, and I'll get some one who has.

Dowsett

(*Angrily.*) I refuse to be treated in this manner, Mr. Starkweather. I have some self-respect—

(*Starkweather grunts incredulously.*) Some decency—

(*Starkweather grunts.*) A position of prominence in my state. You forget, sir, that in our state organization I occupy no mean place.

Starkweather

(*Cutting him off so sharply that Dowsett drops cup and saucer.*) Don't you show your teeth to me. I can make you or break you. That state organization of yours belongs to me.

(*Dowsett starts—he is learning something new. To hide his feelings, he stoops to pick up cup and saucer.*) Let it alone! I am talking to you.

(*Dowsett straightens up to attention with alacrity.*) (*Connie, who has witnessed, rings for Servant.*) I bought that state organization, and paid for it. You are one of the chattels that came along with the machine. You were made senator to obey my orders. Understand? Do you understand?

Dowsett

(*Beaten.*) I—I understand.

Starkweather

223

That bill is to be killed.

Dowsett

Yes, sir.

Starkweather

Quietly, no headlines about it.

(*Dowsett nods.*) Now you can go.

(*Dowsett proceeds rather limply across to join group at tea-table.*) (*Chalmers and Hubbard enter from right, laughing about something. At sight of Starkweather they immediately become sober.*) (*No hands are shaken. Starkweather barely acknowledges Hubbard's greeting.*)

Starkweather

Tom, I want to see you.

(*Hubbard takes his cue, and proceeds across to tea-table.*)

(*Enter Servant. Connie directs him to remove broken cup and saucer. While this is being done, Starkweather remains silent. He consults note-book, and Chalmers stands, not quite at ease, waiting the other's will. At the same time, patter at tea-table. Hubbard, greeting others and accepting or declining cup of tea.*)

(*Servant makes exit*).

Starkweather

(*Closing finger on book and looking sharply at Chalmers.*) Tom, this affair of yours in New York must come to an end. Understand?

Chalmers

(*Starting.*) Hubbard has been talking.

Starkweather

No, it is not Hubbard. I have the reports from other sources.

224

Chalmers

It is a harmless affair.

Starkweather

I happen to know better. I have the whole record. If you wish, I can give you every detail, every meeting. I know. There is no discussion whatever. I want no more of it.

Chalmers

I never dreamed for a moment that I was—er—indiscreet.

Starkweather

Never forget that every indiscretion of a man in your position is indiscreet. We have a duty, a great and solemn duty to perform. Upon our shoulders rest the destinies of ninety million people. If we fail in our duty, they go down to destruction. Ignorant demagogues are working on the beast-passions of the people. If they have their way, they are lost, the country is lost, civilization is lost. We want no more Dark Ages.

Chalmers

Really, I never thought it was as serious as all that.

Starkweather

(*Shrugging shoulders and lifting eyebrows.*) After all, why should you? You are only a cog in the machine. I, and the several men grouped with me, am the machine. You are a useful cog—too useful to lose—

Chalmers

Lose?—Me?

Starkweather

I have but to raise my hand, any time—do you understand?—any time, and you are lost. You control your state. Very well. But never forget that to-morrow, if I wished, I could buy your whole machine out from under

225

you. I know you cannot change yourself, but, for the sake of the big issues at stake, you must be careful, exceedingly careful. We are compelled to work with weak tools. You are a good liver, a flesh-pot man. You drink too much. Your heart is weak.—Oh, I have the report of your doctor. Nevertheless, don't make a fool of yourself, nor of us. Besides, do not forget that your wife is my daughter. She is a strong woman, a credit to both of us. Be careful that you are not a discredit to her.

Chalmers

All right, I'll be careful. But while we are—er—on this subject, there's something I'd like to speak to you about.

(*A pause, in which Starkweather waits non-committally.*) It's this man Knox, and Madge. He comes to the house. They are as thick as thieves.

Starkweather

Yes?

Chalmers

(*Hastily.*) Oh, not a breath of suspicion or anything of that sort, I assure you. But it doesn't strike me as exactly appropriate that your daughter and my wife should be friendly with this fire-eating anarchist who is always attacking us and all that we represent.

Starkweather

I started to speak with her on that subject, but was interrupted.

(*Puckers brow and thinks.*) You are her husband. Why don't you take her in hand yourself?

(*Enters Mrs. Starkweather from rear, looking about, bowing, then locating Starkweather and proceeding toward him.*)

Chalmers

What can I do? She has a will of her own—the same sort of a will that you have. Besides, I think she knows about my—about some of my—indiscretions.

226

Starkweather

(*Slyly.*)

Harmless indiscretions?

(*Chalmers is about to reply, but observes Mrs. Starkweather approaching.*)

Mrs. Starkweather

(*Speaks in a peevish, complaining voice, and during her harrangue Starkweather immerses himself in notebook.*) Oh, there you are, Anthony. Talking politics, I suppose. Well, as soon as I get a cup of tea we must go. Tommy is not looking as well as I could wish. Margaret loves him, but she does not take the right care of him. I don't know what the world is coming to when mothers do not know how to rear their offspring. There is Margaret, with her slum kindergartens, taking care of everybody else's children but her own. If she only performed her church duties as eagerly! Mr. Rutland is displeased with her. I shall give her a talking to—only, you'd better do it, Anthony. Somehow, I have never counted much with Margaret. She is as set in doing what she pleases as you are. In my time children paid respect to their parents. This is what comes of speed. There is no time for anything. And now I must get my tea and run. Connie has to dress for that dinner.

(*Mrs. Starkweather crosses to table, greets others characteristically and is served with tea by Connie.*)

(*Chalmers waits respectfully on Starkweather.*)

Starkweather

(*Looking up from note-book.*) That will do, Tom.

(*Chalmers is just starting across to join others, when voices are heard outside rear entrance, and Margaret enters with Dolores Ortega, wife of the Peruvian Minister, and Matsu Sakari, Secretary of Japanese Legation—both of whom she has met as they were entering the house.*)

(*Chalmers changes his course, and meets the above advancing group. He knows Dolores Ortega, whom he greets, and is introduced to Sakari.*)

(*Margaret passes on among guests, greeting them, etc. Then she displaces Connie at tea-table and proceeds to dispense tea to the newcomers.*)

(*Groups slowly form and seat themselves about stage as follows: Chalmers and Dolores Ortega; Rutland, Dowsett, Mrs. Starkweather; Connie, Mr. Dowsett, and Hubbard.*)

(*Chalmers carries tea to Dolores Ortega.*)

(*Sakari has been lingering by table, waiting for tea and pattering with Margaret, Chalmers, etc.*)

Margaret

(*Handing cup to Sakari.*) I am very timid in offering you this, for I am sure you must be appalled by our barbarous methods of making tea.

Sakari

(*Bowing.*) It is true, your American tea, and the tea of the English, are quite radically different from the tea in my country. But one learns, you know. I served my apprenticeship to American tea long years ago, when I was at Yale. It was perplexing, I assure you—at first, only at first I really believe that I am beginning to have a—how shall I call it?—a tolerance for tea in your fashion.

Margaret

You are very kind in overlooking our shortcomings.

Sakari

(*Bowing.*) On the contrary, I am unaware, always unaware, of any shortcomings of this marvelous country of yours.

Margaret

(*Laughing.*) You are incorrigibly gracious, Mr. Sakari. (*Knox appears at threshold of rear entrance and pauses irresolutely for a moment*)

Sakari

(*Noticing Knox, and looking about him to select which group he will join.*) If I may be allowed, I shall now retire and consume this—tea.

(*Joins group composed of Connie, Mrs. Dowsett, and Hubbard.*)

(*Knox comes forward to Margaret, betraying a certain awkwardness due to lack of experience in such social functions. He greets Margaret and those in the group nearest her.*)

Knox

(*To Margaret.*) I don't know why I come here. I do not belong. All the ways are strange.

Margaret

(*Lightly, at the same time preparing his tea.*) The same Ali Baba—once again in the den of the forty thieves. But your watch and pocket-book are safe here, really they are.

(*Knox makes a gesture of dissent at her facetiousness.*) Now don't be serious. You should relax sometimes. You live too tensely.

(*Looking at Starkweather.*) There's the arch-anarch over there, the dragon you are trying to slay.

(*Knox looks at Starkweather and is plainly perplexed.*) The man who handles all the life insurance funds, who controls more strings of banks and trust companies than all the Rothschilds a hundred times over—the merger of iron and steel and coal and shipping and all the other things—the man who blocks your child labor bill and all the rest of the remedial legislation you advocate. In short, my father.

Knox

(*Looking intently at Starkweather.*) I should have recognized him from his photographs. But why do you say such things?

Margaret

Because they are true.

(*He remains silent.*) Now, aren't they? (*She laughs.*) Oh, you don't need to answer. You know the truth, the whole bitter truth. This *is* a den of thieves. There is Mr. Hubbard over there, for instance, the trusty journalist lieutenant of the corporations.

Knox

(*With an expression of disgust.*) I know him. It was he that wrote the Standard Oil side of the story, after having abused Standard Oil for years in the pseudo-muck-raking magazines. He made them come up to his price, that was all. He's the star writer on *Cartwright's*, now, since that magazine changed its policy and became subsidizedly reactionary. I know him—a thoroughly dishonest man. Truly am I Ali Baba, and truly I wonder why I am here.

Margaret

You are here, sir, because I like you to come.

Knox

We do have much in common, you and I.

Margaret

The future.

Knox

(*Gravely, looking at her with shining eyes.*) I sometimes fear for more immediate reasons than that.

(*Margaret looks at him in alarm, and at the same time betrays pleasure in what he has said.*) For you.

Margaret

(*Hastily.*) Don't look at me that way. Your eyes are flashing. Some one might see and misunderstand.

Knox

(*In confusion, awkwardly.*) I was unaware that I—that I was looking at you——in any way that——

230

Margaret

I'll tell you why you are here. Because I sent for you.

Knox

(*With signs of ardor.*) I would come whenever you sent for me, and go wherever you might send me.

Margaret

(*Reprovingly.*)

Please, please——— It was about that speech. I have been hearing about it from everybody—rumblings and mutterings and dire prophecies. I know how busy you are, and I ought not to have asked you to come. But there was no other way, and I was so anxious.

Knox

(*Pleased.*) It seems so strange that you, being what you are, affiliated as you are, should be interested in the welfare of the common people.

Margaret

(*Judicially.*) I do seem like a traitor in my own camp. But as father said a while ago, I, too, have dreamed my dream. I did it as a girl—Plato's *Republic*, Moore's *Utopia*—I was steeped in all the dreams of the social dreamers.

(*During all that follows of her speech, Knox is keenly interested, his eyes glisten and he hangs on her words.*)

And I dreamed that I, too, might do something to bring on the era of universal justice and fair play. In my heart I dedicated myself to the cause of humanity. I made Lincoln my hero-he still is. But I was only a girl, and where was I to find this cause?—how to work for it? I was shut in by a thousand restrictions, hedged in by a thousand conventions. Everybody laughed at me when I expressed the thoughts that burned in me. What could I do? I was only a woman. I had neither vote nor right of utterance. I must remain silent.

231

I must do nothing. Men, in their lordly wisdom, did all. They voted, orated, governed. The place for women was in the home, taking care of some lordly man who did all these lordly things.

Knox

You understand, then, why I am for equal suffrage.

Margaret

But I learned—or thought I learned. Power, I discovered early. My father had power. He was a magnate—I believe that is the correct phrase. Power was what I needed. But how? I was a woman. Again I dreamed my dream—a modified dream. Only by marriage could I win to power. And there you have the clew to me and what I am and have become. I met the man who was to become my husband. He was clean and strong and an athlete, an outdoor man, a wealthy man and a rising politician. Father told me that if I married him he would make him the power of his state, make him governor, send him to the United States Senate. And there you have it all.

Knox

Yes?—— Yes?

Margaret

I married. I found that there were greater forces at work than I had ever dreamed of. They took my husband away from me and molded him into the political lieutenant of my father. And I was without power. I could do nothing for the cause. I was beaten. Then it was that I got a new vision. The future belonged to the children. There I could play my woman's part. I was a mother. Very well. I could do no better than to bring into the world a healthy son and bring him up to manhood healthy and wholesome, clean, noble, and alive. Did I do my part well, through him the results would be achieved. Through him would the work of the world be done in making the world healthier and happier for all the human creatures in it. I played the mother's part. That is why I left the pitiful little charities of the church and devoted myself to settlement work and tenement house reform, established my kindergartens, and worked for the little men and women who come so blindly and to whom the future belongs to make or mar.

Knox

You are magnificent. I know, now, why I come when you bid me come.

Margaret

And then you came. You were magnificent. You were my knight of the windmills, tilting against all power and privilege, striving to wrest the future from the future and realize it here in the present, now. I was sure you would be destroyed. Yet you are still here and fighting valiantly. And that speech of yours to-morrow—

Chalmers

(*Who has approached, bearing Dolores Ortega's cup.*) Yes, that speech. How do you do, Mr. Knox.

(*They shake hands.*) A cup of tea, Madge. For Mrs. Ortega. Two lumps, please.

(*Margaret prepares the cup of tea.*) Everybody is excited over that speech. You are going to give us particular fits, to-morrow, I understand.

Knox

(*Smiling.*) Really, no more than is deserved.

Chalmers

The truth, the whole truth, and nothing but the truth?

Knox

Precisely.

(*Receiving back cup of tea from Margaret.*)

Chalmers

Believe me, we are not so black as we're painted. There are two sides to this question. Like you, we do our best to do what is right. And we hope, we still hope, to win you over to our side.

(*Knox shakes his head with a quiet smile.*)

Margaret

Oh, Tom, be truthful. You don't hope anything of the sort. You know you are hoping to destroy him.

Chalmers

(*Smiling grimly.*) That is what usually happens to those who are not won over.

(*Preparing to depart with cup of tea; speaking to Knox.*) You might accomplish much good, were you with us. Against us you accomplish nothing, absolutely nothing.

(*Returns to Dolores Ortega.*)

Margaret

(*Hurriedly.*) You see. That is why I was anxious—why I sent for you. Even Tom admits that they who are not won over are destroyed. This speech is a crucial event. You know how rigidly they rule the House and gag men like you. It is they, and they alone, who have given you opportunity for this speech? Why?—Why?

Knox

(*Smiling confidently.*) I know their little scheme. They have heard my charges. They think I am going to make a firebrand speech, and they are ready to catch me without the proofs. They are ready in every way for me. They are going to laugh me down. The Associated Press, the Washington correspondents—all are ready to manufacture, in every newspaper in the land, the great laugh that will destroy me. But I am fully prepared, I have—

Margaret

234

The proofs?

Knox

Yes.

Margaret

Now?

Knox

They will be delivered to me to-night—original documents, photographs of documents, affidavits—

Margaret

Tell me nothing. But oh, do be careful! Be careful!

Mrs. Dowsett

(*Appealing to Margaret.*) Do give me some assistance, Mrs. Chalmers.

(*Indicating Sakari.*) Mr. Sakari is trying to make me ridiculous.

Margaret

Impossible.

Mrs. Dowsett

But he is. He has had the effrontery—

Chalmers

(*Mimicking Mrs. Dowsett.*) Effrontery!—O, Sakari!

Sakari

The dear lady is pleased to be facetious.

Mrs. Dowsett

He has had the effrontery to ask me to explain the cause of high prices. Mr. Dowsett says the reason is that the people are living so high.

235

Sakari

Such a marvelous country. They are poor because they have so much to spend.

Chalmers

Are not high prices due to the increased output of gold?

Mrs. Dowsett

Mr. Sakari suggested that himself, and when I agreed with him he proceeded to demolish it. He has treated me dreadfully.

Rutland

(*Clearing his throat and expressing himself with ponderous unction.*) You will find the solution in the drink traffic. It is liquor, alcohol, that is undermining our industry, our institutions, our faith in God—everything. Yearly the working people drink greater quantities of alcohol. Naturally, through resulting inefficiency, the cost of production is higher, and therefore prices are higher.

Dowsett

Partly so, partly so. And in line with it, and in addition to it, prices are high because the working class is no longer thrifty. If our working class saved as the French peasant does, we would sell more in the world market and have better times.

Sakari

(*Bowing.*) As I understand it then, the more thrifty you are the more you save, and the more you save the more you have to sell, the more you sell, the better the times?

Dowsett

Exactly so. Exactly.

Sakari

The less you sell, the harder are the times?

Dowsett

Just so.

Sakari

Then if the people are thrifty, and buy less, times will be harder?

Dowsett

(*Perplexed.*) Er—it would seem so.

Sakari

Then it would seem that the present bad times are due to the fact that the people are thrifty, rather than not thrifty?

(*Dowsett is nonplussed, and Mrs. Dowsett throws up her hands in despair.*)

Mrs. Dowsett

(*Turning to Knox.*) Perhaps you can explain to us, Mr. Knox, the reason for this terrible condition of affairs.

(*Starkweather closes note-book on finger and listens.*) (*Knox smiles, but does not speak.*)

Dolores Ortega

Please do, Mr. Knox. I am so dreadfully anxious to know why living is so high now. Only this morning I understand meat went up again.

(*Knox hesitates and looks questioningly at Margaret.*)

Hubbard

I am sure Mr. Knox can shed new light on this perplexing problem.

Chalmers

Surely you, the whirlwind of oratorical swords in the House, are not timid here—among friends.

Knox

(*Sparring.*) I had no idea that questions of such nature were topics of conversation at affairs like this.

Starkweather

(*Abruptly and imperatively.*) What causes the high prices?

Knox

(*Equally abrupt and just as positive as the other was imperative.*) Theft!

(*It is a sort of a bombshell he has exploded, but they receive it politely and smilingly, even though it has shaken them up.*)

Dolores Ortega

What a romantic explanation. I suppose everybody who has anything has stolen it.

Knox

Not quite, but almost quite. Take motorcars, for example. This year five hundred million dollars has been spent for motor-cars. It required men toiling in the mines and foundries, women sewing their eyes out in sweat-shops, shop girls slaving for four and five dollars a week, little children working in the factories and cotton-mills—all these it required to produce those five hundred millions spent this year in motor-cars. And all this has been stolen from those who did the work.

Mrs. Starkweather

I always knew those motor-cars were to blame for terrible things.

Dolores Ortega

But Mr. Knox, I have a motor-car.

Knox

Somebody's labor made that car. Was it yours?

Dolores Ortega

Mercy, no! I bought it—— and paid for it.

Knox

Then did you labor at producing something else, and exchange the fruits of that labor for the motor-car?

(*A pause.*)

You do not answer. Then I am to understand that you have a motor-car which was made by somebody else's labor and for which you gave no labor of your own. This I call theft. You call it property. Yet it is theft.

Starkweather

(*Interrupting Dolores Ortega who was just about to speak.*)

But surely you have intelligence to see the question in larger ways than stolen motor-cars. I am a man of affairs. I don't steal motor-cars.

Knox

(*Smiling.*) Not concrete little motor-cars, no. You do things on a large scale.

Starkweather

Steal?

Knox

(*Shrugging his shoulders.*) If you will have it so.

Starkweather

I am like a certain gentleman from Missouri. You've got to show me.

Knox

And I'm like the man from Texas. It's got to be put in my hand.

Starkweather

I shift my residence at once to Texas. Put it in my hand that I steal on a large scale.

Knox

Very well. You are the great financier, merger, and magnate. Do you mind a few statistics?

Starkweather

Go ahead.

Knox

You exercise a controlling interest in nine billion dollars' worth of railways; in two billion dollars' worth of industrial concerns; in one billion dollars' worth of life insurance groups; in one billion dollars' worth of banking groups; in two billion dollars' worth of trust companies. Mind you, I do not say you own all this, but that you exercise a controlling interest. That is all that is necessary. In short, you exercise a controlling interest in such a proportion of the total investments of the United States, as to set the pace for all the rest. Now to my point. In the last few years seventy billions of dollars have been artificially added to the capitalization of the nation's industries. By that I mean water—pure, unadulterated water. You, the merger, know what water means. I say seventy billions. It doesn't matter if we call it forty billions or eighty billions; the amount, whatever it is, is a huge one. And what does seventy billions of water mean? It means, at five per cent, that three billions and a half must be paid for things this year, and every year, more than things are really worth. The people who labor have to pay this. There is theft for you. There is high prices for you. Who put in the water? Who gets the theft of the water? Have I put it in your hand?

Starkweather

Are there no wages for stewardship?

Knox

Call it any name you please.

240

Starkweather

Do I not make two dollars where one was before? Do I not make for more happiness than was before I came?

Knox

Is that any more than the duty any man owes to his fellowman?

Starkweather

Oh, you unpractical dreamer. (*Returns to his note-book.*)

Rutland

(*Throwing himself into the breach.*) Where do I steal, Mr. Knox?—I who get a mere salary for preaching the Lord's Word.

Knox

Your salary comes out of that water I mentioned. Do you want to know who pays your salary? Not your parishioners. But the little children toiling in the mills, and all the rest—all the slaves on the wheel of labor pay you your salary.

Rutland

I earn it.

Knox

They pay it.

Mrs. Dowsett

Why, I declare, Mr. Knox, you are worse than Mr. Sakari. You are an anarchist.

(*She simulates shivering with fear.*)

Chalmers

(*To Knox.*) I suppose that's part of your speech to-morrow.

Dolores Ortega

(*Clapping her hands.*) A rehearsal! He's trying it out on us!

Sakari

How would you remedy this—er—this theft?

(*Starkweather again closes note-book on finger and listens as Knox begins to speak.*)

Knox

Very simply. By changing the governmental machinery by which this household of ninety millions of people conducts its affairs.

Sakari

I thought—I was taught so at Yale—that your governmental machinery was excellent, most excellent.

Knox

It is antiquated. It is ready for the scrap-heap. Instead of being our servant, it has mastered us. We are its slaves. All the political brood of grafters and hypocrites have run away with it, and with us as well. In short, from the municipalities up, we are dominated by the grafters. It is a reign of theft.

Hubbard

But any government is representative of its people. No people is worthy of a better government than it possesses. Were it worthier, it would possess a better government.

(*Starkweather nods his head approvingly.*)

Knox

That is a lie. And I say to you now that the average morality and desire for right conduct of the people of the United States is far higher than that of the government which misrepresents it. The people are essentially worthy of a better government than that which is at present in the hands

242

of the politicians, for the benefit of the politicians and of the interests the politicians represent. I wonder, Mr. Sakari, if you have ever heard the story of the four aces.

Sakari

I cannot say that I have.

Knox

Do you understand the game of poker?

Sakari

(*Considering.*) Yes, a marvelous game. I have learned it—at Yale. It was very expensive.

Knox

Well, that story reminds me of our grafting politicians. They have no moral compunctions. They look upon theft as right—eminently right. They see nothing wrong in the arrangement that the man who deals the cards should give himself the best in the deck. Never mind what he deals himself, they'll have the deal next and make up for it.

Dolores Ortega

But the story, Mr. Knox. I, too, understand poker.

Knox

It occurred out in Nevada, in a mining camp. A tenderfoot was watching a game of poker, He stood behind the dealer, and he saw the dealer deal himself four aces from the bottom of the deck.

(*From now on, he tells the story in the slow, slightly drawling Western fashion.*) The tenderfoot went around to the player on the opposite side of the table.

"Say," he says, "I just seen the dealer give himself four aces off the bottom."

243

The player looked at him a moment, and said, "What of it?"

"Oh, nothing," said the tenderfoot, "only I thought you might want to know. I tell you I seen the dealer give himself four aces off the bottom."

"Look here, Mister," said the player, "you'd better get out of this. You don't understand the game. It's HIS deal, ain't it?"

Margaret

(*Arising while they are laughing.*) We've talked politics long enough. Dolores, I want you to tell me about your new car.

Knox

(*As if suddenly recollecting himself.*) And I must be going.

(*In a low voice to Margaret.*) Do I have to shake hands with all these people?

Margaret

(*Shaking her head, speaking low.*) Dear delightful Ali Baba.

Knox

(*Glumly.*) I suppose I've made a fool of myself.

Margaret

(*Earnestly.*) On the contrary, you were delightful. I am proud of you.

(*As Knox shakes hands with Margaret, Sakari arises and comes forward*).

Sakari

I, too, must go. I have had a charming half hour, Mrs. Chalmers. But I shall not attempt to thank you.

(*He shakes hands with Margaret.*)

(*Knox and Sakari proceed to make exit to rear.*)

(*Just as they go out, Servant enters, carrying card-tray, and advances toward Starkweather.*)

(*Margaret joins Dolores Ortega and Chalmers, seats herself with them, and proceeds to talk motor-cars.*)

(*Servant has reached Starkweather, who has taken a telegram from tray, opened it, and is reading it.*)

Starkweather

Damnation!

Servant

I beg your pardon, sir.

Starkweather

Send Senator Chalmers to me, and Mr. Hubbard.

Servant

Yes, sir.

(*Servant crosses to Chalmers and Hubbard, both of whom immediately arise and cross to Starkweather.*)

(*While this is being done, Margaret reassembles the three broken groups into one, seating herself so that she can watch Starkweather and his group across the stage.*)

(*Servant lingers to receive a command from Margaret.*)

(*Chalmers and Hubbard wait a moment, standing, while Starkweather rereads telegram.*)

Starkweather

(*Standing up.*) Dobleman has just forwarded this telegram. It's from New York—from Martinaw. There's been rottenness. My papers and letter-files have been ransacked. It's the confidential stenographer who has been tampered with—you remember that middle-aged, youngish-oldish woman, Tom? That's the one.—Where's that servant?

245

(*Servant is just making exit.*) Here! Come here!

(*Servant comes over to Starkweather.*) Go to the telephone and call up Dobleman. Tell him to come here.

Servant

(*Perplexed.*) I beg pardon, sir.

Starkweather

(*Irritably.*) My secretary. At my house. Dobleman. Tell him to come at once.

(*Servant makes exit.*)

Chalmers

But who can be the principal behind this theft?

(*Starkweather shrugs his shoulders.*)

Hubbard

A blackmailing device most probably. They will attempt to bleed you—

Chalmers

Unless—

Starkweather

(*Impatiently.*) Yes?

Chalmers

Unless they are to be used to-morrow in that speech of Knox.

(*Comprehension dawns on the faces of the other two men.*)

Mrs. Starkweather

(*Who has arisen.*) Anthony, we must go now. Are you ready? Connie has to dress.

246

Starkweather

I am not going now. You and Connie take the car.

Mrs. Starkweather

You mustn't forget you are going to that dinner.

Starkweather

(*Wearily.*) Do I ever forget?

(*Servant enters and proceeds toward Starkweather, where he stands waiting while Mrs. Starkweather finishes the next speech. Starkweather listens to her with a patient, stony face.*)

Mrs. Starkweather

Oh, these everlasting politics! That is what it has been all afternoon— high prices, graft, and theft; theft, graft, and high prices. It is terrible. When I was a girl we did not talk of such things. Well, come on, Connie.

Mrs. Dowsett

(*Rising and glancing at Dowsett.*) And we must be going, too.

(*During the following scene, which takes place around Starkweather, Margaret is saying good-bye to her departing guests.*)

(*Mrs. Starkweather and Connie make exit.*)

(*Dowsett and Mrs. Dowsett make exit.*)

(*The instant Mrs. Dowsett's remark puts a complete end to Mrs. Starkweather's speech, Starkweather, without answer or noticing his wife, turns and interrogates Servant with a glance.*)

Servant

Mr. Dobleman has already left some time to come here, sir.

Starkweather

Show him in as soon as he comes.

Servant

Yes, sir.

(*Servant makes exit.*)

(*Margaret, Dolores Ortega, and Rutland are left in a group together, this time around tea-table, where Margaret serves Rutland another cup of tea. From time to time Margaret glances curiously at the serious group of men across the stage.*)

(*Starkweather is thinking hard with knitted brows. Hubbard is likewise pondering.*)

Chalmers

If I were certain Knox had those papers I would take him by the throat and shake them out of him.

Starkweather

No foolish talk like that, Tom. This is a serious matter.

Hubbard

But Knox has no money. A Starkweather stenographer comes high.

Starkweather

There is more than Knox behind this. (*Enter Dobleman, walking quickly and in a state of controlled excitement.*)

Dobleman

(*To Starkweather.*) You received that telegram, sir?

(*Starkweather nods.*) I got the New York office—Martinaw—right along afterward, by long distance. I thought best to follow and tell you.

Starkweather

What did Martinaw say?

Dobleman

The files seem in perfect order.

Starkweather

Thank God!

(*During the following speech of Dobleman, Rutland says good-bye to Margaret and Dolores Ortega and makes exit.*)

(*Margaret and Dolores Ortega rise a minute afterward and go toward exit, throwing curious glances at the men but not disturbing them.*)

(*Dolores Ortega makes exit.*)

(*Margaret pauses in doorway a moment, giving a final anxious glance at the men, and makes exit.*)

Dobleman

But they are not. The stenographer, Miss Standish, has confessed. For a long time she has followed the practice of taking two or three letters and documents at a time away from the office. Many have been photographed and returned. But the more important ones were retained and clever copies returned. Martinaw says that Miss Standish herself does not know and cannot tell which of the ones she returned are genuine and which are copies.

Hubbard

Knox never did this.

Starkweather

Did Martinaw say whom Miss Standish was acting for?

Dobleman

Gherst.

(*The alarm on the three men's faces is patent.*)

249

Starkweather

Gherst!

(*Pauses to think.*)

Hubbard

Then it is not so grave after all. A yellow journal sensation is the best Gherst can make of it. And, documents or not, the very medium by which it is made public discredits it.

Starkweather

Trust Gherst for more ability than that. He will certainly exploit them in his newspapers, but not until after Knox has used them in his speech. Oh, the cunning dog! Never could he have chosen a better mode and moment to strike at me, at the Administration, at everything. That is Gherst all over. Playing to the gallery. Inducing Knox to make this spectacular exposure on the floor of the House just at the critical time when so many important bills are pending.

(*To Dobleman.*)

Did Martinaw give you any idea of the nature of the stolen documents?

Dobleman

(*Referring to notes he has brought.*) Of course I don't know anything about it, but he spoke of the Goodyear letters—

(*Starkweather betrays by his face the gravity of the information.*)

the Caledonian letters, all the Black Rider correspondence. He mentioned, too, (*Referring to notes.*) the Astonbury and Glutz letters. And there were others, many others, not designated.

Starkweather

This is terrible!

(*Recollecting himself.*)

Thank you, Dobleman. Will you please return to the house at once. Get New York again, and fullest details. I'll follow you shortly. Have you a machine?

Dobleman

A taxi, sir.

Starkweather

All right, and be careful.

(*Dobleman makes exit*)

Chalmers

I don't know the import of all these letters, but I can guess, and it does seem serious.

Starkweather

(*Furiously.*) Serious! Let me tell you that there has been no exposure like this in the history of the country. It means hundreds of millions of dollars. It means more—the loss of power. And still more, it means the mob, the great mass of the child-minded people rising up and destroying all that I have labored to do for them. Oh, the fools! The fools!

Hubbard

(*Shaking his head ominously.*) There is no telling what may happen if Knox makes that speech and delivers the proofs.

Chalmers

It is unfortunate. The people are restless and excited as it is. They are being constantly prodded on by the mouthings of the radical press, of the muck-raking magazines and of the demagogues. The people are like powder awaiting the spark.

Starkweather

This man Knox is no fool, if he *is* a dreamer. He is a shrewd knave. He is a fighter. He comes from the West—the old pioneer stock. His father drove an ox-team across the Plains to Oregon. He knows how to play his cards, and never could circumstances have placed more advantageous cards in his hands.

Chalmers

And nothing like this has ever touched you before.

Starkweather

I have always stood above the muck and ruck—clear and clean and unassailable. But this—this is too much! It is the spark. There is no forecasting what it may develop into.

Chalmers

A political turnover.

Starkweather

(*Nodding savagely.*) A new party, a party of demagogues, in power. Government ownership of the railways and telegraphs. A graduated income tax that will mean no less than the confiscation of private capital.

Chalmers

And all that mass of radical legislation—the Child Labor Bill, the new Employers' Liability Act, the government control of the Alaskan coal fields, that interference with Mexico. And that big power corporation you have worked so hard to form.

Starkweather

It must not be. It is an unthinkable calamity. It means that the very process of capitalistic development is hindered, stopped. It means a setback of ten years in the process. It means work, endless work, to overcome the setback. It means not alone the passage of all this radical legislation with the consequent disadvantages, but it means the fingers of the mob clutching at

252

our grip of control. It means anarchy. It means ruin and misery for all the blind fools and led-cattle of the mass who will strike at the very sources of their own existence and comfort.

(*Tommy enters from left, evidently playing a game, in the course of which he is running away. By his actions he shows that he is pursued. He intends to cross stage, but is stopped by sight of the men. Unobserved by them, he retraces his steps and crawls under the tea-table.*)

Chalmers

Without doubt, Knox is in possession of the letters right now.

Starkweather

There is but one thing to do, and that is—get them back.

(*He looks questioningly at the two men.*)

(*Margaret enters from left, in flushed and happy pursuit of Tommy—for it is a game she is playing with him. She startles at sight of the three men, whom she first sees as she gains the side of the tea-table, where she pauses abruptly, resting one hand on the table.*)

Hubbard

I'll undertake it.

Starkweather

There is little time to waste. In twenty hours from now he will be on the floor making his speech. Try mild measures first. Offer him inducements—any inducement. I empower you to act for me. You will find he has a price.

Hubbard

And if not?

Starkweather

Then you must get them at any cost.

Hubbard

(*Tentatively.*) You mean—?

Starkweather

I mean just that. But no matter what happens, I must never be brought in. Do you understand?

Hubbard

Thoroughly.

Margaret

(*Acting her part, and speaking with assumed gayety.*) What are you three conspiring about? (*All three men are startled.*)

Chalmers

We are arranging to boost prices a little higher.

Hubbard

And so be able to accumulate more motorcars.

Starkweather

(*Taking no notice of Margaret and starting toward exit to rear.*) I must be going. Hubbard, you have your work cut out for you. Tom, I want you to come with me.

Chalmers

(*As the three men move toward exit.*) Home?

Starkweather

Yes, we have much to do.

Chalmers

Then I'll dress first and follow you.

(*Turning to Margaret.*) Pick me up on the way to that dinner.

(*Margaret nods. Starkweather makes exit without speaking. Hub-bard says good-bye to Margaret and makes exit, followed by Chalmers.*)

(*Margaret remains standing, one hand resting on table, the other hand to her breast. She is thinking, establishing in her mind the connection between Knox and what she has overheard, and in process of reaching the conclusion that Knox is in danger.*)

(*Tommy, having vainly waited to be discovered, crawls out dispiritedly, and takes Margaret by the hand. She scarcely notices him.*)

Tommy

(*Dolefully.*) Don't you want to play any more? (*Margaret does not reply*). I was a good Indian.

Margaret

(*Suddenly becoming aware of herself and breaking down. She stoops and clasps Tommy in her arms, crying out, in anxiety and fear, and from love of her boy.*) Oh, Tommy! Tommy!

Curtain

ACT II. Rooms of Howard Knox at Hotel Waltham

Scene. Sitting room of Howard Knox—dimly lighted. Time, eight o'clock in the evening.

Entrance from hallway at side to right. At right rear is locked door leading to a room which dees not belong to Knox's suite. At rear center is fireplace. At left rear door leading to Knox's bedroom. At left are windows facing on street. Near these windows is a large library table littered with books, magazines, government reports, etc. To the right of center, midway forward, is a Hat-top desk. On it is a desk telephone. Behind it, so that one sitting in it faces audience, is revolving desk-chair. Also, on desk, are letters in their envelopes, etc. Against clear wall-spaces are bookcases and filing cabinets. Of special note is bookcase, containing large books, and not more than five feet high, which is against wall between fireplace and door to bedroom.

Curtain discloses empty stage.

(After a slight interval, door at right rear is shaken and agitated. After slight further interval, door is opened inward upon stage. A Man's head appears, cautiously looking around).

(Man enters, turns up lights, is followed by second Man. Both are clad decently, in knock-about business suits and starched collars, cuffs, etc. They are trim, deft, determined men).

(Following upon them, enters Hubbard. He looks about room, crosses to desk, picks up a letter, and reads address).

Hubbard

This is Knox's room all right

First Man

Trust us for that.

Second Man

We were lucky the guy with the whiskers moved out of that other room only this afternoon.

First Man

His key hadn't come down yet when I engaged it.

Hubbard

Well, get to work. That must be his bedroom.

(*He goes to door of bedroom, opens, and peers in, turns on electric lights of bedroom, turns them out, then turns back to men.*) You know what it is—a bunch of documents and letters. If we find it there is a clean five hundred each for you, in addition to your regular pay.

(*While the conversation goes on, all three engage in a careful search of desk, drawers, filing cabinets, bookcases, etc.*)

Second Man

Old Starkweather must want them bad.

Hubbard

Sh-h. Don't even breathe his name.

Second Man

His nibs is damned exclusive, ain't he?

First Man

I've never got a direct instruction from him, and I've worked for him longer than you.

Second Man

Yes, and you worked for him for over two years before you knew who was hiring you.

Hubbard

(*To First Man.*) You'd better go out in the hall and keep a watch for Knox. He may come in any time.

(*First Man produces skeleton keys and goes to door at right. The first key opens it. Leaving door slightly ajar, he makes exit.*)

(*Desk telephone rings and startles Hubbard.*)

Second Man

(*Grinning at Hubbard's alarm.*)

It's only the phone.

Hubbard

(*Proceeding with search.*) I suppose you've done lots of work for Stark—

Second Man

(*Mimicking him.*) Sh-h. Don't breathe his name.

(*Telephone rings again and again, insistently, urgently.*)

Hubbard

(*Disguising his voice.*) Hello—Yes.

(*Shows surprise, seems to recognize the voice, and smiles knowingly.*)

No, this is not Knox. Some mistake. Wrong number—

(*Hanging up receiver and speaking to Second Man in natural voice.*) She did hang up quick.

Second Man

You seemed to recognize her.

Hubbard

No, I only thought I did.

258

(*A pause, while they search.*)

Second Man

I've never spoken a word to his nibs in my life. And I've drawn his pay for years too.

Hubbard

What of it?

Second Man

(*Complainingly.*) He don't know I exist.

Hubbard

(*Pulling open a desk drawer and examining contents.*)

The pay's all right, isn't it?

Second Man

It sure is, but I guess I earn every cent of it. (*First Man enters through door at right He moves hurriedly but cautiously. Shuts door behind him, but neglects to re-lock it.*)

First Man

Somebody just left the elevator and is coming down the hall.

(*Hubbard, First Man, and Second Man, all start for door at right rear.*)

(*First Man pauses and looks around to see if room is in order. Sees desk-drawer which Hubbard has neglected to close, goes back and closes it.*)

(*Hubbard and Second Man make exit.*)

(*First Man turns lights low and makes exit.*)

(*Sound of locking door is heard.*)

(*A pause.*)

(*A knocking at door to right. A pause. Then door opens and Gilford enters. He turns up lights, strolls about room, looks at watch, and sits down in chair near right of fireplace.*) (*Sound of key in lock of door to right.*) (*Door opens, and Knox enters, key in hand. Sees Gifford.*)

Knox

(*Advancing to meet him at fireplace and shaking hands.*) How did you get in?

Gifford

I let myself in. The door was unlocked.

Knox

I must have forgotten it.

Gifford

(*Drawing bundle of documents from inside breast pocket and handing them to Knox.*) Well, there they are.

Knox

(*Fingering them curiously.*) You are sure they are originals? (*Gifford nods.*)

I can't take any chances, you know. If Gherst changed his mind after I gave my speech and refused to show the originals—such things have happened.

Gifford

That's what I told him. He was firm on giving duplicates, and for awhile it looked as if my trip to New York was wasted. But I stuck to my guns. It was originals or nothing with you, I said, and he finally gave in.

Knox

(*Holding up documents.*) I can't tell you what they mean to me, nor how grateful—

260

Gifford

(*Interrupting.*) That's all right. Don't mention it. Gherst is wild for the chance. It will do organized labor a heap of good. And you are able to say your own say at the same time. How's that compensation act coming on?

Knox

(*Wearily.*) The same old story. It will never come before the House. It is dying in committee. What can you expect of the Committee of Judiciary?— composed as it is of ex-railroad judges and ex-railroad lawyers.

Gifford

The railroad brotherhoods are keen on getting that bill through.

Knox

Well, they won't, and they never will until they learn to vote right. When will your labor leaders quit the strike and boycott and lead your men to political action?

Gifford

(*Holding out hand.*) Well, so long. I've got to trot, and I haven't time to tell you why I think political action would destroy the trade union movement.

(*Knox tosses documents on top of low bookcase between fireplace and bedroom door, and starts to shake hands.*) You're damn careless with those papers. You wouldn't be if you knew how much Gherst paid for them.

Gifford

You don't appreciate that other crowd. It stops at nothing.

Knox

I won't take my eyes off of them. And I'll take them to bed with me to-night for safety. Besides, there is no danger. Nobody but you knows I have them.

Gifford

(*Proceeding toward door to right.*) I'd hate to be in Starkweather's office when he discovers what's happened. There'll be some bad half hours for somebody. (*Pausing at door.*) Give them hell to-morrow, good and plenty. I'm going to be in a gallery. So long. (*Makes exit.*)

(*Knox crosses to windows, which he opens, returns to desk, seats himself in revolving chair, and begins opening his correspondence.*) (*A knock at door to right.*)

Knox

Come in.

(*Hubbard enters, advances to desk, but does not shake hands. They greet each other, and Hubbard sits down in chair to left of desk.*) (*Knox, still holding an open letter, re-volves chair so as to face his visitor. He waits for Hubbabd to speak.*)

Hubbard

There is no use beating about the bush with a man like you. I know that. You are direct, and so am I. You know my position well enough to be assured that I am empowered to treat with you.

Knox

Oh, yes; I know.

Hubbard

What we want is to have you friendly.

Knox

That is easy enough. When the Interests become upright and honest—

Hubbard

Save that for your speech. We are talking privately. We can make it well worth your while—

262

Knox

(*Angrily.*) If you think you can bribe me—

Hubbard

(*Suavely.*) Not at all. Not the slightest suspicion of it. The point is this. You are a congressman. A congressman's career depends on his membership in good committees. At the present you are buried in the dead Committee on Coinage, Weights, and Measures. If you say the word you can be appointed to the livest committee—

Knox

(*Interrupting.*) You have these appointments to give?

Hubbard

Surely. Else why should I be here? It can be managed.

Knox

(*Meditatively.*) I thought our government was rotten enough, but I never dreamed that House appointments were hawked around by the Interests in this fashion.

Hubbard

You have not given your answer.

Knox

You should have known my answer in advance.

Hubbard

There is an alternative. You are interested in social problems. You are a student of sociology. Those whom I represent are genuinely interested in you. We are prepared, so that you may pursue your researches more deeply—we are prepared to send you to Europe. There, in that vast sociological laboratory, far from the jangling strife of politics, you will have every opportunity to study. We are prepared to send you for a period of ten years. You will receive ten thousand dollars a year, and, in addition, the day your steamer leaves New York, you will receive a lump sum of one hundred thousand dollars.

Knox

And this is the way men are bought

Hubbard

It is purely an educational matter.

Knox

Now it is you who are beating about the bush.

Hubbard

(*Decisively.*) Very well then. What price do you set on yourself?

Knox

You want me to quit—to leave politics, everything? You want to buy my soul?

Hubbard

More than that. We want to buy those documents and letters.

Knox

(*Showing a slight start.*) What documents and letters?

Hubbard

You are beating around the bush in turn. There is no need for an honest man to lie even—

Knox

(*Interrupting.*) To you.

Hubbard

(*Smiling.*) Even to me. I watched you closely when I mentioned the letters. You gave yourself away. You knew I meant the letters stolen by Gherst from Starkweather's private files—the letters you intended using to-morrow.

Knox

Intend using to-morrow.

Hubbard

Precisely. It is the same thing. What is the price? Set it.

Knox

I have nothing to sell. I am not on the market.

Hubbard

One moment. Don't make up your mind hastily. You don't know with whom you have to deal. Those letters will not appear in your speech to-morrow. Take that from me. It would be far wiser to sell for a fortune than to get nothing for them and at the same time not use them.

(*A knock at door to right startles Hubbard.*)

Knox

(*Intending to say, "Come in"*) Come—

Hubbard

(*Interrupting.*) Hush. Don't. I cannot be seen here.

Knox

(*Laughing.*) You fear the contamination of my company. (*The knock is repeated.*)

Hubbard

(*In alarm, rising, as Knox purses his lips to bid them enter.*) Don't let anybody in. I don't want to be seen here—with you. Besides, my presence will not put you in a good light.

Knox

(*Also rising, starting toward door.*) What I do is always open to the world. I see no one whom I should not permit the world to know I saw.

(*Knox starts toward door to open it.*) (*Hubbabd, looking about him in alarm, flees across stage and into bedroom, closing the door. During all the following scene, Hubbard, from time to time, opens door, and peers out at what is going on.*)

Knox

(*Opening door, and recoiling.*) Margaret! Mrs. Chalmers!

(*Margaret enters, followed by Tommy and Linda. Margaret is in evening dress covered by evening cloak.*)

Margaret

(*Shaking hands with Knox.*) Forgive me, but I had to see you. I could not get you on the telephone. I called and called, and the best I could do was to get the wrong number.

Knox

(*Recovering from his astonishment.*) Yes. I am glad.

(*Seeing Tommy.*) Hello, Tommy.

(*Knox holds out his hand, and Tommy shakes it gravely. Linda stays in back-ground. Her face is troubled.*)

Tommy

How do you do?

Margaret

There was no other way, and it was so necessary for me to warn you. I brought Tommy and Linda along to chaperon me.

(*She looks curiously around room, specially indicating filing cabinets and the stacks of government reports on table.*) Your laboratory.

Knox

Ah, if I were only as great a sociological wizard as Edison is a wizard in physical sciences.

Margaret

But you are. You labor more mightily than you admit—or dare to think. Oh, I know you—better than you do yourself.

Tommy

Do you read all those books?

Knox

Yes, I am still going to school and studying hard. What are you going to study to be when you grow up?

(*Tommy meditates but does not answer.*)

President of these great United States?

Tommy

(*Shaking his head.*) Father says the President doesn't amount to much.

Knox

Not a Lincoln?

(*Tommy is in doubt.*)

Margaret

But don't you remember what a great good man Lincoln was? You remember I told you?

Tommy

(*Shaking his head slowly.*) But I don't want to be killed.—I'll tell you what!

Knox

What?

Tommy

I want to be a senator like father. He makes them dance.

(*Margaret is shocked, and Knox's eyes twinkle.*)

Knox

Makes whom dance?

Tommy

(*Puzzled.*) I don't know.

(*With added confidence.*) But he makes them dance just the same.

(*Margaret makes a signal to Linda to take Tommy across the room.*)

Linda

(*Starting to cross stage to left.*) Come, Tommy. Let us look out of the window.

Tommy

I'd rather talk with Mr. Knox.

Margaret

Please do, Tommy. Mamma wants to talk to Mr. Knox.

(*Tommy yields, and crosses to right, where he joins Linda in looking out of the window.*)

Margaret

You might ask me to take a seat

Knox

Oh! I beg pardon.

(*He draws up a comfortable chair for her, and seats himself in desk-chair, facing her.*)

268

Margaret

I have only a few minutes. Tom is at father's, and I am to pick him up there and go on to that dinner, after I've taken Tommy home.

Knox

But your maid?

Margaret

Linda? Wild horses could not drag from her anything that she thought would harm me. So intense is her fidelity that it almost shames me. I do not deserve it. But this is not what I came to you about.

(*She speaks the following hurriedly.*) After you left this afternoon, something happened. Father received a telegram. It seemed most important. His secretary followed upon the heels of the telegram. Father called Tom and Mr. Hubbard to him and they held a conference. I think they have discovered the loss of the documents, and that they believe you have them. I did not hear them mention your name, yet I am absolutely certain that they were talking about you. Also, I could tell from father's face that something was terribly wrong. Oh, be careful! Do be careful!

Knox

There is no danger, I assure you.

Margaret

But you do not know them. I tell you-you do not know them. They will stop at nothing—at nothing. Father believes he is right in all that he does.

Knox

I know. That is what makes him so formidable. He has an ethical sanction.

Margaret

(*Nodding.*) It is his religion.

Knox

And, like any religion with a narrow-minded man, it runs to mania.

Margaret

He believes that civilization rests on him, and that it is his sacred duty to preserve civilization.

Knox

I know. I know.

Margaret

But you? But you? You are in danger.

Knox

No; I shall remain in to-night. To-morrow, in the broad light of midday, I shall proceed to the House and give my speech.

Margaret

(*Wildly.*) Oh, if anything should happen to you!

Knox

(*Looking at her searchingly.*) You do care?

(*Margaret nods, with eyes suddenly downcast.*) For Howard Knox, the reformer? Or for me, the man?

Margaret

(*Impulsively.*) Oh, why must a woman forever remain quiet? Why should I not tell you what you already know?—what you must already know? I do care for you—for man and reformer, both—for—

(*She is aflame, but abruptly ceases and glances across at Tommy by the window, warned instinctively that she must not give way to love in her child's presence.*)

270

Linda! Will you take Tommy down to the machine—

Knox

(*Alarmed, interrupting, in low voice.*) What are you doing?

Margaret

(*Hushing Knox with a gesture.*) I'll follow you right down.

(*Linda and Tommy proceed across stage toward the right exit.*)

Tommy

(*Pausing before Knox and gravely extending his hand.*) Good evening, Mr. Knox.

Knox

(*Awkwardly.*) Good evening, Tommy. You take my word for it, and look up this Lincoln question.

Tommy

I shall. I'll ask father about it.

Margaret

(*Significantly.*) You attend to that, Linda. Nobody must know—this.

(*Linda nods.*)

(*Linda and Tommy make exit to right.*)

(*Margaret, seated, slips back her cloak, revealing herself in evening gown, and looks at Knox sumptuously, lovingly, and willingly.*)

Knox

(*Inflamed by the sight of her.*) Don't! Don't! I can't stand it. Such sight of you fills me with madness.

(*Margaret laughs low and triumphantly.*) I don't want to think of you as a woman. I must not. Allow me.

(*He rises and attempts to draw cloak about her shoulders, but she resists him. Yet does he succeed in partly cloaking her.*)

Margaret

I want you to see me as a woman. I want you to think of me as a woman. I want you mad for me.

(*She holds out her arms, the cloak slipping from them.*)

I want—don't you see what I want?——

(*Knox sinks back in chair, attempting to shield his eyes with his hand.*)

(*Slipping cloak fully back from her again.*)

Look at me.

Knox

(*Looking, coming to his feet, and approaching her, with extended arms, murmuring softly.*) Margaret. Margaret.

(*Margaret rises to meet him, and they are clasped in each other's arms.*)

(*Hubbard, peering forth through door, looks at them with an expression of cynical amusement. His gaze wan-ders, and he sees the documents, within arm's reach, on top of bookcase. He picks up documents, holds them to the light of stage to glance at them, and, with triumphant expression on face, disappears and closes door.*)

Knox

(*Holding Margaret from him and looking at her.*) I love you. I do love you. But I had resolved never to speak it, never to let you know.

Margaret

Silly man. I have known long that you loved me. You have told me so often and in so many ways. You could not look at me without telling me.

Knox

272

You saw?

Margaret

How could I help seeing? I was a woman. Only, with your voice you never spoke a word. Sit down, there, where I may look at you, and let me tell you. I shall do the speaking now.

(*She urges him back into the desk-chair, and reseats herself.*) (*She makes as if to pull the cloak around 'her.*) Shall I?

Knox

(*Vehemently.*) No, no! As you are. Let me feast my eyes upon you who are mine. I must be dreaming.

Margaret

(*With a low, satisfied laugh of triumph.*) Oh, you men! As of old, and as forever, you must be wooed through your senses. Did I display the wisdom of an Hypatia, the science of a Madam Curie, yet would you keep your iron control, throttling the voice of your heart with silence. But let me for a moment be Lilith, for a moment lay aside this garment constructed for the purpose of keeping out the chill of night, and on the instant you are fire and aflame, all voluble with love's desire.

Knox

(*Protestingly.*) Margaret! It is not fair!

Margaret

I love you—and—you?

Knox

(*Fervently and reverently.*) I love you.

Margaret

Then listen. I have told you of my girlhood and my dreams. I wanted to do what you are so nobly doing. And I did nothing. I could do nothing.

I was not permitted. Always was I compelled to hold myself in check. It was to do what you are doing, that I married. And that, too, failed me. My husband became a henchman of the Interests, my own father's tool for the perpetuation of the evils against which I desired to fight.

(*She pauses.*) It has been a long fight, and I have been very tired, for always did I confront failure. My husband—I did not love him. I never loved him. I sold myself for the Cause, and the cause profited nothing. (*Pause.*) Often, I have lost faith—faith in everything, in God and man, in the hope of any righteousness ever prevailing. But again and again, by what you are doing, have you awakened me. I came to-night with no thought of self. I came to warn you, to help the good work on. I remained—thank God!—I remained to love you—and to be loved by you. I suddenly found myself, looking at you, very weary. I wanted you—you, more than anything in the world.

(*She holds out her arms.*) Come to me. I want you—now.

(*Knox, in an ecstacy, comes to her. He seats himself on the broad arm of the chair and is drawn into her arms.*)

Knox

But I have been tired at times. I was very tired to-night—and you came. And now I am glad, only glad.

Margaret

I have been wanton to-night. I confess it. I am proud of it. But it was not—professional. It was the first time in my life. Almost do I regret—almost do I regret that I did not do it sooner—it has been crowned with such success. You have held me in your arms—your arms. Oh, you will never know what that first embrace meant to me. I am not a clod. I am not iron nor stone. I am a woman—a warm, breathing woman—.

(*She rises, and draws him to his feet.*)

Kiss me, my dear lord and lover. Kiss me. (*They embrace.*)

Knox

(*Passionately, looking about him wildly as if in search of something.*)
What shall we do?

(*Suddenly releasing her and sinking back in his own chair almost in collapse.*) No. It cannot be. It is impossible. Oh, why could we not have met long ago? We would have worked together. What a comradeship it would have been.

Margaret

But it is not too late.

Knox

I have no right to you.

Margaret

(*Misunderstanding.*) My husband? He has not been my husband for years. He has no rights. Who, but you whom I love, has any rights?

Knox

No; it is not that.

(*Snapping his fingers.*) That for him.

(*Breaking down.*) Oh, if I were only the man, and not the reformer! If I had no work to do!

Margaret

(*Coming to the back of his chair and caressing his hair.*) We can work together.

Knox

(*Shaking his head under her fingers.*) Don't! Don't!

(*She persists, and lays her cheek against his.*) You make it so hard. You tempt me so.

275

(*He rises suddenly, takes her two hands in his, leads her gently to her chair, seats her, and reseats himself in desk-chair.*) Listen. It is not your husband. But I have no right to you. Nor have you a right to me.

Margaret

(*Interrupting, jealously.*) And who but I has any right to you?

Knox

(*Smiling sadly.*) No; it is not that. There is no other woman. You are the one woman for me. But there are many others who have greater rights in me than you. I have been chosen by two hundred thousand citizens to represent them in the Congress of the United States. And there are many more—

(*He breaks off suddenly and looks at her, at her arms and shoulders.*) Yes, please. Cover them up. Help me not to forget.

(*Margaret does not obey.*) There are many more who have rights in me—the people, all the people, whose cause I have made mine. The children—there are two million child laborers in these United States. I cannot betray them. I cannot steal my happiness from them. This afternoon I talked of theft. But would not this, too, be theft?

Margaret

(*Sharply.*) Howard! Wake up! Has our happiness turned your head?

Knox

(*Sadly.*) Almost—and for a few wild moments, quite. There are all the children. Did I ever tell you of the tenement child, who when asked how he knew when spring came, answered: When he saw the saloons put up their swing doors.

Margaret

(*Irritated.*) But what has all that to do with one man and one woman loving?

276

Knox

Suppose we loved—you and I; suppose we loosed all the reins of our love. What would happen? You remember Gorki, the Russian patriot, when he came to New York, aflame with passion for the Russian revolution. His purpose in visiting the land of liberty was to raise funds for that revolution. And because his marriage to the woman he loved was not of the essentially legal sort worshiped by the shopkeepers, and because the newspapers made a sensation of it, his whole mission was brought to failure. He was laughed and derided out of the esteem of the American people. That is what would happen to me. I should be slandered and laughed at. My power would be gone.

Margaret

And even if so—what of it? Be slandered and laughed at. We will have each other. Other men will rise up to lead the people, and leading the people is a thankless task. Life is so short. We must clutch for the morsel of happiness that may be ours.

Knox

Ah, if you knew, as I look into your eyes, how easy it would be to throw everything to the winds. But it would be theft.

Margaret

(*Rebelliously.*) Let it be theft. Life is so short, dear. We are the biggest facts in the world—to each other.

Knox

It is not myself alone, nor all my people. A moment ago you said no one but I had any right to you. You were wrong. Your child—

Margaret

(*In sudden pain, pleadingly.*) Don't!

Knox

I must. I must save myself—and you. Tommy has rights in you. Theft again. What other name for it if you steal your happiness from him?

Margaret

(*Bending her head forward on her hand and weeping.*) I have been so lonely—and then you—you came, and the world grew bright and warm—a few short minutes ago you held me—in your arms—a few short minutes ago and it seemed my dream of happiness had come true—and now you dash it from me—

Knox

(*Struggling to control himself now that she is no longer looking at him.*) No; I ask you to dash it from yourself. I am not too strong. You must help me. You must call your child to your aid in helping me. I could go mad for you now—

(*Rising impulsively and coming to her with arms outstretched to clasp her.*) Right now—

Margaret

(*Abruptly raising her head, and with one outstretched arm preventing the embrace.*) Wait.

(*She bows her head on her hand for a moment, to think and to win control of herself.*)

(*Lifting her head and looking at him.*) Sit down—please.

(*Knox reseats himself.*)

(A pause, during which she looks at him and loves him.) Dear, I do so love you—

(*Knox loses control and starts to rise.*) No! Sit there. I was weak. Yet I am not sorry. You are right. We must forego each other. We cannot be thieves, even for love's sake. Yet I am glad that this has happened—that I have lain in your arms and had your lips on mine. The memory of it will be sweet always.

(*She draws her cloak around her, and rises.*)

(*Knox rises.*) You are right. The future belongs to the children. There lies duty—yours, and mine in my small way. I am going now. We must not see each other ever again. We must work—and forget. But remember, my heart goes with you into the fight. My prayers will accompany every stroke.

(*She hesitates, pauses, draws her cloak thoroughly around her in evidence of departure.*) Dear—will you kiss me—once—one last time? (*There is no passion in this kiss, which is the kiss of renunciation. Margaret herself terminates the embrace.*)

(*Knox accompanies her silently to the door and places hand on knob.*) I wish I had something of you to have with me always—a photograph, that little one, you remember, which I liked so. (*She nods.*) Don't run the risk of sending it by messenger. Just mail it ordinarily.

Margaret

I shall mail it to-morrow. I'll drop it in the box myself.

Knox

(*Kissing her hand.*) Good-bye.

Margaret

(*lingeringly.*) But oh, my dear, I am glad and proud for what has happened. I would not erase a single line of it.

(*She indicates for Knox to open door, which he does, but which he immediately closes as she continues speaking.*) There must be immortality. There must be a future life where you and I shall meet again. Good-bye.

(*They press each other's hands.*)

(*Exit Margaret.*)

(*Knox stands a moment, staring at closed door, turns and looks about him indecisively, sees chair in which Margaret sat, goes over to it, kneels down, and buries his face.*)

(*Door to bedroom opens slowly and Hubbard peers out cautiously. He cannot see Knox.*)

279

Hubbard

(*Advancing, surprised.*) What the deuce? Everybody gone?

Knox

(*Startled to his feet.*) Where the devil did you come from?

Hubbard

(*Indicating bedroom.*) In there. I was in there all the time.

Knox

(*Endeavoring to pass it off.*) Oh, I had forgotten about you. Well, my callers are gone.

Hubbard

(*Walking over close to him and laughing at him with affected amusement.*) Honest men are such dubs when they do go wrong.

Knox

The door was closed all the time. You would not have dared to spy upon me.

Hubbard

There was something familiar about the lady's voice.

Knox

You heard!—what did you hear?

Hubbard

Oh, nothing, nothing—a murmur of voices—and the woman's—I could swear I have heard her voice before.

(*Knox shows his relief.*) Well, so long.

(*Starts to move toward exit to right.*) You won't reconsider your decision?

280

Knox

(*Shaking his head.*)

Hubbard

(*Pausing, open door in hand, and laughing cynically.*) And yet it was but a moment ago that it seemed I heard you say there was no one whom you would not permit the world to know you saw.

(*Starting.*) What do you mean?

Hubbard

Good-bye.

(*Hubbard makes exit and closes door.*) (*Knox wanders aimlessly to his desk, glances at the letter he was reading of which had been interrupted by Hubbard's entry of first act, suddenly recollects the package of documents, and walks to low bookcase and looks on top.*)

Knox

(*Stunned.*) The thief!

(*He looks about him wildly, then rushes like a madman in pursuit of Hubbard, making exit to right and leaving the door Hying open.*) (*Empty stage for a moment.*)

Curtain

ACT III. A Room in the Washington House of Anthony Starkweather

Scene. The library, used as a sort of semi-office by Starkweather at such times when he is in Washington. Door to right; also, door to right rear. At left rear is an alcove, without hangings, which is dark. To left are windows. To left, near windows, a flat-top desk, with desk-chair and desk-telephone. Also, on desk, conspicuously, is a heavy dispatch box. At the center rear is a large screen. Extending across center back of room are heavy, old-fashioned bookcases, with swinging glass doors. The bookcases narrow about four feet from the floor, thus forming a ledge. Between left end of bookcases and alcove at left rear, high up on wall, hangs a large painting or steel engraving of Abraham Lincoln. In design and furnishings, it is a simple chaste room, coldly rigid and slightly old-fashioned.

It is 9:30 in the morning of the day succeeding previous act.

Curtain discloses Starkweather seated at desk, and Dobleman, to right of desk, standing.

Starkweather

All right, though it is an unimportant publication. I'll subscribe.

Dobleman

(*Making note on pad.*) Very well, sir. Two thousand.

(*He consults his notes.*) Then there is *Vanderwater's Magazine*. Your subscription is due.

Starkweather

How much?

Dobleman

You have been paying fifteen thousand.

Starkweather

It is too much. What is the regular subscription?

Dobleman

A dollar a year.

Starkweather

(*Shaking his head emphatically.*) It is too much.

Dobleman

Professor Vanderwater also does good work with his lecturing. He is regularly on the Chautauqua Courses, and at that big meeting of the National Civic Federation, his speech was exceptionally telling.

Starkweather

(*Doubtfully, about to give in.*) All right—

(*He pauses, as if recollecting something.*) (*Dobleman has begun to write down the note.*) No. I remember there was something in the papers about this Professor Vanderwater—a divorce, wasn't it? He has impaired his authority and his usefulness to me.

Dobleman

It was his wife's fault.

Starkweather

It is immaterial. His usefulness is impaired. Cut him down to ten thousand. It will teach him a lesson.

Dobleman

Very good, sir.

Starkweather

And the customary twenty thousand to *Cartwrights*.

Dobleman

(*Hesitatingly.*) They have asked for more. They have enlarged the magazine, reorganized the stock, staff, everything.

Starkweather

Hubbard's writing for it, isn't he?

Dobleman

Yes, sir. And though I don't know, it is whispered that he is one of the heavy stockholders.

Starkweather

A very capable man. He has served me well. How much do they want?

Dobleman

They say that Nettman series of articles cost them twelve thousand alone, and that they believe, in view of the exceptional service they are prepared to render, and are rendering, fifty thousand—

Starkweather

(*Shortly.*) All right. How much have I given to University of Hanover this year?

Dobleman

Seven—nine millions, including that new library.

Starkweather

(*Sighing.*) Education does cost. Anything more this morning?

Dobleman

(*Consulting notes.*) Just one other—Mr. Rutland. His church, you know, sir, and that theological college. He told me he had been talking it over with you. He is anxious to know.

Starkweather

He's very keen, I must say. Fifty thousand for the church, and a hundred thousand for the college—I ask you, candidly, is he worth it?

Dobleman

The church is a very powerful molder of public opinion, and Mr. Rutland is very impressive. (*Running over the notes and producing a clipping.*) This is what he said in his sermon two weeks ago: "God has given to Mr. Starkweather the talent for making money as truly as God has given to other men the genius which manifests itself in literature and the arts and sciences."

Starkweather

(*Pleased.*) He says it well.

Dobleman

(*Producing another clipping.*) And this he said about you in last Sunday's sermon: "We are to-day rejoicing in the great light of the consecration of a great wealth to the advancement of the race. This vast wealth has been so consecrated by a man who all through life has walked in accord with the word, The love of Christ constraineth me.'"

Starkweather

(*Meditatively.*) Dobleman, I have meant well. I mean well. I shall always mean well. I believe I am one of those few men, to whom God, in his infinite wisdom, has given the stewardship of the people's wealth. It is a high trust, and despite the abuse and vilification heaped upon me, I shall remain faithful to it.

(*Changing his tone abruptly to businesslike briskness.*) Very well. See that Mr. Rutland gets what he has asked for.

Dobleman

Very good, sir. I shall telephone him. I know he is anxious to hear.

(*Starting to leave the room.*) Shall I make the checks out in the usual way?

Starkweather

Yes: except the Rutland one. I'll sign that myself. Let the others go through the regular channels. We take the 2:10 train for New York. Are you ready?

Dobleman

(*Indicating dispatch box.*) All, except the dispatch box.

Starkweather

I'll take care of that myself.

(*Dobleman starts to make exit to left, and Starkweather, taking notebook from pocket, glances into it, and looks up.*)

Dobleman.

Dobleman

(*Pausing.*) Yes, sir.

Starkweather

Mrs. Chalmers is here, isn't she?

Dobleman

Yes, sir. She came a few minutes ago, with her little boy. They are with Mrs. Starkweather.

Starkweather

Please tell Mrs. Chalmers I wish to see her.

Dobleman

Yes, sir.

(*Dobleman makes exit.*) (*Maidservant enters from right rear, with card tray.*)

Starkweather

(*Examining card.*) Show him in.

(*Maidservant makes exit right rear*). (*Pause, during which Starkweather consults notebook.*) (Maidservant re-enters, showing in Hubbard.)

(*Hubbard advances to desk.*) (*Starkweather is so glad to see him that he half rises from his chair to shake hands.*)

Starkweather

(*Heartily.*) I can only tell you that what you did was wonderful. Your telephone last night was a great relief. Where are they?

Hubbard

(*Drawing package of documents from inside breast pocket and handing them over.*) There they are—the complete set. I was fortunate.

Starkweather

(*Opening package and glancing at a number of the documents while he talks.*) You are modest, Mr. Hubbard.—It required more—than fortune.— It required ability—of no mean order.—The time was short.—You had to think—and act—with too great immediacy to be merely fortunate.

(*Hubbard bows, while Starkweather rearranges package.*)

There is no need for me to tell you how I appreciate your service. I have increased my subscription to Cartwright's to fifty thousand, and I shall speak to Dobleman, who will remit to you a more substantial acknowledgment than my mere thanks for the inestimable service you have rendered.

(*Hubbard bows.*)

You—ah—you have read the documents?

Hubbard

I glanced through them. They were indeed serious. But we have spiked Knox's guns. Without them, that speech of his this afternoon becomes a farce—a howling farce. Be sure you take good care of them.

(*Indicating documents, which Starkweather still holds.*) Gherst has a long arm.

Starkweather

He cannot reach me here. Besides, I go to New York to-day, and I shall carry them with me. Mr. Hubbard, you will forgive me—

(*Starting to pack dispatch box with papers and letters lying on desk.*) I am very busy.

Hubbard

(*Taking the hint.*) Yes, I understand. I shall be going now. I have to be at the Club in five minutes.

Starkweather

(*In course of packing dispatch box, he sets certain packets of papers and several medium-sized account books to one side in an orderly pile. He talks while he packs, and Hubbard waits.*) I should like to talk with you some more—in New York. Next time you are in town be sure to see me. I am thinking of buying the *Parthenon Magazine,* and of changing its policy. I should like to have you negotiate this, and there are other important things as well. Good day, Mr. Hubbard. I shall see you in New York—soon.

(*Hubbard and Starkweather shake hands.*)

(*Hubbard starts to make exit to right rear.*)

(*Margaret enters from right rear.*)

(*Starkweather goes on packing dispatch box through following scene.*)

Hubbard

Mrs. Chalmers.

(*Holding out hand, which Margaret takes very coldly, scarcely inclining her head, and starting to pass on.*) (*Speaking suddenly and savagely.*) You needn't be so high and lofty, Mrs. Chalmers.

288

Margaret

(*Pausing and looking at him curiously as if to ascertain whether he has been drinking.*) I do not understand.

Hubbard

You always treated me this way, but the time for it is past. I won't stand for your superior goodness any more. You really impressed me with it for a long time, and you made me walk small. But I know better now. A pretty game you've been playing—you, who are like any other woman. Well, you know where you were last night. So do I.

Margaret

You are impudent.

Hubbard

(*Doggedly.*) I said I knew where you were last night. Mr. Knox also knows where you were. But I'll wager your husband doesn't.

Margaret

You spy!

(*Indicating her father.*) I suppose you have told—him.

Hubbard

Why should I?

Margaret

You are his creature.

Hubbard

If it will ease your suspense, let me tell you that I have not told him. But I do protest to you that you must treat me with more—more kindness.

(*Margaret makes no sign but passes on utterly oblivious of him.*) (*Hubbard stares angrily at her and makes exit*) (*Starkweather, who is finishing packing, puts the documents last inside box, and closes and locks it. To one side is the orderly stack of the several account books and packets of papers.)*

Starkweather

Good morning, Margaret. I sent for you because we did not finish that talk last night. Sit down.

(She gets a chair for herself and sits down.)

You always were hard to manage, Margaret. You have had too much will for a woman. Yet I did my best for you. Your marriage with Tom was especially auspicious—a rising man, of good family and a gentleman, eminently suitable—

Margaret

(Interrupting bitterly.) I don't think you were considering your daughter at all in the matter. I know your views on woman and woman's place. I have never counted for anything with you. Neither has mother, nor Connie, when business was uppermost, and business always is uppermost with you. I sometimes wonder if you think a woman has a soul. As for my marriage—you saw that Tom could be useful to you. He had the various distinctive points you have mentioned. Better than that he was pliable, capable of being molded to perform your work, to manipulate machine politics and procure for you the legislation you desired. You did not consider what kind of a husband he would make for your daughter whom you did not know. But you gave your daughter to him—sold her to him—because you needed him—

(Laughs hysterically.) In your business.

Starkweather

(Angrily.) Margaret! You must not speak that way. *(Relaxing.)*

Ah, you do not change. You were always that way, always bent on having your will—

Margaret

290

Would to God I had been more successful in having it.

Starkweather

(*Testily.*) This is all beside the question. I sent for you to tell you that this must stop—this association with a man of the type and character of Knox—a dreamer, a charlatan, a scoundrel—

Margaret

It is not necessary to abuse him.

Starkweather

It must stop—that is all. Do you understand? It must stop.

Margaret

(*Quietly.*) It has stopped. I doubt that I shall ever see him again. He will never come to my house again, at any rate. Are you satisfied?

Starkweather

Perfectly. Of course, you know I have never doubted you—that—that way.

Margaret

(*Quietly.*) How little you know women. In your comprehension we are automatons, puppets, with no hearts nor heats of desire of our own, with no springs of conduct save those of the immaculate and puritanical sort that New England crystallized a century or so ago.

Starkweather

(*Suspiciously.*) You mean that you and this man—?

Margaret

I mean nothing has passed between us. I mean that I am Tom's wife and Tommy's mother. What I did mean, you have no more understood than you understand me—or any woman.

Starkweather

(*Relieved.*) It is well.

Margaret

(*Continuing.*) And it is so easy. The concept is simple. A woman is human. That is all. Yet I do believe it is news to you.

(*Enters Dobleman from right carrying a check in his hand. Starkweather, about to speak, pauses.*) (*Dobleman hesitates, and Starkweather nods for him to advance.*)

Dobleman

(*Greeting Margaret, and addressing Starkweather.*) This check. You said you would sign it yourself.

Starkweather

Yes, that is Rutland's. (*Looks for pen.*)

(*Dobleman offers his fountain pen.*) No; my own pen.

(*Unlocks dispatch box, gets pen, and signs check. Leaves dispatch box open.*) (*Dobleman takes check and makes exit to right.*)

Starkweather

(*Picking up documents from top of pile in open box.*)

This man Knox. I studied him yesterday. A man of great energy and ideals. Unfortunately, he is a sentimentalist. He means right—I grant him that. But he does not understand practical conditions. He is more dangerous to the welfare of the United States than ten thousand anarchists. And he is not practical. (*Holding up documents.*)

Behold, stolen from my private files by a yellow journal sneak thief and turned over to him. He thought to buttress his speech with them this afternoon. And yet, so hopelessly unpractical is he, that you see they are already back in the rightful owner's hands.

292

Margaret

Then his speech is ruined?

Starkweather

Absolutely. The wheels are all ready to turn. The good people of the United States will dismiss him with roars of laughter—a good phrase, that: Hubbard's, I believe.

(*Dropping documents on the open cover of dispatch box, picking up the pile of several account books and packets of papers, and rising.*) One moment. I must put these away.

(*Starkweather goes to alcove at left rear. He presses a button and alcove is lighted by electricity, discovering the face of a large safe. During the following scene he does not look around, being occupied with working the combination, opening the safe, putting away account books and packets of papers, and with examining other packets which are in safe.*)

(*Margaret looks at documents lying on open cover of dispatch box and glancing quickly about room, takes a sudden resolution. She seizes documents, makes as if to run wildly from the room, stops abruptly to reconsider, and changes her mind. She looks about room for a hiding place, and her eyes rest on portrait of Lincoln. Moving swiftly, picking up a light chair on the way, she goes to corner of bookcase nearest to portrait, steps on chair, and from chair to ledge of bookcase where, clinging, she reaches out and up and drops documents behind portrait. Stepping quickly down, with handkerchief she wipes ledge on which she has stood, also the seat of the chair. She carries chair back to where she found it, and reseats herself in chair by desk.*) (*Starkweather locks safe, emerges from alcove, turns off alcove lights, advances to desk chair, and sits down. He is about to close and lock dispatch box when he discovers documents are missing. He is very quiet about it, and examines contents of box care-fully.*)

Starkweather

(*Quietly.*) Has anybody been in the room?

Margaret

No.

Starkweather

(*Looking at her searchingly.*) A most unprecedented thing has occurred. When I went to the safe a moment ago, I left these documents on the cover of the dispatch box. Nobody has been in the room but you. The documents are gone. Give them to me.

Margaret

I have not been out of the room.

Starkweather

I know that. Give them to me.

(*A pause.*) You have them. Give them to me

Margaret

I haven't them.

Starkweather

That is a lie. Give them to me.

Margaret

(*Rising.*) I tell you I haven't them—

Starkweather

(*Also rising.*) That is a lie.

Margaret

(*Turning and starting to cross room.*) Very well, if you do not believe me—

Starkweather

(*Interrupting.*) Where are you going?

Margaret

Home.

Starkweather

(*Imperatively.*) No, you are not. Come back here.

(*Margaret comes back and stands by chair.*) You shall not leave this room. Sit down.

Margaret

I prefer to stand.

Starkweather

Sit down.

(*She still stands, and he grips her by arm, forcing her down into chair.*) Sit down. Before you leave this room you shall return those documents. This is more important than you realize. It transcends all ordinary things of life as you have known it, and you will compel me to do things far harsher than you can possibly imagine. I can forget that you are a daughter of mine. I can forget that you are even a woman. If I have to tear them from you, I shall get them. Give them to me.

(*A pause.*) What are you going to do?

(*Margaret shrugs her shoulders.*) What have you to say?

(*Margaret again shrugs her shoulders.*) What have you to say?

Margaret

Nothing.

Starkweather

(*Puzzled, changing tactics, sitting down, and talking calmly.*) Let us talk this over quietly. You have no shred of right of any sort to those documents. They are mine. They were stolen by a sneak thief from my private files. Only this morning—a few minutes ago—did I get them back. They are mine, I tell you. They belong to me. Give them back.

Margaret

I tell you I haven't them.

Starkweather

You have got them about you, somewhere, concealed in your breast there. It will not save you. I tell you I shall have them. I warn you. I don't want to proceed to extreme measures. Give them to me.

(*He starts to press desk-button, pauses, and looks at her.*) Well?

(*Margaret shrugs her shoulders.*) (*He presses button twice.*) I have sent for Dobleman. You have one chance before he comes. Give them to me.

Margaret

Father, will you believe me just this once? Let me go. I tell you I haven't the documents. I tell you that if you let me leave this room, I shall not carry them away with me. I tell you this on my honor. Do you believe me? Tell me that you do believe me.

Starkweather

I do believe you. You say they are not on you. I believe you. Now tell me where they are—you have them hidden somewhere—(*Glancing about room.*)—And you can go at once.

(*Dobleman enters from right and advances to desk. Starkweather and Margaret remains silent.*)

Dobleman

You rang for me.

Starkweather

(*With one last questioning glance at Margaret, who remains impassive.*) Yes, I did. Have you been in that other room all the time?

296

Dobleman

Yes, sir.

Starkweather

Did anybody pass through and enter this room?

Dobleman

No, sir.

Starkweather

Very well. We'll see what the maid has to say.

(*He presses button once.*) Margaret, I give you one last chance.

Margaret

I have told you that if I leave this room, I shall not take them with me.

(*Maid enters from right rear and advances.*)

Starkweather

Has anybody come into this room from the hall in the last few minutes?

Maid

No, sir; not since Mrs. Chalmers came in.

Starkweather

How do you know?

Maid

I was in the hall, sir, dusting all the time.

Starkweather

That will do.

(*Maid makes exit to right rear.*) Dobleman, a very unusual thing has occurred.

Mrs. Chalmers and I have been alone in this room. Those letters stolen by Gherst had been returned to me by Hubbard but the moment before. They were on my desk. I turned my back for a moment to go to the safe. When I came back they were gone.

Dobleman

(*Embarrassed.*) Yes, sir.

Starkweather

Mrs. Chalmers took them. She has them now.

Dobleman

(*Attempts to speak, stammers.*) Er—er—yes, sir

Starkweather

I want them back. What is to be done?

(*Dobleman remains in hopeless confusion.*) Well!

Dobleman

(*Speaking hurriedly and hopefully.*) S-send for Mr. Hubbard. He got them for you before.

Starkweather

A good suggestion. Telephone for him. You should find him at the Press Club.

(*Dobleman starts to make exit to right.*) Don't leave the room. Use this telephone. (*Indicating desk telephone.*) (*Dobleman moves around to left of desk and uses telephone standing up.*) From now on no one leaves the room. If my daughter can be guilty of such a theft, it is plain I can trust no one—no one.

Dobleman

(*Speaking in transmitter.*) Red 6-2-4. Yes, please.

(*Waits.*)

Starkweather

(*Rising.*) Call Senator Chalmers as well. Tell him to come immediately.

Dobleman

Yes, sir—immediately.

Starkweather

(*Starting to cross stage to center and speaking to Margaret.*) Come over here.

(*Margaret follows. She is obedient, frightened, very subdued—but resolved.*)

Why have you done this? Were you truthful when you said there was nothing between you and this man Knox?

Margaret

Father; don't discuss this before the—

(*Indicating Dobleman.*)—the servants.

Starkweather

You should have considered that before you stole the documents.

(*Dobleman, in the meantime, is telephoning in a low voice.*)

Margaret

There are certain dignities—

Starkweather

(*Interrupting.*) Not for a thief.

(*Speaking intensely and in a low voice.*) Margaret, it is not too late. Give them back, and no one shall know.

(*A pause, in which Margaret is silent, in the throes of indecision.*)

Dobleman

Mr. Hubbard says he will be here in three minutes. Fortunately, Senator Chalmers is with him.

(*Starkweather nods and looks at Margaret.*) (*Door at left rear opens, and enter Mrs. Starkweather and Connie. They are dressed for the street and evidently just going out.*)

Mrs. Starkweather

(*Speaking in a rush.*) We are just going out, Anthony. You were certainly wrong in making us attempt to take that 2:10 train. I simply can't make it. I know I can't. It would have been much wiser—

(*Suddenly apprehending the strain of the situation between Starkweather and Margaret.*)—Why, what is the matter?

Starkweather

(*Patently disturbed by their entrance, speaking to Dobleman, who has finished with the telephone.*) Lock the doors.

(*Dobleman proceeds to obey.*)

Mrs. Starkweather

Mercy me! Anthony! What has happened?

(*A pause.*) Madge! What has happened?

Starkweather

You will have to wait here a few minutes, that is all.

Mrs. Starkweather

But I must keep my engagements. And I haven't a minute to spare.

(*Looking at Dobleman locking doors.*) I do not understand.

300

Starkweather

(*Grimly,*) You will, shortly. I can trust no one any more. When my daughter sees fit to steal—

Mrs. Starkweather

Steal!—Margaret! What have you been doing now?

Margaret

Where is Tommy?

(*Mrs. Starkwater is too confounded to answer, and can only stare from face to face.*) (*Margaret looks her anxiety to Connie.*)

Connie

He is already down in the machine waiting for us. You are coming, aren't you?

Starkweather

Let him wait in the machine. Margaret will come when I get done with her.

(*A knock is heard at right rear.*) (*Starkweather looks at Dobleman and signifies that he is to open door.*)

(*Dobleman unlocks door, and Hubbabd and Chalmers enter. Beyond the shortest of nods and recognitions with eyes, greetings are cut short by the strain that is on all. Dobleman relocks door.*)

Starkweather

(*Plunging into it.*) Look here, Tom. You know those letters Gherst stole. Mr. Hubbard recovered them from Knox and returned them to me this morning. Within five minutes Margaret stole them from me—here, right in this room. She has not left the room. They are on her now. I want them.

Chalmers

301

(Who is obviously incapable of coping with his wife, and who is panting for breath, his hand pressed to his side.) Madge, is this true?

Margaret

I haven't them. I tell you I haven't them.

Starkweather

Where are they, then?

(She does not answer.)

If they are in the room we can find them. Search the room. Tom, Mr. Hubbard, Dobleman. They must be recovered at any cost.

(While a thorough search of the room is being made, Mrs. Starkweather, overcome, has Connie assist her to seat at left. Margaret also seats herself, in same chair at desk.)

Chalmers

(Pausing from search, while others continue.) There is no place to look for them. They are not in the room. Are you sure you didn't mislay them?

Starkweather

Nonsense. Margaret took them. They are a bulky package and not easily hidden. If they aren't in the room, then she has them on her.

Chalmers

Madge, give them up.

Margaret

I haven't them.

(Chalmers, stepping suddenly up to her, starts feeling for the papers, running his hands over her dress.)

Margaret

(*Springing to her feet and striking him in the face with her open palm.*) How dare you!

(*Chalmers recoils, Mrs. Starkweather is threatened with hysteria and is calmed by the frightened Connie, while Starkweather looks on grimly.*)

Hubbard

(*Giving up search of room.*) Possibly it would be better to let me retire, Mr. Starkweather.

Starkweather

No; those papers are here in this room. If nobody leaves there will be no possible chance for the papers to get out of the room. What would you recommend doing, Hubbard?

Hubbard

(*Hesitatingly.*) Under the circumstances I don't like to suggest—

Starkweather

Go on.

Hubbard

First, I would make sure that she—er—Mrs. Chalmers has taken them.

Starkweather

I have made that certain.

Chalmers

But what motive could she have for such an act?

(*Hubbard looks wise.*)

Starkweather

(*To Hubbard.*) You know more about this than would appear. What is it?

Hubbard

303

I'd rather not. It is too—

(*Looks significantly at Mrs. Starkweather and Connie.*)—er—delicate.

Starkweather

This affair has gone beyond all delicacy. What is it?

Margaret

No! No!

(*Chalmers and Starkweather look at her with sudden suspicion.*)

Starkweather

Go on, Mr. Hubbard.

Hubbard

I'd—I'd rather not.

Starkweather

(*Savagely.*) I say go on.

Hubbard

(*With simulated reluctance.*) Last night—I saw—I was in Knox's rooms—

Margaret

(*Interrupting.*) One moment; please. Let him speak, but first send Connie away.

Starkweather

No one shall leave this room till the documents are produced. Margaret, give me the letters, and Connie can leave quietly, and even will Hubbard's lips remain sealed. They will never breathe a word of whatever shameful thing his eyes saw. This I promise you.

(*A pause, wherein he waits vainly for Margaret to make a decision.*) Go on, Hubbard.

Margaret

(*Who is terror-stricken, and has been wavering.*) No! Don't! I'll tell. I'll give you back the documents.

(*All are expectant She wavers again, and steels herself to resolution.*) No; I haven't them. Say all you have to say.

Starkweather

You see. She has them. She said she would give them back.

(*To Hubbard.*) Go on.

Hubbard

Last night—

Connie

(*Springing up.*) I won't stay!

(*She rushes to left rear and finds door locked.*) Let me out! Let me out!

Mrs. Starkweather

(*Moaning and lying back in chair, legs stretched out and giving preliminary twitches and jerks of hysteria.*) I shall die! I shall die! I know I shall die!

Starkweather

(*Sternly, to Connie.*) Go back to your mother.

Connie

(*Returning reluctantly to side of Mrs. Starkweather, sitting down beside her, and putting fingers in her own ears.*) I won't listen! I won't listen!

Starkweather

(*Sternly.*) Take your fingers down.

Hubbard

Hang it all, Chalmers, I wish I were out of this. I don't want to testify.

Starkweather

Take your fingers down.

(*Connie reluctantly removes her fingers.*) Now, Hubbard.

Hubbard

I protest. I am being dragged into this.

Chalmers

You can't help yourself now. You have cast black suspicions on my wife.

Hubbard

All right. She—Mrs. Chalmers visited Knox in his rooms last night.

Mrs. Starkweather

(*Bursting out.*) Oh! Oh! My Madge! It is a lie! A lie! (*Kicks violently with her legs.*) (*Connie soothes her.*)

Chalmers

You've got to prove that, Hubbard. If you have made any mistake it will go hard with you.

Hubbard

(*Indicating Margaret.*) Look at her. Ask her.

(*Chalmers looks at Margaret with growing suspicion.*)

Margaret

Linda was with me. And Tommy. I had to see Mr. Knox on a very important matter. I went there in the machine. I took Linda and Tommy right into Mr. Knox's room.

Chalmers

(*Relieved.*) Ah, that puts a different complexion on it.

Hubbard

That is not all. Mrs. Chalmers sent the maid and the boy down to the machine and remained.

306

Margaret

(*Quickly.*) But only for a moment

Hubbard

Much longer—much, much longer. I know how long I was kicking my heels and waiting.

Margaret

(*Desperately.*) I say it was but for a moment—a short moment.

Starkweather

(*Abruptly, to Hubbard.*) Where were you?

Hubbard

In Knox's bedroom. The fool had forgotten all about me. He was too delighted with his—er—new visitor.

Starkweather

You said you saw.

Hubbard

The bedroom door was ajar. I opened it.

Starkweather

What did you see?

Margaret

(*Appealing to Hubbard.*) Have you no mercy? I say it was only a moment.

(*Hubbard shrugs his shoulders.*)

Starkweather

We'll settle the length of that moment Tommy is here, and so is the maid. Connie, Margaret's maid is here, isn't she? (*Connie does not answer.*) Answer me!

Connie

Yes.

Starkweather

Dobleman, ring for a maid and tell her to fetch Tommy and Mrs. Chalmer's maid.

(*Dobleman goes to desk and pushes button once.*)

Margaret

No! Not Tommy!

Starkweather

(*Looking shrewdly at Margaret, to Dobleman.*) Mrs. Chalmer's maid will do.

(*A knock is heard at left rear. Dobleman opens door and talks to maid. Closes door.*)

Starkweather

Lock it.

(*Dobleman locks door.*)

Chalmers

(*Coming over to Margaret.*) So you, the immaculate one, have been playing fast and loose.

Margaret

You have no right to talk to me that way, Tom—

Chalmers

I am your husband.

Margaret

You have long since ceased being that.

Chalmers

What do you mean?

Margaret

I mean just what you have in mind about yourself right now.

Chalmers

Madge, you are merely conjecturing. You know nothing against me.

Margaret

I know everything—and without evidence, if you please. I am a woman. It is your atmosphere. Faugh! You have exhaled it for years. I doubt not that proofs, as you would call them, could have been easily obtained. But I was not interested. I had my boy. When he came, I gave you up, Tom. You did not seem to need me any more.

Chalmers

And so, in retaliation, you took up with this fellow Knox.

Margaret

No, no. It is not true, Tom. I tell you it is not true.

Chalmers

You were there, last night, in his rooms, alone—how long we shall soon find out—

(*Knock is heard at left rear. Dobleman proceeds to unlock door.*) And now you have stolen your father's private papers for your lover.

Margaret

He is not my lover.

Chalmers

But you have acknowledged that you have the papers. For whom, save Knox, could you have stolen them?

(*Linda enters. She is white and strained, and looks at Margaret for some cue as to what she is to do.*)

Starkweather

That is the woman.

(*To Linda.*) Come here.

(*Linda advances reluctantly.*) Where were you last night? You know what I mean.

(*She does not speak.*) Answer me.

Linda

I don't know what you mean, sir—unless—

Starkweather

Yes, that's it. Go on.

Linda

But I don't think you have any right to ask me such questions. What if I—if I did go out with my young man—

Starkweather

(*To Margaret.*) A very faithful young woman you've got.

(*Briskly, to the others.*) There's nothing to be got out of her. Send for Tommy. Dobleman, ring the bell.

(*Dobleman starts to obey.*)

Margaret

(*Stopping Dobleman.*) No, no; not Tommy. Tell them, Linda.

(*Linda looks appealingly at her.*)

(*Kindly.*) Don't mind me. Tell them the truth.

Chalmers

(*Breaking in.*) The whole truth.

Margaret

Yes, Linda, the whole truth.

(*Linda, looking very woeful, nerves herself for the ordeal.*)

Starkweather

Never mind, Dobleman.

(*To Linda.*) Very well. You were at Mr. Knox's rooms last night, with your mistress and Tommy.

Linda

Yes, sir.

Starkweather

Your mistress sent you and Tommy out of the room.

Linda

Yes, sir.

Starkweather

You waited in the machine.

Linda

Yes, sir.

Starkweather

(*Abruptly springing the point he has been working up to.*) How long?

(*Linda perceives the gist of the questioning just as she is opening her mouth to reply, and she does not speak.*)

Margaret

(*With deliberate calmness of despair.*) Half an hour—an hour—any length of time your shameful minds dictate. That will do, Linda. You can go.

Starkweather

No, you don't. Stand over there to one side.

(*To the others.*) The papers are in this room, and I shall keep my mind certain on that point.

Hubbard

I think I have shown the motive.

Connie

You are a beast!

Chalmers

You haven't told what you saw.

Hubbard

I saw them in each other's arms—several times. Then I found the stolen documents where Knox had thrown them down. So I pocketed them and closed the door.

Chalmers

How long after that did they remain together?

Hubbard

Quite a time, quite a long time.

Chalmers

And when you last saw them?

Hubbard

They were in each other's arms—quite enthusiastically, I may say, in each other's arms. (*Chalmers is crushed.*)

Margaret

(*To Hubbard.*) You coward.

(*Hubbard smiles.*)

(*To Starkweather.*) When are you going to call off this hound of yours?

Starkweather

When I get the papers. You see what you've been made to pay for them already. Now listen to me closely. Tom, you listen, too. You know the value of these letters. If they are not recovered they will precipitate a turn-over that means not merely money but control and power. I doubt that even you would be re-elected. So what we have heard in this room must be forgotten—absolutely forgotten. Do you understand?

Chalmers

But it is adultery.

Starkweather

It is not necessary for that word to be mentioned. The point is that everything must be as it was formerly.

Chalmers

Yes, I understand.

Starkweather

(*To Margaret.*) You hear. Tom will make no trouble. Now give me the papers. They are mine, you know.

Margaret

It seems to me the people, who have been lied to, and cajoled, and stolen from, are the rightful owners, not you.

Starkweather

Are you doing this out of love for this—this man, this demagogue?

Margaret

For the people, the children, the future.

Starkweather

Faugh! Answer me.

Margaret

(*Slowly.*) Almost I do not know. Almost I do not know.

(*A knock is heard at left rear. Dobleman answers.*)

Dobleman

(*Looking at card Maid has given him, to Starkweather.*) Mr. Rutland.

Starkweather

(*Making an impatient gesture, then abruptly changing his mind, speaking grimly.*) Very well. Bring him in. I've paid a lot for the Church, now we'll see what the Church can do for me.

Connie

(*Impulsively crossing stage to Margaret, putting arms around her, and weeping.*)

Please, please, Madge, give up the papers, and everything will be hushed up. You heard what father said. Think what it means to me if this scandal comes out. Father will hush it up. Not a soul will dare to breathe a word of it. Give him the papers.

Margaret

(*Kissing her, shaking head, and setting her aside.*) No; I can't. But Connie, dearest—

(*Connie pauses.*) It is not true, Connie. He—he is not my lover. Tell me that you believe me.

Connie

(*Caressing her.*) I do believe you. But won't you return the papers— for my sake?

(A knock at door.)

Margaret

I can't.

(*Enter Rutland.*)

(*Connie returns to take care of Mrs. Starkweather.*)

Rutland

(*Advances beamingly upon Starkweather.*) My, what a family gathering. I hastened on at once, my dear Mr. Starkweather, to thank you in person, ere you fled away to New York, for your generously splendid—yes, generously splendid—contribution—

(*Here the strained situation dawns upon him, and he remains helplessly with mouth open, looking from one to another.*)

Starkweather

A theft has been committed, Mr. Rutland. My daughter has stolen something very valuable from me—a package of private papers, so important—well, if she succeeds in making them public I shall be injured to such an extent financially that there won't be any more generously splendid donations for you or anybody else. I have done my best to persuade her to return what she has stolen. Now you try. Bring her to a realization of the madness of what she is doing.

Rutland

(*Quite at sea, hemming and hawing.*) As your spiritual adviser, Mrs. Chalmers—if this be true—I recommend—I suggest—I—ahem—I entreat—

Margaret

Please, Mr. Rutland, don't be ridiculous. Father is only making a stalking horse out of you. Whatever I may have done, or not done, I believe I am doing right. The whole thing is infamous. The people have been lied to and robbed, and you are merely lending yourself to the infamy of perpetuating the lying and the robbing. If you persist in obeying my father's orders—yes, orders—you will lead me to believe that you are actuated by desire for more of those generously splendid donations. (*Starkweather sneers.*)

Rutland

(*Embarrassed, hopelessly at sea.*) This is, I fear—ahem—too delicate a matter, Mr. Starkweather, for me to interfere. I would suggest that it be advisable for me to withdraw—ahem—

Starkweather

(*Musingly.*) So the Church fails me, too.

(*To Rutland.*) No, you shall stay right here.

Margaret

Father, Tommy is down in the machine alone. Won't you let me go?

Starkweather

Give me the papers.

(Mrs. Starkweather rises and totters across to Margaret, moaning and whimpering.)

Mrs. Starkweather

Madge, Madge, it can't be true. I don't believe it. I know you have not done this awful thing. No daughter of mine could be guilty of such wickedness. I refuse to believe my ears—

(Mrs. Starkweather sinks suddenly on her knees before Margaret, with clasped hands, weeping hysterically.)

Starkweather

(Stepping to her side.) Get up.

(Hesitates and thinks.) No; go on. She might listen to you.

Margaret

(Attempting to raise her mother.) Don't, mother, don't. Please get up.

(Mrs. Starkweather resists her hysterically.) You don't understand, mother. Please, please, get up.

Mrs. Starkweather

Madge, I, your mother, implore you, on my bended knees. Give up the papers to your father, and I shall forget all I have heard. Think of the family name. I don't believe it, not a word of it; but think of the shame and disgrace. Think of me. Think of Connie, your sister. Think of Tommy. You'll have your father in a terrible state. And you'll kill me. (Moaning and rolling her head.)

I'm going to be sick. I know I am going to be sick.

Margaret

(Bending over mother and raising her, while Connie comes across stage to help support mother.) Mother, you do not understand. More is at stake than the good name of the family or—*(Looking at Rutland.)*—God. You speak of Connie and Tommy. There are two millions of Connies and Tommys working as child laborers in the United States to-day. Think of them. And besides,

316

mother, these are all lies you have heard. There is nothing between Mr. Knox and me. He is not my lover. I am not the—the shameful thing—these men have said I am.

Connie

(*Appealingly.*) Madge.

Margaret

(*Appealingly.*) Connie. Trust me. I am right. I know I am right.

(*Mrs. Starkweather, supported by Connie, moaning incoherently, is led back across stage to chair.*)

Starkweather

Margaret, a few minutes ago, when you told me there was nothing between you and this man, you lied to me—lied to me as only a wicked woman can lie.

Margaret

It is clear that you believe the worst.

Starkweather

There is nothing less than the worst to be believed. Besides, more heinous than your relations with this man is what you have done here in this room, stolen from me, and practically before my very eyes. Well, you have crossed your will with mine, and in affairs beyond your province. This is a man's game in which you are attempting to play, and you shall take the consequences. Tom will apply for a divorce.

Margaret

That threat, at least, is without power.

Starkweather

And by that means we can break Knox as effectually as by any other. That is one thing the good stupid people will not tolerate in a chosen representative. We will make such a scandal of it—

Mrs. Starkweather

(*Shocked.*) Anthony!

Starkweather

(*Glancing irritably at his wife and continuing.*) Another thing. Being proven an adulterous woman, morally unfit for companionship with your child, your child will be taken away from you.

Margaret

No, no. That cannot be. I have done nothing wrong. No court, no fair-minded judge, would so decree on the evidence of a creature like that.

(*Indicating Hubbard.*)

Hubbard

My evidence is supported. In an adjoining room were two men. I happen to know, because I placed them there. They were your father's men at that. There is such a thing as seeing through a locked door. They saw.

Margaret

And they would swear to—to anything.

Hubbard

I doubt not they will know to what to swear.

Starkweather

Margaret, I have told you some, merely some, of the things I shall do. It is not too late. Return the papers, and everything will be forgotten.

Margaret

You would condone this—this adultery. You, who have just said that I was morally unfit to have my own boy, will permit me to retain him. I had never dreamed, father, that your own immorality would descend to such vile depths. Believing this shameful thing of me, you will forgive and forget it all for the sake of a few scraps of paper that stand for money, that stand for a license to rob and steal from the people. Is this your morality—money?

Starkweather

I have my morality. It is not money. I am only a steward; but so highly do I conceive the duties of my stewardship—

318

Margaret

(*Interrupting, bitterly.*) The thefts and lies and all common little sins like adulteries are not to stand in the way of your high duties—that the end hallows the means.

Starkweather

(*Shortly.*) Precisely.

Margaret

(*To Rutland.*) There is Jesuitism, Mr. Rutland. I would suggest that you, as my father's spiritual adviser—

Starkweather

Enough of this foolery. Give me the papers.

Margaret

I haven't them.

Starkweather

What's to be done, Hubbard?

Hubbard

She has them. She has as much as acknowledged that they are not elsewhere in the room. She has not been out of the room. There is nothing to do but search her.

Starkweather

Nothing else remains to be done. Dobleman, and you, Hubbard, take her behind the screen. Strip her. Recover the papers.

(*Dobleman is in a proper funk, but Hubbard betrays no unwillingness.*)

Chalmers

No; that I shall not permit. Hubbard shall have nothing to do with this.

Margaret

It is too late, Tom. You have stood by and allowed me to be stripped of everything else. A few clothes do not matter now. If I am to be stripped and searched by men, Mr. Hubbard will serve as well as any other man. Perhaps Mr. Rutland would like to lend his assistance.

Connie

Oh, Madge! Give them up.

(*Margaret shakes her head.*)

(*To Starkweather.*) Then let me search her, father.

Starkweather

You are too willing. I don't want volunteers. I doubt that I can trust you any more than your sister.

Connie

Let mother, then.

Starkweather

(*Sneering.*) Margaret could smuggle a steamer-trunk of documents past her.

Connie

But not the men, father! Not the men!

Starkweather

Why not? She has shown herself dead to all shame.

(*Imperatively.*) Dobleman!

Dobleman

(*Thinking his time has come, and almost dying.*) Y-y-yes, sir.

Starkweather

Call in the servants.

Mrs. Starkweather

(*Crying out in protest.*) Anthony!

320

Starkweather

Would you prefer her to be searched by the men?

Mrs. Starkweather

(*Subsiding.*) I shall die, I shall die. I know I shall die.

Starkweather

Dobleman. Ring for the servants.

(*Dobleman, who has been hesitant, crosses to desk and pushes button, then returns toward door.*) Send in the maids and the housekeeper.

(*Linda, blindly desiring to be of some assistance, starts impulsively toward Margaret.*) Stand over there—in the corner.

(*Indicating right front.*)

(*Linda pauses irresolutely and Margaret nods to her to obey and smiles encouragement. Linda, protesting in every fiber of her, goes to right front.*)

(*A knock at right rear and Dobleman unlocks door, confers with maid, and closes and locks door.*)

Starkweather

(*To Margaret.*) This is no time for trifling, nor for mawkish sentimentality. Return the papers or take the consequences.

(*Margaret makes no answer.*)

Chalmers

You have taken a hand in a man's game, and you've got to play it out or quit. Give up the papers.

(*Margaret remains resolved and impassive.*)

Hubbard

(*Suavely.*) Allow me to point out, my dear Mrs. Chalmers, that you are not merely stealing from your father. You are playing the traitor to your class.

Starkweather

And causing irreparable damage.

Margaret

(*Firing up suddenly and pointing to Lincoln's portrait*) I doubt not he caused irreparable damage when he freed the slaves and preserved the Union. Yet he recognized no classes. I'd rather be a traitor to my class than to him.

Starkweather

Demagoguery. Demagoguery.

(*A knock at right rear. Dobleman opens door. Enter Mrs. Middleton who is the housekeeper, followed by two Housemaids. They pause at rear. Housekeeper to the fore and looking expectantly at Starkweather. The Maids appear timid and frightened.*)

Housekeeper

Yes, sir.

Starkweather

Mrs. Middleton, you have the two maids to assist you. Take Mrs. Chalmers behind that screen there and search her. Strip all her clothes from her and make a careful search. (*Maids show perturbation.*)

Housekeeper

(*Self-possessed.*) Yes, sir. What am I to search for?

Starkweather

Papers, documents, anything unusual. Turn them over to me when you find them.

Margaret

(*In a sudden panic.*) This is monstrous! This is monstrous!

Starkweather

So is your theft of the documents monstrous.

Margaret

(*Appealing to the other men, ignoring Rutland and not considering Dobleman at all.*)

You cowards! Will you stand by and permit this thing to be done? Tom, have you one atom of manhood in you?

Chalmers

(*Doggedly.*) Return the papers, then.

Margaret

Mr. Rutland—

Rutland

(*Very awkwardly and oilily.*) My dear Mrs. Chalmers. I assure you the whole circumstance is unfortunate. But you are so palpably in the wrong that I cannot interfere—(*Margaret turns from him in withering scorn.*)—That I cannot interfere.

Dobleman

(*Breaking down unexpectedly.*) I cannot stand it. I leave your employ, sir. It is outrageous. I resign now, at once. I cannot be a party to this.

(*Striving to unlock door.*) I am going at once. You brutes! You brutes!

(*Breaks into convulsive sobbings.*)

Chalmers

Ah, another lover, I see.

Dobleman manages to unlock door and starts to open it.)

Starkweather

You fool! Shut that door!

(*Dobleman hesitates.*) Shut it!

(*Dobleman obeys.*) Lock it!

(*Dobleman obeys.*)

Margaret

323

(*Smiling wistfully, benignantly.*) Thank you, Mr. Dobleman.

(*To Starkweather.*) Father, you surely will not perpetrate this outrage, when I tell you, I swear to you—

Starkweather

(*Interrupting.*) Return the documents then.

Margaret

I swear to you that I haven't them. You will not find them on me.

Starkweather

You have lied to me about Knox, and I have no reason to believe you will not lie to me about this matter.

Margaret

(*Steadily.*) If you do this thing you shall cease to be my father forever. You shall cease to exist so far as I am concerned.

Starkweather

You have too much of my own will in you for you ever to forget whence it came. Mrs. Middleton, go ahead.

(*Housekeeper, summoning Maids with her eyes, begins to advance on Margaret.*)

Connie

(*In a passion.*) Father, if you do this I shall never speak to you again.

(*Breaks down weeping.*) (*Mrs. Starkweather, during following scene, has mild but continuous shuddering and weeping hysteria.*)

Starkweather

(*Briskly, looking at watch.*) I've wasted enough time on this. Mrs. Middleton, proceed.

Margaret

(*Wildly, backing away from Housekeeper.*) I will not tamely submit. I will resist, I promise you.

324

Starkweather

Use force, if necessary.

(*The Maids are reluctant, but Housekeeper commands them with her eyes to close in on Margaret, and they obey.*)

(*Margaret backs away until she brings up against desk.*)

Housekeeper

Come, Mrs. Chalmers.

(*Margaret stands trembling, but refuses to notice Housekeeper.*) (*Housekeeper places hand on Margaret's arm.*)

Margaret

(*Violently flinging the hand off, crying imperiously.*) Stand back!

(*Housekeeper instinctively shrinks back, as do Maids. But it is only for the moment. They close in upon Margaret to seise her.*)

(*Crying frantically for help.*) Linda! Linda!

(*Linda springs forward to help her mistress, but is caught and held struggling by Chalmers, who twists her arm and finally compels her to become quiet.*)

(*Margaret, struggling and resisting, is hustled across stage and behind screen, the Maids warming up to their work. One of them emerges from behind screen for the purpose of getting a chair, upon which Margaret is evidently forced to sit. The screen is of such height, that occasionally, when standing up and struggling, Margaret's bare arms are visible above the top of it. Muttered exclamations are heard, and the voice of Housekeeper trying to persuade Margaret to sub-mit.*)

Margaret

(*Abruptly, piteously.*) No! No!

(*The struggle becomes more violent, and the screen is overturned, disclosing Margaret seated on chair, partly undressed, and clutching an envelope in her hand which they are trying to force her to relinquish.*)

325

Mrs. Starkweather

(*Crying wildly.*) Anthony! They are taking her clothes off!

(*Renewed struggle of Linda with Chalmers at the sight.*)

(*Starkweather, calling Rutland to his assistance, stands screen up again, then, as an afterthought, pulls screen a little further away from Margaret.*)

Margaret

No! No!

(*Housekeeper appears triumphantly with envelope in her hand and hands it to Hubbard.*)

Hubbard

(Immediately.) That's not it.

(*Glances at address and starts.*) It's addressed to Knox.

Starkweather

Tear it open. Read it.

(*Hubbard tears envelope open.*) (*While this is going on, struggle behind screen is suspended.*)

Hubbard

(*Withdrawing contents of envelope.*) It is only a photograph—of Mrs. Chalmers.

(*Reading.*) "For the future—Margaret."

Chalmers

(*Thrusting Linda back to right front and striding up to Hubbard.*) Give it to me. (*Hubbard passes it to him, and he looks at it, crumples it in his hand, and grinds it under foot.*)

Starkweather

That is not what we wanted, Mrs. Middleton. Go on with the search.

(*The search goes on behind the screen without any further struggling.*)

(A pause, during which screen is occasionally agitated by the searchers removing Margaret's garments.)

Housekeeper

(Appearing around corner of screen.) I find nothing else, sir.

Starkweather

Is she stripped?

Housekeeper

Yes, sir.

Starkweather

Every stitch?

Housekeeper

(Disappearing behind screen instead of answering for a pause, during which it is patent that the ultimate stitch is being removed, then reappearing.) Yes, sir.

Starkweather

Nothing?

Housekeeper

Nothing.

Starkweather

Throw out her clothes—everything.

(A confused mass of feminine apparel is tossed out, falling near Dobleman's feet, who, in consequence, is hugely mortified and embarrassed.)

(Chalmers examines garments, then steps behind screen a moment, and reappears.)

Chalmers

Nothing.

(Chalmers, Starkweather, and Hubbard gaze at each other dumbfoundedly.)

(*The two Maids come out from behind screen and stand near door to right rear.*)

(*Starkweather is loath to believe, and steps to Margaret's garments and overhauls them.*)

Starkweather

(*To Chalmers, looking inquiringly toward screen.*) Are you sure?

Chalmers

Yes; I made certain. She hasn't them.

Starkweather

(*To Housekeeper.*) Mrs. Middleton, examine those girls.

Housekeeper

(Passing hands over dresses of Maids.) No, sir.

Margaret

(*From behind screen, in a subdued, spiritless voice.*) May I dress—now?

(*Nobody answers.*) It—it is quite chilly.

(*Nobody answers.*) Will you let Linda come to me, please?

(*Starkweather nods savagely to Linda, to obey.*) (*Linda crosses to garments, gathers them up, and disappears behind screen.*)

Starkweather

(*To Housekeeper.*)

You may go.

(*Exit Housekeeper and the two Maids.*)

Dobleman

(*Hesitating, after closing door.*) Shall I lock it?

(*Starkweather does not answer, and Dobleman leaves door unlocked.*)

Connie

(*Rising.*) May I take mother away?

(*Starkweather, who is in a brown study, nods.*) (*Connie assists Mrs. Starkweather to her feet.*)

Mrs. Starkweather

(*Staggering weakly, and sinking back into chair.*) Let me rest a moment, Connie. I'll be better. (*To Starkweather, who takes no notice.*) Anthony, I am going to bed. This has been too much for me. I shall be sick. I shall never catch that train to-day.

(*Shudders and sighs, leans head back, closes eyes, and Connie fans her or administers smelling salts.*)

Chalmers

(*To Hubbard.*) What's to be done?

Hubbard

(*Shrugging shoulders.*) I'm all at sea. I had just left the letters with him, when Mrs. Chalmers entered the room. What's become of them? She hasn't them, that's certain.

Chalmers

But why? Why should she have taken them?

Hubbard

(*Dryly, pointing to crumpled photograph on floor.*) It seems very clear to me.

Chalmers

You think so? You think so?

Hubbard

I told you what I saw last night at his rooms. There is no other explanation.

Chalmers

(*Angrily.*) And that's the sort he is—vaunting his moral superiority—mouthing phrases about theft—our theft—and himself the greatest thief of all, stealing the dearest and sacredest things—

(*Margaret appears from behind screen, pinning on her hat. She is dressed, but somewhat in disarray, and Linda follows, pulling and touching and arranging. Margaret pauses near to Rutland, but does not seem to see him.*)

Rutland

(*Lamely.*) It is a sad happening—ahem—a sad happening. I am grieved, deeply grieved. I cannot tell you, Mrs. Chalmers, how grieved I am to have been compelled to be present at this—ahem—this unfortunate—

(*Margaret withers him with a look and he awkwardly ceases.*)

Margaret

After this, father, there is one thing I shall do—

Chalmers

(Interrupting.) Go to your lover, I suppose.

Margaret

(*Coldly.*) Have it that way if you choose.

Chalmers

And take him what you have stolen—

Starkweather

(*Arousing suddenly from brown study.*) But she hasn't them on her. She hasn't been out of the room. They are not in the room. Then where are they?

(*During the following, Margaret goes to the door, which Dobleman opens. She forces Linda to go out and herself pauses in open door to listen.*)

Hubbard

(*Uttering an exclamation of enlightenment, going rapidly across to window at left and raising it.*) It is not locked. It moves noiselessly. There's the explanation.

330

(*To Starkweather.*) While you were at the safe, with your back turned, she lifted the window, tossed the papers out to somebody waiting—

(*He sticks head and shoulders out of window, peers down, then brings head and shoulders back.*)—No; they are not there. Somebody was waiting for them.

Starkweather

But how should she know I had them? You had only just recovered them?

Hubbard

Didn't Knox know right away last night that I had taken them? I took the up-elevator instead of the down when I heard him running along the hall. Trust him to let her know what had happened. She was the only one who could recover them for him. Else why did she come here so immediately this morning? To steal the package, of course. And she had some one waiting outside. She tossed them out and closed the window—

(*He closes window.*)—You notice it makes no sound.—and sat down again—all while your back was turned.

Starkweather

Margaret, is this true?

Margaret

(*Excitedly.*) Yes, the window. Why didn't you think of it before? Of course, the window. He—somebody was waiting. They are gone now—miles and miles away. You will never get them. They are in his hands now. He will use them in his speech this afternoon. (*Laughs wildly.*)

(*Suddenly changing her tone to mock meekness, subtle with defiance.*) May I go—now?

(*Nobody answers, and she makes exit.*) (*A moments pause, during which Starkweather, Chalmers, and Hubbard look at each other in stupefaction.*)

Curtain

ACT IV

Scene. *Same as Act I. It is half past one of same day. Curtain discloses Knox seated at right front and waiting. He is dejected in attitude.*

(Margaret enters from right rear, and advances to him. He rises awkwardly and shakes hands. She is very calm and self-possessed.)

Margaret

I knew you would come. Strange that I had to send for you so soon after last night—

(With alarm and sudden change of manner.) What is the matter? You are sick. Your hand is cold.

(She warms it in both of her hands.)

Knox

It is flame or freeze with me.

(Smiling.) And I'd rather flame.

Margaret

(Becoming aware that she is warming his hand.)

Sit down and tell me what is the matter.

(Leading him by the hand she seats him, at the same time seating herself.)

Knox

(Abruptly.) After you left last night, Hubbard stole those documents back again.

Margaret

(Very matter-of-fact.) Yes; he was in your bedroom while I was there.

Knox

(Startled.) How do you know that? Anyway, he did not know who you were.

Margaret

Oh yes he did.

Knox

(*Angrily.*) And he has dared——?

Margaret

Yes; not two hours ago. He announced the fact before my father, my mother, Connie, the servants, everybody.

Knox

(*Rising to his feet and beginning to pace perturbedly up and down.*) The cur!

Margaret

(*Quietly.*) I believe, among other things, I told him he was that myself.

(*She laughs cynically.*) Oh, it was a pretty family party, I assure you. Mother said she didn't believe it—but that was only hysteria. Of course she believes it—the worst. So does Connie—everybody.

Knox

(*Stopping abruptly and looking at her horror-stricken.*) You don't mean they charged——?

Margaret

No; I don't mean that. I mean more. They didn't charge. They accepted it as a proven fact that I was guilty. That you were my—lover.

Knox

On that man's testimony?

Margaret

He had two witnesses in an adjoining room.

Knox

(*Relieved.*) All the better. They can testify to nothing more than the truth, and the truth is not serious. In our case it is good, for we renounced each other.

Margaret

You don't know these men. It is easy to guess that they have been well trained. They would swear to anything.

(*She laughs bitterly.*) They are my father's men, you know, his paid sleuth-hounds.

Knox

(*Collapsing in chair, holding head in hands, and groaning.*) How you must have suffered. What a terrible time, what a terrible time! I can see it all—before everybody—your nearest and dearest. Ah, I could not understand, after our parting last night, why you should have sent for me today. But now I know.

Margaret

No you don't, at all.

Knox

(*Ignoring her and again beginning to pace back and forth, thinking on his feet.*) What's the difference? I am ruined politically. Their scheme has worked out only too well. Gifford warned me, you warned me, everybody warned me. But I was a fool, blind—with a fool's folly. There is nothing left but you now.

(*He pauses, and the light of a new thought irradiates his face.*) Do you know, Margaret, I thank God it has happened as it has. What if my usefulness is destroyed? There will be other men—other leaders. I but make way for another. The cause of the people can never be lost. And though I am driven from the fight, I am driven to you. We are driven together. It is fate. Again I thank God for it.

(*He approaches her and tries to clasp her in his arms, but she steps back.*)

Margaret

(*Smiling sadly.*) Ah, now you flame. The tables are reversed. Last night it was I. We are fortunate that we choose diverse times for our moods—else there would be naught but one sweet melting mad disaster.

Knox

But it is not as if we had done this thing deliberately and selfishly. We have renounced. We have struggled against it until we were beaten. And now we are driven together, not by our doing but Fate's. After this affair this morning there is nothing for you but to come to me. And as for me, despite my best, I am finished. I have failed. As I told you, the papers are stolen. There will be no speech this afternoon.

Margaret

(*Quietly.*) Yes there will.

Knox

Impossible. I would make a triple fool of myself. I would be unable to substantiate my charges.

Margaret

You will substantiate them. What a chain of theft it is. My father steals from the people. The documents that prove his stealing are stolen by Gherst. Hubbard steals them from you and returns them to my father. And I steal them from my father and pass them back to you.

Knox

(*Astounded.*) You?—You?—

Margaret

Yes; this very morning. That was the cause of all the trouble. If I hadn't stolen them nothing would have happened. Hubbard had just returned them to my father.

Knox

(*Profoundly touched.*) And you did this for me—?

Margaret

Dear man, I didn't do it for you. I wasn't brave enough. I should have given in. I don't mind confessing that I started to do it for you, but it soon grew so terrible that I was afraid. It grew so terrible that had it been for you alone I should have surrendered. But out of the terror of it all I caught a wider vision, and all that you said last night rose before me. And I knew that you were right. I thought of all the people, and of the little children. I did it for them, after all. You speak for them. I stole the papers so that you could use them in speaking for the people. Don't you see, dear man?

(*Changing to angry recollection.*) Do you know what they cost me? Do you know what was done to me, to-day, this morning, in my father's house? I was shamed, humiliated, as I would never have dreamed it possible. Do you know what they did to me? The servants were called in, and by them I was stripped before everybody—my family, Hubbard, the Reverend Mr. Rutland, the secretary, everybody.

Knox

(*Stunned.*) Stripped—you?

Margaret

Every stitch. My father commanded it

Knox

(*Suddenly visioning the scene.*) My God!

Margaret

(*Recovering herself and speaking cynically, with a laugh at his shocked face.*) No; it was not so bad as that. There was a screen.

(*Knox appears somewhat relieved.*) But it fell down in the midst of the struggle.

Knox

But in heaven's name why was this done to you?

Margaret

Searching for the lost letters. They knew I had taken them.

(*Speaking gravely.*)

So you see, I have earned those papers. And I have earned the right to say what shall be done with them. I shall give them to you, and you will use them in your speech this afternoon.

Knox

I don't want them.

Margaret

(*Going to bell and ringing.*) Oh yes you do. They are more valuable right now than anything else in the world.

Knox

(*Shaking his head.*) I wish it hadn't happened.

Margaret

(*Returning to him, pausing by his chair, and caressing his hair.*) What?

Knox

This morning—your recovering the letters. I had adjusted myself to their loss, and the loss of the fight, and the finding of—you.

(*He reaches up, draws down her hand, and presses it to his lips.*) So— give them back to your father.

(*Margaret draws quickly away from him.*) (*Enter Man-servant at right rear.*)

Margaret

Send Linda to me.

(*Exit Man-servant.*)

Knox

What are you doing?

Margaret

(*Sitting down.*) I am going to send Linda for them. They are still in my father's house, hidden, of all places, behind Lincoln's portrait. He will guard them safely, I know.

Knox

(*With fervor.*) Margaret! Margaret! Don't send for them. Let them go. I don't want them.

(*Rising and going toward her impulsively.*) (*Margaret rises and retreats, holding him off.*) I want you—you—you.

(*He catches her hand and kisses it. She tears it away from him, but tenderly.*)

Margaret

(*Still retreating, roguishly and tenderly.*) Dear, dear man, I love to see you so. But it cannot be.

(*Looking anxiously toward right rear.*) No, no, please, please sit down.

(*Enter Linda from right rear. She is dressed for the street.*)

Margaret

(*Surprised.*) Where are you going?

Linda

Tommy and the nurse and I were going down town. There is some shopping she wants to do.

Margaret

Very good. But go first to my father's house. Listen closely. In the library, behind the portrait of Lincoln—you know it? (*Linda nods.*)

You will find a packet of papers. It took me five seconds to put it there. It will take you no longer to get it. Let no one see you. Let it appear as though you had brought Tommy to see his grandmother and cheer her up. You know she is not feeling very well just now. After you get the papers, leave Tommy there and bring them immediately back to me. Step on a chair to the ledge of the bookcase, and reach behind the portrait. You should be back inside fifteen minutes. Take the car.

Linda

Tommy and the nurse are already in it, waiting for me.

Margaret

Be careful. Be quick.

(*Linda nods to each instruction and makes exit.*)

Knox

(*Bursting out passionately.*) This is madness. You are sacrificing yourself, and me. I don't want them. I want you. I am tired. What does anything matter except love? I have pursued ideals long enough. Now I want you.

Margaret

(*Gravely.*) Ah, there you have expressed the pith of it. You will now forsake ideals for me—(*He attempts to interrupt.*) No, no; not that I am less than an ideal. I have no silly vanity that way. But I want you to remain ideal, and you can only by going on—not by being turned back. Anybody can play the coward and assert they are fatigued. I could not love a coward. It was your strength that saved us last night. I could not have loved you as I do, now, had you been weak last night. You can only keep my love—

Knox

(*Interrupting, bitterly.*) By foregoing it—for an ideal. Margaret, what is the biggest thing in the world? Love. There is the greatest ideal of all.

Margaret

(*Playfully.*) Love of man and woman?

Knox

What else?

Margaret

(*Gravely.*) There is one thing greater—love of man for his fellowman.

Knox

Oh, how you turn my preachments back on me. It is a lesson. Nevermore shall I preach. Henceforth—

Margaret

Yes.

(*Chalmers enters unobserved at left, pauses, and looks on.*)

Knox

Henceforth I love. Listen.

Margaret

You are overwrought. It will pass, and you will see your path straight before you, and know that I am right. You cannot run away from the fight.

Knox

I can—and will. I want you, and you want me—the man's and woman's need for each other. Come, go with me—now. Let us snatch at happiness while we may.

(*He arises, approaches her, and gets her hand in his. She becomes more complaisant, and, instead of repulsing him, is willing to listen and receive.*) As I have said, the fight will go on just the same. Scores of men, better men, stronger men, than I, will rise to take my place. Why do I talk this way? Because I love you, love you, love you. Nothing else exists in all the world but love of you.

Margaret

(*Melting and wavering.*) Ah, you flame, you flame.

(*Chalmers utters an inarticulate cry of rage and rushes forward at Knox*)

(*Margaret and Knox are startled by the cry and discover Chalmer's presence.*)

Margaret

(*Confronting Chalmers and thrusting him slightly back from Knox, and continuing to hold him off from Knox.*) No, Tom, no dramatics, please. This excitement of yours is only automatic and conventional. You really don't mean it. You don't even feel it. You do it because it is expected of you and because it is your training. Besides, it is bad for your heart. Remember Dr. West's warning—

(*Chalmers, making an unusually violent effort to get at Knox, suddenly staggers weakly back, signs of pain on his face, holding a hand convulsively clasped over his heart. Margaret catches him and supports him to a chair, into which he collapses.*)

340

Chalmers

(*Muttering weakly.*) My heart! My heart!

Knox

(*Approaching.*) Can I do anything?

Margaret

(*Calmly.*) No; it is all right. He will be better presently.

(*She is bending over Chalmers, her hand on his wrist, when suddenly, as a sign he is recovering, he violently flings her hand off and straightens up.*)

Knox

(*Undecidedly.*) I shall go now.

Margaret

No. You will wait until Linda comes back. Besides, you can't run away from this and leave me alone to face it.

Knox

(*Hurt, showing that he will stay.*) I am not a coward.

Chalmers

(*In a stifled voice that grows stronger.*) Yes; wait I have a word for you.

(*He pauses a moment, and when he speaks again his voice is all right.*)

(*Witheringly.*) A nice specimen of a reformer, I must say. You, who babbled yesterday about theft. The most high, righteous and noble Ali Baba, who has come into the den of thieves and who is also a thief.

(*Mimicking Margaret.*) "Ah, you flame, you flame!"

(*In his natural voice.*) I should call you; you thief, you thief, you wife-stealer, you.

Margaret

(*Coolly.*) I should scarcely call it theft.

Chalmers

(*Sneeringly.*) Yes; I forgot. You mean it is not theft for him to take what already belongs to him.

Margaret

Not quite that—but in taking what has been freely offered to him.

Chalmers

You mean you have so forgotten your womanhood as to offer—

Margaret

Just that. Last night. And Mr. Knox did himself the honor of refusing me.

Knox

(*Bursting forth.*) You see, nothing else remains, Margaret.

Chalmers

(*Twittingly.*) Ah, "Margaret."

Knox

(*Ignoring him.*) The situation is intolerable.

Chalmers

(*Emphatically*). It is intolerable. Don't you think you had better leave this house? Every moment of your presence dishonors it.

Margaret

Don't talk of honor, Tom.

Chalmers

I make no excuses for myself. I fancy I never fooled you very much. But at any rate I never used my own house for such purposes.

Knox

(*Springing at him.*) You cur!

Margaret

(*Interposing.*) No; don't. His heart.

342

Chalmers

(*Mimicking Margaret.*) No dramatics, please.

Margaret

(*Plaintively, looking from one man to the other.*) Men are so strangely and wonderfully made. What am I to do with the pair of you? Why won't you reason together like rational human beings?

Chalmers

(*Bitterly gay, rising to his feet.*) Yes; let us come and reason together. Be rational. Sit down and talk it over like civilized humans. This is not the stone age. Be reassured, Mr. Knox. I won't brain you. Margaret—

(*Indicating chair,*) Sit down. Mr. Knox—

(*Indicating chair.*) Sit down.

(*All three seat themselves, in a triangle.*) Behold the problem—the ever ancient and ever young triangle of the playwright and the short story writer—two men and a woman.

Knox

True, and yet not true. The triangle is incomplete. Only one of the two men loves the woman.

Chalmers

Yes?

Knox

And I am that man.

Chalmers

I fancy you're right.

(*Nodding his head.*) But how about the woman?

Margaret

She loves one of the two men.

343

Knox

And what are you going to do about it?

Chalmers

(*Judicially.*) She has not yet indicated the man.

(*Margaret is about to indicate Knox.*) Be careful, Madge. Remember who is Tommy's father.

Margaret

Tom, honestly, remembering what the last years have been can you imagine that I love you?

Chalmers

I'm afraid I've not—er—not flamed sufficiently.

Margaret

You have possibly spoken nearer the truth than you dreamed. I married you, Tom, hoping great things of you. I hoped you would be a power for good—

Chalmers

Politics again. When will women learn they must leave politics alone?

Margaret

And also, I hoped for love. I knew you didn't love me when we married, but I hoped for it to come.

Chalmers

And—er—may I be permitted to ask if you loved me?

Margaret

No; but I hoped that, too, would come.

Chalmers

It was, then, all a mistake.

Margaret

Yes; yours, and mine, and my father's.

Knox

We have sat down to reason this out, and we get nowhere. Margaret and I love each other. Your triangle breaks.

Chalmers

It isn't a triangle after all. You forget Tommy.

Knox

(*Petulantly.*) Make it four-sided, then, but let us come to some conclusion.

Chalmers

(*Reflecting.*) Ah, it is more than that. There is a fifth side. There are the stolen letters which Madge has just this morning restolen from her father. Whatever settlement takes place, they must enter into it.

(*Changing his tone.*) Look here, Madge, I am a fool. Let us talk sensibly, you and Knox and I. Knox, you want my wife. You can have her—on one consideration. Madge, you want Knox. You can have him on one consideration, the same consideration. Give up the letters and we'll forget everything.

Margaret

Everything?

Chalmers

Everything. Forgive and forget You know.

Margaret

You will forgive my—I—this—this adultery?

Chalmers

(*Doggedly.*) I'll forgive anything for the letters. I've played fast and loose with you, Madge, and I fancy your playing fast and loose only evens things up. Return the letters and you can go with Knox quietly. I'll see to that. There won't be a breath of scandal. I'll give you a divorce. Or you can stay on with me if you want to. I don't care. What I want is the letters. Is it agreed?

(*Margaret seems to hesitate.*)

Knox

(Pleadingly.) Margaret.

Margaret

Chalmers

(*Testily.*) Am I not giving you each other? What more do you want? Tommy stays with me. If you want Tommy, then stay with me, but you must give up the letters.

Margaret

I shall not go with Mr. Knox. I shall not give up the letters. I shall remain with Tommy.

Chalmers

So far as I am concerned, Knox doesn't count in this. I want the letters and I want Tommy. If you don't give them up, I'll divorce you on statutory grounds, and no woman, so divorced, can keep her child. In any event, I shall keep Tommy.

Margaret

(*Speaking steadily and positively.*) Listen, Tom; and you, too, Howard. I have never for a moment entertained the thought of giving up the letters. I may have led you to think so, but I wanted to see just how low, you, Tom, could sink. I saw how low you—all of you—this morning sank. I have learned—much. Where is this fine honor, Tom, which put you on a man-killing rage a moment ago? You'll barter it all for a few scraps of paper, and forgive and forget adultery which does not exist—

(*Chalmers laughs skeptically.*)—though I know when I say it you will not believe me. At any rate, I shall not give up the letters. Not if you do take Tommy away from me. Not even for Tommy will I sacrifice all the people. As I told you this morning, there are two million Tommys, child-laborers all, who cannot be sacrificed for Tommy's sake or anybody's sake.

(*Chalmers shrugs his shoulders and smiles in ridicule.*)

Knox

Surely, Margaret, there is a way out for us. Give up the letters. What are they?—only scraps of paper. Why match them against happiness—our happiness?

Margaret

But as you told me yourself, those scraps of paper represent the happiness of millions of lives. It is not our happiness that is matched against some scraps of paper. It is our happiness against millions of lives—like ours. All these millions have hearts, and loves, and desires, just like ours.

Knox

But it is a great social and cosmic process. It does not depend on one man. Kill off, at this instant, every leader of the people, and the process will go on just the same. The people will come into their own. Theft will be unseated. It is destiny. It is the process. Nothing can stop it.

Margaret

But it can be retarded.

Knox

You and I are no more than straws in relation to it. We cannot stop it any more than straws can stop an ocean tide. We mean nothing—except to each other, and to each other we mean all the world.

Margaret

(*Sadly and tenderly.*) All the world and immortality thrown in.

Chalmers

(*Breaking in.*) Nice situation, sitting here and listening to a strange man woo my wife in terms of sociology and scientific slang.

(*Both Margaret and Knox ignore him.*)

Knox

Dear, I want you so.

Margaret

(*Despairingly.*) Oh! It is so hard to do right!

Knox

(*Eagerly.*) He wants the letters very badly. Give them up for Tommy. He will give Tommy for them.

Chalmers

No; emphatically no. If she wants Tommy she can stay on; but she must give up the letters. If she wants you she may go; but she must give up the letters.

Knox

(*Pleading for a decision.*) Margaret.

Margaret

Howard. Don't tempt me and press me. It is hard enough as it is.

Chalmers

(*Standing up.*) I've had enough of this. The thing must be settled, and I leave it to you, Knox. Go on with your love-making. But I won't be a witness to it. Perhaps I—er—retard the—er—the flame process. You two must make up your minds, and you can do it better without me. I am going to get a drink and settle my nerves. I'll be back in a minute.

(He moves toward exit to right.) She will yield, Knox. Be warm, be warm.

(*Pausing in doorway.*) Ah, you flame! Flame to some purpose. (*Exit Chalmers.*)

(*Knox rests his head despairingly on his hand, and Margaret, pausing and looking at him sadly for a moment, crosses to him, stands beside him, and caresses his hair.*)

Margaret

It is hard, I know, dear. And it is hard for me as well.

348

Knox

It is so unnecessary.

Margaret

No, it is necessary. What you said last night, when I was weak, was wise. We cannot steal from my child—

Knox

But if he gives you Tommy? Margaret

(*Shaking her head.*) Nor can we steal from any other woman's child—from all the children of all the women. And other things I heard you say, and you were right. We cannot live by ourselves alone. We are social animals. Our good and our ill—all is tied up with all humanity.

Knox

(*Catching her hand and caressing it.*) I do not follow you. I hear your voice, but I do not know a word you say. Because I am loving your voice—and you. I am so filled with love that there is no room for anything else. And you, who yesterday were so remote and unattainable, are so near and possible, so immediately possible. All you have to do is to say the word, one little word. Say it.—Say it.

(*He carries her hand to his lips and holds it there.*)

Margaret

(*Wistfully.*) I should like to. I should like to. But I can't.

Knox

You must.

Margaret

There are other and greater things that say must to me. Oh, my dear, have you forgotten them? Things you yourself have spoken to me—the great stinging things of the spirit, that are greater than you and I, greater even than our love.

Knox

I exhaust my arguments—but still I love you.

Margaret

And I love you for it.

(*Chalmers enters from right, and sees Margaret still caressing Knox's hair.*)

Chalmers

(*With mild elation, touched with sarcasm.*) Ah, I see you have taken my advice, and reached a decision.

(*They do not answer. Margaret moves slowly away and seats herself.*) (*Knox remains with head bowed on hand.*) No?

(*Margaret shakes her head.*) Well, I've thought it over, and I've changed my terms. Madge, go with Knox, take Tommy with you.

(*Margaret wavers, but Knox, head bowed on hand, does not see her.*) There will be no scandal. I'll give you a proper divorce. And you can have Tommy.

Knox

(*Suddenly raising his head, joyfully, pleadingly.*) Margaret!

(*Margaret is swayed, but does not speak.*)

Chalmers

You and I never hit it off together any too extraordinarily well, Madge; but I'm not altogether a bad sort. I am easy-going. I always have been easy-going. I'll make everything easy for you now. But you see the fix I am in. You love another man, and I simply must regain those letters. It is more important than you realize.

Margaret

(*Incisively.*) You make me realize how important those letters are.

Knox

Give him the letters, Margaret

350

Chalmers

So she hasn't turned them over to you yet?

Margaret

No; I still have them.

Knox

Give them to him.

Chalmers

Selling out for a petticoat. A pretty reformer.

Knox

(*Proudly.*)

A better lover.

Margaret

(*To Chalmers.*)

He is weak to-day. What of it? He was strong last night. He will win back his strength again. It is human to be weak. And in his very weakness now, I have my pride, for it is the weakness of love. God knows I have been weak, and I am not ashamed of it. It was the weakness of love. It is hard to stifle one's womanhood always with morality. (*Quickly.*)

But do not mistake, Tom. This of mine is no conventional morality. I do not care about nasty gossipy tongues and sensation-mongering sheets; nor do I care what any persons of all the persons I know, would say if I went away with Mr. Knox this instant. I would go, and go gladly and proudly with him, divorce or no divorce, scandal or scandal triple-fold—if—if no one else were hurt by what I did. (*To Knox.*)

Howard, I tell you that I would go with you now, in all willingness and joy, with May-time and the songs of all singing birds in my heart—were it not for the others. But there is a higher morality. We must not hurt those others. We dare not steal our happiness from them. The future belongs to them, and we must not, dare not, sacrifice that future nor give it in pledge for our own happiness. Last night I came to you. I was weak—yes; more than that—I was ignorant. I did not know, even as late as last night, the monstrous vileness, the consummate wickedness of present-day conditions. I learned that today, this morning, and now. I learned that the morality of the Church was a pretense. Far deeper than it, and vastly more powerful, was the morality of the dollar. My father, my family, my husband, were willing to condone what they believed was my adultery. And for what? For a few scraps of paper that to them represented only the privilege to plunder, the privilege to steal from the people.

(*To Chalmers.*) Here are you, Tom, not only willing and eager to give me into the arms of the man you believe my lover, but you throw in your boy—your child and mine—to make it good measure and acceptable. And for what? Love of some woman?—any woman? No. Love of humanity? No. Love of God? No. Then for what? For the privilege of perpetuating your stealing from the people—money, bread and butter, hats, shoes, and stockings—for stealing all these things from the people.

(*To Knox.*) Now, and at last, do I realize how stern and awful is the fight that must be waged—the fight in which you and I, Howard, must play our parts and play them bravely and uncomplainingly—you as well as I, but I even more than you. This is the den of thieves. I am a child of thieves. All my family is composed of thieves. I have been fed and reared on the fruits of thievery. I have been a party to it all my life. Somebody must cease from this theft, and it is I. And you must help me, Howard.

Chalmers

(Emitting a low long whistle.) Strange that you never went into the suffragette business. With such speech-making ability you would have been a shining light.

Knox

(*Sadly.*) The worst of it is, Margaret, you are right. But it is hard that we cannot be happy save by stealing from the happiness of others. Yet it hurts, deep down and terribly, to forego you. (*Margaret thanks him with her eyes.*)

Chalmers

(*Sarcastically.*) Oh, believe me, I am not too anxious to give up my wife. Look at her. She's a pretty good woman for any man to possess.

Margaret

Tom, I'll accept a quiet divorce, marry Mr. Knox, and take Tommy with me—on one consideration.

Chalmers

And what is that?

Margaret

That I retain the letters. They are to be used in his speech this afternoon.

Chalmers

No they're not.

Margaret

Whatever happens, do whatever worst you can possibly do, that speech will be given this afternoon. Your worst to me will be none too great a price for me to pay.

Chalmers

No letters, no divorce, no Tommy, nothing.

Margaret

Then will you compel me to remain here. I have done nothing wrong, and I don't imagine you will make a scandal.

(*Enter Linda at right rear, pausing and looking inquiringly.*) There they are now.

(*To Linda.*) Yes; give them to me.

(*Linda, advancing, draws package of documents from her breast. As she is handing them to Margaret, Chalmers attempts to seise them.*)

Knox

(*Springing forward and thrusting Chalmers back.*) That you shall not!

(*Chalmers is afflicted with heart-seizure, and staggers.*)

Margaret

(*Maternally, solicitously.*) Tom, don't! Your heart! Be careful!

(*Chalmers starts to stagger toward bell*) Howard! Stop him! Don't let him ring, or the servants will get the letters away from us. (*Knox starts to interpose, but Chalmers, growing weaker, sinks into a chair, head thrown back and legs out straight before him.*) Linda, a glass of water.

(*Linda gives documents to Margaret, and makes running exit to right rear.*) (*Margaret bends anxiously over Chalmers.*) (*A pause.*)

Knox

(*Touching her hand.*) Give them to me.

(*Margaret gives him the documents, which he holds in his hand, at the same time she thanks him with her eyes.*) (*Enter Linda with glass of water, which she hands to Margaret.*) (*Margaret tries to place the glass to Chalmer's lips.*)

Chalmers

(*Dashing the glass violently from her hand to the floor and speaking in smothered voice.*) Bring me a whiskey and soda.

(*Linda looks at Margaret interrogatively. Margaret is undecided what to say, shrugs her shoulders in helplessness, and nods her head.*)

(*Linda makes hurried exit to right.*)

Margaret

(*To Knox.*) You will go now and you will give the speech.

Knox

(*Placing documents in inside coat pocket.*) I will give the speech.

Margaret

And all the forces making for the good time coming will be quickened by your words. Let the voices of the millions be in it.

(*Chalmers, legs still stretched out, laughs cynically.*)

You know where my heart lies. Some day, in all pride and honor, stealing from no one, hurting no one, we shall come together—to be together always.

Knox

(*Drearily.*) And in the meantime?

Margaret

We must wait

Knox

(*Decidedly.*) We will wait.

Chalmers

(*Straightening up.*) For me to die? eh?

(*During the following speech Linda enters from right with whiskey and soda and gives it to Chalmers, who thirstily drinks half of it. Margaret dismisses Linda with her eyes, and Linda makes exit to right rear.*)

Knox

I hadn't that in mind, but now that you mention it, it seems to the point. That heart of yours isn't going to carry you much farther. You have played fast and loose with it as with everything else. You are like the carter who steals hay from his horse that he may gamble. You have stolen from your heart. Some day, soon, like the horse, it will quit We can afford to wait. It won't be long.

Chalmers

(*After laughing incredulously and sipping his whiskey.*) Well, Knox, neither of us wins. You don't get the woman. Neither do I. She remains under my roof, and I fancy that is about all. I won't divorce her. What's the good? But I've got her tied hard and fast by Tommy. You won't get her.

(*Knox, ignoring hint, goes to right rear and pauses in doorway.*)

Margaret

Work. Bravely work. You are my knight. Go.

(*Knox makes exit.*)

(*Margaret stands quietly, face averted from audience and turned toward where Knox was last to be seen.*)

Chalmers

Madge.

(*Margaret neither moves nor answers.*) I say, Madge.

(*He stands up and moves toward her, holding whiskey glass in one hand.*) That speech is going to make a devil of a row. But I don't think it will be so bad as your father says. It looks pretty dark, but such things blow over. They always do blow over. And so with you and me. Maybe we can manage to forget all this and patch it up somehow.

(*She gives no sign that she is aware of his existence.*) Why don't you speak? (Pause.)

(He touches her arm.) Madge.

Margaret

(*Turning upon him in a blaze of wrath and with unutterable loathing.*)

Don't touch me!

(*Chalmers recoils.*)

Curtain

About Author

John Griffith London (born **John Griffith Chaney**; January 12, 1876 – November 22, 1916) was an American novelist, journalist, and social activist. A pioneer in the world of commercial magazine fiction, he was one of the first writers to become a worldwide celebrity and earn a large fortune from writing. He was also an innovator in the genre that would later become known as science fiction.

His most famous works include The Call of the Wild and White Fang, both set in the Klondike Gold Rush, as well as the short stories "To Build a Fire", "An Odyssey of the North", and "Love of Life". He also wrote about the South Pacific in stories such as "The Pearls of Parlay", and "The Heathen".

London was part of the radical literary group "The Crowd" in San Francisco and a passionate advocate of unionization, workers' rights, socialism, and eugenics. He wrote several works dealing with these topics, such as his dystopian novel The Iron Heel, his non-fiction exposé The People of the Abyss, The War of the Classes, and Before Adam.

Family

Jack London's mother, Flora Wellman, was the fifth and youngest child of Pennsylvania Canal builder Marshall Wellman and his first wife, Eleanor Garrett Jones. Marshall Wellman was descended from Thomas Wellman, an early Puritan settler in the Massachusetts Bay Colony. Flora left Ohio and moved to the Pacific coast when her father remarried after her mother died. In San Francisco, Flora worked as a music teacher and spiritualist, claiming to channel the spirit of a Sauk chief, Black Hawk.

Biographer Clarice Stasz and others believe London's father was astrologer William Chaney. Flora Wellman was living with Chaney in San Francisco when she became pregnant. Whether Wellman and Chaney were legally married is unknown. Stasz notes that in his memoirs, Chaney refers to London's mother Flora Wellman as having been his "wife"; he also cites an advertisement in which Flora called herself "Florence Wellman Chaney".

According to Flora Wellman's account, as recorded in the San Francisco Chronicle of June 4, 1875, Chaney demanded that she have an abortion. When she refused, he disclaimed responsibility for the child. In desperation, she shot herself. She was not seriously wounded, but she was temporarily deranged. After giving birth, Flora turned the baby over for care to Virginia Prentiss, an African-American woman and former slave. She was a major maternal figure throughout London's life. Late in 1876, Flora Wellman married John London, a partially disabled Civil War veteran, and brought her baby John, later known as Jack, to live with the newly married couple. The family moved around the San Francisco Bay Area before settling in Oakland, where London completed public grade school.

In 1897, when he was 21 and a student at the University of California, Berkeley, London searched for and read the newspaper accounts of his mother's suicide attempt and the name of his biological father. He wrote to William Chaney, then living in Chicago. Chaney responded that he could not be London's father because he was impotent; he casually asserted that London's mother had relations with other men and averred that she had slandered him when she said he insisted on an abortion. Chaney concluded by saying that he was more to be pitied than London. London was devastated by his father's letter; in the months following, he quit school at Berkeley and went to the Klondike during the gold rush boom.

Early life

London was born near Third and Brannan Streets in San Francisco. The house burned down in the fire after the 1906 San Francisco earthquake; the California Historical Society placed a plaque at the site in 1953. Although the family was working class, it was not as impoverished as London's later accounts claimed. London was largely self-educated.

In 1885, London found and read Ouida's long Victorian novel Signa. He credited this as the seed of his literary success. In 1886, he went to the Oakland Public Library and found a sympathetic librarian, Ina Coolbrith, who encouraged his learning. (She later became California's first poet laureate and an important figure in the San Francisco literary community).

In 1889, London began working 12 to 18 hours a day at Hickmott's Cannery. Seeking a way out, he borrowed money from his foster mother Virginia Prentiss, bought the sloop Razzle-Dazzle from an oyster pirate named French Frank, and became an oyster pirate himself. In his memoir, John Barleycorn, he claims also to have stolen French Frank's mistress Mamie. After a few months, his sloop became damaged beyond repair. London hired on as a member of the California Fish Patrol.

In 1893, he signed on to the sealing schooner Sophie Sutherland, bound for the coast of Japan. When he returned, the country was in the grip of the panic of '93 and Oakland was swept by labor unrest. After grueling jobs in a jute mill and a street-railway power plant, London joined Coxey's Army and began his career as a tramp. In 1894, he spent 30 days for vagrancy in the Erie County Penitentiary at Buffalo, New York. In The Road, he wrote:

> Man-handling was merely one of the very minor unprintable horrors of the Erie County Pen. I say 'unprintable'; and in justice I must also say undescribable. They were unthinkable to me until I saw them, and I was no spring chicken in the ways of the world and the awful abysses of human degradation. It would take a deep plummet to reach bottom in the Erie County Pen, and I do but skim lightly and facetiously the surface of things as I there saw them.
>
> —Jack London, The Road

After many experiences as a hobo and a sailor, he returned to Oakland and attended Oakland High School. He contributed a number of articles to the high school's magazine, The Aegis. His first published work was "Typhoon off the Coast of Japan", an account of his sailing experiences.

As a schoolboy, London often studied at Heinold's First and Last Chance Saloon, a port-side bar in Oakland. At 17, he confessed to the bar's owner, John Heinold, his desire to attend university and pursue a career as a writer. Heinold lent London tuition money to attend college.

London desperately wanted to attend the University of California, located in Berkeley. In 1896, after a summer of intense studying to pass certification exams, he was admitted. Financial circumstances forced him to leave in 1897 and he never graduated. No evidence has surfaced that he ever wrote for student publications while studying at Berkeley.

While at Berkeley, London continued to study and spend time at Heinold's saloon, where he was introduced to the sailors and adventurers who would influence his writing. In his autobiographical novel, John Barleycorn, London mentioned the pub's likeness seventeen times. Heinold's was the place where London met Alexander McLean, a captain known for his cruelty at sea. London based his protagonist Wolf Larsen, in the novel The Sea-Wolf, on McLean.

Heinold's First and Last Chance Saloon is now unofficially named Jack London's Rendezvous in his honor.

Gold rush and first success

On July 12, 1897, London (age 21) and his sister's husband Captain Shepard sailed to join the Klondike Gold Rush. This was the setting for some of his first successful stories. London's time in the harsh Klondike, however, was detrimental to his health. Like so many other men who were malnourished in the goldfields, London developed scurvy. His gums became swollen, leading to the loss of his four front teeth. A constant gnawing pain affected his hip and leg muscles, and his face was stricken with marks that always reminded him of the struggles he faced in the Klondike. Father William Judge, "The Saint of Dawson", had a facility in Dawson that provided shelter, food and any available medicine to London and others. His struggles there inspired London's short story, "To Build a Fire" (1902, revised in 1908), which many critics assess as his best.

His landlords in Dawson were mining engineers Marshall Latham Bond and Louis Whitford Bond, educated at Yale and Stanford, respectively. The brothers' father, Judge Hiram Bond, was a wealthy mining investor. The Bonds, especially Hiram, were active Republicans. Marshall Bond's diary mentions friendly sparring with London on political issues as a camp pastime.

London left Oakland with a social conscience and socialist leanings; he returned to become an activist for socialism. He concluded that his only hope of escaping the work "trap" was to get an education and "sell his brains". He saw his writing as a business, his ticket out of poverty, and, he hoped, a means of beating the wealthy at their own game. On returning to California in 1898, London began working to get published, a struggle described in his novel, Martin Eden (serialized in 1908, published in 1909). His first published story since high school was "To the Man On Trail", which has frequently been collected in anthologies. When The Overland Monthly offered him only five dollars for it—and was slow paying—London came close to abandoning his writing career. In his words, "literally and literarily I was saved" when The Black Cat accepted his story "A Thousand Deaths", and paid him $40—the "first money I ever received for a story".

London began his writing career just as new printing technologies enabled lower-cost production of magazines. This resulted in a boom in popular magazines aimed at a wide public audience and a strong market for short fiction. In 1900, he made $2,500 in writing, about $77,000 in today's currency. Among the works he sold to magazines was a short story known as either "Diable" (1902) or "Bâtard" (1904), two editions of the same basic story; London received $141.25 for this story on May 27, 1902. In the text, a cruel French Canadian brutalizes his dog, and the dog retaliates and kills the man. London told some of his critics that man's actions are the main cause of the behavior of their animals, and he would show this in another story, The Call of the Wild.

In early 1903, London sold The Call of the Wild to The Saturday Evening Post for $750, and the book rights to Macmillan for $2,000. Macmillan's promotional campaign propelled it to swift success.

While living at his rented villa on Lake Merritt in Oakland, California, London met poet George Sterling; in time they became best friends. In 1902, Sterling helped London find a home closer to his own in nearby Piedmont. In his letters London addressed Sterling as "Greek", owing to Sterling's aquiline nose and classical profile, and he signed them as "Wolf". London was later to depict Sterling as Russ Brissenden in his autobiographical novel Martin Eden (1910) and as Mark Hall in The Valley of the Moon (1913).

In later life London indulged his wide-ranging interests by accumulating a personal library of 15,000 volumes. He referred to his books as "the tools of my trade".

First marriage (1900–04)

London married Elizabeth "Bessie" Maddern on April 7, 1900, the same day The Son of the Wolf was published. Bess had been part of his circle of friends for a number of years. She was related to stage actresses Minnie Maddern Fiske and Emily Stevens. Stasz says, "Both acknowledged publicly that they were not marrying out of love, but from friendship and a belief that they would produce sturdy children." Kingman says, "they were comfortable together... Jack had made it clear to Bessie that he did not love her, but that he liked her enough to make a successful marriage."

London met Bessie through his friend at Oakland High School, Fred Jacobs; she was Fred's fiancée. Bessie, who tutored at Anderson's University Academy in Alameda California, tutored Jack in preparation for his entrance exams for the University of California at Berkeley in 1896. Jacobs was killed aboard the USAT Scandia in 1897, but Jack and Bessie continued their friendship, which included taking photos and developing the film together. This was the beginning of Jack's passion for photography.

During the marriage, London continued his friendship with Anna Strunsky, co-authoring The Kempton-Wace Letters, an epistolary novel contrasting two philosophies of love. Anna, writing "Dane Kempton's" letters, arguing for a romantic view of marriage, while London, writing "Herbert Wace's" letters, argued for a scientific view, based on Darwinism and eugenics. In the novel, his fictional character contrasted two women he had known.

London's pet name for Bess was "Mother-Girl" and Bess's for London was "Daddy-Boy". Their first child, Joan, was born on January 15, 1901, and their second, Bessie (later called Becky), on October 20, 1902. Both children were born in Piedmont, California. Here London wrote one of his most celebrated works, The Call of the Wild.

364

While London had pride in his children, the marriage was strained. Kingman says that by 1903 the couple were close to separation as they were "extremely incompatible". "Jack was still so kind and gentle with Bessie that when Cloudsley Johns was a house guest in February 1903 he didn't suspect a breakup of their marriage."

London reportedly complained to friends Joseph Noel and George Sterling:

> [Bessie] is devoted to purity. When I tell her morality is only evidence of low blood pressure, she hates me. She'd sell me and the children out for her damned purity. It's terrible. Every time I come back after being away from home for a night she won't let me be in the same room with her if she can help it.

Stasz writes that these were "code words for fear that was consorting with prostitutes and might bring home venereal disease."

On July 24, 1903, London told Bessie he was leaving and moved out. During 1904, London and Bess negotiated the terms of a divorce, and the decree was granted on November 11, 1904.

War correspondent (1904)

London accepted an assignment of the San Francisco Examiner to cover the Russo-Japanese War in early 1904, arriving in Yokohama on January 25, 1904. He was arrested by Japanese authorities in Shimonoseki, but released through the intervention of American ambassador Lloyd Griscom. After travelling to Korea, he was again arrested by Japanese authorities for straying too close to the border with Manchuria without official permission, and was sent back to Seoul. Released again, London was permitted to travel with the Imperial Japanese Army to the border, and to observe the Battle of the Yalu.

London asked William Randolph Hearst, the owner of the San Francisco Examiner, to be allowed to transfer to the Imperial Russian Army, where he felt that restrictions on his reporting and his movements would be less severe. However, before this could be arranged, he was arrested for a third time in four months, this time for assaulting his Japanese assistants, whom

365

he accused of stealing the fodder for his horse. Released through the personal intervention of President Theodore Roosevelt, London departed the front in June 1904.

Bohemian Club

On August 18, 1904, London went with his close friend, the poet George Sterling, to "Summer High Jinks" at the Bohemian Grove. London was elected to honorary membership in the Bohemian Club and took part in many activities. Other noted members of the Bohemian Club during this time included Ambrose Bierce, Gelett Burgess, Allan Dunn, John Muir, Frank Norris, and Herman George Scheffauer.

Beginning in December 1914, London worked on The Acorn Planter, A California Forest Play, to be performed as one of the annual Grove Plays, but it was never selected. It was described as too difficult to set to music. London published The Acorn Planter in 1916.

Second marriage

After divorcing Maddern, London married Charmian Kittredge in 1905. London had been introduced to Kittredge in 1900 by her aunt Netta Eames, who was an editor at Overland Monthly magazine in San Francisco. The two met prior to his first marriage but became lovers years later after Jack and Bessie London visited Wake Robin, Netta Eames' Sonoma County resort, in 1903. London was injured when he fell from a buggy, and Netta arranged for Charmian to care for him. The two developed a friendship, as Charmian, Netta, her husband Roscoe, and London were politically aligned with socialist causes. At some point the relationship became romantic, and Jack divorced his wife to marry Charmian, who was five years his senior.

Biographer Russ Kingman called Charmian "Jack's soul-mate, always at his side, and a perfect match." Their time together included numerous trips, including a 1907 cruise on the yacht Snark to Hawaii and Australia. Many of London's stories are based on his visits to Hawaii, the last one for 10 months beginning in December 1915.

366

The couple also visited Goldfield, Nevada, in 1907, where they were guests of the Bond brothers, London's Dawson City landlords. The Bond brothers were working in Nevada as mining engineers.

London had contrasted the concepts of the "Mother Girl" and the "Mate Woman" in The Kempton-Wace Letters. His pet name for Bess had been "Mother-Girl;" his pet name for Charmian was "Mate-Woman."Charmian's aunt and foster mother, a disciple of Victoria Woodhull, had raised her without prudishness.Every biographer alludes to Charmian's uninhibited sexuality.

Joseph Noel calls the events from 1903 to 1905 "a domestic drama that would have intrigued the pen of an Ibsen.... London's had comedy relief in it and a sort of easy-going romance." In broad outline, London was restless in his first marriage, sought extramarital sexual affairs, and found, in Charmian Kittredge, not only a sexually active and adventurous partner, but his future life-companion. They attempted to have children; one child died at birth, and another pregnancy ended in a miscarriage.

In 1906, London published in Collier's magazine his eye-witness report of the San Francisco earthquake.

Beauty Ranch (1905–16)

In 1905, London purchased a 1,000 acres (4.0 km2) ranch in Glen Ellen, Sonoma County, California, on the eastern slope of Sonoma Mountain.He wrote: "Next to my wife, the ranch is the dearest thing in the world to me." He desperately wanted the ranch to become a successful business enterprise. Writing, always a commercial enterprise with London, now became even more a means to an end: "I write for no other purpose than to add to the beauty that now belongs to me. I write a book for no other reason than to add three or four hundred acres to my magnificent estate."

Stasz writes that London "had taken fully to heart the vision, expressed in his agrarian fiction, of the land as the closest earthly version of Eden ... he educated himself through the study of agricultural manuals and scientific tomes. He conceived of a system of ranching that today would be praised for its ecological wisdom." He was proud to own the first concrete silo in California, a circular piggery that he designed. He hoped to adapt the wisdom of Asian sustainable agriculture to the United States. He hired both Italian and Chinese stonemasons, whose distinctly different styles are obvious.

The ranch was an economic failure. Sympathetic observers such as Stasz treat his projects as potentially feasible, and ascribe their failure to bad luck or to being ahead of their time. Unsympathetic historians such as Kevin Starr suggest that he was a bad manager, distracted by other concerns and impaired by his alcoholism. Starr notes that London was absent from his ranch about six months a year between 1910 and 1916 and says, "He liked the show of managerial power, but not grinding attention to detail .... London's workers laughed at his efforts to play big-time rancher the operation a rich man's hobby."

London spent $80,000 ($2,280,000 in current value) to build a 15,000-square-foot (1,400 m2) stone mansion called Wolf House on the property. Just as the mansion was nearing completion, two weeks before the Londons planned to move in, it was destroyed by fire.

London's last visit to Hawaii, beginning in December 1915, lasted eight months. He met with Duke Kahanamoku, Prince Jonah Kūhiō Kalaniana'ole, Queen Lili'uokalani and many others, before returning to his ranch in July 1916. He was suffering from kidney failure, but he continued to work.

The ranch (abutting stone remnants of Wolf House) is now a National Historic Landmark and is protected in Jack London State Historic Park.

Animal activism

London witnessed animal cruelty in the training of circus animals, and his subsequent novels Jerry of the Islands and Michael, Brother of Jerry included a foreword entreating the public to become more informed about this practice. In 1918, the Massachusetts Society for the Prevention of Cruelty to Animals and the American Humane Education Society teamed up to create the Jack London Club, which sought to inform the public about cruelty to circus animals and encourage them to protest this establishment. Support from Club members led to a temporary cessation of trained animal acts at Ringling-Barnum and Bailey in 1925.

368

Death

London died November 22, 1916, in a sleeping porch in a cottage on his ranch. London had been a robust man but had suffered several serious illnesses, including scurvy in the Klondike. Additionally, during travels on the Snark, he and Charmian picked up unspecified tropical infections, and diseases, including yaws. At the time of his death, he suffered from dysentery, late-stage alcoholism, and uremia; he was in extreme pain and taking morphine.

London's ashes were buried on his property not far from the Wolf House. London's funeral took place on November 26, 1916, attended only by close friends, relatives, and workers of the property. In accordance with his wishes, he was cremated and buried next to some pioneer children, under a rock that belonged to the Wolf House. After Charmian's death in 1955, she was also cremated and then buried with her husband in the same spot that her husband chose. The grave is marked by a mossy boulder. The buildings and property were later preserved as Jack London State Historic Park, in Glen Ellen, California.

Suicide debate

Because he was using morphine, many older sources describe London's death as a suicide, and some still do. This conjecture appears to be a rumor, or speculation based on incidents in his fiction writings. His death certificate gives the cause as uremia, following acute renal colic.

The biographer Stasz writes, "Following London's death, for a number of reasons, a biographical myth developed in which he has been portrayed as an alcoholic womanizer who committed suicide. Recent scholarship based upon firsthand documents challenges this caricature." Most biographers, including Russ Kingman, now agree he died of uremia aggravated by an accidental morphine overdose.

London's fiction featured several suicides. In his autobiographical memoir John Barleycorn, he claims, as a youth, to have drunkenly stumbled overboard into the San Francisco Bay, "some maundering fancy of going out with the tide suddenly obsessed me". He said he drifted and nearly succeeded in drowning before sobering up and being rescued by fishermen. In the dénouement of The Little Lady of the Big House, the heroine, confronted by the pain of a mortal gunshot wound, undergoes a physician-assisted suicide by morphine. Also, in Martin Eden, the principal protagonist, who shares certain characteristics with London, drowns himself.

Plagiarism accusations

London was vulnerable to accusations of plagiarism, both because he was such a conspicuous, prolific, and successful writer and because of his methods of working. He wrote in a letter to Elwyn Hoffman, "expression, you see—with me—is far easier than invention." He purchased plots and novels from the young Sinclair Lewis and used incidents from newspaper clippings as writing material.

In July 1901, two pieces of fiction appeared within the same month: London's "Moon-Face", in the San Francisco Argonaut, and Frank Norris' "The Passing of Cock-eye Blacklock", in Century Magazine. Newspapers showed the similarities between the stories, which London said were "quite different in manner of treatment, patently the same in foundation and motive." London explained both writers based their stories on the same newspaper account. A year later, it was discovered that Charles Forrest McLean had published a fictional story also based on the same incident.

Egerton Ryerson Young claimed The Call of the Wild (1903) was taken from Young's book My Dogs in the Northland (1902). London acknowledged using it as a source and claimed to have written a letter to Young thanking him.

In 1906, the New York World published "deadly parallel" columns showing eighteen passages from London's short story "Love of Life" side by side with similar passages from a nonfiction article by Augustus Biddle and J. K. Macdonald, titled "Lost in the Land of the Midnight Sun". London noted the World did not accuse him of "plagiarism", but only of "identity of time and situation", to which he defiantly "pled guilty".

370

The most serious charge of plagiarism was based on London's "The Bishop's Vision", Chapter 7 of his novel The Iron Heel (1908). The chapter is nearly identical to an ironic essay that Frank Harris published in 1901, titled "The Bishop of London and Public Morality". Harris was incensed and suggested he should receive 1/60th of the royalties from The Iron Heel, the disputed material constituting about that fraction of the whole novel. London insisted he had clipped a reprint of the article, which had appeared in an American newspaper, and believed it to be a genuine speech delivered by the Bishop of London.

Views

Atheism

London was an atheist. He is quoted as saying, "I believe that when I am dead, I am dead. I believe that with my death I am just as much obliterated as the last mosquito you and I squashed."

Socialism

London wrote from a socialist viewpoint, which is evident in his novel The Iron Heel. Neither a theorist nor an intellectual socialist, London's socialism grew out of his life experience. As London explained in his essay, "How I Became a Socialist", his views were influenced by his experience with people at the bottom of the social pit. His optimism and individualism faded, and he vowed never to do more hard physical work than necessary. He wrote that his individualism was hammered out of him, and he was politically reborn. He often closed his letters "Yours for the Revolution."

London joined the Socialist Labor Party in April 1896. In the same year, the San Francisco Chronicle published a story about the twenty-year-old London's giving nightly speeches in Oakland's City Hall Park, an activity he was arrested for a year later. In 1901, he left the Socialist Labor Party and joined the new Socialist Party of America. He ran unsuccessfully as the high-profile Socialist candidate for mayor of Oakland in 1901 (receiving 245 votes) and 1905 (improving to 981 votes), toured the country lecturing on socialism in 1906, and published two collections of essays about socialism: The War of the Classes (1905) and Revolution, and other Essays (1906).

Stasz notes that "London regarded the Wobblies as a welcome addition to the Socialist cause, although he never joined them in going so far as to recommend sabotage." Stasz mentions a personal meeting between London and Big Bill Haywood in 1912.

In his late (1913) book The Cruise of the Snark, London writes about appeals to him for membership of the Snark's crew from office workers and other "toilers" who longed for escape from the cities, and of being cheated by workmen.

In his Glen Ellen ranch years, London felt some ambivalence toward socialism and complained about the "inefficient Italian labourers" in his employ. In 1916, he resigned from the Glen Ellen chapter of the Socialist Party, but stated emphatically he did so "because of its lack of fire and fight, and its loss of emphasis on the class struggle." In an unflattering portrait of London's ranch days, California cultural historian Kevin Starr refers to this period as "post-socialist" and says "... by 1911 ... London was more bored by the class struggle than he cared to admit."

Race

London shared common concerns among many European Americans in California about Asian immigration, described as "the yellow peril"; he used the latter term as the title of a 1904 essay. This theme was also the subject of a story he wrote in 1910 called "The Unparalleled Invasion". Presented as an historical essay set in the future, the story narrates events between 1976 and 1987, in which China, with an ever-increasing population, is taking over and colonizing its neighbors with the intention of taking over the entire Earth. The western nations respond with biological warfare and bombard China with dozens of the most infectious diseases. On his fears about China, he admits, "it must be taken into consideration that the above postulate is itself a product of Western race-egotism, urged by our belief in our own righteousness and fostered by a faith in ourselves which may be as erroneous as are most fond race fancies."

By contrast, many of London's short stories are notable for their empathetic portrayal of Mexican ("The Mexican"), Asian ("The Chinago"), and Hawaiian ("Koolau the Leper") characters. London's war correspondence from the Russo-Japanese War, as well as his unfinished novel Cherry, show he admired much about Japanese customs and capabilities. London's writings have been popular among the Japanese, who believe he portrayed them positively.

In "Koolau the Leper", London describes Koolau, who is a Hawaiian leper—and thus a very different sort of "superman" than Martin Eden—and who fights off an entire cavalry troop to elude capture, as "indomitable spiritually—a ... magnificent rebel". This character is based on Hawaiian leper Kaluaikoolau, who in 1893 revolted and resisted capture from forces of the Provisional Government of Hawaii in the Kalalau Valley.

An amateur boxer and avid boxing fan, London reported on the 1910 Johnson–Jeffries fight, in which the black boxer Jack Johnson vanquished Jim Jeffries, known as the "Great White Hope". In 1908, London had reported on an earlier fight of Johnson's, contrasting the black boxer's coolness and intellectual style, with the apelike appearance and fighting style of his Canadian opponent, Tommy Burns:

> [What won] on Saturday was bigness, coolness, quickness, cleverness, and vast physical superiority ... Because a white man wishes a white man to win, this should not prevent him from giving absolute credit to the best man, even when that best man was black. All hail to Johnson. ... superb. He was impregnable ... as inaccessible as Mont Blanc.

Those who defend London against charges of racism cite the letter he wrote to the Japanese-American Commercial Weekly in 1913:

> In reply to yours of August 16, 1913. First of all, I should say by stopping the stupid newspaper from always fomenting race prejudice. This of course, being impossible, I would say, next, by educating the people of Japan so that they will be too intelligently tolerant to respond to any call to race prejudice. And, finally, by realizing, in industry and

government, of socialism—which last word is merely a word that stands for the actual application of in the affairs of men of the theory of the Brotherhood of Man.

In the meantime the nations and races are only unruly boys who have not yet grown to the stature of men. So we must expect them to do unruly and boisterous things at times. And, just as boys grow up, so the races of mankind will grow up and laugh when they look back upon their childish quarrels.

In 1996, after the City of Whitehorse, Yukon, renamed a street in honor of London, protests over London's alleged racism forced the city to change the name of "Jack London Boulevard"[failed verification] back to "Two-mile Hill".

Eugenics

London supported eugenics, including forced sterilization of criminals or those deemed feeble minded. His novel Before Adam(1906–07) has been described as having pro-eugenic themes.

London wrote to Frederick H. Robinson of the periodical Medical Review of Reviews, stating, "I believe the future belongs to eugenics, and will be determined by the practice of eugenics."

Works

Short stories

Western writer and historian Dale L. Walker writes:

London's true métier was the short story ... London's true genius lay in the short form, 7,500 words and under, where the flood of images in his teeming brain and the innate power of his narrative gift were at once constrained and freed. His stories that run longer than the magic 7,500 generally—but certainly not always—could have benefited from self-editing.

374

London's "strength of utterance" is at its height in his stories, and they are painstakingly well-constructed. "To Build a Fire" is the best known of all his stories. Set in the harsh Klondike, it recounts the haphazard trek of a new arrival who has ignored an old-timer's warning about the risks of traveling alone. Falling through the ice into a creek in seventy-five-below weather, the unnamed man is keenly aware that survival depends on his untested skills at quickly building a fire to dry his clothes and warm his extremities. After publishing a tame version of this story—with a sunny outcome—in The Youth's Companion in 1902, London offered a second, more severe take on the man's predicament in The Century Magazine in 1908. Reading both provides an illustration of London's growth and maturation as a writer. As Labor (1994) observes: "To compare the two versions is itself an instructive lesson in what distinguished a great work of literary art from a good children's story."

Other stories from the Klondike period include: "All Gold Canyon", about a battle between a gold prospector and a claim jumper; "The Law of Life", about an aging American Indian man abandoned by his tribe and left to die; "Love of Life", about a trek by a prospector across the Canadian tundra; "To the Man on Trail," which tells the story of a prospector fleeing the Mounted Police in a sled race, and raises the question of the contrast between written law and morality; and "An Odyssey of the North," which raises questions of conditional morality, and paints a sympathetic portrait of a man of mixed White and Aleut ancestry.

London was a boxing fan and an avid amateur boxer. "A Piece of Steak" is a tale about a match between older and younger boxers. It contrasts the differing experiences of youth and age but also raises the social question of the treatment of aging workers. "The Mexican" combines boxing with a social theme, as a young Mexican endures an unfair fight and ethnic prejudice to earn money with which to aid the revolution.

Several of London's stories would today be classified as science fiction. "The Unparalleled Invasion" describes germ warfare against China; "Goliath" is about an irresistible energy weapon; "The Shadow and the Flash" is a tale about two brothers who take different routes to achieving invisibility; "A

Relic of the Pliocene" is a tall tale about an encounter of a modern-day man with a mammoth. "The Red One" is a late story from a period when London was intrigued by the theories of the psychiatrist and writer Jung. It tells of an island tribe held in thrall by an extraterrestrial object.

Some nineteen original collections of short stories were published during London's brief life or shortly after his death. There have been several posthumous anthologies drawn from this pool of stories. Many of these stories were located in the Klondike and the Pacific. A collection of Jack London's San Francisco Stories was published in October 2010 by Sydney Samizdat Press.

Novels

London's most famous novels are The Call of the Wild, White Fang, The Sea-Wolf, The Iron Heel, and Martin Eden.

In a letter dated December 27, 1901, London's Macmillan publisher George Platt Brett, Sr., said "he believed Jack's fiction represented 'the very best kind of work' done in America."

Critic Maxwell Geismar called The Call of the Wild "a beautiful prose poem"; editor Franklin Walker said that it "belongs on a shelf with Walden and Huckleberry Finn"; and novelist E.L. Doctorow called it "a mordant parable ... his masterpiece."

The historian Dale L. Walker commented:

Jack London was an uncomfortable novelist, that form too long for his natural impatience and the quickness of his mind. His novels, even the best of them, are hugely flawed.

Some critics have said that his novels are episodic and resemble linked short stories. Dale L. Walker writes:

The Star Rover, that magnificent experiment, is actually a series of short stories connected by a unifying device ... Smoke Bellew is a series of stories bound together in a novel-like form by their reappearing protagonist, Kit Bellew; and John Barleycorn ... is a synoptic series of short episodes.

Ambrose Bierce said of The Sea-Wolf that "the great thing—and it is among the greatest of things—is that tremendous creation, Wolf Larsen ... the hewing out and setting up of such a figure is enough for a man to do in one lifetime. "However, he noted, "The love element, with its absurd suppressions, and impossible proprieties, is awful."

The Iron Heel is an example of a dystopian novel that anticipates and influenced George Orwell's Nineteen Eighty-Four. London's socialist politics are explicitly on display here. The Iron Heel meets the contemporary definition of soft science fiction. The Star Rover (1915) is also science fiction.

Apocrypha

Jack London Credo

London's literary executor, Irving Shepard, quoted a Jack London Credo in an introduction to a 1956 collection of London stories:

> I would rather be ashes than dust!
>
> I would rather that my spark should burn out in a brilliant blaze than it should be stifled by dry-rot.
>
> I would rather be a superb meteor, every atom of me in magnificent glow, than a sleepy and permanent planet.
>
> The function of man is to live, not to exist.
>
> I shall not waste my days in trying to prolong them.
>
> I shall use my time.

The biographer Stasz notes that the passage "has many marks of London's style" but the only line that could be safely attributed to London was the first. The words Shepard quoted were from a story in the San Francisco Bulletin, December 2, 1916, by journalist Ernest J. Hopkins, who visited the ranch just weeks before London's death. Stasz notes, "Even more so than today journalists' quotes were unreliable or even sheer inventions," and says no direct source in London's writings has been found. However, at least one line, according to Stasz, is authentic, being referenced by London and written in his own hand in the autograph book of Australian suffragette Vida Goldstein:

> Dear Miss Goldstein:–
>
> Seven years ago I wrote you that I'd rather be ashes than dust. I still subscribe to that sentiment.
>
> Sincerely yours,
>
> Jack London
>
> Jan. 13, 1909

In his short story "By The Turtles of Tasman", a character, defending her "ne'er-do-well grasshopperish father" to her "antlike uncle", says: "... my father has been a king. He has lived .... Have you lived merely to live? Are you afraid to die? I'd rather sing one wild song and burst my heart with it, than live a thousand years watching my digestion and being afraid of the wet. When you are dust, my father will be ashes."

"The Scab"

A short diatribe on "The Scab" is often quoted within the U.S. labor movement and frequently attributed to London. It opens:

> After God had finished the rattlesnake, the toad, and the vampire, he had some awful substance left with which he made a scab. A scab is a two-legged animal with a corkscrew soul, a water brain, a combination backbone of jelly and glue. Where others have hearts, he carries a tumor of rotten principles. When a scab comes down the street, men turn their backs and Angels weep in Heaven, and the Devil shuts the gates of hell to keep him out....

In 1913 and 1914, a number of newspapers printed the first three sentences with varying terms used instead of "scab", such as "knocker", "stool pigeon" or "scandal monger"

This passage as given above was the subject of a 1974 Supreme Court case, Letter Carriers v. Austin, in which Justice Thurgood Marshall referred to it as "a well-known piece of trade union literature, generally attributed to author Jack London". A union newsletter had published a "list of scabs," which was granted to be factual and therefore not libelous, but then went on to quote the passage as the "definition of a scab". The case turned on the question of whether the "definition" was defamatory. The court ruled that "Jack London's... 'definition of a scab' is merely rhetorical hyperbole, a lusty and imaginative expression of the contempt felt by union members towards those who refuse to join", and as such was not libelous and was protected under the First Amendment.

Despite being frequently attributed to London, the passage does not appear at all in the extensive collection of his writings at Sonoma State University's website. However, in his book The War of the Classes he published a 1903 speech entitled "The Scab", which gave a much more balanced view of the topic:

> The laborer who gives more time or strength or skill for the same wage than another, or equal time or strength or skill for a less wage, is a scab. The generousness on his part is hurtful to his fellow-laborers, for it compels them to an equal generousness which is not to their liking, and which gives them less of food and shelter. But a word may be said for the scab. Just as his act makes his rivals compulsorily generous, so do they, by fortune of birth and training, make compulsory his act of generousness.
>
> [...]
>
> Nobody desires to scab, to give most for least. The ambition of every individual is quite the opposite, to give least for most; and, as a result, living in a tooth-and-nail society, battle royal is waged by the ambitious individuals. But in its most salient aspect, that of the struggle over the division of the joint product, it is no longer a battle between individuals, but between groups of individuals. Capital and labor apply

themselves to raw material, make something useful out of it, add to its value, and then proceed to quarrel over the division of the added value. Neither cares to give most for least. Each is intent on giving less than the other and on receiving more.

Legacy and honors

Mount London, also known as Boundary Peak 100, on the Alaska-British Columbia boundary, in the Boundary Ranges of the Coast Mountains of British Columbia, is named for him.

Jack London Square on the waterfront of Oakland, California was named for him.

He was honored by the United States Postal Service with a 25¢ Great Americans series postage stamp released on January 11, 1986.

Jack London Lake (Russian), a mountain lake located in the upper reaches of the Kolyma River in Yagodninsky district of Magadan Oblast.

Fictional portrayals of London include Michael O'Shea in the 1943 film Jack London, Jeff East in the 1980 film Klondike Fever, Aaron Ashmore in the Murdoch Mysteries episode "Murdoch of the Klondike" from 2012, and Johnny Simmons in the 2014 miniseries Klondike. (Source: Wikipedia)

NOTABLE WORKS

NOVELS

The Cruise of the Dazzler (1902)

A Daughter of the Snows (1902)

The Call of the Wild (1903)

The Kempton-Wace Letters (1903) (published anonymously, co-authored with Anna Strunsky)

The Sea-Wolf (1904)

The Game (1905)

White Fang (1906)

Before Adam (1907)

The Iron Heel (1908)

Martin Eden (1909)

Burning Daylight (1910)

Adventure (1911)

The Scarlet Plague (1912)

A Son of the Sun (1912)

The Abysmal Brute (1913)

The Valley of the Moon (1913)

The Mutiny of the Elsinore (1914)

The Star Rover (1915) (published in England as The Jacket)

The Little Lady of the Big House (1916)

Jerry of the Islands (1917)

Michael, Brother of Jerry (1917)

Hearts of Three (1920) (novelization of a script by Charles Goddard)

The Assassination Bureau, Ltd (1963) (left half-finished, completed by Robert L. Fish)

SHORT STORIES

"An Old Soldier's Story" (1894)

"Who Believes in Ghosts!" (1895)

"And 'FRISCO Kid Came Back" (1895)

"Night's Swim In Yeddo Bay" (1895)

"One More Unfortunate" (1895)

"Sakaicho, Hona Asi And Hakadaki" (1895)

"A Klondike Christmas" (1897)

"Mahatma's Little Joke" (1897)

"O Haru" (1897)

"Plague Ship" (1897)

"The Strange Experience Of A Misogynist" (1897)

"Two Gold Bricks" (1897)

"The Devil's Dice Box" (1898)

"A Dream Image" (1898)

"The Test: A Clondyke Wooing" (1898)

"To the Man on Trail" (1898)

"In a Far Country" (1899)

"The King of Mazy May" (1899)

"The End Of The Chapter" (1899)

"The Grilling Of Loren Ellery" (1899)

"The Handsome Cabin Boy" (1899)

"In The Time Of Prince Charley" (1899)

"Old Baldy" (1899)

"The Men of Forty Mile" (1899)

"Pluck and Pertinacity" (1899)

"The Rejuvenation of Major Rathbone" (1899)

"The White Silence" (1899)

"A Thousand Deaths" (1899)

"Wisdom of the Trail" (1899)

"An Odyssey of the North" (1900)

"The Son of the Wolf" (1900)

"Even unto Death" (1900)

"The Man with the Gash" (1900)

"A Lesson in Heraldry" (1900)

"A Northland Miracle" (1900)

"Proper "GIRLIE"" (1900)

"Thanksgiving on Slav Creek" (1900)

"Their Alcove" (1900)

"Housekeeping in the Klondike" (1900)

"Dutch Courage" (1900)

"Where the Trail Forks" (1900)

"Hyperborean Brew" (1901)

"A Relic of the Pliocene" (1901)

"The Lost Poacher" (1901)

"The God of His Fathers" (1901)

""FRISCO Kid's" Story" (1901)

"The Law of Life" (1901)

"The Minions of Midas" (1901)

"In the Forests of the North" (1902)

"The "Fuzziness" of Hoockla-Heen" (1902)

"The Story of Keesh" (1902)

"Keesh, Son of Keesh" (1902)

"Nam-Bok, the Unveracious" (1902)

"Li Wan the Fair" (1902)

"Lost Face"

"Master of Mystery" (1902)

"The Sunlanders" (1902)

"The Death of Ligoun" (1902)

"Moon-Face" (1902)

"Diable—A Dog" (1902), renamed Bâtard in 1904

"To Build a Fire" (1902, revised 1908)

"The League of the Old Men" (1902)

"The Dominant Primordial Beast" (1903)

"The One Thousand Dozen" (1903)

"The Marriage of Lit-lit" (1903)

"The Shadow and the Flash" (1903)

"The Leopard Man's Story" (1903)

"Negore the Coward" (1904)

"All Gold Cañon" (1905)

"Love of Life" (1905)

"The Sun-Dog Trail" (1905)

"The Apostate" (1906)

"Up the Slide" (1906)

"Planchette" (1906)

"Brown Wolf" (1906)

"Make Westing" (1907)

"Chased by the Trail" (1907)

"Trust" (1908)

"A Curious Fragment" (1908)

"Aloha Oe" (1908)

"That Spot" (1908)

"The Enemy of All the World" (1908)

"The House of Mapuhi" (1909)

"Good-by, Jack" (1909)

"Samuel" (1909)

"South of the Slot" (1909)

"The Chinago" (1909)

"The Dream of Debs" (1909)

"The Madness of John Harned" (1909)

"The Seed of McCoy" (1909)

"A Piece of Steak" (1909)

"Mauki" (1909)

"The Whale Tooth" (1909)

"Goliath" (1910)

"The Unparalleled Invasion" (1910)

"Told in the Drooling Ward" (1910)

"When the World was Young" (1910)

"The Terrible Solomons" (1910)

"The Inevitable White Man" (1910)

"The Heathen" (1910)

"Yah! Yah! Yah!" (1910)

"By the Turtles of Tasman" (1911)

"The Mexican" (1911)

"War" (1911)

"The Unmasking of the Cad" (1911)

"The Scarlet Plague" (1912)

"The Captain of the Susan Drew" (1912)

"The Sea-Farmer" (1912)

"The Feathers of the Sun" (1912)

"The Prodigal Father" (1912)

"Samuel" (1913)

"The Sea-Gangsters" (1913)

"The Strength of the Strong" (1914)

"Told in the Drooling Ward" (1914)

"The Hussy" (1916)

"Like Argus of the Ancient Times" (1917)

"Jerry of the Islands" (1917)

"The Red One" (1918)

"Shin-Bones" (1918)

"The Bones of Kahekili" (1919)

SHORT STORY COLLECTIONS

Son of the Wolf (1900)

Chris Farrington, Able Seaman (1901)

The God of His Fathers & Other Stories (1901)

Children of the Frost (1902)

The Faith of Men and Other Stories (1904)

Tales of the Fish Patrol (1906)

Moon-Face and Other Stories (1906)

Love of Life and Other Stories (1907)

Lost Face (1910)

South Sea Tales (1911)

When God Laughs and Other Stories (1911)

The House of Pride & Other Tales of Hawaii (1912)

Smoke Bellew (1912)

A Son of the Sun (1912)

The Night Born (1913)

The Strength of the Strong (1914)

The Turtles of Tasman (1916)

The Human Drift (1917)

The Red One (1918)

On the Makaloa Mat (1919)

Dutch Courage and Other Stories (1922)

AUTOBIOGRAPHICAL MEMOIRS

The Road (1907)

The Cruise of the Snark (1911)

John Barleycorn (1913)

NON-FICTION AND ESSAYS

Through the Rapids on the Way to the Klondike (1899)

From Dawson to the Sea (1899)

What Communities Lose by the Competitive System (1900)

The Impossibility of War (1900)

Phenomena of Literary Evolution (1900)

A Letter to Houghton Mifflin Co. (1900)

Husky, Wolf Dog of the North (1900)

Editorial Crimes — A Protest (1901)

Again the Literary Aspirant (1902)

The People of the Abyss (1903)

How I Became a Socialist (1903)

The War of the Classes (1905)

The Story of an Eyewitness (1906)

A Letter to Woman's Home Companion (1906)

Revolution, and other Essays (1910)

Mexico's Army and Ours (1914)

Lawgivers (1914)

Our Adventures in Tampico (1914)

Stalking the Pestilence (1914)

The Red Game of War (1914)

The Trouble Makers of Mexico (1914)

With Funston's Men (1914)

POETRY

A Heart (1899)

Abalone Song (1913)

And Some Night (1914)

Ballade of the False Lover (1914)

Cupid's Deal (1913)

Daybreak (1901)

Effusion (1901)

George Sterling (1913)

Gold (1915)

He Chortled with Glee (1899)

He Never Tried Again (1912)

His Trip to Hades (1913)

Homeland (1914)

Hors de Saison (1913)

If I Were God (1899)

In a Year (1901)

In and Out (1911)

Je Vis en Espoir (1897)

Memory (1913)

Moods (1913)

My Confession (1912)

My Little Palmist (1914)

Of Man of the Future (1915)

Oh You Everybody's Girl (19)

On the Face of the Earth You are the One (1915)

Rainbows End (1914)

Republican Rallying Song (1916)

Sonnet (1901)

The Gift of God (1905)

The Klondyker's Dream (1914)

The Lover's Liturgy (1913)

The Mammon Worshippers (1911)

The Republican Battle-Hymn (1905)

The Return of Ulysses (1915)

The Sea Sprite and the Shooting Star (1916)

The Socialist's Dream (1912)

The Song of the Flames (1903)

The Way of War (1906)

The Worker and the Tramp (1911)

Tick! Tick! Tick! (1915)

Too Late (1912)

Weasel Thieves (1913)

When All the World Shouted my Name (1905)

Where the Rainbow Fell (1902)

Your Kiss (1914)

PLAYS

Theft (1910)

Daughters of the Rich: A One Act Play (1915)

The Acorn Planter: A California Forest Play (1916)

CPSIA information can be obtained
at www.ICGtesting.com
Printed in the USA
LVHW111418050920
665176LV00005B/63

9 789390 230952